Ollie A. J. Carter

The War of Terratopia

Olympia Publishers
London

w.olympiapublishers.com
OLYMPIA PAPERBACK EDITION

Copyright © Ollie A. J. Carter 2024

The right of Ollie A. J. Carter to be identified as author of
this work has been asserted in accordance with sections 77 and 78 of the
Copyright, Designs and Patents Act 1988.

All Rights Reserved

No reproduction, copy or transmission of this publication
may be made without written permission.
No paragraph of this publication may be reproduced,
copied or transmitted save with the written permission of the publisher,
or in accordance with the provisions
of the Copyright Act 1956 (as amended).

Any person who commits any unauthorised act in relation to
this publication may be liable to criminal
prosecution and civil claims for damage.

A CIP catalogue record for this title is
available from the British Library.

ISBN: 978-1-80439-422-9

This is a work of fiction.
Names, characters, places and incidents originate from the writer's
imagination. Any resemblance to actual persons, living or dead,
is purely coincidental.

First Published in 2024

Olympia Publishers
Tallis House
2 Tallis Street
London
EC4Y 0AB

Printed in Great Britain

Dedication

For the SUMT 'old team'. I miss you all.

Table of Content

Part I - The Makings of War 7
    Chapter 1 10
    Chapter 2 15
    Chapter 3 20
    Chapter 4 29
    Chapter 5 35
    Chapter 6 40
    Chapter 7 45
    Chapter 8 54
    Chapter 9 59
    Chapter 10 66
    Chapter 11 73
    Chapter 12 79
    Chapter 13 85
    Chapter 14 91
    Chapter 15 98
    Chapter 16 103
    Chapter 17 110

Part II - Rise and Betrayal 113
    Chapter 1 114
    Chapter 2 120
    Chapter 3 129
    Chapter 4 135
    Chapter 5 143
    Chapter 6 149
    Chapter 7 155
    Chapter 8 159
    Chapter 9 165

Chapter 10	176
Chapter 11	183
Chapter 12	190
Chapter 13	197
Chapter 14	204
Part III - The Deity	**212**
Chapter 1	213
Chapter 2	216
Chapter 3	219
Chapter 4	223
Chapter 5	230
Chapter 6	236
Chapter 7	243
Chapter 8	249
Chapter 9	253
Chapter 10	260
Chapter 11	269
Chapter 12	275
Chapter 13	282
Chapter 14	290
Chapter 15	296
Chapter 16	301
Chapter 17	308
War of Terratopia Timeline	319

Part I
The Makings of War

Chapter 1

The Combined Union of Terratopia

The archipelago of Terratopia was truly a land to behold, a truly magnetic place. The world of Terra Tearia was still early on in its summer, only one age had passed since its declared beginning from the Celestial Starda and it showed. Terratopia was a true haven to inhabit for all races and beings of Terra Tearia. Mountain sides were bathed in warm sunlight and the snow top peaks glistened like stars to the lands below. Forests, woods and trees were vibrant shades of green, their leaves gently swayed in the calm constant winds, creating a consistent wave of ever-changing shades of emerald. Cool fresh rivers rushed down their watery roads to clear deep blue seas that perfectly reflected the skies above. Kingdoms of Men, Elves, Valkyries, Merpeople, Dwarves, Gnomes, Fairies, Pixies, Samsons, Goliaths, Centaurs, and even Giants and Great Owls sprawled across the archipelago and surrounding seas; all of which lived in a close, friendly harmony. These many kingdoms constantly grew closer together and continually intergraded in the name of friendship, trade, aid, and all things good as time marched peacefully on and on.

After a couple of centuries of this continued peace and harmony, the Men and Elves of the grand kingdom city of Roccano proposed that all separate kingdoms of Terratopia should combine into a single union of kingdoms, where the aim of helping one another for the benefit of all could be put at the forefront of a combined effort from all peoples from across all lands; because, although they were all of different races, from different kingdoms, with different cultures, they were all still one people, the people of Terratopia. The proposed idea spread quickly throughout the land and garnered tremendous support. All peoples of Terratopia could harmonise even further and with much greater ease as kingdoms on opposite sides of the archipelago would effectively have the same access to each other as if they were neighbouring kingdoms. Although still different and unique, every kingdom would now be a part of the same union, a single community bigger and better than anyone kingdom alone.

With resounding support, Thyzus Hobbes, the Lordbaron of Roccano and one of the first Elves to ever awaken in Terra Tearia, spearheaded the creation of the Terratopia Union. He did this as the unions original idea was his to begin with, theorizing it after studying much philosophy and scared texts within the Merpeople kingdom of Aquatatia.

Thyzus's kingdom city of Roccano, beneath the titanic Mount Roccano, became the collective capital of the Terratopia Union. This was because it was by far the grandest kingdom in all the land but also, more importantly, because the immense Mount Roccano, for which the entire kingdom wide city was built around, was the most central point of the Terratopia archipelago. The titanic mountain was a uniting landmark for all Terratopia's peoples, as historically its slopes were where the Chroniclers spirits descended and delivered their news from the Celestial Heavens above and it was also rumoured to be where some of these spirits even resided at all times, atop the tallest peak where no being had ever seen. A grand parliament building was built within Roccano, from which the entire Terratopia Union operation flowed through. This huge ziggurat complex was filled with representatives from across all kingdoms of Terratopia, to carry out any and all aspects of the goings on within the union. All kingdoms within the union also sent their wisest, most prominent inhabitants to the parliament. These wise, powerful members became the Lord Delegates of their respected kingdoms and they collectively, in their parliament chamber, led the Terratopia Union to the best possible greatness, prosperity, and harmonisation they could, solving any and all problems that faced the union the best they could with their great wisdom and ability to reason.

Roccano itself was an ancient, glorious kingdom city of Men

and Elves. Awaking early in the spring of the World, together the fairness of the Elves and ingenuity of Men created one of the first permanent settlements in all of Terra Tearia's history. This settlement continued to grow and grow over the entire spring of the World; and by the coming of Terra Tearia's summer, it had grown into an entire kingdom sized city filled with fine distinguished lines of Men and Elves. As Roccano was a kingdom of two races, it was collectively agreed that two leaders would be needed to run it most fairly. Being the fairest race of all beings in the world, the leader of the Elves was agreed to be the primary leader of the kingdom, the Lordbaron. But the leader of Men would always be second in command over the kingdom, the Premier; with much of their power being equal to that of the Lordbaron in nearly all regards. The Lordbaron was primarily tasked to and run the kingdom most fairly and wisely; and the Premier, always being from the most adaptive, creative race, Men, was primarily tasked with continually advancing the kingdom to further and further greatness, continually bringing new fresh ideas to the immortal wise Elves, who themselves made sure these new ideas remained fair to all.

As the Terratopia Union took hold, it became Roccano's sole purpose to support it, to be the central hub and beating heart of it, as well as being the driving force of any and all actions the Lord Delegates agreed on, pushing them out into the combined wider kingdoms of Terratopia. Thyzus Hobbes was unanimously made the Prime Lord Delegate, a role of not proposing ideals to the Lord Delegates and the union, but instead chiefly guiding their ideals, leading them in action and upholding what the union stood for. As the historic Elf leader of the Roccano, his wisdom was unparallel and his views impartial, his only bias being the continued support and prosperity of the union, and not that of his own kingdom as Roccano's kingdom purpose was to the support of the union anyway. Many other influential leaders of Roccano were appointed to impartial roles within the union's parliament as well; the Premier of Roccano was to be the Speaker of the parliament, maintaining its order and leading the Lord Delegates in session.

This system, as revolutionary as it was, wasn't perfect; and for some was just too much. The simpler and more rudimentary race of Centaurs found the union of kingdoms too bureaucratic and sophisticated and soon led their woodland kingdoms to leave the union. With Centaurs being a race caring not as much for the goings on outside of their forest realms and their realms not being particularly affected by the wider goings on outside them either, the Centaurs actions didn't surprise many nor did they shake the collective belief in the union. As well as this, time would go on to show that although not in the union, the Centaur woodland kingdoms were by no means unfriendly with the union, they just simply choose not to fully be a part of the union instead. A more surprising early departure from the Terratopia union was the kingdom of Fairies and Pixies. Being races of mending, healing, and love, their wishes to not be a part of a movement where such qualities were at the forefront of its purpose confused the remaining kingdoms within the union. The Fairies and Pixies were however in absolute agreement with the aims of the union, but they felt they needed to be a part of no such system to fulfil their race's natural qualities. In addition, the Fairies and Pixies felt that a consequence of being in such a union would be that their roles would become relied and expected on, believing such a scenario to be against their way of life. Even though they were assured by Thyzus personally that such ways of thinking would not manifest, the Fairies and Pixies still wished to remain out of the union, but assured that they would forever be friends to all in Terratopia and help in any way they saw fit. Understanding this, Thyzus and the Lord Delegates respected their wishes and departure.

Over the millennia, the Terratopia union worked exceedingly well, the collective kingdoms of Terratopia all prospering beyond imagination working together with one another through the close fluid companionship of the union. As an immortal Elf, Thyzus remained the Prime Lord Delegate and his popularity only grew as his wisdom and guidance over the Lord Delegates in charge of the union remained positive and constant, never swerving from the positions purpose of supporting and empowering the Terratopia Union. The Premier of Roccano however, as from the mortal race of Men, changed over the generations and, as a consequence, the Speaker of the Parliament changed with it. This however only seemed to benefit the union further as new fresh leadership to lead the Lord Delegates was always replenished and as a result never allowed the union parliament to dwell on old ways of thinking or be the same way twice but to instead constantly change, adapt, and improve with time.

The inhabitants of the kingdoms in Terratopia only saw benefits from the union as their quality of life only ever seemed to improve and their enjoyment of living in Terratopia never faltered. All peoples, even the Giants who had come to feel their qualities of immense strength and size had become reliant upon, felt that the combined archipelago of Terratopia was the grandest, most magnificent, awe-inspiring land in all of Terra Tearia. This however would not last.

Chapter 2

The Sons of Thyzus

The Terratopia Union was the idea of Thyzus Hobbes. He came across such an apprehending by studying in the great libraries of Aquata, the underwater capital city of the Merpeople kingdom of Aquatatia. Thyzus was a wise Elf by the summer of the World, having lived throughout the worlds Spring, founding Roccano with neighbouring Men near springs very beginning and ruling it for many lifetimes, leading his people to greatness over this time. He had also grown into a very powerful sorcerer; delving deep into the wizarding magics of Terra Tearia, pioneering the discovery of more and more powerful spells and accomplishing more and more powerful feats; at some point even having the magical prowess to levitate a Giant to the very peak of Mount Roccano, though the Giant reported that up at such heights the snow and wind was too much to see anything at all. Thyzus shared all he learned and discovered regarding the magic of the world with his people, transforming Roccano into a kingdom of powerful mages and wizards. Thyzus took great enjoyment in the discovery of new knowledge and then sharing that with the world at large; it was because of this quality that he fell into close friendship with the Merpeople, not least of all, the Merpeople of Aquatatia and their leaders, Magistrate Solomon and his descendants, all of whom were also named Solomon. Being the race of Measus, the wisest Celestial, Merpeople were the greatest thinkers and philosophers in Terra Tearia, spending their days ponding and theorising on all aspects of life. Over the spring of the world the Merpeoples growing amounts of philosophical texts filled grand halls in their cities and Aquata had the largest most magnificent collection of them all. A collection that just called out irresistibly to an Elf like Thyzus. Casting a magical enchantment over himself to be able to breath, live, and function underwater, Thyzus spent a great many years within the walls of Aquata, spending the majority of his time in the grand philosophical text halls and libraries in the city, reading all he could.

The more Thyzus read, the more he fell into deep deliberation, ponding intently on all the mind-opening ideals he read upon. Yet his rumination had no direction or purpose, he would just fall into a deep thought over anything he read as the works and ideals within them were all so monumental to behold. This all changed however when he met the head curator of the halls. A graceful Mermaid named Mia. Mia guided Thyzus though his thoughts and led him to even greater understandings of what he read and how it all could all be potentially applied into the world at large. The two grew close, finding great comfort and enjoyment in each other's company, even finding that their philosophical debates with one another led them to even greater appreciation of their sometimes-opposing views. Thyzus was incredibly grateful to have met Mia, her wisdom being greater than that of his own and her understanding, patience, and guidance seemingly unending. Before long Thyzus fell in love with her, he began to share his knowledge of magic with her and before long she too fell in love with him; the two connecting over their mutual love of knowledge and of wanting to share it with the world. When Thyzus requested Mia join him as his wife when he would return to his surface kingdom, Mia, in her love for Thyzus and her longing to share her knowledge and to explore the world beyond her underwater kingdom, graciously accepted.

    The two eventually journey back to Roccano. Thyzus ended his enchantment upon himself but also taught Mia how to enchant herself to be able to breath on land. Upon arriving back to Roccano, Thyzus magically transformed Mia's elegant mermaid fishtail into an exquisite lower body, comparable to the most beautiful Elves and matching her own beauty exceedingly well. Together the two wed and transformed Roccano into an even greater kingdom, even opening and presiding over a large philosophy academy in the kingdom. After a few years living together, talking deeply every night, Thyzus pieced together his plan to unite Terratopia into a combined union of kingdoms, which Mia highly endorsed and helped to final out in theory and planning.

    Not long after the creation of the Terratopia Union and the finishing of the grand parliament complex, Mia became pregnant and gave birth to a son, whom was named Kyzus

Hobbes. A Half-elf, and the first Half-elf in history to be half Merman, half Elf. Kyzus was alike to Elves in every way, in look, appearance, and soul; however, he also had the soul of a Merman, having a love of philosophy, wisdom, and thinking as well as a deep longing love of the sea. Kyzus was even able to breathe underwater alike to his Merpeople ancestors. Thyzus was overjoyed with his gift of a son, and together with Mia, resolved to teach him everything they knew, so that he would grow into an even more powerful and wise person than even themselves. A century later, Mia again gave birth to another son, Lyzus Hobbes. Similar to Kyzus, both Thyzus and Mia were overjoyed with the addition of another into their family and also resolved to teach him all they knew and guide him to greatness.

Time marched on within Terratopia and the brothers Kyzus and Lyzus grew into incredibly accomplished Half-elves. They both grew into very mature handsome brothers, being as wise and understanding as their mother and as powerful and fair as their father. In their inherit longing to explore, they journeyed throughout the archipelago of Terratopia, spending years in every kingdom, intermingling with its peoples and learning their cultures, coming to appreciate their ways of life. The brothers revisited many of the kingdoms numerous times, sometimes together, sometimes as individuals. Sometimes they did this one behalf of their father and the Terratopia Union on business or political grounds as they had grown into quite significant and influential figures within the union, holding much respect and support from all peoples across the land. Other times they revisited simply out of their own will for the pleasure and enjoyment to experience the particular kingdom once more.

As the summer of the world continued to pass the sons of Hobbes continued to grow as individuals. Their power, knowledge, and wisdom eventually surpassing that of their parents and their names becoming even more prominent, well-known, and respected. Kyzus even surpassed his father in reputation in the union for all his work done as a representative and advisor to the Terratopia Union.

As similar the two brothers were however, their differences as individuals did gradually begin to show. Lyzus began to be more and more like his mother; spending years, if not centuries underwater, exploring the seas and residing in the underwater Merpeople kingdoms, living among them. Lyzus in fact brought the four Merpeople kingdoms of Terratopia even closer together, drawing up the Merpeople Kingdom Alliance and convincing its people to sign it. Due to Lyzus, the kingdoms of Aquatatia, Reeforiris, the Great Eastern Bay and the Shore Mountains Atoll had never been closer, effectively having their own underwater union within the wider Terratopia Union.

Kyzus however, began to become more and more like his father. He became the most powerful sorcerer in Terratopia, seeking to learn all he could to then share and guide all he could as well. Kyzus began dedicating his life to the support and empowerment of the union, similar to his father before him. He came to believe in it stanchly. Kyzus became a chief advisor to the Lord Delegates chamber as well as the main face of the union, representing it out in the wider kingdoms outside of Roccano. Recognising this, Kyzus was appointed the new Prime Lord Delegate, by the suggestion of Thyzus and the unanimous agreement of the Terratopia Union Parliament. Thyzus and Kyzus also agreed that Thyzus should keep his role as the Lordbaron of Roccano as he could then focus more on running the kingdom city which could potentially further improve its support of the Terratopia Union; likewise, Kyzus could then focus wholly on the Terratopia union itself and, with his excellent relationship with Thyzus, could work closely with his father to empower the union to further greatness and prosperity.

Lyzus, in his commitment to his love of the sea, as well as his stronger desire to explore beyond his kingdom, inherited from his mother Mia, met the first ever Gnarth and Cherub in Terra Tearia on his explorations far from Terratopia, who coincidentally were seeking him out. He then joined them in their task to create the 'Baubles of Terra Tearia'. Three precious jewels representing the three aspects of a being's life within Terra Tearia; Body, Soul, and Spirit. Together the three traversed the world and succeeded in their plan and indeed created the most magical, beautiful, precious, and monumental gemstones in Terra Tearia. However, so magnificent and magic where the stones, even more so when bundled together, that the three creators could not part ways with their creations, nor bare to separate them, for all who witnessed them became transfixed by them. Because of this, they all named themselves the 'Baubles Guardians' and decided to house and protect them for all time. The agreed upon place to keep the gemstones was a dedicated palace in the capital city of the Sky Islands of Valhalla, the high capital of the Valkyries and the home of the Cherub. Lyzus explained all this to his family, and with a heavy but happy heart, left his family, Roccano, and Terratopia behind for good, to reside in Valhalla for the rest of his days. Thyzus and Mia never saw him again.

Chapter 3

The Giants Rebellion

As the ages of the summer of the world passed, the kingdoms of Terratopia continued to prosper. Kyzus and the Speakers of the Parliament led the Terratopia Union through the ages, dealing with any challenge that faced the land or any one kingdom, and constantly improved the union to greater prosperity and harmonisation each passing year. The peoples of the Terratopia however were about to face their greatest challenge yet; the coming of autumn. Its arrival foreseen or foretold by no one.

One day while awakening to the brightening morning sun, the peoples of Terratopia, and indeed the entire world of Terra Tearia at large, noticed a lot had changed. The sun was not as bright as it once was. Its light dimmer and its warmth less than what it used to be the previous day. In addition, the winds were cooler, the sky was darker, and as days and weeks passed, the rains became more constant. The rivers and seas where much darker and less transparent and the forests, woods and trees less vibrant; their leaves gradually changing to magnificent brilliant fiery shades of yellow, orange, red and gold.

No one knew what had happened and mass panic spread across Terratopia. Immense strain was placed onto the union and none felt it more than Kyzus. The collective parliament fell into chaos and no one individual or group had the outright authority to end it, which aggravated Kyzus for he believed he could, but he hadn't the legitimate power to as Prime Lord Delegate. After much consideration and consoling with Thyzus and Mia, the three deduced that the likely cause of events was due to Terra Tearia passing from its summer to autumn of the World, similar to how a great many ages earlier it had done so from spring to summer. They all took for granted that the summer would never end as it had been countless tens of thousands of years but they now believed it apparently just had.

Their suspicions were made correct when the Chroniclers

eventually descended onto the slopes of Mount Roccano once more and foretold of the terrible deeds of the terrific demonic Gathaku, named Gathgauge, and the poisoning of the Celestial Atlas, dooming Terra Tearia for eventual and ultimate destruction in due time. But that due time was a great, near uncountable number of ages away, practically forever, especially for mortal races like Men, whose lifetimes wouldn't even come close to Terra Tearia's doom. Yet the news still saddened the vast majority of the peoples of Terratopia. Despite, from a disassociated, logical and rational point of view, nothing really had changed for the archipelago and its inhabitants, widespread sadness, panic, and despair still infected all kingdoms across the lands and the union parliament itself. All of this continually aggravated Kyzus more and more whom didn't have the authority to place everyone back in line and rationally listen to the wisdom of the Merpeople and Elves who were handling the news far better than all other races, going about their lives as normally as they could. There was also the added threat that the Evil spirit of the fallen Celestial Morur was now much stronger and able to infiltrate and corrupt the peoples of the world far easier. Something the current chaotic and panic swept atmosphere presented the perfect conditions for peoples to buy into his Evil which only worsened the chaos.

    Panic and chaos continued to sweep the union and the lands of Terratopia. Everyone seemed to fall into a cycle of needless bickering. Inhabitants of kingdoms in their despair sought for avenues to place their built-up turmoil, which all too often came out as anger towards the Terratopia Union itself for not taking action. Yet action could not be taken as the parliament was still largely in turmoil also, with representatives and Lord Delegates becoming less and less judicial and instead becoming more and more emotional, angry, and sometimes hate filled. They bickered with one another needlessly, getting nothing substantial done while also then growing more and more frustrated that nothing was achieved, only to then blame one another for the union's inactivity; a vicious negative spiral which only led the people of Terratopia to lose more and more confidence in their leaders and the union. It was as if trust and faith in one another had disappeared overnight.

Kyzus's annoyance at the Terratopia Union and its members continued to grow and his respect for the inhabitants of the kingdoms, kingdoms he had personally lived in for a time and revisited for pleasure, went down. He began to feel let down by the mass panic and chaos across the lands and let down by the needless arguing. He felt this even more upon discovering that many were calling for the dissolvement of the union and that kingdoms should go their own way; reversing all the work his father and himself had dedicated their lives towards over countless years and lifetimes. Such illogical calls made little sense to Kyzus, his wisdom and great sense of fairness to all truly struggled to understand the reasonings behind these demands of union dissolvement. He could not grasp the conclusions the peoples of Terratopia were coming to, they knew that the world was now going to be a much harder place to live in and Evil more able to take hold, and so for that they wanted to break apart an ancient union built on friendship and helping one another to make the lands a better place; truly a baffling concept to Kyzus. The fact many different kingdoms were making the same calls and gaining much support for them baffled Kyzus further and he wished nothing more than to put a stop to it all and revert things back to normal as it was in the height of the Summer of the world, a time of near perfection and a time where people seemed to be far understanding and trustworthy, of their leaders and of one another.

Alas Kyzus hadn't the authority and power to accomplish what he desired, instead he was limited to what the Speaker and Lord Delegates proposed, which in the grand scheme of things were nearly always irrelevant and not going to solve the real underlying problems facing them. Kyzus continually highlighted this but his wisdom continually fell on death ears. In addition, the proposals brought up were most often a reflection or a consequence of the wider kingdoms' inhabitants. Proposals were; emotional, fuelled by distrust, fear, anger, despair, and irrationality; they were illogical in nature and reversed all the Terratopia Union had accomplished. All the unions strengths and achievements were seemingly forgotten about and people focused on any weakness they could find, or fabricate, to then expose and then ultimately make worse, further creating more problems and weaknesses which were then further exposed and made worse. The governance of the Terratopia Union became seen as inadequate, its issues snowballing beyond its control and it all being all fuelled by the distrusting, panicked people of the kingdoms. Terratopia had become a boiling pot and Kyzus knew it, he grew even sadder that he could do nothing about it. He knew something would soon boil over and that its consequences would be disastrous. Sure enough, something terrible did happen and it had drastic life changing consequences for Kyzus and indeed the whole of Terratopia at large.

Szar, the King of Giants was the most vocal advocate for the disillusionment of the Terratopia Union. His kingdom of Giants had all become fed up of the unions perceived rule over them. In addition, they came to despise the kingdom of Roccano in particular, perceiving it to be an overbearing capital, directly ruling the whole of Terratopia for its own personal gain, the kingdoms nothing more than puppets for the Elven inhabitants to satisfy their secret wish to rule the entire archipelago for themselves. Szar began to regard Thyzus as a tyrant and Kyzus a puppet of his, as it was Thyzus who created the union in the first place. Fuelled by a new found hatred and anger, a direct result of Morur's Evil spirit, Szar gathered his Giants court and recalled his Lord Delegate back to his kingdom. Together the Giants all plotted a terrible plan...

Upon returning back to Roccano, the Giants Lord Delegate, Mur, called that an extended meeting should take place, a meeting between all the Lord Delegates of the union, as well as all the respected leaders of the kingdoms; to collectively discuss a solution to the current crisis. Seeing some potential in the proposition to finally get things back to normal, Kyzus did all in his power to make the proposed idea happen; which it did. It was decided that a year from that day, all leaders and Lord Delegates from across all Terratopia would meet on the slopes of Mount Roccano to discuss, what Kyzus had dubbed 'the Autumn crises.'

In the course of the year before the proposed extended meeting, during a dark yet peaceful night while Kyzus was working late at the union parliament building, Thyzus and Mia were sitting in their respected chairs in their large open study. A warm crackling log fire burned as the husband and wife sat and discussed the current matters of Terratopia and what they could do about it, if anything even could be; a type of evening that had become a regular occurrence for the both of them. During this dark and peaceful night, interrupting their discussion, a cold wind blew through the study and eerily extinguished the fire in an instant. As the room dimmed a black cloudy figure manifested itself; draped in long ebony flowing robes and a hood so large that the figures face, if it had one, could not be seen. The black spirit floated in front of the fireplace in-between the mildly confused couple. Levitating calmly, its arms by its side and its skeleton-like hands resting on its black belt, the manifestation spoke;

"Do not be afraid Thyzus and Mia Hobbes," said a rich voice, speaking reassuringly and raising one of its bony arms openly. "I am a servant of the Celestial Thoseus and I come bringing news of your unfortunate futures."

"What do you mean?" asked Thyzus. "You're a Grim Reaper spirit aren't you? But we are still alive! We have no need to be escorted to the Halls of Thilore!"

"You misunderstand," said the Demi-god of Thoseus, again in a rich but calm voice. "I am afraid both of your deaths and its drastic consequences have been foreseen by my Celestial master and I am here to share this foresight with you as its consequences deem you both worthy to know."

Puzzled and concerned, the couple looked at one another, registering the worry in each other's eyes. "What do you mean?" asked Mia. "We are both far before our years of deaths from old age and have no broken soul, we could not possibly die!"

"And Terratopia is a peaceful place, it may be in slight chaos but there is no war among its peoples. Why do you bring us this news spirit?" Thyzus then added.

The Grim Reaper replied, "A war there is not currently no. But one is coming. It starts with the death of you both. Much foreseen pain, suffering, anguish, chaos, and death arises because of it." Thyzus and Mia rose to their feet at the news, the Demi-god continued, "Terratopia and its peoples, including your son Kyzus, are woefully underprepared for the insuring conflict. It will break your son and Morur's Evil will flourish in the ensuring environment of the war-torn archipelago."

Thyzus and Mia had come together to hold each other, Thyzus begged, "Spirit, are our deaths certain? How do we even die? What can we do to avert such a future you have foreseen? Is Evil really doomed to control our beloved home?"

"Your deaths are inevitable yes and I cannot tell you how they come about," the Grim Reaper responded. "However, its consequences can of course be changed..."

After the Grim Reaper said this, Kyzus had arrived home, the sound of him closing their grand palace home doors rocked through the study. As soon as the echoing stopped, Thyzus and Mia had come to realise the Grim Reaper before them had vanished where it floated and the log fire had burst back into flames, warming the room once more.

Thyzus and Mia decided not to tell their beloved son about their foreseen deaths, they could not bring themselves too, but they did however try the best they could to prepare him for a world without their presence, guidance, and love. In addition, Thyzus and Mia began to train themselves in the ways of combat and collectively began to arm Roccano and close friendly kingdoms; proclaiming that; 'in as hostile and uncertain of a world such as their own, as a safety net, having a defensive standing force to keep the peace could only benefit a kingdom.' Mia's home kingdom of Aquatatia began to arm itself and build a navy. The nearby cities to Roccano in the kingdom of Rodus, Filnethias and Rime, as close friends of Thyzus began to follow in his example as well, building up powerful forces of high Men and Elves to protect their cities in the chaotic climate.

Sure, enough the year passed and all the relevant peoples gathered on Mount Roccano slopes as previously agreed upon a year earlier. Importantly for the sinister purposes of the Giants Szar and Mur, Thyzus also joined the meeting, hoping to share his wisdom on the coming discussion. The collection of powerful leaders and Lord Delegates all sat down and began to discuss the current situation and what should be done about it. Talks seemed to be going well with leaders and Lord Delegates agreeing on more things than they had since autumns coming and were also conversing far more calmly as well, showing to Kyzus in particular a clear desire for peace and prosperity within them all. This would not last however. Szar and Mur, who had been mostly quiet up until this point, simply nodding in agreement to everything said, rose to their feet suddenly, towering over their fellow beings below on the mountain slopes. They proclaimed that Roccano's rule of Terratopia was at an end and that the supreme independence of the combined kingdoms had begun. Szar let out an almighty roar and Mur smashed his huge fists down onto the mountain slopes, aiming directly for Thyzus. Before the ancient Elf could even register what was going on, Thyzus was crushed beneath the huge fists of Mur in a sudden moment of horrific violence. Mur then approached Kyzus with his fists raised again. Kyzus however instinctively, though with much effort, magically froze Mur, and then Scar in place. All other members of the gathering naturally froze in place as well in sheer horror at the scene. Their state of shock only was only shaken away when the battle cry of more Giants could be heard in the distance. Kyzus screamed at them all to run back to the city, which they all promptly did, being closely followed by Scar who managed to overpower Kyzus's spell. Mur then followed suit as Kyzus tired and dropped to his knees in exhaustion.

    The remaining members of the now chaotic meeting ran for their lives into back into the city of Roccano being followed by the two homicidal Giants. Loud horns started to blow and screams of panic and dread started to erupt. Kyzus was the only person left on the mountainside. The weight of his father's death then suddenly hit him and, in a trace, he stumbled over to the new crater created in the mountainside where the dead body of his father lay. Upon climbing the ridge of the crater and looking down into it, he saw the mangled, squashed body of Thyzus, a mere glimpse of its former self. In an even deeper trance, Kyzus drifted down to his dead fathers' side and, upon reaching the horrific site that was Thyzus's squashed remains, passed out in shock, falling flat next to his father's body.

    Kyzus was woken days later by a patrol of Men and Elves sent to look for him. He still couldn't believe what had happened. His entire life had been spent in a peaceful, harmonised land where the most violent act he had ever saw was the hunting of deer. Still in a semi-trance-like state from the shock, Kyzus was escorted to the current Premier of Roccano, Joell. Not accounting for Kyzus's clear dazed state, Joell hurriedly attempted to catch Kyzus up on what had transpired since his father's death. An army of Giants had attacked Roccano however, the grand gates of the kingdom were too robust, and the combined Elves and Men's defence too strong, for them to break through. However, Szar and Mur had rampaged through the city kingdom, causing complete mayhem, destruction, and death in their wake. Eventually, Mur was brought down through the skill of the Elven mages and the bravery of the Men soldiers. Szar, however, continued his rampage only to be halted by the defiant defence of Mia. The mentioning of his mother brought Kyzus straight back to reality who had so far not taken in anything Joell had said. His eyes darted straight to make contact with Joell's and he immediately asked where his mother was. Joell sighed, dropping his head, and tearing his gaze away from Kyzus's and to the ground. He removed his crowned helmet and toldKyzus how his mother had perished duelling Szar on the grand steps leading to their palace home built into the mountain side. Kyzus instantly dropped to his knees in despair and shock, zoning straight back into the dazed trance he was in as his father died days earlier. He didn't hear how epic and valiant his mother's duel was, or how she had in fact defeated Szar, slicing his neck only to be crushed by his enormous dead body as it collapsed onto the mountain side steps where she had landed from her fatal attack.

 No anger or desire for revenge passed over Kyzus. He just simply couldn't comprehend how this had all happened. How the events from the coming of autumn had transcribed into what they currently were. How had needless bickering turned to conspiracy and murder? In sheer disbelief Kyzus rose to his feet and drifted to his mountainside home, away from the cries of Joell. The Premier followed, explaining how he had assembled a large, grand army and was ready to march on the Giants Lands and destroy every last one of them for their terrible act of war. Kyzus nodded slightly and waved his hand in an approving way, but barely acknowledged anything Joell was really saying. Joell then butted directly in front of Kyzus, blocking his path. He announced that as the new Lordbaron of Roccano he should lead his troops and followers into war, after all he was also the most powerful sorcerer in all the land. Joell explained that they even had the eager support of the high Elves of Filnethias, the high Men of Rime, and the Merpeople of Aquatatia, none of these words registering with Kyzus until the mentioning of Mia's home kingdom. He stood up from his hunched position but still with his head hung down, Kyzus then grabbed Joell's crowned helm from his hands and placed it on Joell's head. He announced in a sombre voice that as the new Lordbaron of the kingdom of Roccano, he commanded the Premier take the grand army he spoke of and do with it as he saw fit. Kyzus saw no point in this coming war but his will was too broken to argue against it. Kyzus then commanded for his parent's bodies be sent to his palace home and then for him not to be disturbed until he came out again. Until then any roles originally filled by the Lordbaron were to fall into the Premier of Roccano.

After saying this first decree as Lordbaron of Roccano, Kyzus continued to drift his way towards his palace home, carelessly sailing over the corpse of the Giant king Szar that lay on his palace's grand steps. On reaching the doors to his home he paused, let out a sigh of sheer pain before then pushing them open, stepping inside and closing the doors behind him, locking them upon their closure. The distinct depressing metallic sound that could be heard across the whole moaning kingdom.

Chapter 4

The Re-Sparking of Hope

A few days later a small sombre company of Men and Elves arrived at Kyzus's doors with his parent's bodies within sublime golden and wooden coffins. The leader of this company was a young woman named Robin. When arriving at Kyzus's doors she hesitated but, being encouraged on by her fellow Men and Elves in the company, she banged on the large metal knocker on the palace's door. A resounding voice quickly replied;

"Are you the bringers of my doomed parents?"

"Yes, my Lordbaron," Robin replied. "We have created lavish coffins to rest such great leaders in and brought them to you as requested," she paused but then continued. "My Lordbaron, the people miss you. We are all devastated at the loss of such monumental icons of our great kingdom city and none of us can imagine what it must be like for you, it cannot be easy. Please come out and let us all say farewell to our former heroes together."

Robin's voice was as kind and reassuring as her words, she then took a step back to eagerly await Kyzus's response from behind the door. Silence followed before eventually being broken by a response;

"The peoples worry is most appreciated but I have my way of dealing with this loss and saying farewell alone in my own palace is how it shall be done. Thank you, my dear friend, from behind the door, but please leave."

Robin's company all sighed but understood and so turned to walk back down the palace steps. Robin too turned and began to walk away, except with her back turned to Kyzus's doors she stopped, she felt too sorry for Kyzus to walk away so she doubled back and spoke to the door again;

"My Lordbaron, you need a friend. No one should face what you're facing alone. You may be a Half-elf of ancient times, with wisdom beyond comprehension; but I know you are hurting and are upset right now. You must be feeling immense grief and be filled with sorrow. Any being would be. Let me help you."

Robins request seemingly fell on death ears until the doors peered open slightly and a finely dressed figure could be seen through the small gap in-between the slightly ajar doors. Robin bowed her head at Kyzus's presence but he reached out towards her delicate chin and gently lifted her head to make eye contact with her.

"Never would I have expected such comforting wise words to come out of a lady seemingly so young."

Robin darted her eyes back and forth between Kyzus's own and the ground;

"Thank you my Lordbaron," she replied.

"Please call me Kyzus my dear, now who might you be?" Kyzus inquired.

"I am Lady Robin my Lordbar- Kyzus; I am the secretary of the Speaker Joell; we have met in passing in parliament but never been fully acquainted."

Opening the doors further Kyzus exclaimed, "I knew I recognised you somewhere! You will have to forgive my ignorance, please come inside."

Robin did so, passing by Kyzus and stopping in his palaces lobby, amazed by its splendour. Kyzus walked around to face Robin once more.

"You have the spitting image of my dear mother," Kyzus said. "You are what I imagine she looked like in her younger years before she had even met my father."

Robin blushed. "You are too kind Kyzus, I'm sure I couldn't come close to the beauty of the Lady Mia."

Kyzus chuckled, "Yes that may be true, but beautiful nonetheless you are and so kind and wise for looking so young."

Robin blushed even more and chuckled back, "You yourself don't look as old as I'd have thought for a being of your age, knowledge and wisdom."

This was true, for as old Kyzus was, he was still in the younger prime of his life in respect of Half-elven immortality. He began to smile and stepped closer to then take Robins hands with his own.

"Come, Robin," he said happily, "let me show you something."

The two then walked into the grand living hall of the palace, its walls covered in fine art and sculptures and candle chandeliers daggled from the high ceiling bathing the hall is warm magical candlelight. A huge lavish polished table was also in the centre of the room, dominating its floor space. In the far corner of this room however floated a seemingly sentient dark red hooded robe that's fabrics swayed gently as if blown by a light wind. This sight startled Robin at first before then being reassured by Kyzus of what it was. It was a Wraith, a servant of the Celestial Zella. Robin began to calm as Kyzus explained what it was, how it had come to him and how it had helped him deal with his parents' deaths.

The Wraith arrived in Kyzus's presence the day he locked himself in his palace home. Through his knowledge of Terra Tearia's mythology and history, Kyzus knew what the Wraith was and why it had come to him. He willingly accepted the Wraith's presence despite the fact that it could not speak nor did it have any recognisable features besides its dark red hooded robe seemingly covering an invisible floating body, which was completely invisible outside the spirit world. The Wraith brought much comfort and relief to Kyzus, seemingly sucking his pain and sorrow away with its close presence and invisible touch. Kyzus once again thanked Robin for her caring words but he explained how he was not alone, he had a Wraith, personally sent by the Celestial Zella, he did not need the help of anyone else. However, as he said this, the robe dropped to the floor like a rag; the Wraith had disappeared. It had phased back into the spirit realm, leaving only its dark red robe in its wake.

Speechless Robin then explained to Kyzus that he could not rely on the gifts of the Celestials and spirit Demi-gods to mend his sorrow filled broken heart and will. Kyzus needed to come back to the real world, he needed to let go of his desisted parents, overcome it and move on; to fulfil his duties as the new Lordbaron of Roccano and the Prime Lord Delegate of the Terratopia Union, both things being in utter turmoil since the Giants rebellion. These wise words filled Kyzus with hope, he stood up proud and announced that Robin was right, explaining how her words were as if Mia herself were there saying them to him right now. He once more held Robin's hands and this time asked her to say with him in his palace. He was not yet ready to go outside and rule Roccano as Lordbaron, but he felt great comfort, friendship, and happiness with Robin and so wanted her to stay with him. Robin sincerely accepted Kyzus's request, feeling it to be a great honour, but also feeling a strong bond between herself and Kyzus, and she wanted to explore it further.

Over the next fifty years the two lived together in Kyzus's palace. The pair brung the best out of each other and became incredibly happy in each other's company. They began a courtship after several years and, although never officially marrying, several years later had three children together. A set of twin brothers, whom were named Tyzus and Hyzus, and a younger daughter, Mia-Myzus. Kyzus, just as his father Thyzus had done before him, resolved to raise his children the best he possibly could, teaching them all he could in the ways of wisdom, fairness, and magic. When Hyzus and Tyzus were ten years old and Mia-Myzus six, Kyzus had never been happier, his soul was filled with hope for the future once more. Kyzus finally felt ready to venture back outside into the world with his new family by his side; which on his children's birthday he did. The opening of his palace doors and his advance through the streets of Roccano was a truly monumental occasion for all in the kingdom as well as for Kyzus's family. Kyzus took up his duties as the Lordbaron of Roccano and officially married the Lady Robin, her young beauty still somehow persisting throughout her time together with Kyzus, the close companionship to him magically keeping her in her younger youthful years of when first meeting him all those years ago, similar to how Mia was also kept young by close companionship Thyzus as well.

The Premier Joell had unfortunately perished in the on-going war against the Giants however the latest Premier, Jowell, the son of Joell, welcomed Kyzus back with much enthusiasm and eagerly awaited the coming years with a true Lordbaron to lead Roccano once more. Jowell also explained the current state of affairs in Terratopia to Kyzus. With the outbreak of the war against the Giants and the decimation of Roccano at the hands of Szar and Mur, on top of the current disorder the Terratopia Union was already in, it was agreed that the union was to be placed on hold until the wars end. All of its standing framework was to be upheld but no more union activity was to happen, the parliament was agreed to be disbanded until the war had come to its conclusion. In addition, a new capital for the union was built from the ground up to try and remove the image of the unions own old capital being attacked and its previous former Prime Lord Delegate slain. The new capital of the Terratopia Union was named Embirith, after the tremendous river it was built along. It was a grand, marvellous, and immaculate city and its parliament buildings were among the most dignified, grandiose, and exulted in all Terra Tearia. It truly was a monumental way to reignite the failing union, restoring it upon its eventual return after the war.

The war between Men, Elves, Merpeople, and Giants, which became known as the war between Roccano, and Giants or 'the war for the sake of Thyzus', was going exceedingly well for the allied forces of Roccano, Rodus, and Aquatatia. The Giants were all but defeated, their forces near spent. Despite the war lasting over half a century the Giants had not been able to venture far out their kingdoms borders of the Stepping Hills for over thirty years and Jowell estimated that only a few more campaigns through the Giant Lands were required to fully end the war. Even their capital city, their only city, the City of Giants, had been destroyed by the forces of high Men and Elves from Rodus, its immense oversized buildings being reduced to massive ruins. Upon learning all this, Kyzus felt that the war had gone on long enough, not even wanting to know the cost of life it had caused. He proposed a peace treaty be drawn up and signed. Such an agreement was welcomed by his allies but rejected by the Giants; however, a year later a temporary end to the fighting was agreed and a peace treaty signing arranged.

Kyzus and Jowell's forces continued to surround the Stepping Hills, making sure no rogue Giants could escape and reck havoc on Terratopia. An entourage of Giants agreed to meet with Kyzus and Jowell in the nearby fortress city of Cronmpt, the capital of the nearby kingdom of Arway and a stronghold Jowell's forces had been using as a forward staging post all of the war's duration. In his desire to raise his children to best he could and to help them eventually grow to be great Half-elven leaders like him, Kyzus brought his children with him to Cronmpt to witness the diplomatic event, under the care of Robin. The Giants latest leader, the king Dimz, soon arrived at the tall foreboding walls of Cronmpt along with his entourage, his head being the perfect height to see Kyzus, his family, Jowell, and numerous other important players in the allied forces that had all but defeated his kingdom as they all stood atop the mighty walls of Cronmpt. King Dimz looked war torn and angry, his bread was a rich dreaded black and his eyes orange like fire. As he stood right up next to the walls of Cronmpt he stared directly into Kyzus's eyes.

"So, you are the Lordbaron who hasn't showed his face for over fifty years?" Dimz's said, his deep voice booming across the surrounding plains of Arway. "I have come to accept your surrender, weak son of Thyzus Hobbes. Surrender or continue this war till your own death."

Chapter 5

The Grave Betrayal

Somewhat stunned, Kyzus disregarded Dimz's words and announced;

"As the Lordbaron of Roccano and the leader of the forces against you king Dimz, I have come to put an end to this war, so as to stop the fighting and death between our kingdoms."

Dimz scowled, his giant eyebrows and nose wrinkling in fury. Kyzus continued, "Despite the actions by your old king and Lord Delegate and their betrayal of my fathers and my peoples trust and respect, I have not come to ascertain a surrender from you with any conditions. I, along with my fellow leaders, wish for peace to once again return to Terratopia, we wish for you to sign this peace treaty to return things to how they were not half a century ago. No sanctions will be placed onto your kingdom and you will be welcomed back into the restored Terratopia Union if you so wished."

Dimz roared with rage, "My grandfather Szar and his cousin Mur are heroes for their actions against your kingdom and your family! You are foolish to forgive them. We Giants would all do the same. We care not for your supposed restored union; we see it as the front it really is; a corrupt way for the leaders of Roccano to rule and control the entire archipelago of Terratopia along with its peoples! We will not become slaves!"

Kyzus was amazed at the audacity of the Giant king. His claims could not be further from the truth with no factual merit behind them at all. Jowell then exclaimed;

"Lies, absolutely none of that is true and you know it! Roccano had no control over Terratopia, it supported the union, that is all! And besides, Roccano is no longer the capital of the restored union. It is its own independent kingdom within the union now, a new, truly independent, capital has been made. The city of Embirith. A city built over the River Embirith, on the Rodus slopes, lying on the outskirting pastures of the kingdom of Nindir!"

Dimz laughed maniacally. "Change what you will about the

union, we would never voluntarily join an ideal where our control is taken away and given to a far-reaching distant city under the control of races other than our own."

"Your own race is just as much as in control of the union as any other! But that's fine!" Kyzus stated, "no one is forcing you join the restored union and your people will be treated no differently whether you do or do not. Our aims are the peace and prosperity of all, which is why we are here requesting you end this war between our peoples."

Dimz rebutted, "I will never agree to a peace between our peoples, not unless it was through your surrender to us!"

Jowell yelled out, "You cannot be serious you dim-witted Giant, you are defeated! We have every right to push for your unconditional surrender, we could fully occupy your whole kingdom and yet we only ask for an end to the fighting! Your city is in ruins and your people all but slain! End this war before you are all killed because of it!"

Dimz renounced, lifting his arms high above his head, "We are the Giants of the Giant Lands of Terratopia. As long as we stand, Mount Harpgar and the Great Owls as our witness, we shall never surrender!"

"The war shall continue then," stated Kyzus, tired of Dimz ignorance and turning to walk away towards his family.

"Don't you turn your back on me son of Thyzus Hobbes," Grunted Dimz. "I offer you one last chance to surrender; for your family's sake."

With a sense of anger finally passing over him, Kyzus turned around and exclaimed, "My family have seen all they need to see to understand my decision to continue to wage war against you and your ignorant peoples. We have no need to surrender, we can and will defeat you. You will regret not accepting our mercy when you had the chance, now countless more must unnecessarily die because of it, most of them your own race!"

Dimz smirked, "Death to all then."

He stepped back but then kicked Cronmpt's walls with the sole of his mighty boots. "I declare an end to the temporary truce, let the fighting commence once more!" Dimz then shouted.

He once again kicked the fortress city walls. So thunderous was his strikes that they shook everyone standing on them to their knees. Dimz noticed this and continued to do it, seeing an opportunity to break Kyzus's will once more as Robin with her children by her side all began to stumble close to the walls interior edge. Dimz continued to strike at the colossal walls of Cronmpt, shaking Robin to the very edge. Kyzus saw exactly what was happening and rushed to her aid, managing to magically catch and levitate her as she eventually fell off the walls. She then screamed at Kyzus to save their children whom were also now about to fall. As they did Kyzus magically suspended them as well, beginning to then slowly lower all his family down to the safe ground below. Aggravated at his foiled plan, Dimz rushed to climb the wall; while his accompanying Giants fought against the Elven guard and defence of Men. An opening in the walls defences soon occurred and Dimz leaped at it, he clambered half up the wall and, after spying Kyzus, swung his hammer to strike Kyzus down. Jowell saw this and charged for Kyzus, pushing the Half-elf out the way just in time but not fast enough to save himself and he was crushed beneath Dimz's almighty blow.

Saved Kyzus was, but the actions of Jowell disrupted him so much that his magical grip on Robin and his children failed and they all continued to plummet to the streets of Cronmpt below. Immediately Kyzus re-cast his spells and magically caught Mia-Myzus, then Tyzus, then Hyzus. But for Robin it was too late. For his children all had fallen into streets in-between buildings below the walls; but Robin fell directly over a tall church spire. Kyzus managed to catch her, but not before the spires point had impaled her through her torso. Half alive, Robin begged Kyzus to lower their children to safety and then to let her go.

Tears flooded Kyzus's eyes, his pain and anguish even more intense than from the loss of his father and mother. He lowered his children to the ground and then magically cast a mystical foggy bubble around them so that they could not see the sight of their dying mother. Kyzus exclaimed in terror how he could not allow Robin to die, especially at his own hand. He knew he could not magically heal her wounds but he cried to her that he would find a way; he simply could not bear to lose her as well. Tears flooded Robin's eyes as well. She calmly told Kyzus how it was all right, how he could never hurt her and how it was now time for him to let her go. Kyzus still shook his head in tears. He exclaimed how he couldn't do it, he had never let go of the loss of his parents and needed Robin to cope with it as well, she brought so much happiness and stability to his life, there was no possible chance he was going to let her go; literally or figuratively. Robin again calmly and bravely looked Kyzus in the eyes, saying how it was ok, her time had unfortunately come and that it was time to let her go. Still Kyzus could not do it, drawing out every moment as long as he possibly could.

Dimz saw all that was going on and proceeded to throw his hammer at the church spire and Robin. Kyzus cried out and strained to magically hold Robin in her critical position with one hand while also attempting to stop the flight of the enormous Giant king's hammer with his other. Move the hammers trajectory away from Robin with a magical force Kyzus could but alas he could not stop it and it struck the church spires base, crumbling it to the ground and Robin along with it. Still held in place impaled on the churches spire by Kyzus's magical grip, Robin tumbled into the imploding collapsing tower and soon disappeared from Kyzus's view; hidden behind the clouds of dust and rumble.

Kyzus once again fell into the same dazed trance he fell into from his parent's death. He screamed out in sorrow and lay on his back, staring up into the grey overcast skies. The high kings of Filnethias and Rime eventually managed to slay Dimz and then proceeded to call for the extermination of all Giants for their grave betrayal. They leaped to their steeds and rode for the Stepping Hills to signal their armies to wipe out the Giants and to scorch their lands. Kyzus did not even register the severity of what they had ordered and set off to do, instead he just lay on the tall city walls in grief and sorrow feeling incredibly intense emotions but somehow also feeling nothing at all but numbness. Before long Hyzus, Tyzus and Mia-Myzus arrived by his side breaking him out his daze. They all hugged him in fear and began to ask where their mother was.

Being as strong and brave as he could for his children, trying not to show how broken his will truly was, Kyzus explained how their mother had unfortunately had to go and be by Zatos Zendar's side. Kyzus explained how Robin was just too amazing and compassionate and that the god Zatos Zendar needed more Angels like her and so she had peacefully gone to be an Angel beyond even the heavens of Terra Tearia, to now overlook the whole universe for all time. With tears in his eyes Kyzus looked at his children, whom now too were tearing up, he told them that they weren't going to see their mother again for a very long time, but that she was always going to be watching over them and was extraordinarily proud of them all and always would be. And with that Tyzus, Hyzus, and Mia-Myzus all cuddled up as tight as they could to their father Kyzus and they all felt comfort in each other's arms as rain then slowly started to pour down on them all.

Chapter 6

The Children of Kyzus

Kyzus and his children all set out to return back home to their kingdom of Roccano. Their journey was long, slow and sombre. Kyzus decided not to journey by sea back home, not wanting to accept the help of the Aquatatia Merpeople and their fast ships as it would remind him too much of Mia, whom he had also began to grieve over once more. Instead Kyzus and his children travelled by land. They rode in a large luxurious carriage pulled by pure white unicorns. They travelled slowly and mostly in silence, all holding each other tight as the only form of comfort they all had. Together they remembered Robin and all she had done for all of them. Their journey took them through the kingdom of Arway and over the Kondit Hills, they followed the path of the Kondit River, passing through the kingdom of Kondit Point and riding pass the rich grand mansion city of Men, the city of Kondit. When they made it to the coast, through the magic of Kyzus and the unicorns, the carriage flew over the areas of sea in between Kondit Point and the Connecting Isles. They halted their journey in the capital of the Connecting Isles, Xephex, for a couple of days to restore their supplies and strength as their journey was only half complete.

While in Xephex, Kyzus received an invitation from the Elf Lord Folore, leader of the kingdom of Lemlee. He wished to offer his condolences and offer to help in any way he could. Kyzus wished only to get back home, but he would not refuse the offer of help like he had done with Robin all those years ago for he knew none would be as persistent as her to help. He accepted the invitation, believing it also to beneficial to his children to receive loving support from the fair woodland Elves of Lemlee as well. In their unicorn drawn carriage they all rode and flew to the capital of Lemlee, Wefalime, where they were greeted by Lord Folore and his wife the Lady Elwii. Kyzus's children were amazed by the forest city and the entire tree covered forest islands that surrounded it. An entire set of islands completely covered in dense woodlands with trees as old as time and leaves as colourful and striking as fire.

They were all escourted to Folore and Elwii's residence, a marvellous wooden chateau built high up in the tree top canopy, which also brought wonder to the young children's eyes and they began to smile again for the first time since arriving at Cronmpt. Kyzus saw this, realising at that moment that his children had not yet seen the wonder and beauty of the varying kingdoms of Terratopia as they had not spent lifetimes exploring the archipelago as he had done with his brother many ages ago. Kyzus requested that his children be allowed to go explore and play in the peaceful wonderous Elven city which Lord Folore graciously allowed, advising them to go find the fountains of Lemlee in the city centre of Wefalime. He called for two of his entourage guards to watch over the children as they ran off to explore and play. When alone, Kyzus, Folore and Elwii began talking, the Elves offering their condolences and support to Kyzus as friends and asked how he was coping. Not soon after this however, horns of Valkyries could be heard as a host from Melian, the Sky Mountains of Terratopia capital, arrived riding flying Pegasus's over the treetops and gracefully landing in Kyzus's presence. The Queen of Valkyries, Heroyn, unmounted from her Pegasus and approached Kyzus. She bowed and told how sorry she was for his loss and wished to help in any way she could. Kyzus thanked her before Heroyn then continued for, she also came bearing news. Glorthelian and Johnathan III, the High kings of Elf and Man of Filnethias and Rime had won the war against the Giants. Filled with a little hope, Kyzus asked if the Giants had finally surrendered but Heroyn signed, explaining how the Giants fought till the very end and had now been completely wiped out. The last Giant in Terratopia being slain by Glorthelian and Johnathan III personally that very morning.

Kyzus fell onto the seat he was standing next too. He couldn't believe it. He had no idea that's what his forces were doing and he did not wish for this to have happened. The weight of being the leader of a combined army that had wiped out an entire kingdom and race hit Kyzus as if a mountain had been dropped onto his shoulders. The feelings of comfort he was beginning to feel from being in Wefalime and in the company of the Elves and Valkyries were violently ripped away. Kyzus once again wished to return home and think about all that had transpired since his parent's deaths. He wished for nothing like this to ever be possible to happen ever again within the lands of Terratopia. He wished for a Terratopia where, no more bloodshed could occur and no one would ever feel the pain and sorrow he was feeling currently or had felt historically. Kyzus desired for nothing more than to return Terratopia and its peoples to their state of former happiness and prosperity apparent in the summer of the world as he could not remember anything being wrong with the world until its summer ended.

Kyzus was torn though, as he also felt an even stronger duty to the raising of his children as he had resolved to do alongside Robin at their births; but he also firmly believed he could never raise them to be the best beings they possibly could be in the current climate of Terratopia. He was truly uncertain about what to do. Kyzus, Heroyn, Folore, Elwii, and the surrounding Elves and Valkyries all stood facing one another in silence and dismay, the news of the Giants total genocide lingering in the air, even the ambient singing of Lemlee's woodland birds seemed to halt.

This silence was soon broken however by the innocent giggles and squeals of glee from Kyzus's children as they came running to Kyzus. They all stopped suddenly however, and starred as their eyes lay sight on the beautiful, formidable winged women that were the Valkyries. Their mouths dropped in bewilderment and their eyes widened in astonishment. Mia-Myzus asked if they were Angels like her mother now was and Heroyn replied, her voice and expression filled with kindness and compassion. She explained how they were Valkyries from a faraway floating city called Melian. The children all slowly made their way to their fathers welcoming embrace, their attention still fixed on the magnificent winged women as Heroyn explained herself. They all begged Kyzus to be able to visit Heroyn's kingdom and explore the Sky Mountains they now learned about; their pleas giving Kyzus the beginnings of an idea. He enthusiastically agreed, requesting Heroyn take them all to her floating kingdom, which she willing did.

Flying in their unicorn drawn carriage and alongside the Valkyries and their Pegasus's, Kyzus and his children flew over the sea separating West from Central and East Terratopia, travelling from the Isles of Lemlee to the Sky Mountains of Terratopia, the Valkyries kingdom. They eventually arrived at the mesmerising collection of floating islands in the sky and upon them, the city of Melian. Melian was a grandiose city, similar to Roccano being built around a mountain, Mount Melian. However, Melian was built up far higher and onto far steeper slopes than Roccano was. The city had no streets, it was instead like a monumental collection of bird nests constructed into a large interconnected branched tree; however, the nests were entire buildings, castles, and towers made of golden and white stone, and the branches of the tree were outcrops of rock on the sheer slopes of the mountain sides.

The lofty, glorious kingdom fascinated Kyzus's children and the family spent a whole year within the skies of Melian, exploring and living in the city. Hyzus, Tyzus, and Mia-Myzus loved every moment and Kyzus was happy to see his children enjoy themselves, yet his thoughts from Lemlee still plagued his mind and he soon wished to put his ideas into floriation. He gathered his children one day and explained to them how they were still very young and had extremely promising lives ahead of them. Kyzus told how he wished for them to become as knowledgeable, wise, understanding, fair, compassionate, and magically powerful as their ancestors before them. Kyzus's children resoundingly agreed saying that they wanted to be just like their father and mother as well as live up to the legends of their grandparents. Kyzus explained to them the journey him and his brother took to become the Half-elves they were today; studying intensively over many lifetimes in the library halls of Aquata and exploring all the kingdoms of Terratopia, living among their peoples, learning from them and their cultures, similar to how they were living right now in Melian. This news all greatly excited the children whom were eager to explore Terratopia and grow up to be just like their ancestors. Mia-Myzus asked Kyzus if he learnt all that he learnt from the peoples of Terratopia or whether his parents had helped him as well. Kyzus replied that Thyzus and Mia were a huge reason behind the Half-elf that he was currently, however he felt that without them and without Robin, he could not do this to same degree and felt that the outside kingdoms of Terratopia were to be more beneficial to them than his own teaching. He also added that he needed to spend some time to study and contemplate by himself as he wished to come up with a 'grand plan' to better Terratopia and restore it to be just like how it was in the Summer of the world, long before any of them were born.

The twins Tyzus and Hyzus understood this and looked forward to their lives ahead. Lives of learning and exploring Terratopia and they looked forward to their father's plan to restore the lands to their mythical summer like prime told now only through stories. Mia-Myzus however was less enthusiastic. As the youngest she felt far closer to Kyzus than her brothers and did not want to spend lifetimes away from his side exploring the archipelago. She wished to be personally raised and taught by him instead of by far away kingdoms. Kyzus understood this and, touched by his daughters love for him, her pleas also gave him a further idea and opportunity for his somewhat foreseen plans and so Kyzus agreed.

Kyzus determined that Mia-Myzus should come back with him to Roccano where he would personally teach her all he knew as well as reflect on all that happened to them, to study, and to contemplate and rationalise out his 'grand plan' which he felt his children would be a huge part of. His twin sons however where to be sent to the underwater Merpeople city of Aquata where they would be raised and tutored by the wisdom of their grandmother Mia's people. Once grown up they would be sent out to explore and live in the numerous kingdoms of Terratopia, just as how Kyzus and Lyzus had done before them.

Before the Hobbes family parted ways, Kyzus assured his children that they were free to go visit each other anytime but that they should also study and work hard as they would play paramount parts in his coming plan. His children all excitedly understood and promised to devote themselves to become the best Half-elves they could be. Vowing themselves to the service of Kyzus's ensuring plan, sealing magical oaths with every word they said.

Chapter 7

The Deity

Over the next one hundred and fifty years much happened and changed in the archipelago of Terratopia. The twins Hyzus and Tyzus lived an entire century in Aquata studying under the Merpeople tutors and grew into exceptionally wise Half-elves. Mia-Myzus also grew up to be an incredibly wise Half-elf as well as a powerful sorceress under Kyzus's personal and rigorous schooling. Tyzus and Hyzus went on to explore Terratopia's kingdoms just like how their father and uncle had done before them, venturing everywhere from the deep dwarven kingdoms of Dwaria and Kossorlim to the woodland realms of Orthelian and Rodus Forest, meeting with the Centaurs that ruled them. The twins spent time and lived in every kingdom of Terratopia, from the grandiose high Elf capital of Filnethias to the humble, homely Fungi Forest villages belonging to the Gnomes. Mia-Myzus spent several years exploring Terratopia also, but never as much as her brothers and never staying too long in any of the kingdoms, preferring instead to reside in Roccano and with Kyzus; being by his side and learning all she could from him. There was one exception to this however, the kingdom of Sabare. This island kingdom was the kingdom of Goliaths and Samsons and Mia-Myzus was mesmerised by them; their culture and their way of life there. The city of Sabare, built around the mountain twin peaks of Samson and Goliath, was triumphant. It was a kingdom centred around a culture of beings that were the greatest, most powerful, and mighty warriors and guardians in all of Terra Tearia but also beings of immense laughter, play, joy, and love. The delicate balance between warrior like power and gentle, playful love the Samsons and Goliaths possessed enthralled Mia-Myzus and she re-visited the Samson and Goliath kingdom at least once a year for the latter thirty years, spending nearly all the rest of her time with Kyzus in Roccano, as well as visiting her brothers, wherever they were on their journeys.

The Terratopia Union had indeed been restored, although Kyzus played no part in it and allowed the Premier to dictate and fulfil all the roles necessary for it, as Roccano was now just another Lord Delegate and representative sending kingdom within the union, just like every other. The restored Terratopia Union did indeed run out of the newly built, purposely constructed, grand city of Embirith however, it was effectively running the same as it was before the war for the sake of Thyzus. A central parliament was filled with a diverse range of representatives from peoples all across Terratopia that operated and managed all aspects of the union, from ethics to finances, to laws to trade. The running and governance of the union; creating all the unions laws, actions, stances, and direction was down to the Chamber of Lord Delegates. Every kingdom that was a part of the union sent one Lord Delegate to represent their kingdom in the chamber. Kingdoms could also send up to three Advisors with their Lord Delegates whom were also a part of the chamber except they had no voting power, simply more being voices of advice for all the Lord Delegates and voices of insight into the home kingdoms they came from. Being the Speaker of the Parliament was now no longer exclusively for the Premier of Roccano, instead it was now a position with a term limit and speakers had to be selected through a majority decision from the whole parliament. It was a similar story for the Prime Lord Delegate, the position no longer being exclusive for the Lordbaron of Roccano but a position selected by the Lord Delegates Chamber every term. The Speakers role remained the same; the impartial duties of controlling the Chambers sessions, selecting what was on the session's agenda through suggestions from the whole parliament as well as from the Lord Delegates, leading discussion in session and trying to make everything as orderly as possible. The role of the Prime Lord Delegate also remained the same, the role being impartial and also one of not being allowed to propose agendas to the Speaker or Chamber, instead their role holding the most weight and power within the Chamber itself, guiding proposed ideals to the best to their ability and leading the Chamber and union parliament in action.

The union continued to be of some success, continuing much of the work of Thyzus and Kyzus as panic and chaos had begun to subside; however, the union still reached nowhere near the heights of its prosperity and harmony it reached in the summer of the world. Progress was painfully slow and often the unions actions involved backtracking, altering, and reversing proposals and ideals as different leaders of the union with different personal agendas came into and out of power. This itself partly being due to Morur's corrupting influence on union members, but also on the peoples of the union kingdoms themselves they ruled over and that held the union up. Due to Terra Tearia's autumn, Terratopia's peoples themselves bickered and divided and continually demanded different changes constantly, leading to no one ever being satisfied with anything. The lack of noticeable, lasting, and sustainable progress, and sense of uselessness, inevitably began to aggravate the people of the kingdoms within the union once more as well. Some kingdoms slowly began to consider leaving, and in fact some did leave, most noticeably the kingdom of Sabare. The kingdom of Thruckland, an influential merchant sea-bearing kingdom of Men too also started to become far less active in the union as well as the Merpeople kingdoms, them instead falling back into their own union created by Lyzus Hobbes long ago. Only Aquatatia remained as active as it could, its representatives seeing the potential of the Terratopia Union if its people could only solve its devastating issues of distrust and power, and needless bureaucratic bickering.

The overall climate of Terratopia had also continued to change greatly in the autumn of the world compared to its summer. Although kingdoms still all largely remained 'Good', rebellions and extremist groups began to sprout in many kingdoms, largely due to small minorities of inhabitants with their misguided intentions falling to Morur's temptations and choosing actions, or even lives, of Evil. Outside of city, town and village walls the landscape became a dangerous place to wander. Ruffians, bandits, pirates, and marauders attacked, looted, and pillaged all they could get away with. Crime became a serious, but somewhat manageable, problem faced by all kingdom leaders. City wide mobs, kingdom wide mafias, and cross kingdom wide crime syndicates appeared and began to flourish, although very delicately. The rule of law and respect for it began to falter as vast majorities of people began to distrust it and the ones who set and enforced it. Disputes, fighting, and death became far more common place across the lands, though it was still frowned upon. There was still much good in Terratopia and its people happy, but the lands had changed much from their perfectly peaceful, friendly, far more prosperous days in the utopia of summer.

In addition, rumours and stories began to spread of Evil creatures and monsters appearing and attacking travellers and even small settlements. These rumours were confirmed to be true by the enlightening of the Chroniclers, as there were now Colossus's and Tyrants roaming the lands, evil creations from servants and practitioners of Morur's evil twisted magics; Warlocks and Witches.

None of this had gone unnoticed by Kyzus, indeed he had foreseen much of this happening through his great wisdom and understanding. Over the one hundred and fifty years since he arrived back in Roccano with his daughter and sending his twin sons to Aquata, Kyzus had done much. Being the Lordbaron of Roccano he ruled the kingdom with the Premiers. He progressively tried to bring his rule more into the background of Roccano's image as well as progressively altering Roccano's role within the wider Terratopia union. The kingdom became far less influential and active in the union; it faded to the background and became far more neutral in action and largely unaffected by the union's actions and the union unaffected its. Kyzus taught his daughter vehemently in studies and trained her intensely in the magical arts. The two also became exceptional in the way of combat, transforming themselves into extremely powerful combatants and sorcerers. Finally, over the century and a half, as well as doing all that, Kyzus remained largely in his mountain palace home. He studied texts and works from his parents as well as formed his own. He contemplated and reflected deeply on all that had happened in Terratopia, Kyzus aimed to try to fully understand why things were the way they were and deeply pondered for days on end. Eventually he came up with an idea to complete his goal of bringing Terratopia back to its summer levels of prosperity...

Kyzus spent years rationalising out his new overall theory and even more years plotting out his scheme to turn his theory into a reality. And finally, at this time of one hundred and fifty years after arriving back in Roccano, Kyzus believed he had finally finished his 'grand plan' and called all his children back to his palace to share with them his completed works, to explain to them their roles in his plan and to start putting it all into motion.

With Tyzus, Hyzus, and Mia-Myzus all soon back home together, Kyzus gathered them in his large, cluttered study filled with scrolls, texts, books and notes. Lit by a plethora of old disfigured candles, He announced to them all;

"My children, it has been over a century and a half since the tragic death of your mother and my wife, the Lady Robin."

He paused for a moment of silence for the most important person in their collective lives, before then continuing;

"The coming of autumn signified a significant change in the world of Terra Tearia and indeed within our lands of Terratopia. The collective kingdoms of the lands fell into chaos and the union built on friendship and trust between all failed. The death our great leaders, Thyzus and Mia, brought about a devastating war which avoidably led much death and to the extinction of an entire race within these archipelago isles."

He paused again, the weight of ultimately being responsible for the Giants extinction weighing on him before then continuing;

"Since then, life in Terratopia has become chaotic, unfair, nasty, brutish, and short. The very state of the people's nature has changed due to Morur's increased power and the infiltration of his Evil presence in all. The people are far more shellfish now and do not trust anyone but themselves, choosing 'every man for himself' like options over selfless 'helping one another for the benefit of all' like options, as such options require a basic unfounding level of trust in one another, trust that is no longer there. With Autumns arrival, the people had begun to realise something... they all already knew that they were all capable of achieving truly monumental things, but as well as this, the people realised that they were all a threat to each other's goals and aspirations because they were ALL capable of standing in each other's way. The people of Terratopia have all realised they had the power to make or break anyone's aims, and anyone had the exact same power to do the same to them. A very primitive mentality my children as the faith in one another seemingly left them all and everyone came to expect the worst of everyone else." Kyzus affirmed before then continuing. "Many, however, have seen past this and tried to rise and strive to all work together and is why the restored union is still functioning... somewhat... as the people do also have this inherit desire for peace and prosperity and to rise above their primitive natural state. Though the unions progress only seems to be going nowhere or sometimes backwards," Kyzus pointed out and looking to see if his children were still with him before then continuing on. "The problem is that collectively, we as people, as living beings are flawed. The people are all flawed. It is life's condition to be flawed because of the very fact we are alive and free to do whatever we want at any moment. Temptation affects all and all have their own agenda and priorities, everyone's is different from everyone else's, sometimes the goals of some may align slightly but it never lasts and they always diverge eventually and on top of that, like I keep saying people just cannot trust each other regardless of their aligned goals." Kyzus said before then continuing once more; "Any power in anyone's hands corrupts all, causing further Evil like tendencies like greed and jealously to arise, it has become unavoidable. Morur's Evil is here and cannot be gotten rid off. Like I said before, the people knew that they are capable of amazing things and their own agendas will reflect that. However, with autumn they have relapsed and come to realise that their fellow inhabitants are also capable of amazing things and have their own agenda, which primitively, though inevitably, means everyone perceives everyone as a threat to their own selfish desires meaning no one trusts one another any more. No one will work together for the collective good of everyone any more because anyone could betray anyone else at any time for their own gain. Furthermore, they will not trust one another, even if working together for collective good. The people will find reasons to not believe or trust each other, even if what they are doing equally benefits them both. People alone will only work towards the good of themselves personally, not the good of themselves as a community. That is the state of our world now that Evil exists, it cannot be changed because it is a fundamental flaw of life"

Kyzus paused again, looking intently at his children who all seemed to be following and in awe at their fathers' words, before then continuing again:

"People have lost their faith in one another; they all mistrust one another far more. Competition has become more prevalent as well as the prevailing goal of most. Now, over much deliberation, I now know that there is only thing to control and solve these issues that Terratopia faces... An untied society with strict laws and consequences. Strict laws and consequences that raise us as a people out of the state of nature and do nothing but encourage the collective good for all. Strict laws that take some power away from the people to force that trust and allow for prosperity." announced Kyzus grandly with his arms out wide.

"It would bring about an aura of peace, trust and, sanctuary, the primitive state of nature we currently all live in becoming irrelevant as the society with its laws would be in place to mitigate the state of nature's flaws and distrust therefore meaning that for one to choose to go against them would be choosing to be irrational and the choosing worst-off option, even to the most primitive of desires, it would in fact harm them more to go against this society and its laws. It would be safer, more peaceful and allow them to achieve their goals, where shellfish or not, within this society." Kyzus then detailed further; "If all peoples gave up the some of the same equal freedoms, they all currently have access to in this current chaotic, unfair, nasty, brutish, and short state of nature, to live in this united society under its laws, the society and its peoples would collectively flourish, just as Terratopia did in the Summer of the world. This would happen because as I said before, the people collectively do desire peace and prosperity and it would happen indefinitely so long as the society was run justly and fairly and its laws reflected that. As long as the society respected the rights of the people it ruled over, the people would hold the society aloft. Laws aiming for the individual prosperity of all and prevention of the state of nature appearing would allow all this to happen. If the running of the united society did not reflect this, if any one law was even slightly detrimental to this, then it would simply fail as it would in fact be more beneficial for the peoples to live their lives in the current chaotic, unfair, nasty, brutish, and short state of nature they are currently in now." Kyzus stated before affirming a final statement; "The peoples of Terratopia, if living in the united society I describe, would want to live in it and obey its laws, they would feel obligated to do so as it would protect them all from the inherit primitive flaws present in one another and allow them to flourish, knowing in good faith that no one would be a threat to their agendas as the society and it laws would protect them. The lands, the kingdoms and the peoples would be stable and would prosper, it would be just like the summer of the world!" Kyzus exclaimed, again with his arms out wide and his head tilted up to the sky.

"In fact, the only reason the summer of the world never required such a society was because Morur's Evil wasn't apparent, the primitive state of nature felt by all today not realised as the peoples were already above it. Because they expected good in one another and trusted one another. Morur's Evil relies on and plays on the flaws of us living people. But during the summer, we were all already above them. We were better, we trusted one another and the Evil effects of power had little to no effect as we weren't shellfish enough to buy into them. We knew they existed, but we were collectively good enough to not buy into them. But with autumns coming and Morur's Evil increased, infiltrated presence, the state of nature within all was made apparent as distrust rose. Therefore, all that is needed to revert things back to the days of Terratopia's summer is that the state of nature needs to be made rationally insignificant to abide by once again. Its ways of life mitigated, it becoming against common sense for people to follow it. It needs to become detrimental for one to buy into their newly discovered primitive, shellfish desires, just as it was during the summer and trust needs to be re-established again. This is what my united society would do!" exclaimed Kyzus, finally concluding his speech of philosophical theory and reasoning.

Hyzus, Tyzus, and Mia-Myzus who had all sat and listened intently, were astonished by the enlightened theory of Kyzus, his words astonished them all.

"How would this united society be run?" asked Hyzus. "How are its laws and consequences determined to sustain itself and allow itself to flourish? How would the society truly be able to create laws to render living by the state of nature insignificant, illogical and irrelevant? The autumn so far has shown that we as a people simply can't do that any longer even if they truly do have this desire for peace! After all, surly the laws would have to be created by people which the state of nature corrupts, therefore making the laws inevitably corrupt as well and on top of all that, nobody would trust them? Nobody would trust the society and its laws. Surely? Who could possibly be wise and trusted enough by the people to come up with strict laws that every being should abide by but also want to abide by and see no flaw in?" the children of Kyzus Hobbes all inquired.

"You are right my children," replied Kyzus. "But I know exactly how the problems you pose will be solved... The Deity."

Chapter 8

The Plan of Kyzus

It had been an entire year since any of the Hobbes family had been seen since their summoning to the Lordbaron of Roccano's mountainside palace by Kyzus. The peoples of the kingdom city began to worry, their Lordbaron had once again disappeared from the people's eye and now his children too also vanished, their lack of presence being felt by all. The minds of Elves and imaginations of Men began to wander; perhaps they were never going to come out their palace home? Roccano and indeed Terratopia had not been the same since Kyzus's very active presence in aiding rule had diminished, whether over his kingdom or the union; perhaps it would never be the same again. The atmosphere of Terratopia had certainly changed and nothing ever seemed to be done about it, nor did it seem anyone know what to do about it, instead everyone endlessly argued, bickered and complained.

When the mood of Roccano couldn't be any duller, Kyzus and his children emerged through the grand imposing wooden doors of their mountainside palace. They appeared with much enthusiasm on their faces and they all paraded through the streets to the Ruling Castle, the building from where Roccano's rule was coordinated through the Lordbaron and Premier's offices with their nobles and advisors. Kyzus and his children caused quite a stir within the kingdom, amassing large crowds behind them as they journeyed to the Ruling Castle, announcing to all that they had new proclamations to say to the kingdom. Once at the kingdoms governmental building, the Hobbes family journeyed up to the 'Regulatory Balcony' on the main castles keep which overlooked the castles courtyard and was where announcements where traditionary made to the peoples of the kingdom since the days of old under Thyzus. Once in the balcony, overlooking the now packed courtyard, Kyzus raised both his hands and spoke, announcing powerfully;

"My people of the great kingdom of Roccano, I have been letting you all down in recent times as I have not been fully involved in my role as your Lordbaron, however, I must assure you all that my absence from my ruling throne alongside the current Premier Joell III has not been a wasted time for me nor my people. I have been in deep council, with my parent's texts, my wise children and my own rationalisation and reflection. I have devised a scheme; a lofty, dignified grand plan to not only bring prosperity and well-being back to the kingdom of Roccano but to the restored Terratopia union and every other kingdom in our great archipelago to former glory!"

The crowds cheered with support as Kyzus nodded and waved graciously at them all, his children stood behind him in powerful, stoic stances.

"There is much to do!" Kyzus proclaimed. "Much to do and it will take a long time, it will not be an easy period for us my kingdom, but by the end Roccano will once again be the most grandiose kingdom in all of Terratopia and it will lead and empower all other kingdoms to flourish!"

The crowds once again cheered and Kyzus began to announce even more;

"Mia-Myzus, the daughter of Hobbes, will take my place as Lordbaron of our great kingdom as I will step down and become an advisor to the kingdom." As Kyzus said this Mia-Myzus stepped forward and gestured to the crowd, she announced;

"I will run this kingdom to the best of my ability as your Lord baroness, I have spent my lifetime learning from the teaching and wisdom of my father and I will use that to not only run this kingdom, but to refurbish it and reinstate its standing in the world to match that of its legacy!"

The crowd once again cheered and welcomed their new leader gratuitously. Kyzus then stepped forward once more for another announcement;

"My two sons, Tyzus and Hyzus, the twins of Hobbes will end their studies and travels of the lands and instead enter the political world of the Terratopia Union, representing our kingdom as advisors to our Lord Delegate, the Lord Delegate Petar. There, in the union's capital of Embirith they will start the long arduous journey of transforming the union to support Terratopia to flourish once again!"

Similar to their sister, as Kyzus announced them, Hyzus and Tyzus stepped forward, acknowledging the supporting crowd. They both exclaimed;

"We have learnt much from our travels of the archipelago's kingdoms and cultures, living among the peoples and understanding their ways of life. Similar to our grandfather Thyzus before us, we have spent a lifetime within the philosophical halls of Aquata and learnt much from the Merpeople there. Our knowledge and wisdom is like that of our sister and comparable to that of our wise father Kyzus! We will succeed where Terratopia seems to be failing, we will bring noticeable action to the union and positive change for its kingdoms once more!"

The crowds once again erupted in cheer as the twins stepped back behind their father. Kyzus announced that this was only the beginning of his plan, but there was already much to do, he requested the help and cooperation of the people of Roccano which was vehemently agreed to with cries of cheer and Kyzus announced that the Hobbes family would once more bring prosperity to the kingdom with the people's assistance and held aloft by their power. Kyzus then, along with his children, stepped down from the balcony and waited within the castle for the crowds to disperse. As they did this, they were greeted by the Premier Joell III and other ruling nobles and advisors. They all told how they looked forward to this new reignited rule from the Hobbes family, welcoming Mia-Myzus as their new Lord baroness ruler and wishing Hyzus and Tyzus well in their coming time serving in the Terratopia Union as Lord Delegate advisors, offering their help and support to all of Kyzus's children.

Before long, the crowds had subsided from the Ruling Castles courtyard and talks with the Premier and his accompany came to a logical end. Kyzus and his children gradually began to make their way back to their home and once there and indoors they all hugged themselves with a sense of glee and achievement;

"My children," Kyzus said, "You have done well and my plan is now in motion. You are all vital to it as you are by now aware and I hope you are all up to the challenge of making it succeed, for the good of the peoples of Terratopia."

"We are, father," his children replied. "We shall endeavour to make good on your plans and to fulfil them to their full potential. We will keep to our vows we took in the city of Melian." As they said this a magical mystical whisp of green cloud emitted out them out but quickly faded away, a side effect of oaths taken under magic, making clear to all how serious the oath is when uttered.

"Good! Good!" Kyzus exclaimed. "Now there isn't a fleeting moment to waste! Daughter, go! Leave us, prepare for your rule as Lordbaroness of our great kingdom, run it and propel it to glory! Learn all you can as well about ruling!"

"Yes father," Mia-Myzus said running off to her chambers within the Hobbes's family palace.

"And my twins! Go, leave for Embirith. Join Lord Delegate Petar, advise him, advise the Lord Delegates Chamber, make good the union but most importantly, advance your political careers. Being the twins of Hobbes makes you influential figures within the union already as my brother and I were formerly as sons of Hobbes. But still, advance your significance, become imperative to the union and high up in the parliament. Garner cult-like support. You both having swaying control of the union is vital to my plan of creating the united society."

"Yes father, we will father." Tyzus and Hyzus replied. They went on to ask Kyzus a question that had been plaguing their minds since hearing their father's plan;

"Father, what about 'The Deity' you speak of? We all know our parts of the plan, infiltrating the union and bringing it closer and closer together and advancing our political standing, and our sisters' role of empowering Roccano to supreme greatness once more, but what of the Deity? How does the Deity fit into the united society? Who or what even is this Deity? How do we come by it?"

Kyzus chuckled, "My twins, worry you should not about these hefty thoughts, you both have enough on your agendas as it is! The Deity is the central role of the coming united society I plan to create, but worry not about the who or what or how, leave the Deity to me..."

And with that reassurance, Hyzus and Tyzus nodded before then leaving for their unicorns and making for Embirith.

Chapter 9
The Role of the Daughter of Hobbes

Another fifty years passed and the beginnings of Kyzus's plan were put into motion, his children devoted their lives to their father's instructions. Tyzus and Hyzus did indeed become prominent figures in the union; advancing their significance in the parliament through moving powerful speeches, persuasive proposals, wise council, and advice to the Lord Delegate Chamber and through close work with their Roccano Lord Delegate Petar. Additionally, they even advanced their standing through more sinister means; gaining the undevoted loyalty of many other parliament representatives, advisors, and even some Lord Delegates; doing this through expert manipulation, bribery, and blackmail. Corrupt as some of Hyzus and Tyzus's actions were, it was all under the guise and advice of their father Kyzus who continually pushed for every method possible for his twin sons to increase their power and prominence in the parliament. They were no longer in the civilised times of summer, they needed to be ruthless and utilise all options. "The options are available, they are a part of politics now, better you use them well over someone else using them against you" Kyzus continually reasoned to them.

Through the efforts of the twins of Hobbes actions, the Terratopia union did indeed start to take steps forward again, ideas proposed by the Lord Delegate Petar and empowered by Hyzus and Tyzus and their political power base started to transform the union to a less chaotic entity and kingdoms once again began to see minor reform and positive effects to themselves and others. Action was beginning to take place. There were yet still however many serious fundamental underlying issues within the union, the most rife being the far more widespread corruption and cronyism. The integrity of the union was nothing like what it used to be in the summer of the world, its members became far more greedy, abusing their power for their own gain not for the union itself or even really for the gain of their own home kingdoms. Methods of gaining the support of fellow members went beyond the respectable confounds of debate and council. Bribery, underhand favours, and blackmail became its own currency and held far more notable power if wielded correctly. Another continued fundamental issue of the union was that its members and kingdoms themselves still did not trust each other, they were all largely out for themselves and not for the benefit of all. Kingdoms leaders saw and sought to utilise the Terratopia Union as a tool for their own kingdoms gain, consequentially permanently stunting the effectiveness and progress the union could ever have, just as Kyzus had foretold.

A trend had also begun to emerge with the Prime Lord Delegates and the Speakers of the parliament. At the very founding of the restored union these positions weren't meant to souly fall to one kingdom to continually fill as term limits were set and new people from different kingdoms were supposed to be voted in, this however didn't seem to happen. The representatives from Filnethias always seemed to become the Prime Lord Delegates and representatives from Rime always seemed to become the Speakers; these events mirroring quiet similarly to the old union as the Prime Lord Delegate was the Lord baron of Roccano, a powerful leader of Elves, and the Speaker the Premier of Roccano, a powerful leader of Men. Now the Prime Lord Delegate was always from the high Elven capital of Filnethias and the Speaker from the high capital of Men, Rime. The fact both these cities were in the same high kingdom of Rodus furthered this issue of mirroring the old union as it meant the leaders of the union were from the same kingdom. This caused calls for the dissolvement of the union to emerge and gain momentum once again in what came to be known as 'Liberalist' movements, purely due to these movements wanting to 'Liberate' kingdoms from the union.

It was no coincidence history seemed to be repeating itself again, just under different names, and it was largely happening so quickly due to the subversive efforts of the twins of Hobbes, under Kyzus's guide. They had indeed become powerful voices and figures in the union, controlling much sway and holding much power in the parliament. The Lord Delegate Petar through

Mia-Myzus's own rule of back in Roccano, empowered the kingdom to much higher prominence in the union, and thus empowered himself to higher prominence as a consequence as well. Consequentially through Tyzus, Hyzus, Mia-Myzus, and Petar's, combined efforts, the union was becoming increasingly under their own regulation from behind a metaphorical curtain. A curtain some even suspected to exist but chose to ignore.

Mia-Myzus set about ruling Roccano just as she stated she would. She coordinated rule alongside the Premier Joell III within the Ruling Castle, ruling the kingdom through day-to-day life, but she also empowered Roccano and built it up to great prosperity once more. The kingdom rebuilt itself fully from the ruined wakes of the Giants Szar and Mur destruction. Buildings grew larger, taller, and more grandiose. The city grew in size, sprawling completely around Mount Roccano and its surrounding lands, as well sprawling up the sides of the great mountain. New levels of city were carved and created around the more gradual lower slopes of the mountainside turning the kingdom into a monumental tiered city around a truly breath-taking mountain whose steep peak couldn't even be remotely seen from even the highest tiers of the city. A new glorious, imposing wall was also built along the banks of the Roccano River, completely encircling the front of the city and blocking all access to the kingdom by land. The only way in or out was now through the stupendous gates that had previously held the Giants army at bay many years ago at the start of their war. The walls surrounding the kingdom were lofty and magnificent and built with pure white stone and marble. As a consequence, these majestic walls reflected the suns light from above and illuminated the entire kingdom and surrounding lands in a sea of warm white light. Roccano's prominence in Terratopia rose as well. Its trade of unique luxurious goods tantalising, its aid to fellow kingdoms was unmatched, as well as its military might. Roccano became home to some of the most skilled knights of Men and powerful Elven mages, its standing army was unmatched in splendour, glory, and power. And all of this was thanks to Mia-Myzus's efforts under Kyzus's guise.

Kyzus continually kept a close watchful eye over Roccano,

the union, and Terratopia at large, constantly surveying the landscape and climate of the lands and instructing the actions of his children accordingly. As well as this, Kyzus spent the majority of his time hidden from sight once again; spending days, weeks, months, and sometimes years within the confines of his palace home without ever being seen. What Kyzus spent his time doing was unknown to all, even his children had little idea of his activities. He made a point of making sure none knew as well, never allowing his children to visit him but instead himself going to them or summoning them to meetings in a secret cavern within the hills of the Thruck Range.

Kyzus spent his time alone, obsessing over his plan, making sure all went off without a hitch and was constantly adapting it to the current situation of Terratopia. He also spent his time studying once more, but now researching magics. Deep, powerful, rare, sometimes unknown magics, some forms of it considered to be unnatural if known to the wider world. Kyzus was engrossed with it all. Although he was already the most powerful sorcerer in all Terratopia, but he sought to be more powerful, he sought to become all-powerful. Over the fifty years, his magical aura and presence began to become so powerful that it was unavoidable to hide. His children all noticed this apparent advancement in magical power from their father but they knew not for what end. When asked to share his advancements by his children, Kyzus did not, instead ordering his children to advance their skills in combat, which they diligently did.

Mia-Myzus was always the most talented and the best of the three siblings, being taught relentlessly by Kyzus himself from such a young age. But all three of them became terrifying combatants, their skill with Elven weaponry near unmatched and enough to rival the greatest warriors and duellist in all Terratopia and perhaps even in all the world of Terra Tearia.

Kyzus had on the other hand had been discreetly visiting the great Dwarven realm of Kossorlim, beneath the vast 'Dividing Mountains' mountain range, disguised as an old mysterious hooded figure. Kyzus kept his identity hidden from the Dwarves through deception and magic as he wished not to be recognised nor his actions noticeable or traceable back to him. Kyzus came to the Dwarves of Kossorlim as they were the greatest craftsmen and smiths in all of Terratopia; he needed their skills to craft for him magical artifacts he had previously read about in ancient abstract texts. Under the guise of an old man called Awalatar, Kyzus tasked the Dwarven smiths to create for him crystal seeing stones for which he paid extremely handsomely for and even more handsomely to keep a secret from the wider lands. The Dwarves of Kossorlim agreed to this whole-heartedly, fuelled by their love for crafting, as well as for riches and wealth. After a great many years, the Dwarves had created thirty-two seeing stones for Awalatar. These perfectly spherical crystal balls, made out of the rare precious crystal stone Magiccora, were highly magical objects. During their creation Kyzus infused powerful enchantments into them, enchantments he was in total control over and the type of which were mostly unknown to the entire world of Terra Tearia. The balls all gently illuminated warm light and eradiated vibrant colours of varying types. They were almost irresistible not to touch when seen and when in fact touched, they would unleash their enchantments onto the hands that bore them. So magnificent of a creation were the stones that the Dwarves nearly broke off their deals with Kyzus, wanting to keep them for themselves and distribute them to friends around the land. Kyzus half expected this and never allowed it either, as through a combination of power, might, intimidation, and a lot of gold, the Dwarves relented their claims on the seeing stones. Kyzus kept the seeing stones in a designated hall within his palace, keeping them hidden from all until it was the right time.

When Kyzus's final crystal seeing stone was crafted and finished by the Dwarves, he moved onto the next step in his grand plan, He thusly summoned Mia-Myzus to his palace. Mia-Myzus knew this coming meeting with her father was going to be an important one as it was the first time anyone would have been allowed to step foot in the Hobbes mountainside palace in fifty years, although she did wonder why her brothers hadn't also been invited. When she arrived, Mia-Myzus was directed towards the hall filled with seeing stones by a sentient talking cloud of yellow mist, a fun, common, and useful spell cast by Kyzus and one often used to entertain children or guests by sorcerers across the world. As Mia-Myzus approached the hall, she was astounded by the rainbow-like glow given off before even entering through the door. As she did enter, her eyes were nearly blinded by the changing, flowing array of colourful lights emanating from the crystal balls. Once her eyes had adjusted to the bright rainbow lit room, she felt the warmth of magic rush over her, making her realise that there was a great deal of powerful magic concentrated in the hall from all the mysterious the spherical stones. Mia-Myzus finally then noticed Kyzus standing at the end of the hall in flowing grey robes and holding one of the stone balls in his arm with the other outstretched to greet her;

"Greetings daughter," Kyzus said. Mia Myzus noticed a slight change in her father's voice since she had last spoke to him, his voice almost sounded like three overlapping different voices that all echoed off each other as they projected across the hall. "You have done well and you have made me proud."

"Thank you father," she replied, slowly crossing the hall to approach him. "I have done all I can to keep my oath," the mystical magic mist again emitting from her as she said this. "I, alongside Joell III, have ruled Roccano to prosperity and I alone have propelled Roccano to greatest once more, our kingdom city is the greatest in all of Terratopia once again. The kingdoms of the archipelago both admire and fear us, just as you requested father."

"Good... Gooood!" chanted Kyzus "All is going according to my plan. You are now ready to start the next phase of it. I will again need your undevoted loyalty for it once more."

"I am ready father; you have and always will have my loyalty to your great vision," Mia-Myzus paused. "But what of my brothers? When will they be ready?" she then questioned as she slowly continued to approach Kyzus.

Kyzus chuckled, "Oh daughter, they are ready, it is just that my plan dictates you go on a different journey to them. You are on different paths, you always have been since Melian, but you all journey towards the same goal, a goal only reachable by you all wandering your separate paths alone. Besides, I have taught and raised you personally daughter, you are the most suited to the coming tasks ahead of you. You are the most fearsome combatant and the most magically powerful of your siblings. You are truly formidable. You have also fifty years of experience ruling a kingdom and empowering it to greatness; all attributes most desirable to your coming new role."

Mia-Myzus bowed her head, her person now reaching her father. She stood in front of him and held his outstretched hand;

"Thank you father, what is it you have me do?"

"You have spent a considerable amount of time in the Samson and Goliath kingdom of Sabare, living among the peoples there. It is there I need you to go. I will be reprising my role as Lordbaron in your wake"

Mia-Myzus was excited to be heading back to her favourite kingdom and gleefully asked;

"What am I to do there, father?"

Kyzus replied "Sabare is an island kingdom on the far eastern reaches of Terratopia, it is largely isolated from the mainland kingdoms and the mainland kingdoms isolated from it. There is minimal contact now to Sabare as it is no longer in the union. Little is known about its going on and, more importantly, little is cared about it as well. But I know that Sabare has been suffering recently from extremist rebel activity. The insurgents there wish to rule over Sabare and transform the kingdom into a fearsome, military state, potentially to wage war on the rest of Terratopia."

"And you want me to put a stop to it?" Mia-Myzus butted in assuredly.

Kyzus laughed; "Oh daughter! I want you to cause it!" he exclaimed. While saying this Kyzus outstretched his hand holding the seeing stone to Mia-Myzus; "And this will help you."

Chapter 10

The Death of Mia-Myzus

Kyzus explained to Mia-Myzus the next stage of his plan. He explained how over the past fifty years, he had been using his children to move all the right pieces across Terratopia into place and how he had also been moving other pieces into place personally in the background as well, such as with the creations of the magic seeing stones. Now it was time to for action.

"I still don't understand what you want me to do father," Mia-Myzus said. "Why do you want me to cause a kingdom to have a revolution and become militarised? Surely that will only worsen Terratopia's state of nature?"

"Because my dear daughter that's exactly what Terratopia needs, a war is coming. A terrible war. It will begin and it will spread across the whole of Terratopia. All will be affected by it." Kyzus explained.

"But surly that goes against all the progress my brothers are making in the union to untie it further! I thought that is what your plan was about! To unite Terratopia, not aid in its division and collapse into war!" Mia-Myzus exclaimed.

Kyzus, chuckled. "On the contrary daughter, Terratopia is not yet ready to be united, its people would never freely accept my united society as they would never see the rationale behind it, they would not comprehend or refuse to comprehend its logic and they will feebly want to believe that they are above the state of nature I say they are all in. But they are not above it. They are all too short sighted, shellfish and, more importantly, would never trust in it. My united society is an extreme at the end of a spectrum. The good extreme, the other extreme being utter and total chaos. To reach the good extreme, it would need be bred from the opposite extreme, when the state of nature couldn't be more cruel, unfair, nasty, brutish, and short. People flip to extremes when pushed to them and currently that is not the case. The people desire order, true order, the type of order that comes with peace. Right now, there is only chaos with the illusion of order as kingdoms supposedly work together in the union, but they do not work together for the benefit of them all. They work together for the benefit of themselves. The people need to see how flawed everything truly is. How wrong they truly are. How bad it really can be and will eventually be without my society. They need to experience its short comings in the worst way. Any attempt at the true order and peace of my united society would never be successful because of this illusion. The people would perceive the chaotic shellfish state of nature to be more beneficial to them as they have not experienced how bad it can truly become, thusly making my united society unsustainable. The next stage of my plan is to help push Terratopia in the right direction, one small step backward to allow for one giant great leap forward. Think of it as a hard reset. And for that to happen I need you to fulfil my instructions to carry out your side of the plan."

"I understand father," Mia-Myzus said. "But how do you know war is coming? And how do my efforts fit into it? More importantly, how am I even supposed to achieve a kingdom wide revolution in a kingdom filled with races of the greatest guardians and warriors in all the world?"

Kyzus explained "Through the efforts of your brothers, Terratopia will collapse into civil war, of this I am certain. Terratopia is on the brink of it, its people just don't know it yet. Your brothers will give them the push they need. Your efforts are vital to making sure the war has the outcomes perfect for the uniting of my society. Your efforts will ensure that the war causes as much chaos as possible, you will ensure the state of nature in Terratopia couldn't be more shellfish, cruel, unfair, nasty, brutish, and short. You will do all this from your new home of Sabare and with your devoted followers of Samsons and Goliaths."

"Forgive me father, you may have taught me well and I may be skilful and powerful enough alone to take over some kingdoms like those of Gnomes and even some Men, but Sabare is a truly stoic kingdom, how am I to take it over? Even with this extremist support you speak of, assuming the rebels will even follow me." Mia-Myzus said, questioning herself and Kyzus.

"You are right, I have taught you well, Mia-Myzus. Hear me now daughter, you will gain the support of the Rebels. Don't pretend you don't think I know about why you loved visiting Sabare so much. The Samsons and Goliaths enthral you; they fascinate you. You have grown into a fine, irresistible Half-elf, as attractive as you are powerful. A deadly concoction for a warrior race like Samsons and Goliaths to be intoxicated by, and especially for warrior extremist. I'm sure you will have no trouble gaining the support of the insurgents, use whatever means come most naturally to you." Kyzus said, giving his daughter a knowing look.

He then continued; "In the ways of staging a revolution, you are correct, the extremists have not the strength nor the support to take over the kingdom but that is only the final goal. After all, your aim is to fuel the war, your efforts will have limited impact from Sabare alone, but not all kingdoms will take a side in this coming war, of that I am certain, if they are controlled properly, they will be useful tools for you to feed the war effort for both sides" Kyzus said knowingly again. "In addition, the underworld of crime has become a league of its own, its power perhaps more significant than even that of the current Terratopia Union and it has the potential for so much more if it was only organised and controlled properly from a single coordinator with a clear goal." Kyzus again said with a knowing look.

"I think I see what you are saying father!" Mia-Myzus exclaimed, a sinister smile sweeping over her face as she came to endure herself to her coming tasks more and more.

Kyzus continued; "You will use this rebel group of Samson and Goliath insurgents to gain control over the crime syndicates that have spread across the lands. Some may fight you; others may willingly join. Crime lords, families, syndicates, mobs, mafias, everything! Everything must and will fall under your control; you will collectivise them and use this to become a mighty criminal queen with the most powerful crime empire Terra Tearia has ever seen! With this crime empire under your rule, you will use it to help the rebels take over the kingdom of Sabare where you will run your sinister empire from the shadows for the benefit of the war effort and the suffering of all."

"From the shadows? The suffering of all?" Mia-Myzus enquired.

"True power comes from ruling from the shadows, controlling all with all being unaware of it" Kyzus replied eerily, his face leaning back from the light of the hall. "Besides the inhabitants of Sabare would never allow for you to be their ruler. They are a proud race. They would never follow a chieftain who isn't of their own flesh and blood." Kyzus replied before continuing; "You are not a Samson or Goliath, but your rebel followers are. Use their leader, use them as a figurehead, a puppet from you to rule Sabare and transform it into the capital for your vast crime empire. The power you would hold on the grand stage that is Terratopia would be unmatched with a militarised state of the greatest warriors in all the land at your disposal as well as the ability to control the entire criminal underworld and the pivotal, vital war effort." Kyzus paused after he said this, before then continuing to answer Mia-Myzus's other concern; "The suffering of all is necessary to see how terrible the state of nature can be. Remember, one step backwards for a great leap forward. We push them to one extreme so that they will welcome and embrace the other. Besides. All of this is inevitable anyway. If you don't do as I say, I guarantee someone else will rise to at some point in the near or far future. Terratopia will descend into the suffering you impose anyway; all you are doing is hurrying the process up and making sure it happens under my control for my plan." Kyzus explained.

"I will do as you command father! I look forward to my coming journey." Mia-Myzus said again with a sinister smile. "I am the most powerful of your descendants and I will make you proud, I will control the neutral kingdoms of the coming war, I will rule over the criminal underworld, I will command over the military state and warrior kingdom of Sabare. I will do all this to fuel the war, I will make Terratopia a truly chaotic and evil place."

Mia-Myzus final remarks roused Kyzus but also concerned him slightly and made his eyes widen in surprise.

"Good daughter! But be careful not to stray from my

plan though. I will keep in contact with you and continue to INSTRUCT your efforts to best serve MY plan. When the time is right, the war will end and all will unite into my society under the Deity, vanquishing Evil indefinitely. Remember, we do not want to make Terratopia an Evil place. We are merely showing its people how Evil it truly could become if they continue to buy into the cruel, chaotic, unfair, nasty, brutish, and short state of nature and how terribly Evil they all can really be."

"Yes father, of course father," Mia-Myzus repented, her gaze surreptitiously avoiding his.

"I am proud of you, you truly are a magnificent daughter, if only Robin was here to see you now. There is yet one more thing I need you to make sure of Mia-Myzus," Kyzus said.

"What is it father?" she asked, a tear in her eye from Kyzus's earlier kind words.

"Terratopia cannot know of your efforts, they cannot know of your dealings in the criminal underworld, they cannot know of your shadowy rule over Sabare, they cannot know of your control over the neutral kingdoms. Not even your own brothers. The plan will not work if anyone, other than myself, know of your workings, your true identity must be kept secret and unknown. Rule from the shadows."

Mia-Myzus paused. She completely understood why no one could know her identity from her coming rule and control but she also knew what would have to be done to ensure such a thing;

"I'm going to have to disappear, aren't I?" Mia-Myzus said, more tears in her eyes, although this time tears of sorrow.

Kyzus sighed and hung his head "No my dear daughter, your brothers will never believe you just to have vanished. You must perish, it will only drive them further to avenge you, as well as drive your beloved citizens of Roccano."

Mia-Myzus gasped and tore her hands away from her father.

"Come now daughter," Kyzus said in an assuring tone. "When you took your oath to me all those years ago, I did say it will not be easy. It will be all right, your sacrifice now will be for the benefit of all, even your brothers; and when this is all over and my plan complete, the pain felt now will pale in comparison to the joy felt in the future as you all unite once more in my prosperous society."

Mia-Myzus remained silent for a while, the oaths mystical magic mist appearing once more upon Kyzus's mentioning of the oath before it suddenly being whisked away by Mia-Myzus drawing her blade. She raised it above her head before then suddenly slicing it behind her back and then across her head and face faster than she could blink. In front of Kyzus's unphased expression and stance, Mia-Myzus's cape fell to her feet being cut from her shoulders and a huge sliced cut developed across her face. From the right top of her forehead to the bottom left of her cheek, the perfectly straight cut missed both her eyes and cleaved perfectly centrally over her nose bridge and in-between her eyes. Mia-Myzus refused to flinch at the pain as blood began to seep down her face. She bent down to grab her cape and then washed it in her blood that was dripping onto the stone floor and then rose it up to messily wipe down her bloodied face. She then handled the blooded cape to Kyzus and reaffirmed her oath to him;

"I, the daughter of Hobbes, once again vow to make it my lives purpose to serve you father and fulfil your plan to the best of my ability or death take me." The oaths green mist billowed more thickly from her as she said this and spiralled around her to then dissipate soon after silence.

Kyzus grinned at the sight, he took Mia-Myzus bloody robe and gave her the seeing stone he was holding.

"Excellent daughter, you never disappoint. Here, take this magical seeing stone. The crystal ball will allow you to see anywhere in Terratopia when holding it. Your sight will be limitless, able to see from east to west, through mountains, around trees and under the seas. You will also be able to communicate with me personally so long as I too am holding a crystal stone as well. There are other magical enchantments in all these stones but you need not worry about them as they serve no purpose to your aims. Now go!

Leave for Sabare daughter! And I will break the news of your 'tragic death' by the hands of ruffians and marauders to the land and your brothers."

And with that Mia-Myzus took the crystal ball seeing stone, cast a magical invisibility enchantment over herself so as not to be seen by any and then made for the kingdom of Sabare...

Chapter 11

The Role of the Twins of Hobbes

After his daughter's departure, Kyzus summoned his twin sons to his palace. By this time, the twins had now risen to become the leaders of the Terratopia Union parliament, as per their father's latest instructions. Hyzus had become the Prime Lord Delegate and Tyzus the Speaker. Along with Lord Delegate Petar, the three effectively controlled the union; in power and in loyalty and following. Some days after their summoning by Kyzus they arrived back in Roccano, riding on their unicorn's steeds. They were excited to be returned home and looked forward to seeing their sister again. However, when not being immediately greeted by her as they arrived at the stupendous gates of Roccano, the twins were at first surprised before then starting to be filled with dread as Roccano itself seemed to be a gloomier place since their last visit. Black flags and banners were hung atop every rooftop and along every window ledge and floated gently in the wind. The people of Roccano were miserable and the twins were not greeted by their sister their entire journey through the streets up to Kyzus's mountainside palace.

As they climbed their stairs, they heard their fathers voice projected into their heads in a loud, resounding statement;

"Tyzus. Hyzus. Twins of Hobbes. Your dear sister, Mia-Myzus, the only daughter of Hobbes, is dead. Come, meet me in my study, we have much to discuss."

The twin brothers felt immense grief and anguish surge through them. The cold hand of sorrow passed over them both and left their hearts heavy and hurt. They looked at one another in disbelief and stayed there, frozen in grief on the steps leading up to the palace doors. Sometime later Kyzus's voice was once again projected into their heads, echoing in their ears;

"Come! There will be time for mourning later!"

This snapped Hyzus and Tyzus out their trance and they continued their climb to meet with their father. Each step upwards became more and more heavy and the tall wooden palace doors seemed all but immoveable to them. Eventually they made their way into Kyzus's study, the room being completely covered in scattered opened books and unwrapped scrolls. It was as if a blanket of paper and ink was placed over the study, no surface nor part of flooring was not covered by some form of paper and writing. Kyzus stood in the centre of the room, draped in long, dark grey, flowing robes with another seeing stone held in one arm, partially hidden from view, being tucked away inside the overly large sleeves of his gown.

"Welcome my sons. Come sit with me, we have much to discuss." Kyzus said in a sombre voice.

The twins swept some scrolls off two exquisite wooden seats before then sitting on them, they too also noticed the difference in their father's voice. It was deeper, it was also as if he was speaking two or three different voices at once at the same time that all overlapped and echoed off one another.

"What happened to our sister?" they both asked diligently.

"She was slaughtered," Kyzus replied. "I sent her on a diplomatic mission to Sabare to improve relations with the distant kingdom but she was ambushed. She was waylaid and assaulted by wandering ruffians and maunders; primitive, wild men that prey on the unsuspecting traveller."

Tyzus gasped and asked how could such a thing have happened? Hyzus replied before Kyzus could get a chance too.

"Because Terratopia is not what it used to be! Like father said before, it is a savage, brutish, and cruel place now, these are but common occurrences across the land and it is why we must unite the kingdoms into our father's planned great society! So as this terrible state of nature would be no more!" he said angrily, not necessarily meaning to be angry to his brother but just venting the wave of grieving emotions he was feeling.

"I know that!" Tyzus snapped back. "I more meant how can a band of lowlife criminals, lost in the wilderness manage to slay our sister? She could beat both of us in combat with ease. In a duel she could defeat us two on one in less than three minutes without the aid of her magical prowess. She was the most skilled with an elven blade in all of Terratopia and her capability with magic went beyond unnatural, how could she be killed?"

Kyzus sighed. He produced her bloodied cape and threw it towards Tyzus who instantly recognised it as his sisters. He threw it to the ground in anger and heartbreak. Kyzus then spoke;

"How my beloved daughter, whom I loved and tutored her whole life and taught nearly everything I know, came to be brutally murdered by the likes of common bandits is a mystery to even me my sons. But it has happened. Our Mia-Myzus is no longer to walk among us in the land of the living and her absence will be noticed and missed dearly."

"How does this effect your plan father?" Hyzus asked

"It does not," Kyzus mumbled in an uninspired tone. "Mia-Myzus's role as Lordbaron and ruler of Roccano will now fall to me and I will continue her role in my plans as if she was still here. In the meantime, these tragic events only highlight how out of hand events in Terratopia have become and the need for my united society under the Deity. The time has now come to move onto the next stage of my plan."

Tyzus and Hyzus sat up from their grief-stricken slouches in the wooden seats they sat on upon hearing their father mention his plan moving onto its next stage. They edged forward ready once more to fulfil their oaths and now do so for the revenge of their dear death departed sister.

Tyzus and Hyzus sat for hours listening to Kyzus detail the next part of his plan and his explanations as to why it should happen and what it would cause. Although confused at first, the twins slowly they came round to understanding Kyzus's theory and philosophy for the greater good.

The twins learned that there was to be war. War that would be fuelled to be the most chaotic, most cruel, most brutal and most savage in all imagination by the peoples of Terratopia own primitive short-sighted desires of being out for themselves and no one else. It would be the perfect stage for the state of nature to fully rear its ugly head and for the people to purse it to its absolute worseness, to then also desire it to end, when its consequences become too much to bear in their inherit desire for peace. Kingdoms would fall, hundreds of thousands would die from all races, great sacrifices would be made, evil aspects from all peoples would be exposed, some may even purse them. But from the chaos and ashes of a war ruined Terratopia, peace, prosperity and order would arise, or so Kyzus told. All the death and suffering caused from the war would be made void by the thriving welfare of the lands when united in eternal peace within Kyzus's planned society under the Deity. The sacrifice of some, over a relatively short period, for the prosperity of all for the rest of all time reasoned Kyzus.

The power over the union concentrated in the hands of the twins of Hobbes, and indeed in the hands of Roccano no less, caused great division within the union. Some saw it as a positive situation; harking back to the former prosperity of the old union when it was ruled by the Lordbaron and Premier of Roccano and by the great former leaders Thyzus and Kyzus himself. However, many saw it once more as Roccano attempting to claim power and rule over all kingdoms, just as the Giants had 'told' and fought for years earlier; before their extinction from Terratopia in the resultant war. Liberalist movements started to gain serious traction in many kingdoms and within the parliament itself. Many kingdoms from different races starting calling for dissolvement of the union once more and the free liberation of the land, for all kingdoms to be at their own independent liberty. These kingdoms did not want to answer to anyone but themselves, their own peoples, and their own needs. They wanted to not be 'restricted' or 'controlled' by the union. It was this division that Kyzus instructed his twin sons to exploit and make worse.

Hyzus was instructed by Kyzus to pursue all 'Unionist' movements; to make it his goal to fanatically unite the union at all costs and, most importantly, to consider any ideals, movements, or proposals of a Liberalist nature to be null and void. He was to consider any kingdom that now left the union and demanded the union be disbanded an illegitimate kingdom and not to one be friends with. That kingdom instead to either be cohered into joining the union or face the same fate of the kingdom of Giants. Any liberalist kingdoms actions of attempting to leave, or claiming to have left the union would also be illegitimate and face the same consequences. Tyzus, on the other hand, was instructed by Kyzus to purse actions of the complete opposite nature than that of his brother. He was to become the figurehead of the Liberalist movement. To pioneer its actions and to fight everything his brother would stand for, to ultimately call for the union to be dissolved forever. Together the two would create such extreme polarised division within the union that only one course of action was inevitable. War. A fanatical civil war across all of Terratopia that was to be illustrated out to be the ultimate matter for life or death.

Tyzus was to lead the kingdoms of a liberalist nature to leave the union, to 'liberate themselves and others' from any kingdoms rule but their own. These kingdoms and their actions would of course be considered illegitimate by Hyzus and his union. Together under Tyzus's leadership the Liberalist kingdoms would leave the union and would form a military alliance to stand with each other with the goal of only one thing, to fight the Terratopia Union and for their survival. To fight against the unions domination and to ultimately destroy it. Hyzus would consider such actions of Tyzus's kingdoms an act of war against the union itself and its kingdoms and so Terratopia thusly would collapse into a devastating conflict. Kyzus with his rule over Roccano would make sure his kingdom stayed neutral in the insuring conflict so as he could continue his work for later stages of his plan and to not lend Roccano's vast forces to any one side as they would then surely be victorious. Some other kingdoms would also inevitably choose to stay neutral, not getting caught up in the twin's fanatical division and Tyzus and Hyzus were ordered to allow and respect this as their neutrality would serve a value purpose in fuelling the war to greater lengths and severity.

After many days of listening, learning, planning, and fine tuning their fathers' scheme and their roles within it, under the close guidance of Kyzus, Tyzus and Hyzus set out and rode back to Embirith to begin growing the already planted seeds of war. Upon their unicorn steeds the Prime Lord Delegate and the Speaker of the Terratopia Union parliament rode back towards the union capital to cause its downfall; to divide the kingdoms of Terratopia and collapse them all into horrific civil war.

Chapter 12

War Begins

The Terratopia Union soon fell into complete chaos and division as the twins Hyzus and Tyzus set about fulfilling their roles to Kyzus's plan. Hyzus worked closely with Lord Delegate Petar in getting him to continually propose more and more extreme and fanatical unionist ideals and reforms for Hyzus to then pile his full weight and support behind. This had the desired outcome Kyzus hoped for. It brought about more liberalist resistance and, more importantly, it pushed and forced members, representatives, Lord Delegates, and entire kingdoms to choose now distinct sides, dividing the union clearly. The polarised parliament was no longer about kingdoms helping one another in a union and figuring out the best ways to do it. It was now about choosing a side, an ideology to stand behind and protect and fight for. Kingdoms and their people were either 'Unionist' or 'Liberalist'. Either wanting the Union to unite further, or for it to be completely abandoned. There was no in-between, each side seeing their own as perfect and the other as clearly deviant and malevolent.

Some kingdoms saw the escalating divisive issue unfolding and chose to not to be a part of it, joining the kingdoms that had already left the union long before, just as Kyzus foretold. The two Dwarven kingdoms of Kossorlim and Dwaria, caring little for whether the lands outside their mountain and underground kingdoms were in a union or not, departed from the union and the divisive entity it had become, simply not caring enough about either ideology to join it.

The other notable departure from the union was the kingdom of Thruckland, the kingdom of sea bearing Men that was controlled by the capital city of Thruck under the leadership of Viceroy Charles VIII. The city of Thruck was home to Port Thruck, a harbour district the size of most cities within Terratopia and it was the trading capital of the archipelago; being situated with best access to West, Central and East Terratopia, by boat or by land, as well as to the Connecting Isles. It was a central hub of trade that nearly all goods and peoples passed through when travelling across Terratopia. Thruckland was an extremely wealthy kingdom as a result of this, and, as both of the ideologies within the union would harm its riches and wealth, Thruckland also totally left the union, declaring itself a neutral but friendly state to both sides.

Similar to the Dwarves, the two kingdoms of Gnomes, the Giant Mushroom Forest, and the Fungi Forest, simply did not care enough about either extreme side of the current ideological scale that had developed within the union and so too left.

These kingdoms that left however were not considered illegitimate by Hyzus, just as their father requested, nor were they considered Liberalists as they simply did not care about either side of the division, they did not call for the unions dissolvement but they didn't want to be a part of a union divided against itself either. They did not particularly care if the union united further or was completely disbanded but they also could not bear the divisive issue the conflict was becoming, not wanting to be drawn into it and so left.

There still remained a great many kingdoms within the union and both sides became more and more divisive and hostile towards one another. Hyzus continually pushed for greater and greater unity and for more extreme actions to be taken against its opposition. Tyzus firmly established himself as the figurehead of the Liberalists by continually fighting everything his brother pushed for, strongly resisting extreme Unionist actions, and instead pushing for his own extreme Liberalist actions like calling for the ultimate dissolvement of the union and total liberation for all kingdoms. Support for either side only grew in ferocity as either side not only began to hate each other and their opinions but they also began seeing the opposing views as extreme and anarchist, their actions making no logical sense at all apart from for the destruction of life as they knew it.

This all came to a head one rowdy evening in the Lord Delegates Chamber after Tyzus, as Speaker, called a meeting into session upon the learning of the news that the Lord Delegate

Petar had been assassinated. Unionist kingdoms accused it as a Liberalist plot as Lord Delegate Petar had always been an avid pusher of Unionist ideals and was at the forefront of the Unionist leadership. Liberalist kingdoms of course denied this, claiming it instead to be a Unionist scheme to help them to push their agenda through the divided distracted parliament.

Behind their respected leaders, Lord Delegates and Advisors roared at each other. Insults and allegations were hurled in a noisy chaos across the Lord Delegates Chamber. Words like; 'corrupt', 'heartless', 'archaists', 'illegitimate' and, 'power hungry' were yelled across the Chamber at each other. Hyzus and Tyzus faced off against one another in a furious, riveting debate; their words so expertly crafted that they only made their followers all the more certain of the side they had chosen, making the divide that split the kingdoms all the more certain as well. Nearly the entire parliament had also gathered outside the Lord Delegates Chamber building and crammed within the building's upper galleries. Members and representatives clashed with one another over their differing opposing stances, yelling at one another and cheering on their respected leadership, a scene that had spilled out into the whole city of Embirith as inhabitants rallied themselves up into a frenzy.

"Outrageous!" Tyzus yelled, "Your actions brother, are outrageous! You still tenaciously choose to purse actions that you know the kingdoms of the union do not want! You try to push us ever closer to a single united state, a nation under one's rule. That rule being Roccano's! Terratopia is not a single nation. It is a wide collection of kingdoms. A beautiful variety of peoples that all live different cultures. You should know this as we spent years living among them all! In order for them all to thrive properly, we must disband this feeble attempt of combining the kingdoms that is holding us all back and draining our resources. If Roccano, or any kingdom for that matter, was to hold even slightly more power over any other, than it would hold all of the power! It would be a minority rule over a majority of differing beings and people. We must liberate the kingdoms, allow them to become fully independent of one another!"

Liberalist roared as Tyzus finished his remarks, cheering on him and belittling the Unionists that faced them on the opposite side of the Chamber floor. Unionist collectively booed and aggressively shouted back, until Hyzus rose up and replied;

"Any attempt to leave this union completely without the majority say of this Chamber will be actions of an illegitimate nature, actions that go against this great unions very founding. Furthermore, as I have kept saying, calls for this great union's abandonment will also be considered treasonous! Terratopia faces problems never before faced and will continue to do so in the near and far future! We must unite in order them face them all together! You are foolish to think otherwise!"

"This supposed great union was born out of bloodshed brother!" Tyzus cried. "It was forged from the weapons of war and baptised in the blood on an entire, now extinct, race! This is not a great union; it is a flawed one. One that is rife with corruption. One that enforces its will through military might from selected kingdoms of Men and Elves and their friends. Unionist actions will never be willingly accepted by a great many kingdoms of Terratopia, they have previously led to war and death and now have led to chaos and division. Surely you can see that the people do not want this!"

Hyzus once again rose and yelled in retaliation;

"It was Liberalist actions that caused previous wars and death. It was the figurehead of the previous Liberalist movement that killed our beloved mother when we were but children! Do not attempt to morally high road us Tyzus. You and your followers are anarchists, intent on the sustainability of chaos that ravages our lands. A Liberalist Terratopia will not solve its issues, only worsen them. Crime rules our kingdoms more than our kingdoms rulers. The lands outside city walls are unsafe, venturing them with anything less than an army a clear death wish as even the most fearsome and powerful of peoples, even our own sister, have shown by being brutally murdered by unknown savages. We must unite further to stop this! For the good of us all!"

Tyzus seemingly grew angry at the mention of his sister's death. He roared;

"A Liberalist Terratopia is the solution! Problems like this within kingdom borders would be solved by the independent kingdoms as well as no one wants them! They would be solved faster because the solutions wouldn't have to go through a corrupt union or be approved by kingdoms that have no personal gain from it. What's more, we are not anarchists for simply choosing to not unite. We only wish for Terratopia to be restored to nationwide peace and prosperity once more. We wish to be able to live freely under our own kingdoms rule, not that under a supposed united state that in reality is a select few kingdoms enforcing its will on all others to satisfy their power-hungry greed, for their own gain and nothing more."

"That is preposterous!" Hyzus replied. "A united Terratopia would be run by all kingdoms! Similar to how it is now in the union except it will have the power to enact change that currently cannot be enacted!"

"The union currently is not run by all kingdoms!" Tyzus barked. "It was run exclusively by Roccano in the times of old, then exclusively run by the high kingdom of Rodus from Filnethias and Rime and it now would once more would be ran by Roccano if it wasn't for my own dedication to all kingdoms and not just my own!"

Liberalist cheered for their leader as he spouted the hypocrisy of Unionist words before letting him continue;

"The Terratopia union has only ever been ran by powerful Men and Elves. Men and Elves who claim to be above all else at that! It has never been ran by kingdoms nor races of any other kind! We grow tired of your corruption and hypocrisy Hyzus." Tyzus stated before continuing on; "I have drawn up a proposal that ten Liberalist kingdoms have signed. It details their immediate departure from the union and its ruling, to become liberated and free to their own internal rule, no one else's. To become freely independent, liberated kingdoms even further away from the unions orbit than the kingdoms that are not currently in the union like the Centaurs, Dwarves, Gnomes or Thruckland. Understand the time of waiting and debate is over Hyzus. These ten kingdoms will leave this union by nightfall and will continue to demand for the union to be abandoned, it is up to you to allow the will of these people, or deny them their liberation. Understand that if you oppose this proposal, I will form an alliance between all these kingdoms and they will stand together in unity to fight the unions rule, and the unions rule alone, not stopping until the union is dissolved!"

The whole chamber gasped and fell silent for a moment after Tyzus's radical words. He then threw the signed proposal to his brother, the important scroll unravelling as it flew through the air and landing perfectly on the table in front of Hyzus. Hyzus started intently at his brother and spoke;

"These actions cannot and will not be considered legitimate by this great union. Your actions of defiance show the clear anarchism that flows through all your minds, your promise to form an alliance to stand against this great union is treasonous in nature and only seals the archaists you all are. Morur has clearly corrupted you all. Should you follow the path you have stated" Hyzus paused briefly to gather his breath and to sound as imposing as possible, "A state of war will exist us. Between the grand Combined Union of Terratopia and the radical Liberalist Alliance."

The chamber fell silent once more as all eyes turned to Tyzus for his response. He stood up proudly, his head high, chest out and hand on his blade;

"War it is then!" he announced triumphantly, drawing his blade, impaling it deep into the table before him and pinning the unravelled Liberalist proposal of departure that lay on it in place.

Chapter 13

The Foundations Laid

War had now been declared and Terratopia was about to begin its long and savage civil war. Tyzus and nearly all members from the Liberalist kingdoms left Embirith promptly and headed straight for their own home kingdoms to inform them of the news and to prepare for the upcoming conflict. The remaining Unionist members left in Embirith all roared hatred for the Liberalist's and of their leader Tyzus at each other, greatly intensifying the hostile atmosphere of the parliament. They were all eventually silenced by Hyzus who spoke in a commanding voice;

"Loyal and faithful members of Terratopia. We are now in a civil war against foolish anarchists that wish for nothing more than our downfall. Not just our own personal downfall, but the downfall of civilisation, the downfall of all we have worked for and all our ancestors have worked for before us! We cannot allow this to happen. The union survived and won one war, we will survive and win another! We must subdue these illegitimate kingdoms and make them pay for their crimes of treason against us! We cannot afford to lose, for the sake of our societies!"

The parliament cheered for Hyzus and began calling him their leader, chanting his name and chanting ruler. Hyzus spoke once more;

"It is important we do not allow this coming war to lower our standards! We are the grand Union of Terratopia! We stand for everything Terratopia should be and so thusly should not and cannot allow for any actions that are detrimental to this. We shall not lower ourselves even one bit to the Liberalist level. We will respect the neutral kingdoms. We will not commit crimes against all peoples and beings. We will fight everything Morur's Evil stands for. We will win this war and we will win it right. The way one wins a war matters and we will win it the right way. You all chant for me as your leader, but a ruler I am not. I will remain in my position of power for the duration of this war, to best lead us against my brother, unless I am deposed by you all. And rest be assured that when this war ends the Terratopia Union will be ruled by all kingdoms, just as it was in the times of my grandfather Thyzus!"

Cheers once more erupted for Hyzus, the volume deathening and shaking to the bone.

"Now go! Send for your kingdoms! Prepare them for this war!" Hyzus commanded and sure enough representatives for all Unionist kingdoms left for their homes to prepare for war.

Riots broke out in the streets of Embirith as the Liberalist leaning inhabitants of the city, that had not left, fought for their cause and against the decrees of Hyzus whose words had turned the Unionist inhabitants even more hostile towards them. Streets were filled to the bursting with violence as rioters from both sides clashed. But the riots did not last long, being completely stopped by the overwhelming Unionist public in Embirith as well as its standing garrison which was loyal to Hyzus and the union. The homes and businesses of the Liberalist families were ransacked, looted, and even destroyed and the Liberalist rioters were either killed in the chaos or imprisoned indefinitely, there only hope to be released on a wagon back to friendly Liberalist kingdoms.

Some days later, during the dawn of twilight, Hyzus and Tyzus met in the secret cavern in the Thruckland Range hills they historically had always met in to see their father. They greeted each other enthusiastically and embraced each other tightly in a brotherly hug of congratulations. They were ecstatic, the plan had gone off without a hitch, Terratopia was at war and they were the respected leaders of each side and with a fanatical following. The narrative they had orchestrated to cause the war was excellent. They had made the situation out to be life or death. The decision to end all decisions. And the information they spat only made their fanatical followers more sure of the side they had chosen, regardless how truthful what was said was. The twins then both walked into the dark, dimly lit cavern together where their father Kyzus was waiting.

"We have good news for you father!" They both said excitedly "War has begun. You were right, the kingdoms didn't even resist it, they wanted it!"

"Excellent" Kyzus boomed in his deep echoing voices, the echoes of his magical voice standing out even more in the deep cavern, becoming even more foreboding. "We must now make sure this war has the desired effects on Terratopia and its peoples. You must both inform each other exactly what both of your sides are doing, planning, and preparing for. Confrontations must be devastating with no winners. Conflict must always be deadly and costly but ultimately change nothing. This war must drag out its full course. This cavern will continue to be our meeting place whenever I summon you both, but while away leading your factions, use these to communicate." As Kyzus said this, he presented two seeing stones from his robes, one in each hand. They glowed brightly in the dark cavern; their changing rainbow colourations magnificent to behold and beautifully illuminating the whole cave in a rainbow sea of light. "These seeing stones will allow you to see anywhere in Terratopia; through mountains, over forests and under seas, your minds imagination is the limit. Touch it and your vision shall travel where ever your minds desire. Additionally, you can communicate with each other with them, if you are both touching them you will be able to establish a connection to talk should you both want to. You may also be able to do this with me if I am holding my own. Never let these seeing stones leave your side."

Hyzus and Tyzus's eyes widened the more Kyzus detailed the warm colourful stone gifts he presented and they thanked him for them as well. Hyzus then asked;

"Father, what of the neutral kingdoms? How do we ensure they won't be detrimental to your plans? If they favour any one side or refuse to help at all I fear the war may be short lived."

Kyzus replied "Worry not about such thing's son, that is a role Mia-Myzus would have filled but now it falls to me. The neutral kingdoms will fuel this war to utter devastation I will make sure of it."

"And what of the other powers of these lands father?" Tyzus asked. "What about the wild bandits, ruffians, and pirates? What about the crime syndicates? I hear rumours that a crime empire is rising in the far east of Terratopia the other side of the Dividing Mountains, will this matter to us?"

Kyzus smiled. "You are wise dear son, but you forget, the journey of crime is a journey of selfishness, all those on the path are on it for their own benefit and nothing more. They will welcome this war as it brings opportunity and they will ensure its devastation to all through their own cruel nature. Do not concern yourself with their actives. Welcome them in fact. Don't rely on them and do not align yourself with them but by all means use them!"

Satisfied all they were unsure about was answered, the twins of Hobbes asked Kyzus for their next instructions which he then began to explain;

"Tell me, what are the borders of Terratopia now? What kingdoms belong to the Liberalist Alliance?"

"We have four kingdoms of Men Father, three more Elves and a further three of Merpeople. We all but rule the seas and the lands of Western Terratopia. The kingdoms of Gweston, Suitear, Arway, Kondit Point, the Connecting Isles, Lurtha, Orthelian, Reeforiris, the Shore Mountain Atoll and the Kingdom of the Great Eastern Bay are all Liberalist and have pledged themselves to my military alliance" replied Tyzus.

"Good, good, okay," Kyzus said, clearly in thought. "Since Western Terratopia is so strongly Liberalist and I believe only two Unionist kingdoms within it stand in your way from dominating it completely, I want you to build a Liberalist stronghold there. A grand fortress city from which you will reside in and control over the Liberalist Alliance from. It should be known as 'Jassett' and it should be a rallying point for the Liberalist movement, a defiant landmark against the Unionists. I want you to build it near the Elven capital of Gweston, Lendspen. Build it on the Lendspen arm as it is deep in Liberalist territory but also close to the Sky Mountains kingdom which has chosen to be Unionist. Such close proximity to the Valkyries will cause much chaos throughout the war, I am sure" Kyzus finished before moving onto address his other son; "And you Hyzus, return to Embirith. Rule the Unionist forces from there. Central Terratopia is completely dominated by the Union so your war is all about fighting to make sure all Unionist kingdoms isolated by Liberalists do not fall! You must not allow Tyzus to gain the upper hand anywhere! Both of you ensure you know exactly what either side is attempting and planning. There should a balanced dance of bloodshed and death between you both."

"Yes father," they both said before turning and leaving the cavern.

When left seemingly all alone in the cavern, Kyzus then spoke into the darkest corner of the cavern; "You can come out now." A hooded female then emerged with a sinister smile on her scared face. "Ahh daughter. You have indeed done well and have aided your brothers greatly, I'm sure they would be most grateful."

"Thank you, father, I accomplished your bidding without question and with ease. None suspected it was I who assassinated Lord Delegate Petar as per your command and I have seduced the leader of the insurgent Samson and Goliath group and I have the insurgents completely under my authority. We have begun our conquest of the crime syndicates, soon they will ALL bow to me" proclaimed Mia-Myzus.

"Good daughter, excellent in fact, you are proving yourself more and more each passing day. I have clearly taught you well and now I have your next task."

Mia-Myzus bowed to one knee, inquiring what her next orders were.

"I need you to pay the Viceroy of Thruck, Charles VIII a visit." Kyzus said. "Make sure he knows it is in his best interests to serve you and no other side in this coming civil war. Oh, and take this, you may find it useful to give to the Viceroy, it will help you greatly in your task ahead," as Kyzus finished his sentence he presented and handed another seeing stone to Mia-Myzus.

"I will father. Consider the kingdom of Thruckland under my control and non-others and thank you, I'm sure this will be most useful." Mia-Myzus replied as she accepted the seeing stone from her father.

And with these as her parting words Mia-Myzus swiftly left the cavern and headed for the city of Thruck in the dark dead of night. Once out of sight Kyzus let out a terrific laugh. A foreboding yet joyous laugh as his plan was now fully in motion, it was going perfectly smoothly and no one was none the wiser in the slightest. It was only a matter of time before he could unite Terratopia under the rule of the Deity, restoring it to its former glory in the summer of the world. Kyzus could not help but smile at the fact he knew that in less than half a millennium, for the rest of eternity no one would ever again face any of the pain or suffering he had faced. Everyone would only know what it was like to live in a near perfect, summer like Terratopia. And with that comforting thought, Kyzus magically teleported back to his Roccano palace home and fell asleep in front of a warm burning fire, peacefully sleeping for the first time since Autumn had first begun over two and a half centuries ago. He dreamt of the prosperous society he was in the process of creating and it brought him much joy and relief in his sleep which was filled with wonderful dreams from the Dream Spirits.

Chapter 14

The Beginnings of the Civil War in Terratopia

Tyzus and Hyzus left the cavern within the Thruckland Range they had just spoke to their father in, brandishing their seeing stone gifts and emerging into the cold dark night.

"I guess this is farewell brother?" Tyzus said in a semi-optimistic tone.

"I guess so," Hyzus replied. "Though it sounds like we will be in close contact all too often" he then joked.

"Ah yes. I'll be on the other side of the archipelago and I still won't be able to get away from you!" Tyzus sarcastically replied. "Anyway...what now brother? The war is only a few days old and the world is our oyster!"

"Well," Hyzus replied. "I think it would be most beneficial to our father's plans if the Liberalist Alliance are the aggressors in this coming conflict. Your actions in Embirith have already made the Liberalists seem that way to the wider world anyway. Besides, just as father said; my Unionist kingdoms are mostly concentrated in Central Terratopia with only a few kingdoms isolated outside that, they themselves are at the mercy of your Liberalist kingdoms. You should be the aggressors and attack these isolated kingdoms while I will do all I can to make sure these kingdoms do not fall!"

"Agreed," Tyzus said. "Silvor and Silvoud shall be my primary targets in Western Terratopia. Carlin will be my target in the Eastern Terratopia. And Lemlee will be my target in the Connecting Isles region."

The twins shook on this arrangement before Hyzus then said;

"But what about Aquatatia? It is also the only Merpeople kingdom to side with the Unionists and it is completely surrounded. Reeforiris to its south, the Shore Mountains Atoll to its west, the Liberalist controlled Connecting Isles to its north and only neutral Roccano and Thruckland to its east."

"Ordinarily I would say Aquatatia is in a prime position to be completely overrun, especially as it is a kingdom of tutors, academics, and philosophers, not warriors. It would be a perfect way to start of the war! An early victory for my Liberalists and a devastating early defeat to motivate your Unionists with utter vengeance." Tyzus said before pausing and then continuing; "But it is a grand kingdom, perhaps the most splendid of all the Merpeoples. It was also our home for a large portion of our youth as well as the favourite kingdom of our uncle Lyzus and of course it is the ancient home of our grandmother Mia."

"Exactly," Hyzus replied. "There is no other kingdom within Terratopia apart from Roccano itself that holds any greater meaning to us and the Hobbes family."

"I say we both decree separately to our factions that war effort is not allowed to cross over into Aquatatia territory. It simply holds to much meaning for either of us to allow our armies to bring the war inside its underwater borders." Tyzus suggested before then adding; "as well as that, Aquata itself is home to the greatest collections of records and works within Terratopia, perhaps all of Terra Tearia; this is a truly priceless asset that our archipelago cannot afford to lose."

"This is true," Hyzus said in a pondering tone. "But the Merpeople of Aquatatia are among the most avid supporters of the Terratopia Union, asking them for their kingdom not to partake in this war may be an impossible task. They will want to fight the Liberalist Merpeople kingdoms that surround it and they will want to support their closest Unionist neighbour, Lemlee, as much as they are able."

"Ummm," Tyzus hummed to himself while he pondered on what to do. "I instead suggest we stick with my original idea except with one difference. The city of Aquata is where that kingdoms' grandiose lies, as well as all the meaning to our family. We should instead decree that war does not pass into the city boundaries of Aquata, for the same reasons we have both already given, but the wider kingdom of Aquatatia shall have no such restrictions."

"That seems like a far more feasible request for me to ask of the Aquatatia Merpeople. I doubt they would want the war to ever reach their capital either, whether Liberalist or Unionist in nature!" Hyzus replied.

"Excellent! It is agreed then!" Tyzus resounded. "Now I must get going and return to the west, I have an entire fortress city to build afterall!"

"Good luck with that!" Hyzus remarked. "I shall make sure Silvor and Silvoud don't bother you too much while you do that, as well as the sky mountain Valkyries, but it will obviously be a challenge, I'm sure" he then said knowingly with a wink.

"Thank you Hyzus" Tyzus nodded. "I will also be immediately ordering assaults on Lemlee and Carlin at this time as well, to keep the war efforts mostly focused on the Connecting Isles and the far east at the moment."

"All right Tyzus," Hyzus replied "I shall make sure they are ready for you!"

The twins then departed on their unicorns, hugging each other goodbye before they left. Hyzus headed straight back towards Embirith while Tyzus made for Port Thruck to then sail west.

Tyzus's journey took him to Port Thruck where in the bustling harbours he found a large ship destined for Xephex, the capital of the Liberalist controlled Connecting Isles kingdom. It was upon this vessel that Tyzus travelled, arriving in the Connecting Isles capital city after only a few days sailing. Upon arriving, Tyzus was greeted and welcomed graciously; being treated as a hero and as if he was the Count of Xephex himself. Tyzus did not stay in the city long however, instead sailing straight to Lendspen along the coastline of Western Terratopia on an incredibly fast Merpeople ship sent by the Shore Mountains Atoll kingdom.

All of the other leaders of the Liberalist kingdoms in Western Terratopia were already in the grand Elvish city, awaiting Tyzus's arrival. When at the ornate gothic capital of Gweston and with all the gathered Liberalist leaders, Tyzus advocated for the creation of the fortress city of Jassett and for it to be the symbol of the Liberalist Alliances stoic defiance against the Terratopia Union and Embiriths rule, a monument to liberty. Tyzus also gave his decree that the war effort was forbidden to touch the city of Aquata as he personally could not allow any harm to come to such an important city of his and his family's past, as well citing the preservation of Aquata's priceless records as another reason.

The gathered Liberalist Alliance leaders agreed resoundingly to these announcements made by Tyzus but also affirmed to him that they should also quickly strike at some of the isolated Unionist kingdoms while the war was still in its youth, suggesting Silvor and Silvoud as prime targets. Tyzus rebuked this however, expounding that the western Liberalist kingdoms should focus their resources on the construction of Jassett, further reasoning that if they were to instead divert attention to the two Unionist kingdoms, the vital quick completion of Jassett would be jeopardised. In addition, Tyzus inferred that if they were to focus attack on Silvor and Silvoud, Unionist presence and pressure in the west would also increase, especially from the Valkyries from the Sky Mountains which, as Tyzus again pointed out, would further hinder Jassett's construction. Tyzus also remarked that the two isolated Unionist kingdoms were in no position to attack any of the surrounding Liberalist kingdoms and so they should instead just be left alone for now and cut off from the rest of the Unionists. Tyzus instead commanded all attention in the west instead focused on the assembling of Jassett. Agreeing to this, the Liberalist leaders were then instructed that attacks should instead be centred around the isolated kingdoms of Lemlee and Carlin for now. Tyzus ordered that Reeforiris should send word to the Kingdom of the Great Eastern Bay for them to besiege Carlin by sea and for them to tell the kingdoms of Lurtha and Orthelian to do that same on land. As well as this, the Connecting Isles kingdom were ordered to start an offensive on the woodland isles of Lemlee with the Merpeople from the Shore Mountains Atoll to assist them.

    And so, it was done. Tyzus's first orders as the leader of the Liberalist Alliance were given and representatives from all the western Liberalist kingdoms left for their home kingdoms to proclaim Tyzus's orders and to start preparations to fulfil them. A large, combined, impressive navy from Xephex and Kondit Point began assaulting Lemlee, with armies also being sent to attempt to invade any of the forest islands that they could. With the assistance of the Merpeople from the Shore Mountain Atoll, a blockade was also set up around Lemlee in an attempt to stave the woodland kingdom islands into submission. Although the blockade did come to face continual resistance and attack from Aquatatia constantly.

A Merpeople taskforce from Reeforiris eventually made its way to their fellow Merpeople kingdom in the east, the Kingdom of the Great Eastern Bay, and delivered the orders of attacking Carlin. Orders which were also in turn delivered to the kingdoms of Lurtha and Orthelian. Carlin was then continually assailed by armies of Men, Elves and Merpeople from the three Liberalist kingdoms that surrounded it. The Unionist kingdom barely managed not to fall in the first few days of the campaign. Carlins lands were invaded and ravaged by the Liberalist armies but its walled-up capital, Cufle, remained an unconquerable stronghold that the Liberalist forces could not penetrate.

Hyzus coordinated Unionist responses to the war extremely well. He had prepared Carlins and Lemlee's armies and defences well for assault and besiegement, pouring effectively all the readily available central Unionist kingdoms forces, support, and resources into them; the two kingdoms and their capitals of Wefalime and Cufle were transformed into formidable strongholds as a result. In addition, the Viceroy of Thruck and the Dwarf king of Kossorlim where both extremely cooperative and helpful to Hyzus's in his efforts to support his fellow Unionist kingdoms under siege by his brother Tyzus as well. These two neutral kingdoms going so far as to even providing weapons and resources to his Unionist, resources that Hyzus otherwise wouldn't have had, as well as unique access through their lands, but it all came at an exceptionally high financial cost to his Unionists.

Around the Isles of Lemlee, the indominable, stubborn defiance of the Elves in their wooden kingdom, continually rebuked any and all attacks and invasions sent by the armies of Men from Kondit Point and the Connecting Isles. Huge Liberalist landings where continually planned and attempted, sometimes with the assistance of Merpeople but every time the Liberalist forces were repelled; their established hard-fought beachheads turning into slaughter grounds with all invaders eventually being snuffed out.

Lemlee was kept supplied with some Unionist supplies and reinforcements being transported in shipments from Thruck, the convoys being able to pass through the established blockade when it was slightly broken from devastating coordinated attacks from Aquatatia. These navel battles that took place above and below the water were horrific for all involved, being extremely costly and futile in nature as any breaks in the blockade were always stitched back up within a day or two, often with reinforcements arriving to seas still having a red tinge from the blood spilled previously. Still, these small windows in the blockade for Thruck's ships to pass through became the much needed, vital lifeline of Lemlee, its inhabitants kept alive from them. Yet, there was never enough supplies to prevent the decline and suffering of the Elven inhabitants of the kingdom. Lord Folore's and Lady Elwii's kingdom remained in their hands, but at the cost of the starvation and suffering of their people, as well as the terribly high death rates of their soldiers, fighting desperately in the defence of their woodland islands.

The kingdom of Carlin was in a similar situation. It faced invasion and assault from all directions from three separate kingdoms of three separate races. Merpeople from the Great Eastern Bay ravaged the coast and rivers. Men from Lurtha pillaged and plundered all across the kingdom's lands, even burning entire towns and villages to the ground. Elves from Orthelian also overwhelmed the landscape as well as becoming the primary force besieging the kingdoms capital of Cufle. Cufle itself soon became the only Unionist part of Carlin to not fall to the Liberalist Alliance and while it stood unconquered, the kingdom of Carlin too remained the same. Cufle's staunch resistance and survival was kept alive from relief forces continually sent by Central Terratopia passing through Kossorlim. These relief armies where almost always totally defeated, but their campaigns into Liberalist lands and sometimes into Carlin itself diverted enough Liberalist forces away for Cufle's siege to be broken and aid given, most often in the form of trade caravans driven by Gnomes and Centaurs. Their services and contents already paid for by Embirith.

Just as was the case in Lemlee, both sides suffered tremendously from the war efforts in the east. Countless lives from all races were lost on all sides. Kingdoms lands were ravaged, their inhabitants made homeless, lives made redundant or being ended outright. The people's within Cufle faced starvation as barely enough supplies ever made it safely into the city and the Elven besiegers rarely had the resources to mount meaningful offensives onto the city, yet they were always ordered too by Tyzus and were always repelled with exceedingly high losses by Hyzus.

The war continually raged on. Morur's evil presence throughout Terratopia flourished and despite no kingdoms ever totally falling to either side; the pain, devastation, and death suffered by all often made some wish the fighting would stop and peace to return.

After three years passed in the awful conflict, a major change in fighting was about to occur as the Liberalist Alliance fortress city of Jassett was finally completed.

Chapter 15

A Change in Strategy

Tyzus stood proud on top of the highest tower in Jassett and overlooked his magnificent, now fully completed, fortress city. The circular stronghold stood on the banks of the River Harpgar's estuary and on the shores of Gweston Bay. The city overlooked the bays waters to see the shimmering trees of the Silver wood at the most southern point of the kingdom of Suitear. The oversized grey stone fortress was also built right at the beginning of the 'Lendspen Arm', the peninsula that the lustrous capital of Gweston, Lendspen, stood at the very end of; which could itself be seen when looking from Jassett's eastern walls and towers. The westerns walls and towers overlooked the exquisite rolling plains of Gweston, the far horizon only being broken by the monstrous peaks of the Harpgar Mountains and Mount Harpgar itself further towering over them, punching high into the sky, the second highest mountain in all of Terratopia, after Mount Roccano.

The construction of Jassett had been no easy feat for Tyzus and his Liberalists either. All the timber required was easily transported from the nearby friendly forest kingdom of Suitear, but getting the vast amounts of stone required was a far more difficult task. The Harpgar Mountains were where the Great Owls of Terratopia resided and they did not allow for any quarrying to take place in their home, especially for the war effort which they vehemently opposed. Any attempt by the Liberalists to take stone from the Harpgar Mountains was always hampered by the Great Owls who killed any that ventured into their lofty rocky home. Stone instead had to be transported from quarries in Arway or imported from the Dwarves of Dwaria at extortionate costs, as Gweston itself had no stone deposits being a lush kingdom of flood plains. Both of these options also faced further impediment as Unionist kingdoms stood in between Arway, Dwaria, and Gweston where Jassett was being built. Stone from Arway had to pass through Silvor, which the fearsome cavalry of the kingdom the Liberalist retaliate and stab into the Unionists own heartlands to assail their own kingdoms. Tyzus listened to all the demands and suggestions from the Liberalist leaders, pondering on their ideas and trying to come up with a strategy that would not only satisfy the leaders, but also be able to be countered effectively from his brother, as he could not allow for his Liberalist forces to totally overrun any of Hyzus's Unionist kingdoms.

After some thought, Tyzus finally came up with a solution. He, in a powerful, uplifting speech, played on the anger felt by the Liberalist leaders, manipulating them to desire nothing more than revenge on the Unionist kingdoms for all the death and suffering that they had caused. Tyzus knew that any offensive launched at Silvor or Silvoud in the west would likely succeed as they were too isolated for Hyzus to effectively support substantially without a lot of prior warning, so he knew he had to keep the wars attention on them to a minimum. To do this, Tyzus declared that the Liberalists should strike at the core of the Unionists, to create offensives into Central Terratopia itself. Under Tyzus's incredible manipulating ability, the Liberalist leadership thunderously agreed. Efforts on Lemlee and Carlin would continue as normal but now invasions into the high kingdom of Rodus were planned. Forces from Reeforiris where to assault the grand coastal cities of Filnethias and Rime while invasion forces from Gweston, Suitear and Arway would strike deep into Rodus, their primary target being the Unionists capital of Embirith at the far side of the kingdom's borders.

The gathered Liberalists leaders loved this plan, seeing it as the perfect revenge strategy towards the Unionists as well as an effective approach to ultimate victory; for if Embirith could fall, the whole of the Terratopia Union, and thusly the Unionists, would surely quickly follow suit. With this strategy agreed, Tyzus ordered that preparations for their new approach be immediately put underway, which they diligently were.

Later that day, Tyzus retired to his private quarters within Jassett where he attempted to contact his brother, as well as father, to inform them of the radical change in the Liberalist offensive. Kyzus and Hyzus answered Tyzus's call almost instantly.

"Brother, father, I have news of radical change in the Liberalist approach to the civil war. We are beginning preparations for an invasion into the high kingdom of Rodus and onto Embirith! Filnethias and Rime will be assaulted from the sea by Reeforiris while forces from Gweston, Suitear and Arway will all sail and invade into Rodus." Tyzus reported.

"Interesting," Kyzus remarked. "That is a bold move my son, well done on convincing the Liberalists to commit to such an offensive. Hyzus! I want you to make sure no Merpeople are able to set foot into the cities of Filnethias and Rime."

"What about the invading forces into Rodus father?" asked Hyzus.

"I want you to allow them in." Kyzus replied. "Let them ravage the whole landscape, let them consume the whole kingdom, they would not dare to touch Roccano, Tyzus will make sure of that. I want you to even let them cross the River Embirith and draw up to the outskirts of Embirith."

"Are you sure father? So close to my capital? The Unionist will be close to losing the war if this happens." Hyzus questioned.

Kyzus replied; "this is the perfect opportunity to induce terrible suffering on the all peoples in Central Terratopia that have so far largely been left out of the civil war's devastation, besides the economic downturn they have experienced. Plus, it also gives you both the perfect opportunity to obliterate each other's forces to no accomplishment what so ever. Tyzus... I want you to pour everything the western Liberalist kingdoms have into this invasion. Make them feel this victory is certain, but all must be committed to it in order to succeed. And Hyzus... I want you to do everything to make sure Embirith does not fall, but also that the Central Unionist forces will be all but wiped out from the eventual battle with Tyzus's invading Liberalist."

Both the twins smiled to themselves at the sadistic genius of Kyzus's orders.

"Yes father," they both replied before the three then let go of their seeing stones to go and prepare for this monumental coming assault and battle.

Chapter 16

The Invasion of Rodus

Before long the Liberalist invasion forces were on their way to the high kingdom of Rodus, sailing across the expansive sea that divided Western and Central Terratopia. Tyzus had indeed poured everything the Liberalist in the west had into this invasion force, creating an uncountable number of new ships to transport the vast armies of Men and Elves. The seas surface was barely blue when looked at from above, the watery waves being near impossible to see because of the sheer amount of wooden sailing ships that covered them. When looking from above, the sea was not blue, it was instead brown, white, black, and silver from the ship's decks, sails, and the armed-up forces upon them, hellbent on war.

The Liberalist invasion fleet was so large that it comprised of three separate forces. First were legions of Merpeople from the Kingdom of Reeforiris that advanced largely underwater towards the grand cities of Filnethias and Rime. Second was the force sent from Arway. Slews of ships filled with knights and soldiers of Men and some mercenary forces of Centaurs from the '10,000-Tree Wood' left Kondit Point and made for the coastline in-between Roccano and Filnethias. The final force was by far the biggest and it headed for the long stretch of coast in-between Filnethias and Rime. Wades of ships, filled to the brim with Elves from Suitear and Gweston left from the Lendspen arm, cruising towards Rodus; it was with this force that Tyzus himself also sailed with.

When approximately halfway to their destination, disaster struck the behemoth Liberalist fleet as battalions of Merpeople sent from Aquatatia clashed with the outlying legions from Reeforiris underwater as well as also raiding parts of the huge navy from Arway. Entire segments of the Arway invasion force where assailed, with a great many ships being sunk and a great many more knights and soldiers being killed or drowned by the ruthless forces of Aquatatia. The cramped, slow-moving ships, being so crammed close together on the water's surface were near defenceless sitting ducks for the Unionist attackers to prey upon. A similar situation occurred to the colossal detachment of Elves from Gweston and Suitear, as sections of this huge force were attacked from the sky. A huge army of Valkyries riding Pegasus's from the Sky Mountains of Terratopia bombarded and ransacked the compacted Elven ships that mercilessly floated on the sea.

Complete devastation spread across the assaulted areas of the Liberalist invasion forces, with panic and fear spreading even further throughout the massive fleet as the forces of Men and Elves watched on helplessly, and in horror, at the ships being pillaged bombarded and sunk all around them. The Men and Elves directly under attack fought for their lives, relentlessly attempting to fend of the armies of Merpeople or Valkyries that attacked them; ruthlessly firing arrows into the sky or throwing harpoons and spiked weighted nets into the sea in any attempt to dispel their attackers. This brutal battle that spread across the sea raged on for many hours, nearly an entire day, killing and sinking huge amounts of the Liberalist invasion fleet. However, so massive was the collection of Liberalist ships, all armed for war, that eventually they savagely fought off the continual onslaughts of Unionist attacks, completely annihilating the armies that attacked them, but at a tremendous cost.

Still, the greatly hindered, butchered invasion fleet pressed on, spurred by the fact they had defeated a huge Unionist attempt to stop them, seeing it as a sign of their inevitable victory. The Merpeople of Reeforiris were the first to meet their destinations, emerging out of the sea and assaulting the harbours and ports of Filnethias and Rime. They faced immediate and stiff resistance however as the elite high Men and Elf guards fiercely defended their capital homes. On the shore boarders of these two incredible immaculate cities of high Men and Elves, a cruel battle emerged as the great military might of Reeforiris, the largest Merpeople kingdom, fought the garrisoned forces of well-prepared high Men and Elves that protected their grand cities.

On the empty shores of Rodus, in-between these great cities

however, a whole different scenario occurred as entire armies of Men and Elves disembarked from their ships and almost immediately penetrated straight into the kingdom they sought to invade. Vast armies marched throughout the kingdom of Rodus, intending to advance all the way to Embirith, occupying as much land and causing as much mayhem as they could along the way.

It took over a week for the Liberalist invasion fleet to completely empty itself onto the shores of Rodus, in which time, the already alighted armies had completely ravaged the majority of the kingdom. Liberalist battalions caused utter devastation from the Southern Highlands and Rodus Forest all the way up to the Thruckland range. The forces of Men, Elves, and mercenary Centaurs scorched the lands that they advanced across and met little resistance wherever they ventured. The resistance that these armies did face were no match and were completely overwhelmed by the sheer size and unstoppable nature of the Liberalist divisions. The small towns and villages scattered throughout Rodus never stood a chance and where near totally destroyed, their inhabitants fleeing as far as fast as they could.

No Liberalist forces dared to advance anywhere near Roccano, Tyzus himself also ordering no such attempts be made. Additionally, although Filnethias and Rime still withheld from their aquatic assaults from the sea. Tyzus however, ordered no encirclements and land-based attacks on the cities be made, instead ordering all of his forces to press onto Embirith. Which they did and within days the grand capital of the Terratopia Union was within Liberalist sights and grasp. On the outskirts of the city Tyzus ordered his armies hold, so as they could fully regroup and reform with all of their forces that had spread across Rodus as well as the ones that had yet to still fully leave their ships on the coast. Refugees from across Rodus could be seen fleeing into the city for days, their own lands now destroyed and them hoping and seeking for refuge and safety from the overwhelming Liberalist force. Over this time, Tyzus devised his plan of attack, communicating his strategy with Hyzus so that he knew what to expect and could organise his Unionist defence accordingly. Tyzus arranged for his invasion force to be further split into three separate armies to attack Embirith from three separate directions. The battalions of Elves from Gweston were to attack from the Southern highlands, the forces from Arway to attack from over the River Embirith further to the north and the armies from Suitear to attack from over the Rodus Slopes.

Finally, the day came and Tyzus ordered an all-out attack on Embirith, all three of his huge armies advancing quickly and converging around the great Unionist capital. But, to the storming Liberalist forces horror, they found that they had severely underestimated the defences of the city and the number of Unionist forces within it. Formidable divisions of high Men and Elves armed with shinning weapons and armour sprung out the city and formed an impenetrable host around Embirith. Hyzus had in fact, to boost the already standing garrison of Embirith, halved Filnethias and Rimes forces before the Liberalist invasion even set foot on Rodus, leaving half to defend against the Merpeople assault and retreating the other half back to defend Embirith, ascertaining the remaining soldiers of high Men and Elves scattered throughout Rodus to defend the city as well. The gathered host of warriors from the high kingdom of Rodus and the garrison already within Embirith were more than a match for the overwhelming invading Liberalist armies.

Inevitably the two enormous Liberalist and Unionist hosts clashed. The two forces fully unleashing themselves on one another, committing everything they had to slay their opposing foes. It was carnage. Complete and utter bloodshed. The largest gathering of Men and Elves and the largest military might's that had so far converged on one another in all of Terra Tearia's history raged deadly all-out warfare at each other, turning the green pastures outside the grand city of Embirith into a boggy brown and black slaughter ground, bathed in dark red blood and littered with dead, deformed, and dismembered bodies.

Tyzus and Hyzus surveyed the horrific sight from afar, safe in their observing positions. The twins communicated and coordinated attacks with one another and to their clashing armies for the maximum amount of desolation, with the minimum amount of gain. When the battle around Embirith was at its height, the death toll suffered from both sides immeasurable, the Liberalists, with their hugely superior numbers began to overrun the defending Unionist host and push them back into their city. Embirith was now under siege, its walls being battered by a rush of unrelenting Liberalist attacks. Tyzus ordered his forces to fully commit to breaking down the final defences of Embirith and for them to press on with their offensive throughout the night. Panic and fear now swept across Embirith as its inhabitants began to fear for their safely and lives as flaming projectiles, shot from the war machines of Arway's Men, smashed against the walls of the city as well as over them and into the streets and buildings. It was during this dark chaotic night, lit up only by the burning destruction across Embirith, that Hyzus revealed his next move to the intruding Liberalist forces. A second Unionist force appeared from the north, advancing as silently as they could with no torch light illuminating them. An enormous army of woodland Elves from Nindir and Nindar advanced on the Liberalist forces that surrounded the burning city of Embirith. Tyzus knew of this coming force, but made sure to place all the attention of his armies to the besiegement of Embirith and not to watching their flanks. The march of the relief Elven force was also drowned out from the tumultuous noise of battle as it advanced with near invisibility.

  Soon though, the armies of Nindir and Nindar came so close to Embirith that their sight could not be missed or ignored. Liberalist battle commanders cried out and ordered their armies to prepare for the new attack coming from behind. The Liberalist forces scattered in a chaotic desperate attempt to switch their lines from facing Embirith to facing their new attackers from the north. As soon as their silent cover was blown however, the massive Unionist wood Elf army lit their torches to show their full size and numbers and charged straight into battle, attempting to take full advantage of the surprised, disorganised, Liberalists armies. Once again, huge Unionist and Liberalist armies clashed in devastating battle as Elven brethren from different kingdoms fought one another in deadly duels that caused nothing but death and despair for both sides. The Knights of Men from Arway continued to lead their assault on Embirith but their efforts became futile as the grand city of Embirith would not fall to the now greatly diminished sieging force. They simply no longer had the military might to take the city, even with its crumbling and burning defences.

Throughout the night the battle continued to rage, its sheer magnitude and monstrosity only being truly seen when the golden light of the morning sun glared over the field of violence and death below it. The land around Embirith could no longer be seen; it was instead covered in dead bodies layered on top of one another for nearly as far as the eye could see. Every square inch of ground was covered in layers of corpses and yet still the surviving Unionist and Liberalist soldiers fought on against one another in a fatigued desperate state. The opposing forces were mere glimpses of their former selves, in size and in splendour and the peoples that had made up both sides of the battle had fundamentally changed to the core. Morur's Evil had infiltrated every single person's soul, fuelled by the anger and grief within them all and catalysed by the temptations and power Morur's Evil spirit held, making buying into it irresistible for the war-ravaged rage-filled soldiers.

The infernal, hellish sight that the battlefield around Embirith had become and the terrible, barbaric situation that had occurred was only now becoming clear to the twins of Hobbes as they both looked over the hell that was the battlefield they had commanded over together and caused. The monumental horror of what they saw in and around Embirith could not be described as it was so unlike anything anyone could have possibly imagined. An uneasy feeling passed over them both as they realised the truly evil thing that occurred and that they were both largely responsible for. The sheer weight of emotions that passed over them drowned them both and they fell into a drunken daze of confusion, feeling sick to even breath and guilty to even remotely feel alive. They both reached for their seeing stones and called for one another; without exchanging any words, they both knew exactly what the other was thinking. This was enough. Letting go of their stones and shaking themselves out of their daze, Hyzus and Tyzus ordered their forces retreat, commanding them all leave the battlefield at once and to return home; which, by the end of the day, happened, as the surviving peoples from both sides all collectively began their return home, every one of them in a seemingly hungover, drunken state of despair, grief, and regret. Every person, whether Man or Elf, whether Unionist or Liberalist in faction was covered in mud, blood, and entrails; they were all of them truly exhausted and in a trance of confusion, anger, grief, and remorse. Slowly and sombrely, they all made their way back to their homes to truly attempt to process what had just happened.

Chapter 17

The Reinforcement of Kyzus

On his journey back to the coast where his ships lay, Tyzus held his stone and called for his brother; who coincidentally held his own and called for Tyzus as well. Feeling each other's presence through their magical connection, neither twin could bring themselves to speak, themselves being truly speechless in what to say. They tried to take comfort in one another's presence and they travelled their vision to be able to see one another. During this connected silence between them both, that went on for quite some time, Kyzus pick up his own seeing stone and connected to both his sons.

"My boys! I am so proud of you both! I have seen what you did, it was perfect. You should both be very proud!" Kyzus announced in an impressed tone.

Tyzus and Hyzus did not reply, instead staying in their dazed state, overwhelmed with emotions.

"I can see and sense these events have taken a heavy toll on you both. For that I am sorry. But stay strong my sons! What you are doing now is for the benefit of all who will ever live for all eternity! Remember that." Kyzus spoke again.

His twin sons however remained silent and Kyzus spoke once more in a more assuring understanding tone;

"I ask you both to cast your minds back to your youths, when you first took your vows, and to before the beginning of this war my sons. Remember why you are doing this. You must trust in me that this is the right thing to do. I am the only one to see it and we together are all the only ones with the power and will to make it so. Situations like this were inevitable in the state of nature Terratopia was in anyway, it would have slowly descended to this anyway. This was always going to happen. What we are doing here is rushing it to its worse to then break it. Remember why we are doing this my sons. Peace, prosperity, and happiness will return to all of Terratopia, that I promise you. You just need to stay strong."

Still the twins of Hobbes remained silent but their father's words did raise them out of their drowning sea of emotions, offering to them a solid rope of clarity to grasp upon. Sensing this change with his sons, Kyzus spoke to them both one final time;

"I shall leave you both to discuss things with each other and process all this. I am very proud of you, my children. I love both and you are well on your way to fulfilling your oaths you took to me all those years ago."

And with these parting words, Kyzus let go of his stone and his connection to Tyzus and Hyzus, who both began to emanate the oaths magical mist as their father mentioned it. The twin brothers then finally spoke to one another.

"Are we sure we are doing the right thing here brother?" Hyzus said.

Tyzus replied "I only know the answer to that as much as you know it brother. I am unsure."

"That was truly monstrous and evil what occurred at Embirith right? We can agree on that?" Hyzus asked.

"Indeed, it was brother." Tyzus replied. "I certainly feel it was. I had no idea this is what the cost of war truly felt like. It's so easy to cope and deal with it when in our cosy capitals and the battles raging far from our homes with people, we have never known nor even seen."

"I know!" Hyzus cried. "My city lies in ruins, my inhabitants scared. The lands of Nindir and Rodus are scorched and filled with death. My armies are all but wiped out! My armies comprised of loyal followers I have known for hundreds of years!"

"I know my brother I know. Many of the people that have given their lives for both of us where my friends as well." Tyzus replied apathetically. "And as well as that, think of all the families that have been affected and must have lost at least one person thanks to this invasion of mine. I bet every single family in Terratopia has been affected by this battle. So much death. So much suffering. I'm not okay with it"

"And our soldiers themselves," Hyzus added. "This war has clearly fundamentally changed them all. I could not have imagined anyone would be capable of such heinous acts and yet everyone committed them! Continuously! For days!"

"I think that brings us to seriously consider our fathers words. This war and its devastation was inevitable right? We've just given it a serious push and been so detached to realising what it has truly caused up until this point. But the savagery of fighting, the evil nature of it, it cannot be on us, right? We didn't order this to happen? Not to this level of barbaric cruelness." Tyzus said, seeking the assurance of his brother.

Hyzus agreed, saying "Absolutely! After all... this is for the greater good right? In the grand scheme of things, the suffering of these people will surely not outweigh the eternal happiness and prosperity of all people for all time under our father's untied society, right?"

"Yeah... yeah!" Tyzus replied. "This is for the greater good as father says! What we are feeling right now is just a period of weakness, we cannot allow it to deviate us for our oaths!"

"Agreed!" shouted Hyzus. "Like father said, we only need to stay strong. We are the only ones with the will to bring about the united society. We are saving Terratopia!"

Feeling much better about themselves, the twin brothers bid each other farewell and let go of their seeing stones, taking up a new enthusiastic command of their opposing sides in the civil war making sure it continued until Kyzus deemed it to stop.

Part II
Rise and Betrayal

Chapter 1

A Final Farewell

Mia-Myzus had just swore her undying loyalty to her father's plan once more and had left her old life behind. All those that knew her and knew of her now would believe her to be dead; her presence and rule now becoming all but a memory. With an invisibility enchantment cast over herself, Mia-Myzus left the city of Roccano, the kingdom she ruled over all but a few hours ago. She needed not any of her belongings where she was going, although she did wish she could take some of her fine clothes and most precious treasured trinkets; but alas, their missing presence would undoubtably be noticed by her brothers, jeopardising her father's plan. Her journey ahead to the kingdom of Sabare was going to be long and she had little time to spare, and so Mia-Myzus thought carefully about how to arrive at the Samson and Goliath kingdom in as little as time as possible while also keeping her identity unknown to all.

The grand city of Embirith was the central hub of the Terratopia Union and so consequently the beating heart to nearly all kingdoms on the archipelago. With this in mind, Mia-Myzus deduced that from the heart of the Union, there must be connecting vessels that travel to even the most eastern kingdoms like Carlin or the Gnomes Fungi Forest where she could then easily cross the Sabare Strait to her destination. And so, Mia-Myzus's route was settled, from Roccano she would make for Embirith where she would find passage to the kingdoms of Carlin or the Fungi Forest to then cross into Sabare via boat.

Mia-Myzus strode through Rodus's lands with speed and purpose, the warm sun above her heating her face pleasantly and its light reflecting off Roccano's distant grand white walls making the entire countryside charmingly bright to a point of almost dazzlement. While crossing the lush green rolling countryside of the high kingdom of Rodus, on the main road between Roccano and Embirith, Mia-Myzus grew tired of her invisibility enchantment and so decided to unveil it. Seeing as no one else was within sight, Mia-Myzus did so without worry, but no later than her postponement of the spell, that she then heard the faint galloping of hooves. Although far away, the galloping was thunderous and approaching fast, the sounds volume rising steadily. Mia-Myzus considered re-casting the invisibility enchantment over herself but then a better idea sprung to her mind. The galloping sound had a distinct sound to it, it sounded as if two horses rode towards her, yet they approached too fast to be two normal horses, even if they were towing no cart or chariot; furthermore, the consistency of the galloping steps was too precise to be two separate horses. The unique, thunderous melody that rode towards Mia-Myzus was instantly recognisable to her, it was clearly the stride of a Sleipnirs, the majestic, fast 8-legged race of horses, and it was coming from Roccano's direction. Mia-Myzus knew of only one Sleipnirs in all of the kingdom and it belonged to Kyzus's right-hand, his personal messenger and representative. Barriel was her name and she had been a close friend of Mia-Myzus since they were both young.

 Mia-Myzus knew that her father had obviously summoned his sons to him to break the news of her own 'death' and that Barriel was sent to deliver Kyzus's summoning, as was her role and as she had done many times before for similar summoning's. Mia-Myzus derived that Barriel must be heading for Embirith where her brothers were and thusly would be of much help to her in speeding up her own travels to that grand city.

 The Sleipnirs galloping drew ever closer and just before Barriel passed into sight, Mia-Myzus cast a new powerful enchantment over herself; not one that would hide her presence or appearance, but one that would hide her identity. Mia-Myzus now looked, sounded, and could act the same as she always had done yet now no one would be able to recognise her true identity, unless so magically powerful that they'd be able to recognise and break down her spell.

 As Barriel rode over the small ridge that Mia-Myzus was the other side of, she noticed what looked like to her a lone female

Elf travelling on the side of the dirt gravel road towards Embirith. As she approached her, she slowed her steed and called out;

"Hello there, traveller! Are you heading to Embirith? I am, myself, on my way there and there is still yet a way to go, if you are heading to the same destination as I but have no steed, may I please offer you a lift with me upon my own?"

Mia-Myzus smiled at the sight of her close friend and replied;

"You are most kind my lady, I am indeed on my way to Embirith to visit my husband who is a representative at the Union parliament, my horse was stolen from me by bandits soon after I left my home of Filnethias. I thought I was going to have to travel all the way there by foot!"

"Oh, that is dreadful!" Barriel said sympathetically "These lands are not as safe or kind as they use to be. These bandits are getting braver, stealing the horse of a high Elf no less! You are lucky I found you, wandering these lands alone without an escort is a mighty dangerous feat. Please tell me your name and I will take you to see your husband without hassle."

"My name is Delilah," Mia-Myzus replied, coming up with the name without even having to think, as if it was second nature to her, "And thank you so much! It would be an honour to ride upon a Sleipnirs." As she mounted up behind Barriel, she then asked "Forgive me, but are you not Barriel? The messenger of Kyzus Hobbes himself?"

Barriel set off her Sleipnirs mount and smiled, "I am indeed," she replied. "I am in fact on my way right now to summon his twin sons to him as Kyzus has called for them."

"How exciting," Mia-Myzus replied, trying to sound as enthusiastic as possible. "Do you happen to know why?"

Barriel paused and her head sank, she turned to face Mia-Myzus with a small tear in her developing in her eye, she said with a heavy tone; "Mia-Myzus, his daughter, has been murdered."

Mia-Myzus was touched by how upset her close friend was telling of her own passing, she was filled with sympathy and only wished she could tell her she was in fact all right. As compassionately as possible she reached around and hugged Barriel in the way she always used to which brought more tears to Barriel's watery eyes.

"I am so sorry to hear that," Mia-Myzus said, trying to cover up her own whimpering of how sorry, but moved, she felt for and by Barriel. "Was she a close friend of yours?"

"She was indeed," Barriel sobbed. "A very close friend, we grew up together, I considered her a sister in all but blood and was so proud of how she had transformed Roccano to glory once more."

Mia-Myzus's heart sank even further at these kind, flattering words and only wished that she could thank her friend for them. She hugged Barriel even tighter and said "This must be very hard for you, but I'm sure she knows how proud you are of her and that she too would consider you her sister and be proud to."

Mia-Myzus felt herself then getting too emotional and pulled herself away from her best friend, her father's plan flashed before her eyes and her vows to it. She reassured herself that nothing would get in the way of her oath, not even touching heart wrenching encounters like this.

"Thank you Delilah," Barriel said, wiping the last tears from her eyes. "You are a good person, a fine high Elf. Your husband is very lucky, I hope you find him easily and if you are ever in Roccano, please seek me out, it would be a pleasure to meet you again."

Mia-Myzus felt her heart, with tragic delight, sink even more. "You are too kind Barriel, I hope we do see each other again, I really do," she said, meaning every word.

Before long the two left the green grassy countryside of Rodus, riding around the far tip of the Rodus slopes and crossing the River Embirith to arrive at the grand capital of the Terratopia Union; arriving far quicker than any other traveller could have as the speed and endurance of the Sleipnirs race was unmatched. The two made their way through the bustling wide-open streets of the city to the huge, formidable, wonderous parliament complex. From there Barriel and Mia-Myzus then rode up to the grandiose Lord Delegates Chamber building where Hyzus and Tyzus undoubtably were. As they arrived at the extravagant chamber building; which was big enough, lavish enough, and golden enough to put a king's palace to shame; Barriel blew on her horn and the twins promptly appeared at the oversized grandiose front doors and began making their way down the lofty steps towards the streets below where Barriel and her passenger stood. Barriel then dismounted along with Mia-Myzus. As Barriel dismounted, she subtly turned to Mia-Myzus and spoke;

"My master Kyzus has specifically requested not to tell his sons the reasoning for their summoning as he wants to break the news himself, please Delilah, do not mention anything about their sister's death and try to seem as if you don't know"

"Of course, Barriel, of course," Mia-Myzus said comfortably, holding Barriel's shoulder as Hyzus and Tyzus approached.

"Barriel!" Tyzus exclaimed "What news comes from Roccano?"

"Your father Kyzus summons you to his palace, that is all I know, you are to leave immediately" Barriel replied in a no-nonsense manner.

"Immediately?" Hyzus said. "Huh, must be important. Send for our unicorns!" he then shouted up into the chamber building as four servant boys scrambled inside to ready their masters' mounts.

"And who is your friend Barriel?" Tyzus said enthusiastically.

"This is Delilah, she has come from Filnethias to meet her husband, she arrives with me as her horse was stolen by bandits on the journey." Barriel replied. Mia-Myzus smiled, nodded, and curtsied graciously.

Hyzus sighed. "These lands aren't as safe as they used to be, I'm sorry for your troubles."

"Delilah?" Tyzus said in an inquiring tone. "What a beautiful name, very fitting of a fine high Elf like yourself."

Mia-Myzus chuckled at her brother's amorous remarks, "if only he knew," she thought to herself, her brother always had been the more bashful of them all. "You are too kind," she replied, before turning to Hyzus and saying "Indeed, these are scary times, but there are rumours your father has a grand plan to solve it! It's why he spends so much time in his palace is it not? I look forward to the times ahead, especially with you both in the positions you now are in the union!"

Hyzus, Tyzus and Barriel where all semi-shocked at 'Delilah's' remarks as only them three, as well as Mia-Myzus, had been told directly by Kyzus that he had a secret plan they were all working towards. But alas they were all flattered by her kind words.

"Now if you don't mind, I must go, my husband will be expecting me." Mia-Myzus said quickly. As she left, she hugged Barriel again whispering "It's going to be okay Barriel, I hope to see you again soon" before then turning to her brothers and promptly hugging them both as well, the way she always had done before; reaching round, grabbing, and holding them both before they could even react and then burying her head into their shoulders. Briefly she could feel a tear coming as she knew her brothers had absolutely no idea about the terrible news they were about to receive from Kyzus, but she fought it back, determined not to let anything on. As she let go, she began walking away, turning around briefly to say "I really do hope to see you all again!" Before then again turning and pacing away out of sight, disappearing into the crowded streets.

"What was that all about?" Hyzus chuckled

"She is totally into me!" Tyzus teased. "She just hugged you so you wouldn't feel left out."

Barriel roared with laughter and Hyzus pushed his brother lightly in response laughing as well, the three then made their way to their steeds and promptly left for Roccano.

Mia-Myzus smiled with glee, she felt much closure and happiness to have spent some final moments with the closet three people in her life, even if they did not know it was with her. She also felt immense pride that she didn't let on her true identity and kept to Kyzus's orders. She felt as if she had been tested and that she had passed. Nothing was going to stop her accomplishing her tasks set by her father.

Chapter 2

Useful Encounters

Early the next day, while wandering through the bustling marketplaces of Embirith, looking for new capes and hoods to buy as well as other supplies for her journey, Mia-Myzus spotted some shady figures begin to tail her. Curious at the development she kited them all into a dark, secluded alley before then instantly killing one of them with a slick slash of her blade across their throat, and taking another hostage before any of others could register what was going on. One of her arms was holding a knife to the hostage's throat, and the other was pointing her blade towards the remaining hooded figures as a pool of blood from their dead companion seeped towards them and around their boots.

"Whoa Whoa Whoa!" the man taken hostage exclaimed. "What the? How? How did this just happen?" he said as he reached for his own sword. Mia-Myzus noticed this however and so promptly magically levitated the sword out of its scabbard and chopped the man's reaching hand off effortlessly. "Ahgh!" he yelled in pain, "Who are you witch?"

Mia-Myzus forcefully flung the levitating sword away, imbedding it deep within the alleys wall right by the remaining hooded figures. She then thrust the man into his remaining followers and moved to block the alleys only entrance and exit.

"But more importantly, who are you?" she replied, taking down her hood and showing her long flowing hair, the scar across her face and her sinister smirk. The man clutching a rag onto the stump on his forearm where his hand was cut off from growled in anger and pain as blood seeped through the material and dripped to the ground;

"We are representatives of the Kuk Crime Clan and you have just made yourself an extremely powerful enemy Elf! Give up now and the syndicate may have mercy on you; or at the very least make your death quick."

"The Kuk's you say?" Mia-Myzus said in a curious tone. "How very interesting... well anyway I better get going." As soon as she said this, Mia-Myzus summoned a thick cloud of grey smoke around herself and then shot out of the alley way, throwing her knife back and impelling and killing another of the shady figures as she leaped away to the rooftops, leaving the remaining Kuk's in total shock and disarray.

Mia-Myzus then returned to the vast teeming marketplace, blending into the crowds seamlessly. After purchasing all she required as well as an exquisite new knife from a Valkyrie vender, Mia-Myzus then began to look for some way to quickly get to the far eastern stretches of Terratopia. She wandered the city for quite some time before eventually coming across some Gnomes napping in a shaded, quiet area of downtown. Mia-Myzus approached in a cordial manner and asked if they knew of any way to get to the Fungi Forest kingdom. The Gnomes were very friendly and indeed helpful to her and they directed Mia-Myzus to another area of the city that ran caravans to the giant mushroom kingdom in the far east. These caravans were led by Centaurs from the Orthelian Woods and the operation was under the leadership of an old Wolfhound called Rox. Mia-Myzus thanked the Gnomes for their help and soon found a rundown walled up compound filled with Gnomes, Centaurs, and wagons with tall round fabric roofs. Figuring that this complex must have been the place, Mia-Myzus entered through the rusty main gate only to be stopped by an imposing Centaur clad in armour and wielding a sword as tall as herself. Mia-Myzus was stunned by the surprisingly foreboding stature of the Centaur as well as his impressive armour. She went on to explain that she wished to travel to the Fungi Forest kingdom as she had business in the kingdom of Sabare, but the Centaur seemingly didn't accept her explanation and gestured strongly for her to leave repeatedly, despite her insistence. This was until they both heard a booming bark.

They both turned to find a largely grey Wolfhound with strains of white hair leave its overly sized dog bed surrounded by clumsy Gnomes holding large fans or bowls filled with food. The Wolfhound introduced himself as Rox in an old but commanding rich voice and approached Mia-Myzus. The overly large, scruffy, grey, wirerey haired dog had a prestigious presence, being large enough that his head was the same height as Mia-Myzus's own, even though he was on all four legs. Mia-Myzus smiled and tried to seem as friendly as possible as she explained again that she wished to travel to the Fungi Forest as she had business in Sabare. Rox was far more accommodating to Mia-Myzus, allowing her passage on the next caravan convoy to the Gnomes kingdom if she paid; which she happily did, paying handsomely with a brown leather bag of gold she had previously swiped from the markets. Mia-Myzus knew exactly the kind of language Rox spoke, no nonsense, no hassle and, all that mattered was gold. Rox was satisfied with the exchange and mentioned that if Mia-Myzus ever wanted to use his services again, she was more than welcome to. The old Wolfhound went onto claim that he had the best connections and access from Embirith to the east over the Dividing Mountains in all of Central Terratopia, better than even the Viceroy of Thruck. Mia-Myzus was certainly very glad to have met Rox and learn of his operation, giving her name of Delilah to him and adding how she would keep his words in mind. She knew that, even from her short interaction with the esteemed Wolfhound, that she liked his character. Rox was clearly old but somehow commanded respect, authority, and insight, something Mia-Myzus admired greatly.

 A couple of hours later a convoy heading for the Fungi Forest left the compound. Several rickety wooden wagons pulled by Centaurs, filled with Gnomes and cargo, and escorted by more Centaurs left Embirith on the large main road crossing Nindir to the Dwarven Realm of Kossorlim. The caravan headed towards the Dwarven realm as it was the quickest and safest route through the Dividing Mountains. The Dwarven kingdom was entirely within and under five linear mountain peaks that spanned across the monstrous, unforgiving range, effectively positioning the kingdom as the choke point between the central kingdoms and eastern kingdoms of Terratopia. The Dwarves of Kossorlim had always been more than happy to allow travel through their realm but, ever since the coming of autumn, they made sure their position did not go unexploited; demanding substantial regulations, taxes, and tolls before passage was granted to anyone.

The caravan travelled throughout the night and by first light the next day it had arrived at the entrance of Kossorlim. The Dwarven realms entrance was no mere doorway, it was in fact an entire fortress, built half into the mountain ranges side. Salient, stately, and striking, the solid stone lofty towers and walls stood tall and proud in front of the giant mountains that towered further above; a pleasing yet, oxymoronic sight considering the stunted heights of the guards that occupied the fortress. The gates of this stone fortress were stone also, having exquisite Dwarven runes and imagery engraved into them. But the massive stone doors were closed tightly shut.

The rickety convey was stopped in front of the fortresses gates and inspected by a team of Dwarf guards. Mia-Myzus noticed the familiar manner the inspection was carried out in, a manner that suggested it had been done many times before. Some of the Gnomes and Dwarves even called each other by first name and commented on their new beard braids, further indicating the familiar relationship they all had to Mia-Myzus's observation. Mia-Myzus's presence did heighten tensions slightly however, being an irregularity to the norm, but a signed note from Rox vouching for her and her own addition of a few gold and silver coins quickly smoothed things over with the Dwarf guards.

The giant stone gates were commanded open, a remarkable sight to behold as the huge thick stone slab doors, as tall as a family's house, slid open smoothly, with a pleasing grinding sound, like rubbing two pebbles together. The caravan then continued on its journey towards the Fungi Forest. Passage through the enormous, lengthy, underground Dwarven realm was remarkably quick as there was an expertly crafted, completely straight, long, and wide cobble bridge that went straight from the west to east of the subterranean kingdom. The smooth road was constructed with great skill from stone and metal and was seemingly its own separate platform from the entire kingdom, as very few buildings were dotted on either side on it. Instead, a great many other ramps and stairways connected from above and below to the road bridge. These additional passages onto the straight road connected it to the wider underground stone kingdom that surrounded all around it and was crafted and craved from and into the mountains themselves. This stone road that ran perfectly straight, horizontal, and true that the caravan travelled along was like a highway straight through the hollowed-out mountain range that the magnificent Dwarven realm completely eclipsed all around in every direction, with several entrances and exits on and off it into the breath-taking Dwarf kingdom.

The journey through Kossorlim took less than a day and it was still light outside as the caravans emerged through the eastern gate, which itself was a perfect mirror image of the western one. The convoy was now in the lands of Lurtha and made for a ford crossing over the Lurtha River that led to the Orthelian Forest where the caravan would stop for rest. Once again, they all travelled throughout the day and night and by noon the next day the caravan had arrived at the borders of the forest, being greeted by even more Centaurs. Some wagons were then unloaded and new cargo loaded up once more. The Centaurs that had so far been pulling and escorting the caravan switched with new ones, ones clad in heavier armour and weaponry and that seemed like great warriors to Mia-Myzus's eye. The convoy then split into two, the wagons carrying new cargo headed back towards Kossorlim and the remaining ones continued onto the Fungi Forest, heading towards the roaming hilltops just visible on the eastern horizon.

These hills were the Carlin Highlands and they were the only thing standing in the way between the caravan and its destination, they were also the border to the kingdom of Carlin. The caravan gradually journeyed its way towards them until early evening and no sooner than the caravan had surpassed the first hill of the highlands that it was ambushed by marauders in the narrow valley it travelled down. The Gnomes all quickly hid in the wagons, pulling up large wooden shields around them, effectively turning the wagons all into wooden bunkers. The Centaurs all sprang into action as well, charging into the ambushers and slaying as many as they could. The sight was fascinating to Mia-Myzus as the might of Centaurs was put on full show to her in ways she had never seen. The Centaurs rode with such excellence and power, wielding giant swords with skills comparable to some Elven soldiers with their much smaller blades that Mia-Myzus previously had known and whom had trained with for centuries. Some Gnomes also periodically opened up gaps in their wooden wagon bunkers to shoot small magical projectiles at their attackers with surprising success. The daughter of Kyzus stood firm and in awe, dodging any arrows fired at her and sniping them back at the archers that had fired them in vengeance for disrupting her view of the battle. Not long after the skirmish had begun, it was all over as the surviving marauders scattered in an attempt to preserve their numbers and lives. Once safe again the Gnomes took down their large wooden shields, the Centaurs took up the wagons once more and they all continued on their way towards the Fungi Forest as if nothing had happened.

A few hours later, as nightfall approached, the caravan stopped once more, being halted by the leading Centaur after a sparrow landed on his shoulder. To Mia-Myzus's pleasant surprise, the small bird spoke the common tongue, a rarity among Pheseus's wild animals. The sparrow warned of an ambush lying in waiting ahead of them and detailed that this ambush wasn't one from common ruffians attempting to plunder the convoy like earlier. What lay ahead of the convoy were renegade Samsons and Goliaths, wanderers banished from their own kingdom of Sabare. Mia-Myzus overheard this and was secretly overjoyed, she knew that these must be the insurgents her father had spoken off, finding them was going to be much easier than she had originally worried as they had brought themselves right to her, or rather she had brought herself right to them. However, upon learning of this news, the head Centaur did not want to procced, he knew his followers and the Gnomes he was meant to protect were no match for Samson's and Goliath's. He knew they'd all be killed or at the very least, have all the wagons goods stolen for sure, as had happened from previous ambush's countless times before. Mia-Myzus could not have this however and so convinced the caravan to procced, she reasoned that, thanks to the sparrow, they now had the element of surprise and could outflank the ambushers, catching them unawares. She detailed that the escort should leave the convoy and circle behind the Samsons and Goliaths lying-in wait ahead. As the Samsons and Goliaths attack the convoy, the Centaurs could then attack them from behind, completely ruining the ambush and the insurgents' chance of success. The head Centaur agreed to this, eager to claim a victory over the greatest warrior beings in Terra Tearia that had for so long ravaged his caravans and killed many of his people. And so, the caravan proceeded with Mia-Myzus's plan.

As the caravan crossed into the next valley and continued into a more wooded area, the Samsons and Goliaths revealed themselves. Firing arrows into the convoy, hurling large rocks at it and a number of them all charging forward into it as well. As they did so however, the encircling Centaurs then revealed themselves and charged into the Samson and Goliath ranks from behind, to the ambushers own shock. As the battle began to ensue, Mia-Myzus then revealed herself and flexed the true magical prowess she held. She lifted all the wagons into the air and then froze all the Centaurs and Gnomes in place against their will, lifting many of them into the air as well. Stunned, the Samsons and Goliaths ambushers all stood in confused amazement. Once the entire caravan was lifted high above her head and all the Centaurs all levitated together as a group, Mia-Myzus's face turned sinister and she flung all cargo out of the wagons, squashing the frozen Gnomes underneath them, the impacts making horrific squelching sounds and exploding the Gnomes bodies across the woodland floor. She then disassembled the wooden carriages into pieces and then further split some of the floating wood into long, sharp deadly splinters. Without hesitation she turned the splinters into devastating projectiles, firring them into the frozen, hovering Centaur huddle covering them all from head to hoof in wooden fragments, impaling them all deeply and fatally, as if they were rained on by wooden swords. After this, Mia-Myzus relaxed her power and all came crashing down spectacularly around her, the wreckage snapping the ambushers out of their amazed trance.

The Samsons and Goliaths all promptly rushed towards and around her; their weapons pointed straight at her face.

"Who are you?" a Samson demanded.

"My name is Delilah and I have come in search of you all. I have an interesting proposition for your leader" Mia-Myzus replied confidently.

This led many to laugh and one Goliath even let loose an arrow towards Mia-Myzus, but she moved her body out of the way at an unnatural speed and then grabbed the arrow right out of the air in front of her with ease. She started sharply at the Goliath archer and scowled before then flinging the arrow straight back at him and magically impaling it deep into his chest faster then as if it was shot with a bow. She then magically picked up some debris from a wagon and flung it towards him, crashing the wagons remains into him and sending the Goliath hurtling backwards into a tree. Laying on the ground, contorted in pain with broken bones, Mia-Myzus then rose the same wagon parts up above the wounded Goliath and then crashed them down with immense force, killing him instantly. Silence followed, only to then be interrupted by the tree the now dead Goliath had smashed into then falling down onto the piled-up wagon parts the Goliaths body lay underneath, further squashing it. Mia-Myzus then spoke;

"I will repeat myself; I have come to speak to your leader, I have a proposition I'm sure you all would like to hear."

Impressed at the show of force and might by the high Elf Delilah, the Samsons and Goliaths all gradually lowered their weapons and agreed to take her to their camp. The ambushers gathered their blood-stained spoils from the convoy and as they all left, Mia-Myzus noticed a Gnome that had survived the encounter, hiding behind a bush. As the Gnome saw he was spotted, he began running away for safety. Mia-Myzus then quickly magically caught and gripped the Gnome bringing him towards her. The Samsons and Goliaths watched on in awe as Mia-Myzus proceeded to apologise to the old wriggling white bearded Gnome before impaling him on her blade.

"Can't be having any witnesses to my actions," she said facing the approving onlooking Samsons and Goliaths.

"Why did you apologise so sincerely though?" asked a Samson.

Mia-Myzus explained, "Because they are sweet, peaceful beings just trying to make their way in the world, over my travels with them I have grown fond of them and their simplistic lives and desires."

"Interesting," replied the Samson in a semi sarcastic tone. "Over my many raids of them I have grown fond of their cargo they haul. Their food is delightful and their Mushrooms and Herbs are extremely pleasurable and satisfying to the mind."

"Indeed," Mia-Myzus chuckled, trying to seem as agreeable as possible. The group then wandered off into the night, carrying the cargo from the caravan, towards their camp, leading Mia-Myzus along with them.

Chapter 3

The Beginnings of a Crime Empire

Soon the insurgent Samsons and Goliaths, along with Mia-Myzus, all arrived at their camp deep in the woodland. It was a semi-permanent settlement with spiked stakes in the ground in front of log walls that surrounded the whole camp. Some crudely built wooden buildings were present but the camp was largely entirely filled with tents and other fabric shelters, some utilising trees as support, but all of them half-heartedly put together. The camp was entirely lit a warm but flickering orange by torch light and fire pits that were themselves dotted around inconsistently. The inhabitants were all battle harden Samsons and Goliaths that had clearly been living off the wilderness for a long time. Their beards and hair were ragged and messy and they all wore minimum clothing, but what they did wear only enhanced the mighty appearance they all possessed. They were all over seven-foot-tall beings with incredibly large, vibrant muscles all over their bodies that were as well defined as other features like their noses and eyes. Their own rugged appearance contrasted greatly with their weapons which were kept in exceptional condition, looking as if they had all just been newly forged and polished earlier that same day. Some wore parts of armour that were again in similar condition to their weapons; but the armour wore by all was inconsistent in type and placement. Some wore leather, some steel, some wore helmets and others shoulder pauldrons or chest plates. The ambush party all marched to the very centre of the camp where the largest fire pit was, which was itself surrounded by tree stumps and logs doubling as seats and benches. It was here where the largest tent was.

 As the ambush party arrived at the large central fire pit, two beings walked confidently out of the tents entrance. An imposing black haired and bearded Goliath, standing taller and broader than all others, and a stately blond haired and bearded Samson, equally prestigious in appearance. Bathed in the orange hue of the firepit, they presented themselves to the recently returned band of warriors. Both wore a red half-cape over their left shoulders that finished at their knees height and gently blew in the wind, lending to their already very stately presence.

"Welcome back brothers! I trust your efforts where a success?" boomed the blond Samson in a rich deep voice.

"And who is this fine specimen you have brought back with you?" The Goliath added. "A delicate gorgeous Elf? What a find brothers!"

Before any of the Samsons or Goliaths could say anything, Mia-Myzus stepped forward assuredly and spoke, holding her blade in one hand, making sure it was in full view for all to see;

"I am Delilah. A high Elf of Filnethias" she said as she lit a magical blue flame in her other hand. "I have come to speak to your leader about a proposition to you."

The crowd all gasped in harmony in a very masculine manner and then roared with mocking laughter. The blond Samson and accompanying Goliath looked at each other and also began to laugh.

"What could a puny, regal, high Elf witch possibly offer us?" The Goliath laughed

"It was a mistake coming here," the Samson said "There are not many females among our group and you are mighty fine my dear Delilah" he finished, looking her up and down.

Mia-Myzus flirtatiously giggled and said "Oh I have no doubt, why else do you think I have come here but to finally meet the most fearsome warriors in all of Terratopia." But as she finished saying this her expression instantly turned from amorous to malevolent and she unleashed the small blue flame controllably at the Goliath and launched her knife at the Samson. The black beard was singed off the Goliath and the long blond flocks of the Samson were hair cut short. The blue flame and knife then returned to Mia-Myzus's grasp as the two victims of its strike realised what had just happen. The Goliath reached for his axe and the surrounding crowd also advanced hastily on Mia-Myzus. The blond Samson however didn't take any hostile actions, he instead bent down to pick up some of his chopped hair and smiled to himself in admiration towards Delilah. He rose his hand and commanded all to stop.

"Forgive me Delilah, I may have underestimated your might. We don't often see a beautiful flower with thorns deadly enough to impress us. My name is Daiv and this is my brother-in-law, Vaid," he said gesturing to the Goliath holding an axe menacingly besides him, "We are both the leaders of this clan."

"Pleasure to meet you both," Mia-Myzus said in a kind soft tone before switching to a more commanding one. "May I join you both to discuss the proposal I have brought to you?"

Vaid smirked before asking "What have you come to offer us?"

Mia-Myzus stepped towards him and gently held his arm when she was close enough, she then whispered; "I have come to offer myself." She said this loud enough for Daiv to also hear while looking towards him as well before then grabbing his arm and pulling him close to her hips. Sandwiched in-between the two strapping beings Mia-Myzus then turned to face the large crowd that had gathered around the fire pit; the whole camp had now in fact been drawn to the mysterious high Elf new comer. When facing them all she announced; "And I have come to offer you all the chance to rule the kingdom from which you were all wrongly banished! I will make Sabare rightfully yours!"

The camps inhabitants all roared and cheered. Daiv and Vaid both looked at each other, delightfully smiling. They both looked at Mia-Myzus slightly below and in-between them. As if telepathically agreeing, they nodded at each other before then picking Mia-Myzus up by the waist, turning and waltzing into their tent.

The three spent all night awake and in the tent together. It was late the next morning when they all finally emerged, smiling with messy hair. Mia-Myzus stood behind Daiv and Vaid with nothing but a large fur cloth around her. Vaid then announced;

"My brothers, we have ourselves a new ally! Delilah will assist us in our efforts to claim Sabare as our own. She agrees with our views that we are the warrior race of this world and our kingdom should reflect that! It is to be the military bane of Terratopia!"

The camp all cheered once more before Daiv then spoke;

"We have not the numbers nor resources to start nor win a revolution in our kingdom, but Delilah has enlightened us to upcoming events within Terratopia as well as her own plan to give us the power necessary to claim Sabare for our own!" The camp all roared once more before Daiv then spoke again, "The three of us will make for the city of Hinneb, to begin Delilah's plot, I need volunteers to come with us!"

Vaid then also added, "We also need a number of you to infiltrate back into Sabare once more. Start gathering support for our cause and sow the seeds of revolution in the minds of all that will listen! Appeal to the warrior pride deep inside all in both of our races!"

Once again, the camp all roared in praise and enthusiasm; the whole camp was now present at the central fire pit. Large numbers then eagerly volunteered for both tasks set by their leaders and before long the camps population was split into three. Some staying behind to guard over their base and to continue to pillage and gather supplies in the Carlin Highlands. Some headed for the Sabare Strait and back to their home island. The rest followed Vaid, Daiv and Mia-Myzus as they left for the kingdom of Lurtha and its capital, Hinneb.

Travelling on make shift rafts by the rapid fast flowing River Carlin and then by foot, the band arrived at Hinneb by nightfall and stealthily entered the city. Lit by touch light, the narrow, dingy city streets of Men were dusty, dark, and desolate. Mia-Myzus led her Samson and Goliath followers to a run down and secluded building. It was surrounded by the silhouettes of hooded figures residing all around on surrounding rooftops or within alleyways. There were shady guards at the entranceway of the building as well, all of whom grew restless as the hostile looking group led by Daiv and Vaid approached.

"Back off you lot," a guard exclaimed. "You are encroaching on 'The Sons of the East' territory and we do not take kindly to trespassers."

Mia-Myzus gestured her hand at Vaid who then promptly grabbed the guard by his neck and lifted him high off the ground. More hooded guards then ran towards the band of

Samson's and Goliath's who also readied themselves for a fight but then Mia-Myzus flicked her hand and froze all the guards heading towards them in place. One by one, still fully conscious but their bodies frozen in place, the guards all dropped dead as Goliaths walked up to them and stabbed them all in the hearts or stomachs with their fearsome large sharp weapons. Fear swept over the guards' eyes that Vaid held by the neck as Daiv approached him and muttered;

"Now my dear fellow, we know exactly where we are. We are right where we want to be. Now call off your goons that stalk us in the rooftops and let us through."

Vaid then dropped the guard and he collapsed to the floor gasping for air.

"Lower your weapons, let them through!" he grunted into the surrounding darkness before scrabbling to his feet and opening the door he was guarding, gesturing for the intruders to all to head inside.

The party did so, led by Mia-Myzus and surrounded by Samsons holding large polished metal shields on all sides. Walking swiftly through the dark, dimly lit building, they made their way through cramped corridors into the main central room where a large, long rectangular table sat in its centre. At the table sat seven figures, all draped in large robes with overexaggerated shoulders garments and tall collars that reached above their own heads. They all rose to their feet in astoundment as they all saw the intruding hostile band, and countless guards rushed into the chamber as the invading party arrived.

"What is the meaning of this?" A man who stood at the head of the table shouted.

Without replying Daiv threw his twin bladed sword into the air, it being perfectly parallel to the flat tables edge below it. Mia-Myzus then thrust the weapon forward along the table with a powerful magical force. The weapon travelled effortlessly the full length of the table, its two sword tips floating over either table side, and then stopped just before hitting the man at its head. Six distinct thuds could then be heard as the heads of the six men standing at the table's sides hit the floor, being sliced off by the blades of the floating twin bladed sword. Six more thuds followed as the now headless bodies also collapsed to the floor, blood began to seep everywhere, covering the floor in a shiny dark red.

"My name is Delilah and you are now under my control," Mia-Myzus said confidently.

Chapter 4

The Declaration of War

After Mia-Myzus, Daiv and Vaid's efforts in Hinneb, the Sons of the East crime syndicate was completely under their control. Mia-Myzus made sure however, that she was the undisputed leader of it, promising her support with the backing of the crime syndicate to the Samson and Goliath rebel leaders which they agreed to under her cunning and charm. Under the leadership of their new crime boss Delilah, the Sons of the East stepped up their activity dramatically and ruthlessly took out any minor rivals. Every village, town, and city east of the Dividing Mountains had Mafia's set up in them and they all answered to Delilah as their Kingpin.

Over the course of the next several weeks turning to months, crime became the new law of the land in the east as authorities quickly lost control to it, became corrupted by it, and then a part of it, or simply pleaded ignorant to it. Using her seeing stone, as well as her sway over Daiv and Vaid and their warrior followers, Mia-Myzus also hunted down and gained the obedience of nearly all the bandits, marauders, and ruffian groups out in the wilderness, as well as even the pirates within the Great Eastern Bay. Some joined Mia-Myzus's side willingly, others through fear, and those that refused to pledge to her were all killed mercilessly, sending a clear message.

The beginning of Mia-Myzus's crime empire had begun. In one fell and swift swoop, she effectively had full control over Eastern Terratopia's underworld, with all mafia's being a part of her syndicate as well all raiders out in the wilderness answering to her as well. The vast amount of power and resources now at her disposal in so short of a time was astounding.

Spreading westward, over the Dividing Mountains was Mia-Myzus's next challenge. Attempting to control the Dwarves of Kossorlim would be a futile effort for now as they were a proud but extremely stubborn people and finding alternative ways over the mountains would be an extremely lengthy, inefficient, and costly affair as the few known mountain passes were extremely perilous and continually covered by avalanches and rock slides all too often. Luckily however, an opportunity presented itself in the form of Rox and his caravans' operation. The increased criminal activity in the east presented very lucrative black-market opportunities. Opportunities both Rox and Mia-Myzus would greatly benefit from and so sure enough, being the type of Wolfhound Rox was, he requested a presence with the mysterious new kingpin of the Sons of the East crime syndicate, completely unaware of whom it really was.

Mia-Myzus, along with Daiv and two other Goliaths, journeyed on a caravan sent for them by Rox to Embirith to meet with the Wolfhound. Vaid did not join them as Mia-Myzus had manipulated and convinced him to journey to Sabare with ample supplies gifted to him from her syndicate. There in Sabare, Vaid would stay and continue to rally support for his insurgents and fuel the fires of revolution in the kingdom as its time was soon coming.

Mia-Myzus not only did this to make a victorious revolution in Sabare all but inevitable but she wanted time alone with Daiv to seduce him further, to gain his undisputed loyalty to her and her alone, therefore gaining the loyalty of his clan; as although equal leaders in principle, Vaid was seen more as a fearsome warrior and commander in battle, not like Daiv whom was seen more as a natural leader by the rebels. Mia-Myzus knew this and had been skilfully swaying Daiv under her mastery without him realising through her charm and tributes. She continued this seduction all journey but as they left the western gates of Kossorlim she dropped the facade and asked Daiv a very important question;

"Daiv... what would you do for me? With all that I have done for you, for your cause, for your affection, what would you do for me?"

"Delilah," Daiv said semi-shocked, thinking deeply before fully answering. "There isn't anything I wouldn't do for you."

Mia-Myzus smiled longingly at him. "Really? Anything?"

Daiv replied "Yes Delilah. Anything. You clearly want the same thing I do. You share the same enlightenment as I. You see my races of Samsons and Goliaths are meant for more than what we are right now, everything you have done only proves that. You have done much for my cause and for that I could never be more grateful. I really would do anything for you as anything you want could only be what I want also!" Daiv paused, stating deeply into Mia-Myzus's mysterious eyes, and getting lost within them. He then began to speak his mind even further. "Delilah, I consider myself most lucky that you came in search of my clan. A beautiful high Elf like yourself would never have come into my presence so far in the east otherwise. And you are not only beautiful. You are formidable. A fighter like none I have ever seen and a sorcerer more powerful than any I could imagine. Delilah, I have grown increasingly fond of you ever since we spent our first night together, despite Vaid also never being far from us. I have begun to long to have you by my side. Although I have always felt complete with my brother-in-law, I have begun to desire you more Delilah. When Vaid and I are the Chieftains of Sabare, I can think of nothing more that would complete my life than to have you as my spouse. I love you Delilah" Daiv said in a soft tone and holding Mia-Myzus's hands gently.

    Mia-Myzus, for the first time in her life was truly speechless. She was expecting Daiv to confess his love for her, she had after all been seducing and manipulating it to be so for some time. However, she was not expecting him to propose, which she knew in Samson and Goliath culture was an intensely prestigious act. Marriage in their culture was a rarity; males and females preferring the company of each other and the love it entails, but rarely devoting their whole lives to souly and only to one another, instead experiencing love and companionship very loosely with whomever they all liked whenever they all liked. Further adding to Mia-Myzus's speechlessness was that deep inside, she too had completely fallen in love with Daiv. She had been continually repressing these feelings knowing that they could be detrimental to Kyzus's plan and her oath, but also in the assumption that Daiv would never want to marry her anyway, instead choosing to share her with Vaid or casting her away once she was no longer helpful to his cause, as is most often the case in Sabare culture. Mia-Myzus felt her heart racing with romantic love for the first time in her life and immediately flung herself around Daiv and kissed him.

"I would love nothing more my love!" she exclaimed "But this is very sudden, can we please talk more of this after our meeting with Rox?" she asked, doing so to buy herself some time to figure out how to best deal with this latest development in regards to Kyzus's plan.

"Of course my love," Daiv replied affectionately.

The couple spent the rest of the journey in each other embrace, both smiling uncontrollably. But in Mia-Myzus's mind, her thoughts flew around her head faster than she could register them. This wasn't a part of Kyzus's plan, but she also really loved Daiv and did not want to refuse this new found intense feeling that burned inside of her. As best she could, Mia-Myzus attempted to devise how she could still keep to her father's plan while also keeping Daiv as her love.

Upon arriving in Embirith, Mia-Myzus noticed how chaotic the city was compared to the last time she was there. The atmosphere in the streets was far more hostile and there even seemed to be mass gatherings all around with people screaming out ravaging speeches and sometimes hateful speeches about kingdoms independence or anarchist betrayers. Mia-Myzus was almost shocked by how different Embirith was from her last visit, it was as if it had completely flipped to the opposite of what it used to be and supposedly stood for. Soon later the caravan arrived at Rox's walled compound and met with the Wolfhound who was most surprised, yet somehow expected to see 'Delilah' once more. Confused slightly at first, but still fond from their last encounter, Rox listened to all Mia-Myzus had to say and she didn't have to say much to win him over. It was clear to him that cooperating with her would be very good for business and extremely profitable. And so, a relationship was quickly decided and agreed upon. Rox would transport or smuggle any and all things Delilah requested both sides of the Dividing Mountains, gaining shares in all its profits as well as the protection of her up and coming crime empire as well as the Samson and Goliath rebels. For Mia-Myzus, her crime empire would now be empowered and interconnected further with Rox's transport of goods and easy connections both sides of the Dividing Mountains. She could use this as a kickstart to her empires expansion to swell westwards as she now effectively had unimpeded access through Dividing Mountains to move whatever or whomever she wished.

Later that same day, Mia-Myzus had a new order from her father, receiving it through her seeing stone. During the night Mia-Myzus slipped out of Rox's compound where she, along with Daiv and the Goliaths, were residing for the next few days to finalise her new partnership with Rox. Slyly, through the dark of night, Mia-Myzus covertly wandered the streets of Embirith, which were still filled with rabbles of people endlessly ranting to one another. She made her way towards the parliament residences. These buildings were where all the members, representatives, advisors, and Lord Delegates of the Terratopia Union parliament lived their personal lives when not working in the parliament and not back in their home kingdoms. Mia-Myzus skilfully infiltrated these residences with great stealth and with the assistance of her impressive magical prowess. Not a single guard was even remotely aware as to her presence. She was here with only one specific goal in mind and soon Mia-Myzus found exactly what she was looking for as she located the quarters of Lord Delegate Petar. Finding the Lord Delegate from Roccano all alone in his quarters, Mia-Myzus then proceeded to slickly and silently enter his residence from an opened glass window in his roof.

Lord Delegate Petar was sitting comfortably in an arm chair that was in the centre of his living room. He held a book in one hand and smoked a pipe in the other as he quietly read the book that he held, which was one of Thyzus's most popular texts. Mia-Myzus, who had infiltrated into Petar's quarters undetected crept up behind him and then assuredly rested her drawn knife onto the left lower part of his neck where it connected with to his body, near his collarbone.

"Not. A. Word." Mia-Myzus said in a strong yet quiet tone.

Lowering his book and pipe slowly, but remaining seated in his arm chair Petar sighed.

"What kind of pathetic Liberalist intimidation tactic is this?" Petar said assuredly.

Mia-Myzus, still keeping her knife's tip pressed firmly against Petar's lower neck, slowly walked around him to face him, keeping her face incredibly close to Petar's own and then grabbing the top of his head firmly with her other hand.

"And who might you be?" Petar asked in a sarcastic tone. "Tyzus sent some regal high Elf to do his dirty work?"

Mia-Myzus chuckled to herself and clicked her fingers to lift the disguising enchantment she had placed over herself. Immediately Petar's eyes widened as he was able to see his threatener's true identity.

"Mia-Myzus?" he exclaimed. "But you're dead? How is it that you are here?"

Smiling sinisterly to herself, Mia-Myzus replied; "Oh Petar the answer to that is so far beyond your limited understanding you have no idea."

Mia-Myzus's tone didn't sit well with Petar as she seemingly talked down to him as if he was a child.

"There are things in motion that you have absolutely no control over but yet will define the future of Terratopia." Mia-Myzus then continued in the same tone.

"Have you gone completely insane?" Petar asked. "What in Zatos Zendar's name are you talking about?"

"You'll see," Mia-Myzus slyly replied with a malevolent look on her face. "Oh, oh wait... no you won't."

As she said this, Mia-Myzus's expression turned dire and she plunged the knife she held deep into Petar's lower neck until the knife's hilt hit his collarbone. Petar could only gasp in terror and shock as blood attempted to spray out from beneath the knife's hilt and he starred at Mia-Myzus in shock, horror and confusion. Mia-Myzus glared back and maniacally laughed as she sliced her knife from the left side of Petar's lower neck to the right, the hilt scrapping across his collarbone. Blood gushed out of the terrifying gapping chasm that nearly totally separated Petar's head and neck from his chest. Mia-Myzus watched as the life quickly left Petar's eyes and then proceeded to let go of his head which then slumped back over the head rest of his now blood soaked arm chair which tore the already huge cut in-between Petar's neck and body to be even wider, so wide that his spine could be seen, covered in dark red blood. The job was done, Kyzus's latest orders fulfilled. Mia-Myzus briefly smiled to herself, relishing in what she had done and how she did it. She didn't have to taunt Petar like that, and she certainly didn't need to make his death so gruesome. But as she smiled to herself, she realised she was pleased she did, she wanted too. It came so naturally to her. Near instantly after this realisation, she shook herself and her sinister smile turned to an insecure frown, frightened at the realisation she had come too. Was this really who she was? This thought didn't have long to linger however as she heard footsteps outside and so she quickly bolted away disappearing into the night like a phantom.

    The next day Rox held a feast. It was during the evening of this celebratory feast Rox had organised for their new partnership, that Mia-Myzus was summoned by Kyzus through the seeing stone. As quick as she could she thanked Rox for everything, saying that she'd be back soon, and convinced Daiv and the two Goliaths to follow her as she now had different business to attend. The four stole a horse drawn carriage from nearby streets, which in the current chaos no one seemed to notice before then making their way towards the Thruckland Range. When leaving the city, they noticed how the hostile atmosphere was boiling over into conflict as the beginnings of riots began to spread, buildings were ruined and a great many more peoples from all races left the city heading in all directions. Mia-Myzus knew exactly what had happened and explained it to Daiv. War had now officially just been declared, just as she foretold. She couldn't help but smile to herself, happy that her father's plan was coming together and proud of her brothers for orchestrating the war declaration, they really had done an incredible job of turning Terratopia's people against each other, she could see it clear as day.

    The four travelled for three days and three nights before finally arriving at the Thruckland Range, over which time Mia-Myzus had come up with a solution to the problem she faced in regards to her new found love. Kyzus's plan never outlined for there to be two leaders of Sabare anyway, if she could find a way to eliminate Vaid while maintaining Daiv in power as the Chieftain, she could still be his spouse while keeping to Kyzus's plan of using the rebel leader as a puppet figurehead, after all, what better way to be in control of her puppet than to marry it, so Mia-Myzus reasoned to herself. This further bred another sinister idea in Mia-Myzus's mind. A true test of Daiv's loyalty to her and a way to seal him to her side and no one else's. A plan which she would put into motion on their return back to the far east.

When finally arriving at the Thruckland Range, the group drawered up along the side of the monumental hills separating Nindir for Thruckland. Mia-Myzus left the carriage and ordered Daiv and the Goliaths to stay while she went to attend her business, quickly leaving their sight. A couple of hours later she returned with a new found sense of enthusiasm. When Mia-Myzus boarded the carriage, she announced that they had a new destination and task to complete before being able to return home. They were to head for the grand trading city of Thruck.

Chapter 5

The Rising of an Underworld Empire

Two days later Mia-Myzus and her accompany arrived at the bustling grand city of Thruck. She explained to Daiv and his Goliath followers that Thruckland was a purely economic driven kingdom, it only cared about one thing, wealth. Mia-Myzus detailed that Thruck was ruled over by a Viceroy and that the Viceroy would have been brought up in the art of business and exploiting all possible so as to lead their kingdom, and importantly, themselves to greater and greater richness and wealth. She then explained their next task; how the current Viceroy, Charles VIII, would have no interest in joining either side of the war as it is bad for business, but that his position also put him in an extremely influential position. Just as Kossorlim was effectively the single passage between Central and Eastern Terratopia, Thruck was the gateway between Central and Western Terratopia as well as the trading capital of the entire archipelago. Mia-Myzus explained that Charles VIII would distain this new civil war and undoubtably would wish it to end, likely gearing his neutral independent kingdom for the pursuit of peace. However, this would not be through the kindness of his heart but in the knowledge that war was bad for his economic driven kingdom and so he thusly needed it to end. If, however, Mia-Myzus could convince him that, under her control, he could lead Thruck to further fuel the war efforts to best exploit both sides for profit, Thruck and Charles VIII could become rich beyond the wildest of imaginations and far wealthier than if the war was to end sooner rather than later. Wealth that would of course be in the pockets of Mia-Myzus and Daiv as well, wealth that would finance a Sabare revolution. Mia-Myzus further explained that gaining control of Thruck would also in-turn mean gaining control of nearly all of Terratopia's trade, giving them all the supplies that they would ever need and the ability to dictate who got supplies. Mia-Myzus summarised by stating that they were effectively buying the infrastructural power Thruck held over Terratopia by showing its leader the maniacal ways to increase his riches.

Seeing the logic, Daiv and his Goliaths devised and agreed on a plan with Mia-Myzus. The four would infiltrate Thruck, find Charles VIII, gain his obedience and loyalty to the Delilah Crime Empire and then puppet him to fuel the war, exploit both sides and make them all very rich as well as gain control of his kingdoms position of trading power.

And so, the party did just that. With the aid of the seeing stone, Mia-Myzus located Charles VIII in Port Thruck, discussing matters with a governor and being guarded by a company of guards. He was short, but stood assuredly in fine clothes and a white wig that, in its many rolls, reached down to his fabric shoulder pounders. He wore a blue sash over his brown buttoned jacket and expensive jewellery in his ears, on his fingers, and chained onto his clothes. His guards, dressed in bright blue, red, and gold uniforms, stood all around him and kept the perimeter completely clear of any passers-by.

In the busy streets of the port, carrying out Mia-Myzus's task would be difficult if not impossible. Daiv believed him and his men could easily defeat the guards, but that wasn't the issue for Mia-Myzus. Such an encounter out in the open would be too public and jeopardise the whole basis for Kyzus's plan. If Thruck was openly and widely known to be controlled by a criminal empire, neither side of the civil war would seek the key neutral kingdoms help and in fact avoid it. Mia-Myzus explained this and ordered that they all wait until a less public opportunity arose, one with no witnesses. And arose it did. All day the party shadowed and followed the Viceroy, keeping out of his and his guards' sight as he went about his daily business; travelling all over the port and city of Thruck, meeting with a great many governors, merchants, and traders discussing any and all things commerce. But as evening drew close, Charles VIII made his way to his huge, grand, luxurious, brick mansion home. This was where Mia-Myzus and her company would strike. For a couple of hours, the band awaited outside the mansion's boundaries, scouting it out and plotting their next moves but as the dark of night descended, they all made their move. The four were an unstoppable silent force compared to the few nightguards on watch that were slayed effortlessly and quietly. Mia-Myzus and her accompany soon managed to sneak into the Viceroy's exquisite, polished, wooden bedroom quarters without arising any alarm.

Daiv ordered the two Goliaths to pick the sleeping Viceroy up from his luxurious grand oak four poster bed by either arm. As he awoke and the fear struck him from the burly intruders grabbing his arms, Mia-Myzus immediately casted a spell over Charles VIII making it impossible for him to scream or even speak, he was silenced, his mouth completely sealed shut. Fear and panic passed over the leader of Thruck eyes as he took in his surrounding of three fearsome warriors and a shady, powerful high Elf sorceress. Mia-Myzus then spoke in a confident, no-nonsense tone;

"Hello Charles, I am Delilah and I come bearing great news for you. You see, Terratopia is now going to collapse into a long devastating civil war, as I'm sure you know. I know the ones responsible for this and I assure you, it will last an extremely long time, perhaps longer than your lifetime. So why not take advantage of it instead of oppose it? I know you are a man of business so I will make this easy for you to understand. If you pledge yourself to me and do exactly as I say... Exactly. As. I. Say... I can make you and your kingdom one of the most powerful in all of Terratopia, certainly the wealthiest." Mia-Myzus paused to take in the Viceroys expression, hoping it was a cooperative one before then continuing on; "You see, your kingdoms' positioning and purpose in Terratopia is vital to both sides and if you were to use this position to, instead of end the war, draw it out as much as possible, you could bleed both sides coffers economically dry. Thruck could become wealthy beyond your wildest dreams. How does all that sound to you? All you have to do is pledge yourself to me. May I add that this civil war will only increase the criminal underworlds activities which I know you oppose. Be loyal to me and I will give you protection from this."

Charles VIII glared intently at Mia-Myzus. Servery angry and frustrated at her insolence. He was furious at her for invading his quarters and effectively holding him hostage, threatening him to obey her. Mia-Myzus sensed this anger and so waved her hand at Daiv in mild annoyance, sighing as she did. Daiv then grabbed both of Charles VIII legs and began to pull them towards him. The two Goliaths then began to slowly pull on his arms they both held. Slowly and painfully, Charles VIII had his limbs pulled away from his body. Mia-Myzus lifted the magical spell allowing the Viceroy to scream out in pain, she then said;

"All you have to do Charles, is agree serve me. Serve me and this pain would stop, as well as making you rich and protected, it's honestly a mystery to me why you refuse."

Just as Charles VIII limbs were about to be pulled from their sockets he yelled out and agreed to do anything, screaming for them to stop. Daiv and the Goliaths dropped him to the floor and towered over him as he blubbered in pain and cowered in fear. Mia-Myzus approached, stopping just in front of his head. Bearing over him she demanded;

"Pledge your elegance to me! Vow to be loyal to me and me alone! Do this and I will make you and your kingdom prosper over this war as well as guarantee your safety."

"I vow," Charles VIII whimpered. "You have my undying obedience; my will is at your command my lady Delilah."

Mia-Myzus and Daiv smiled sinisterly at the sight. "Kiss my feet," she then replied.

The terrified and reeling in pain Viceroy looked up at her, almost like a desperate plea as to not make him do it, but Mia-Myzus stared back intently in a serious fashion and moved her foot closer to his face. Charles VIII sighed but then kissed the foot in front of him.

"Excellent" Mia-Myzus said in a coy manner. "Welcome to my service. I now have more information to tell you. So, listen carefully. I am the head of a crime empire..."

"WHAT?" the viceroy cried out before then having his lips sealed shut again by Mia-Myzus who started intently at him in anger before continuing;

"A crime empire that will raise its power to totally dominate Terratopia, dominating its underworld and from behind the spot light. Don't worry you will be safe as you are now a part of it, in fact, I can make it useful and profitable to you. In the city of Embirith you will find an old Wolfhound called Rox. I strongly suggest you meet him. Tell him I sent you. I'm sure you'll find partnership between you both most profitable, both on the legitimate and illegitimate markets. You are now in the service of the Delilah Crime Empire! But you must not let anyone know! Anyone who is not also a part of my empire must not know of your true loyalties or of I. You will rule Thruck as I command but you will do it as yourself. As the Viceroy. Not as my pawn. Do I make myself clear?" Mia-Myzus asked seriously, lifting the spell and allowing him to speak

"Yes, my lady," Charles VIII whimpered again, still stuck on the floor in agonising pain and ashamed of his lost dignity.

"Wonderful" Mia-Myzus joyfully, yet threateningly said in an overbearing manner. "I will be in touch, here take this stone," she said as she dropped the seeing stone Kyzus had given to her in the cave a few days ago. "Do not let it left your side. When I wish to talk to you, or you to me simply hold this stone and it will happen." And as soon as she said this, Mia-Myzus cast another spell over the Viceroy sending him into sleep and not allowing him to wake till late the next morning. During which time Mia-Myzus, Daiv and their Goliath followers would have long left Thruck and made for Sabare, via Rox in Embirith; but not before pillaging and ransacking the mansion to make their intrusion look like nothing more than a robbery to the outside world.

When arriving at Rox's compound many days later Mia-Myzus and her accompany were greeted by more than just Rox. A group of shifty looking Men awaited them and they introduced themselves as representatives of Hoda, the Crime Lord of Rodus. They explained that word travels fast in the underworld of Terratopia and that they knew of Delilah and her rising crime empire. But instead of attempt to fight her however, Hoda wished to join her and become a part of her organisation, saying that he recognised the flow of the river had changed and that fighting it would be futile and costly. Surprised but pleased Mia-Myzus welcomed her latest subornments. She introduced them to Rox and, similar to how he had partnered up with the Sons of the East, Hoda and his network would now work closely with Rox and his services. Mia-Myzus's crime empire was truly starting to take hold of Terratopia and her power would only grow even more.

Mia-Myzus warned Rox that he would now also soon be in business with Thruck, which the Wolfhound was most pleased about, eager to further his new entrepreneurial business that his caravans were transforming into. Mia-Myzus then ordered Hoda's representatives to follow what she had done with the Sons of the East, to set up strong organised crime mobs in every settlement across the lands of Rodus and Thruckland, them all answering to her, and to ruthlessly take out all rivals. She also ordered the hunting down of all bandits, marauders, and pirates and to either get them to pledge their loyalty to her crime empire or be crushed.

Once this was done, Central Terratopia would be all but under her control, the only exceptions being the Elven kingdoms of Nindir and Nindar. Mia-Myzus ordered that Rox and Hoda's combined efforts should do all they can to infiltrate and take over these two Elven kingdoms from within. The Elves were far less susceptible to allow crime to flourish in their lands due to their strong natural quality of fairness, but it wasn't impossible, as Mia-Myzus had shown by overrunning the Elven kingdom of Orthelian with the Sons of the East Syndicate where crime there now flourished. The Elves afterall, like all the races of Terra Tearia, were still only as pure as their souls and their souls, like every soul in existence within the universe, was not perfect and would fall to Mia-Myzus's will under the right strain. With the lofty orders given, Mia-Myzus, Daiv, and the Goliaths then hitched a ride of one of Rox's caravans and made their way back home.

With all this power now acquired by Mia-Myzus, the time was right to finally take over Sabare.

Chapter 6

Interesting Developments

During the journey back to Eastern Terratopia, Mia-Myzus began putting her own plan of sealing Daiv to her side while also ruling Sabare into action. She began by again confessing her own love to Daiv and by how happy she felt to be in the position that she was in. Mia-Myzus skilfully however never made Daiv feel he had her head over heels for him; despite the fact she truly was. Mia-Myzus crafted her words and actions in such a way that Daiv knew he would not be the one calling the shots in their coming union of love but yet somehow, he did not mind and also in fact wished it. As powerful as a leader Daiv was, as mighty as a warrior and foreboding as a protector, he was completely in love with the mysterious and powerful high Elf he knew as Delilah. Daiv was infatuated by Mia-Myzus's own power and might, in total admiration at her own intelligence, cunning, and higher understanding of Terratopia at large and he was totally enthralled by her own unparalleled beauty, even with the scar across her face. There was not anything Daiv would not do to be with Delilah and make her happy.

    Mia-Myzus knew all that Daiv was feeling towards her and was secretly delighted, although she would not truly show it. Instead, she would use Daiv's near blinding love for her to make him the key central pawn in her role in Kyzus's plan. He would lead the rebel Samson and Goliath extremists exactly how she dictated; he would rule the kingdom of Sabare exactly as she commanded; he would transform Sabare to become the headquarters of her crime empire exactly how she directed. In doing all this, he would aid her to become the most powerful leader in all of Terratopia, controlling its influential sinister underworld from the shadows, such was her directive. In order to do all of this however, Mia-Myzus needed Daiv's brother-in-law, Vaid, out of the picture and Daiv's total, upmost, blind loyalty to her and no one else, luckily though, she knew exactly how to do this.

While crossing through Kossorlim, Mia-Myzus was going to spring her plan on Daiv but she learned of a development within Kossorlim that made her put her requests to Daiv on hold. Odin II, the king of the other Dwarf kingdom in Terratopia, Dwaria, was on a royal visit to the king of Kossorlim, Thor III, to discuss what the Dwarven race would do about war that had erupted in Terratopia. This was a monumental opportunity that Mia-Myzus knew she had to capitalise on as within Terratopia there were three significant neutral kingdoms that would be the key to making sure that the civil war had the desired effects Kyzus wished for. These kingdoms were Thruckland and the two Dwarven realms of Kossorlim and Dwaria. Mia-Myzus so far only had the control over Thruckland, and easy access through Kossorlim, but she needed the oversight over the Dwarven kingdoms to truly fuel the war effort to its maximal devastating potential. Kossorlim was the gateway between Central and East Terratopia as well as a kingdom of master masons, forgers, and craftsmen. Dwaria, although smaller and far less wealthy than Kossorlim, was a kingdom with the greatest blacksmiths in all of Terratopia; able to create the finest and sturdiest weapons and armour in time and quality unmatched by any other kingdom from any other race. It was a kingdom based on the mining and creation of harsh study vital metals like iron and steel, unlike Kossorlim which was based on mining far more precious materials like gold, silver, emerald, ruby, and Magiccora. Making sure these kingdoms were under the influence of Kyzus's plan was paramount and having both of their kings in the same place, at the same time, coming up with their agenda regarding the civil war could not have been a more perfect opportunity for Mia-Myzus to seize on.

Gaining authority over the Dwarves was still a near, if not totally, impossible task however. The Dwarves were not like the Men of Thruck in the sense that they could be easily dominated over if persuaded and pressured in the right way. They were too proud, but also too stubborn of a race for that; their unbending resolve would never allow such a scheme to happen and their kingdoms were too powerful and too impenetrable to be dominated over by any other. However, the Dwarves were alike to the Men of Thruck in other ways, their lust for wealth and riches. The Dwarves may never be dominated over into doing anyone's biding, but Mia-Myzus believed that they could be bribed, influenced, and tricked into acting in accord with the desires of others, if the reward to themselves was substantial enough. And so, this was exactly how Mia-Myzus planned to win over the Dwarf kings.

Mia-Myzus halted the caravan in Kossorlim as it rode along the long straight bridge connecting the western and eastern gates and requested to be able to meet with the Dwarf kings. A request that was denied by the caravans Dwarven escort. Mia-Myzus continually requested an audience with the kings but was denied every time. To the Dwarves, Mia-Myzus and her Samson and Goliath company were nothing but passengers on the Wolfhounds Rox's caravans, they had little idea that Rox was in fact under Mia-Myzus's own leadership, nor did they have any idea who she even was. The Dwarf captain named Korg was eventually called to the halted caravan, as he was the one in charge of all travel in, out, and through Kossorlim, but he too adamantly refuted Mia-Myzus's requests to see the kings, being even more blunt and less patient. Korg even turned down large sums of gold and jewels as payment for his cooperation, and threatened to throw the caravan out of the gates they had just travelled through, stranding them on the wrong side of the Dividing Mountains.

To Mia-Myzus it was clear that she was never going to be freely allowed to see the kings by the Dwarves, so she devised that she must convene with them another way. When the caravan set off again, Mia-Myzus cast an invisibility enchantment over herself and slipped off the back of the wagon she rode on as it moved along. Too her annoyance though, her missing presence was almost immediately noticed by Korg, who had now joined the caravans Dwarven escort to make sure it left Kossorlim without any further disruptions. The caravan was halted once more and the Dwarf guards all spang into action, looking for the now missing high Elf. Mia-Myzus knew that what was happening was escalating into a serious incident. The Dwarves were clearly being far more protective over their kings than she had originally anticipated. Her actions of surreptitiously leaving to subvertly meet with the kings would do more harm than good now in Mia-Myzus's eyes, as it could cripple the healthy vital relationship Rox and his caravans had with them. So, as quick as she could, she thought of a way to de-escalate tensions while also explaining her absence in as innocent of a way as possible. She immediately rolled her seeing stone from her sleeve onto the ground of the grand stone road and then lifted the invisibility enchantment off herself as she 'chased' after the stone. Mia-Myzus was instantly spotted by Korg who, along with other guards, chased after her and surrounded her. When Mia-Myzus finally caught the seeing stone she had rolled away she turned and faced her Dwarven pursuers with as innocent as a stance and expression as she could, despite the sea of razor-sharp axes that where mere inches from her torso. She sincerely apologised, explaining that she had dropped her seeing stone and had only gone to chase after it. Korg's suspicious, unforgiving snarl turned to surprise as he laid eyes on the mystical, perfectly spherical crystal, becoming mesmerised by it. He had seen it before.

"Awalatar," he mumbled to himself before then looking straight at Mia-Myzus and asking; "How did you come by this?"

Intrigued at the development, but cautious not to reveal any of her father's business by accident, Mia-Myzus replied;

"My father gave it to me for my quests in the east." Slowly cogs began to turn in Mia-Myzus's head. She had always wondered where all the seeing stones that had filled the hall she saw them all in had come from; although she never thought too much of it as if their origins were important, Kyzus surely would have told her. They had clearly been made here by the infamous Kossorlim craftsmen.

"Your father?" Korg inquired. "Is your father the one named Awalatar?"

Further intrigued, Mia-Myzus pieced together that Awalatar must have been the guise Kyzus went under when commissioning the Dwarves to create the seeing stones for him. But she did not know how to answer Korg's question as she knew far too little to answer without risking undermining her father's unknown previous actions.

"Will you not answer?" Korg then demanded

"I will not," Mia-Myzus replied stubbornly with a no-nonsense look on her face.

"Very well," Korg said in annoyance. "Return to your caravan and get out of my kingdom."

Mia-Myzus diligently did so, climbing back onto the wagon and cosying up to Daiv. When she was settled the caravan once more continued on its way.

"What was that all about?" Daiv asked curiously and amusedly.

"I'm not actually sure my love," Mia-Myzus replied in a confused tone. "I don't know at all" she then repeated while starting at the ground in deep thought.

The caravan continued on its way and soon made its way out of the eastern gate of Kossorlim. By that time, it was night and the Centaurs pulling the caravan elected to rest up and await till morning in the secluded mountain foothills before continuing to the Samson and Goliath camp. The travelling band of Gnomes and Centaurs as well as the Goliaths soon fell fast asleep after they camped up the caravan. Daiv and Mia-Myzus also prepared themselves for sleep, curling up close to one another and holding each other lovingly. But as Daiv fell asleep, Mia-Myzus sat up and grabbed her seeing stone. She placed it on her lap and pressed her fingers against its surface. Closing her eyes, she then called out for Kyzus, whom not too long later responded.

"Father. I have come across an issue that I require your guidance on," Mia-Myzus announced. "The Dwarf kings Thor III and Odin II of Kossorlim and Dwaria are currently meeting and in talks together, discussing the Dwarf response to the civil war. I however see no way of reaching them to intervene to make sure our interests are aligned. I cannot be taken to them and I cannot bring myself to them without undermining my current status."

"How interesting," Kyzus replied. "There is really no way you allowed to see them?"

"No father. Their loyalty to the protection of their kings and the secrecy around them is uncompromising and they seem to be far less accommodating to outsiders now that there is an archipelago wide civil war beyond their mountain borders, not even lofty riches help!" Mia-Myzus explained.

"Intriguing," Kyzus said. "But I sense there is more to why you have called me daughter. What else is there?"

Stunned that her father had grown so magically powerful that he could sense her own inner thoughts, Mia-Myzus then explained her exchange with Korg.

"I see," Kyzus said. "Well, you are right daughter, Awalatar was me and it was I who ordered, and assisted in, the creation of the seeing stones, you're lucky Korg didn't try to seize the stone from you! They were close to attempting to do the same to me. I am glad you did not reveal yourself as my daughter also, very wise. The seeing stones and their creator is still a mystery to all then."

"Yes, but Korg seemed fascinated by the crystal ball as well, I wonder if there is a way to use this?" Mia-Myzus inquired

"Excellent thinking daughter," Kyzus replied. "Perhaps 'Awalatar' shall pay Thor and Odin a visit. Leave this to me daughter, focus on taking Sabare with your boyfriend."

And with those final words said, the connection Mia-Myzus had with Kyzus abruptly ended. An uncomfortable feeling then immediately passed over Mia-Myzus. Her father could clearly sense or feel her own inner feelings; he had clearly deduced that she had developed a love for the Samson leader. How Kyzus did this, whether it was through the seeing stone itself or whether his magical prowess had grown that much so as to be able to sense such things from extremely long distances away, was a mystery to Mia-Myzus but it was still unsettling nonetheless, she really could not hide anything from him. Not that Mia-Myzus wanted too, but the development was unsettling all the same. She was also agitated in the fact that her father had clearly been up to far more than he was telling his children. None of them actually knew the full extent of their fathers' plan but now a glimpse into the unknown goings on of Kyzus was revealed to Mia-Myzus and it unnerved her, what was he up to? With these thoughts spiralling around her head Mia-Myzus lay back down to Daiv and attempted to sleep away the troubling thoughts.

Chapter 7

Delilah and the Samson Leader

Early the next morning the caravan awoke and began to continue along its journey at first light. Mia-Myzus attempted to purge the anxious concerns about her encounter with her father rattling around her head from her mind. Comforted by Daiv who saw the agitated state she was in, Mia-Myzus soon felt back to normal and confident enough to finally talk to Daiv about their future together and what she required to be done to make it happen.

"...With the resources from my crime empire, your followers should have all the supplies necessary to stage and win a revolution in Sabare" Mia-Myzus said. "If Vaid has played his part as instructed, Sabare should be a melting pot of turmoil, unrest, and strife, on the brink of uprising."

"I have every confidence in that Vaid will have done all you have requested to your liking my love. Once we arrive back at camp, we can all march to Sabare and take the kingdom for ourselves!" Daiv replied.

"We mustn't be too hasty my love," Mia-Myzus replied "The chieftain's army of Goliaths and Samson guards will still be loyal to him and are still a mighty force to be reconned with. They do have a chance of defeating us in an all-out offensive, especially if drawn out. We must be smart about this. Victory must be quick and decisive."

"Of course Delilah, what would I do without you," Daiv teased.

Giggling in a coy manner Mia-Myzus replied "Probably lounging on that bear fur bed of yours, eating the Gnomes food and enjoying their mushrooms a little too much I should think. Anyway! We should not openly march on Sabare, we should continue to slyly infiltrate the kingdom as we have been doing already. We need to meet with Vaid and discuss a quick plan of attack that will drop Sabare into our hands in less than a day."

"A day!" Daiv cried "You wish to topple an entire kingdom in less than a day! A kingdom belonging to races that are the greatest warriors in all of Terra Tearia! Are you sure it's not you who has been enjoying the Gnomes mushrooms?" Daiv joked but in a serious tone.

"Ye of little faith," Mia-Myzus replied coyly again. "Have I not already created the most powerful crime empire Terratopia has ever known in less time than it takes to walk from one end of it to the other? I have every confidence in my planning and in your followers' ability that we can pull off such a feat. Besides your races have a flaw I intend to exploit. A flaw I have already exploited to get where I am today."

"And what is that?" Daiv asked in a sarcastic tone

"Loyal and brutal you all may be, but you all respect displays of might and power to much and then give the one showing their feats opportunities they'd never be able to get otherwise. This is something I think is most admirable about your culture and one reason I fell in love with it. But it can be exploited. And I intend to" explained Mia-Myzus

Semi-stunned, both flattered and almost insulted, Daiv just looked at Mia-Myzus blankly, not quite sure how to take in her words.

Mia-Myzus continued; "If we can put on such a show of force, such a grand feat of might, the inhabitants of Sabare will not oppose us, in fact they may admire us. Maybe not join us but revere us and definitely not oppose us. The chieftain will have to address our revolution properly, not just simply attempt to put it down, the people would not stand for that, we would 'deserve' to have demands listened to in their eyes. This is where you and Vaid will become the new chieftains my love. You will both challenge the current chieftain to a duel. A duel for the right to rule over Sabare. A duel that will have to be accepted or face complete uproar from the populous."

"This is an excellent plan my love," Daiv said. "But it's flawed. Even together Vaid and I could never defeat Turberus, the current chieftain. There is a reason he is our kingdoms leader. There is talk that he is of our Titans bloodline! We have only a small chance at best and I would not bet the entire result of our efforts on this small chance."

"Oh Daiv, my love. You have a much bigger chance than you give yourself credit for." Mia-Myzus tantalized. "Besides as your future wife I think it is only right and fair I give you some... assistance. Not that the people of Sabare will know of course. I can't be undermining your rightful position to rule now," she then said in a knowing manner and with a now malevolent look over her face.

Daiv, now also with a more ominous expression over his face as well replied; "I like the way you think my love. You really are wife material Delilah."

The two then moved in close together, holding each other in a loving embrace and kissed.

For quite some time, as the caravan journeyed towards the Carlin Highlands, Daiv and Mia-Myzus kissed and caressed one another, happy in their love for each other and grateful they had such similar aspirations. When the feelings of love and affection couldn't be more intense between the two, Mia-Myzus finally sprung the make-or-break part of her own plan to Daiv;

"Daiv my love. Before I marry you, I need you to do something for me."

"Anything Delilah," Daiv replied, whispering gently.

"If you do this for me, you will be the sole ruler of Sabare, the kingdom will be at your command and you will have me by your side for your whole life." Mia-Myzus said, whispering back in an equally gentle, but manipulative tone.

"Go on," Daiv quietly replied.

Mia-Myzus stopped kissing Daiv and looked him straight in the eyes.

"I need you to allow Vaid to die."

Daiv paused, Mia-Myzus's words lingering in the air. He looked into her mystical eyes as she looked back at him in a loving but dependable expression.

"Consider it done my love," Daiv finally replied in a longing tone.

Finally, sometime later, the caravan arrived back at the Samson and Goliath camp. The rebel's settlement had changed much since Daiv and Mia-Myzus were there last. It was far less rickety and over grown and had now amassed into a small wooden fortress town. Still hidden deep in the woodland, the now much thicker, stronger wooden walls stood taller than before and had the odd tower periodically dotted along it. There was now a full-fledged gatehouse over the entrance in and out of the camp and it housed a log portcullis that was raised for the arriving caravan. Inside the base, nearly all the old tents were replaced with wooden and dried mud huts, some even with thatched roofs. An entire community had been built within the wooden walls; a bakers, some storehouses, hunting shacks, a timber mill, and even a large blacksmith had all been built around the new town and they were all occupied by a great many Samsons and Goliaths whom all worked tirelessly. The settlement seemed familiar in many ways, the firepits and walk ways all remained in largely the same place, but it had also changed in so many ways and seemed more alive. It was all possible thanks to the efforts of Mia-Myzus and her crime empires backing.

 Daiv followed by Mia-Myzus, holding each other's hands walked proudly to the central firepit where they had previously first met. The huge tent belonging to Vaid and Daiv still remained, it seemingly being untouched from the surrounding developments but yet it still somehow held the same prowess and authority it did previously. Daiv stood proudly at the entrance of his tent and cried out for the camp to all gather round the large central firepit. Once the camps inhabitants were all there, Daiv announced to his followers his proposal to Delilah, uniting their clan with her crime empire to be even closer. Daiv then also announced that it was time to move to Sabare and start the beginnings of their revolution, he ordered the wagons from Rox's caravans be filled with all the supplies they needed and then for everyone to be ready to depart for Sabare; orders which by nightfall were fulfilled.

 And so, in the darkness of night, only lit by minimal torch light, the insurgents convoy made its way to the Sabare Strait, filled with the supplies and weapons for the revolution the camp had been stocking up.

Chapter 8

The Sabare Revolution

Some days later, the vast majority of the Samson and Goliath insurgents had successfully infiltrated Sabare and were gathering in their head hideout near the centre of the kingdom. The hideout had been kept well supplied, similar to the camp in the Carlin Highlands, thanks to the efforts of Mia-Myzus's crime empires network and resources and there was great deal many more smaller fronts that had sprung up throughout Sabare for the growing rebel movement to gather as well.

In the main hideout, Vaid was catching up Daiv and Mia-Myzus with all he had accomplished in their absence and he detailed to them the goings on within the kingdom. Support for the insurgent's cause had grown tremendously, especially with the outbreak of the civil war. The chieftain had still retained his isolationism policy for the kingdom, in fact tightening it upon hearing the news of the civil wars outbreak. Turberus reasoned that as the mightiest warrior races in all of Terratopia, both sides of the war would seek the support of his kingdom and his armies, potentially even resulting in them being pitted against one another. And so he reiterated that despite being potentially the most formidable armies that would fight in the civil war, the Samson and Goliath races were also races of laughter, play, and love, something that was incompatible with being at war. Turberus was adamant that as a populous of joy, they should not deviate away from it just because the wider world had fallen into war. This had enraged many inhabitants of Sabare with their inner warrior-like desires. These desires were being fuelled to greater extremes by Vaid's efforts. Many within Sabare longed to fight in the war that now raged over Terratopia. This longing to fight was only further increased through Morur's Evil presence, as he sought to spread Evil wherever he could in all that would choose it, at all times.

Once learning of the climate within Sabare as well as learning its layout in detail, Mia-Myzus devised and explained her plan for the revolution to the insurgent leaders. Mia-Myzus detailed that Sabare had several key points within it that if controlled would drop rule over the kingdom into their hands. These were the chieftain's compound, the numerous armouries and blacksmiths through the kingdom, the market places, the warehouses and storage sheds districts, the harbour, and the kingdoms gatehouse. Taking the chieftain's compound would be a near impossible task Mia-Myzus felt, but if all the other buildings and areas could be taken and held, the chieftain would have no choice but to agree to their demands. The demands being a duel for the right to rule over Sabare.

Daiv and Vaid were taken aback by the boldness of Mia-Myzus's plan, Vaid especially, but that only made him like it more and be more eager to execute it. The next issue was the fact that all willing to fight for the rebel's cause in the coming revolution needed to be armed and armed quickly. Turberus knew all too well of the growing extremist movement rising in his kingdom and was beginning to crack down on it harshly, despite not knowing its true scale. The problem Mia-Myzus faced was that if all the rebels willing to fight advanced on their targets, armed with their weapons, kingdom wide, Turberus and his standing garrison would be alerted and ready to defend well before the rebels would get a chance to pull off their revolution quickly and successfully. The element of surprise was the crucial key for a swift takeover. Mia-Myzus needed the insurgents to be unarmed and unassuming while discretely surrounding and amassing on their targets before then suddenly arming themselves and taking their targets before Turberus and his forces could even get word of what was happening.

Mia-Myzus had accounted for this though early on in her planning for the revolution and had cleverly come up with a design that would allow for such a thing to happen. Rox's caravans had been in business with Sabare for quite some time and so were a familiar, unassuming sight. Now that they were under Mia-Myzus's control she could use them to arm the rebels quickly at the very place their targets were. Since being in her crime empire, Rox's caravans had gotten extremely good at hiding cargo when needed for smuggling resources into kingdoms. Mia-Myzus formulated that if some wagons could be posted at the relevant targets, ladened with hidden weapons, the rebels could arm themselves instantly to then quickly take control of their areas and buildings with overwhelming speed and force, facing little to no resistance. And so that is exactly what Mia-Myzus explained was to happen to Daiv, Vaid, and their followers. They already had one caravan of wagons from their journey from their camp and after two more naturally arrived in Sabare on regular business, Mia-Myzus ordered them to stay within the kingdom and not to return to Rox after they had unloaded. With three full caravans worth of wagons, Mia-Myzus split them and distributed them out so that there would be wagons outside every armoury, blacksmith, marketplace, warehouse, and storage shed across the kingdom, as well as the gatehouse and harbour. Daiv then ordered all fighters for the rebel cause to be assigned to targets and then to deliver and leave their weapons with the respected wagons for their target. Once done, a day was set and plan of attack coordinated for the revolution. Once agreed, all details were then relayed to all rebel fighters via the insurgent fronts and they all awaited eagerly for the day of the revolution to begin.

Three days later, the fateful day of the revolution began. Rox's wagons were all deployed to their respect targets by the Centaurs and Gnomes early in the morning, ladened with their hidden deadly cargo where they then remained, looked after by the unassuming Centaurs and Gnomes. The rebel fighters all began to amass on their respect targets as well, spying the weapon ladened wagons and scouting out plans of attack. All morning, kingdom wide, insurgent Samsons and Goliaths assembled unassumingly but ominously around their targets waiting for the chimes of the mid-day bells, thereby signalling the start of the revolution. The morning sun began to light up the fabric, wooden, and stone kingdom, warming the streets in an unusually bright, clear day. Vaid, Daiv, and Mia-Myzus all took up their positions near the kingdom's gatehouse, the three being needed at that particular location as it was the most heavily guarded and most vital target to the revolution. If taken, control in and out the kingdom would be theirs, as well as effective control over the entire kingdom cities walls as there was no other towers or buildings on them. With the glaring sun beating down into the kingdom that surrounded the twin mountain peaks of Samson and Goliath, the anticipation of the insurgent forces built up even more with every passing hour. The atmosphere throughout the kingdom grew tense, the air grew thick enough to be cut by a sword and Turberus noticed. Sensing something wasn't quite right, Turberus was about to order his full army of Goliaths and Samson guards to all arm themselves and patrol the streets, before then suddenly hearing the chimes of the mid-day's bells. An eerie silence followed before then being broken by an eruption of war cries and roars, sounds that were heard kingdom wide.

The rebels all attacked. Arming themselves quickly from Rox's wagons and then launching themselves at their targets. Terror spread across the kingdom as armed and violent Samsons and Goliaths raped the market places, stormed the armouries, ravaged the blacksmiths, invaded warehouses and storage sheds, assaulted the harbour, and assailed the gatehouse. The attackers all faced little to no resistance initially but soon some defiance against their control arose from the chieftain's guards on duty or from the loyalist of inhabitants. The bashing of shields, clashing of swords, clanking of axes, roars of attack, and screams of pain and death all rattled across Sabare, drowning out any other noise that could be heard. The majority of the chieftain's warriors all rushed to his compound, locking it up and taking up defensive positions as quickly as they could to defend against the assumed incoming attack. But as Turberus soon released, an attack never came, nor would it ever come. The fighting was happening out there, in his now somewhat defenceless kingdom instead.

At the gatehouse, fighting was at its deadliest and bloodiest, Vaid led a group of warriors to assault one side of the fortified, heavily guarded building while Mia-Myzus and Daiv advanced on the other side. Vaid heroically led his teams charge up and along the city walls towards the gatehouse, slaying all that stood in his way promptly and brutally. The further he advanced, the louder he roared, the more covered in blood he became, and the more terrifying of a sight he looked. Before long, Vaid became too scary of a force for the guarding chieftains Samsons to face and so they retreated back to the gatehouse and barricaded close the mighty oak door to the walls Vaid was on.

On the opposite side of the gatehouse, the Goliaths led by Daiv fought off the Samson guards on the ground leaving opportunity for Mia-Myzus to magically lift Daiv and some accompanying Samsons to the top of the walls where they all then began their devastating rampage towards the gatehouse. Mia-Myzus slew every Samson and Goliath that attempted to attack her on the ground; spinning as fast as a tornado and as elegantly as a fairy dancing in the wind. Her spiralling robes mystified and dizzied all that saw them and her Elven blade sliced deeply into all flesh it touched. Daiv flourished his twin bladed sword around him like a rotating propeller, intimating all that opposed it, before he would then manage to cut them through with insane force. Steadily, like an unstoppable force, the three leaders and their followers all converged on the gatehouse from the ground and either side of the walls. Soon enough they had it completely surrounded and had crushed all resistance outside of its fortification.

Fallen dead bodies of guards lay scattered all around the gatehouse. The remaining guards all barricaded themselves within the gatehouse, reading themselves for their last stands at all the entrance ways, but Mia-Myzus had different plans. She magically leapt to the very top of the gatehouse's roof, slaying the three Samsons guards positioned there with countless hasty and deadly slashes of her blade, before then lifting Daiv and Vaid up alongside her. The three then smashed through the trapdoor down into the gatehouse and dropped into the building behind the backs of the remaining guards. As quick as lighting, the three launched themselves at the guards, killing many before they had even registered what had happened. In a fatal, yet effortless, beautiful dance, the three choregraphed around each other in a devastating brawl. Defending each other from all angles as well as attacking their enemies from every direction. Mia-Myzus's love for Daiv grew exponentially watching him swing his twin bladed sword around himself and slaughter all he attacked. Likewise, Daiv became even more enthralled by the high Elf Delilah, fighting side by side with her and watching her dispatch the most mighty of foes twice her size with ease in what looked like a ballet dance to her. Her enemies blood sprayed like ocean waves that her long flowing hair then bathed in and Daiv was infatuated. Once all the guards were killed, Mia-Myzus and Daiv sprung into each other's embrace and kissed. Vaid then attempted to join in but Mia-Myzus magically thrust him out one of the barricaded doors without batting an eyelid to Vaid's surprise, which he laughed and shrugged off with no hard feelings. Once Vaid emerged outside, the rebel Samsons and Goliaths that had just finished off the counteracting force outside cheered as the gatehouse was now theirs.

By the end of the day and the dawning of night over Sabare, the rebels had achieved their aims. They had all successfully attacked and held every target labelled by Mia-Myzus. They controlled all the key points of the kingdom. The revolution had begun and was all but finished in less than a day. The inhabitants within the kingdom now didn't oppose the insurgents either, just as Mia-Myzus predicted, instead admiring them greatly for their feats and beginning to question their loyalty to their chieftain Turberus. The inhabitants of Sabare began to sway to the rebels and their cause; which was now being announced ruthlessly within the streets by the orders of Vaid. Turberus couldn't believe the revolution that had just occurred, astounded by its tactics, scale, magnitude, support, and success. Being totally dumbfounded and believing such a thing was impossible by the small extremist group that he had banished previously years ago. Reluctantly, but realising he had no choice, Turberus sent a messenger to the extremist leadership, asking for their demands.

Chapter 9

The Duel between Turberus, Daiv and Vaid

Once getting word from a messenger sent by Turberus asking to meet to hear their demands late that evening, Vaid and Daiv marched with their rebel followers from the gatehouse right up to the chieftain's compound; parading proudly and loudly through the streets lit by touch light. The night was still young but it was already too dark to see anything without the flickering glow of fire. Vaid and Daiv's armed followers grew in size the closer they got to the compound and grew in volume as the loud rabble swelled and their chants intensified. Once arrived at the Turberus's compound, the insurgent leader's entourage, as well as many new followers that had joined post revolution, swarmed around and completely surrounded Turberus's position. The compound was alike to the rebels own wooden camp out in the wilderness of the Carlin Highlands with tall, strong wooden walls surrounding several buildings that housed the chieftain's home and government with only a single entrance in and out. The compound was far more impressive and grand than the rebel's settlement however; its walls were thick oak logs standing on end with spiked whittled tops, there were also towers along the walls and the buildings within the compound were made skilfully from stone and fine timber, looking grandiose and noble.

The heavy and imposing compounds gates were closed shut and the towers and walls were heavily guarded with formidable Samsons and Goliaths soldiers armed to the teeth. Vaid and Daiv strutted proudly up to the gates and stood firm. Slamming his axe down, Vaid fiercely exclaimed;

"Turberus! Chieftain of Sabare. You have failed. Our so-called extremist group you wrongfully banished has staged a revolution that the people no longer fight but welcome!"

"The people of Sabare have spoken! The way in which Sabare is to be run must change Turberus! You are no longer welcomed as our leader." Daiv then proclaimed.

A foreboding, deep, rough voice then replied; equal too, if not louder, than Vaid and Daiv's own;

"I am by all means still your leader! You do not have the support of my people. You have their admiration, as well as my own. Which is why I have summoned you here peacefully to listen to your demands. If you wish for me to step down and hand rule over Sabare to your extremist ways willingly, you have another thing coming!"

"That is exactly what we wish!" Vaid snapped back. "And it will happen. We only want to see our kingdom fulfil its true potential and our leadership will make it so!"

The same powerful voice replied from behind the closed gates; "Your ideals are nothing but extreme and fundamentally flawed. You purse our races deep warrior desires while completely ignoring our other inner qualities of love, laughter, and play. What you would do too Sabare is nothing short of evil and exactly what our great Celestial creators Tunmore and Tankus fight against!"

"You are wrong! We are proud races!" Shouted Daiv. "We are the greatest warriors in all of Terratopia and it is you who completely ignore that! We may be races of love as well, but that love is for our fellow brothers whom we fight side by side with!" Daiv ferociously reasoned back before then continuing; "If you will not willingly step down, you must agree to our alternative demand... I, Daiv, son of Daivud."

"And I, Vaid, son of Vaidiv." Vaid then exclaimed

"Challenge you, Chieftain Turberus, to a duel. A contest of combat for the right to rule over Sabare. To the death." Daiv confidently announced.

Silenced followed, only the gentle whistling of the nights wind and the cracking of torch fire could be heard. Vaid and Daiv eagerly awaited a response along with their rebel followers as well as nearly the whole kingdoms inhabitants that had crampedly gathered to see the exchange. The nights air grew almost as tense as the earlier mid-day bells, but eventually the foreboding gates of the compound creaked open revealing the most formidable Goliath Daiv and Vaid had ever saw. The beast of a being steadily stepped towards the two, his boots stomping menacingly on the ground. It was Turberus, and as Daiv had previously said to Mia-Myzus, there was a clear reason why he was the Sabare's chieftain. Despite Daiv and Vaid being unnaturally tall, broad, and formidable compared to regular Samsons and Goliaths, Turberus literally stood head and shoulders even above them both and his great double-edged sword was nearly as tall as them themselves as he dragged it by his side. Lit only by the inconsistent red and orange hue of fire, the brown haired, black bearded, behemoth of a Goliath towered over Vaid and Daiv as he stopped before them.

"I accept," he said in a brash serious tone.

Showing no fear, Daiv and Vaid starred directly into Turberus's intimidating gaze stoically.

"Excellent," Daiv nodded in a sarcastic manner before turning and walking away.

"We fight at dawn!" he then shouted over his shoulder.

"Kiss your loved one's goodbye," Vaid cheered as he too walked away. "You aren't going to see them again come morning."

Turberus then too turned and walked back to his compound before the gate then closed shut behind him.

When dawn arrived the next day, the sun only just beginning to brighten and bathe Sabare in a light golden glow, the entire kingdom all gathered around the chieftain's compound once more. The inhabitants piled on top of each other and the surrounding buildings to catch a glimpse of the epic duel that was about to commence.

Directly outside the closed compound gates, a semi-circle of densely packed spiked wooden stakes had been driven into the ground, marking out the duel's arena. At the furthest point from the gates within the semi-circle, Vaid and Daiv lay on their backs next to one another watching the sky turn from black to blue to yellow as it transitioned from night to day.

"Won't your lady Elf friend by joining us?" Vaid asked in a light hearted tone

"Oh, she's here, just not in sight. 'It apparently being detrimental to her plans' if she's seen in close contact with us by the kingdom's inhabitants," Daiv responded in a joking manner waving his hands sarcastically, mimicking the tone Mia-Myzus most often used when talking about her mysterious plans and actions.

The two laughed before Vaid then said; "Yeah, she is a strange one. Beautiful, cunning, and powerful. But a strange one nonetheless."

"Agreed," Daiv chuckled. "I love her though."

Vaid chuckled at his brother's words. "If you love her, why don't you marry her?" he then said acerbically.

"I think I might do just that you know brother," Daiv said light heartedly but also in a serious tone

Vaid paused and turned to face Daiv. "Uh, really?"

Daiv turned to face him and nodded.

"Damn," Vaid said in a semi-shocked tone, realising Daiv was serious. "I understand now why she didn't let me join in to kiss her with you earlier" he then said jokingly, laughing as he finished his sentence.

The two then laughed more together before Vaid once again spoke. "Seriously though, good for you brother. I'm happy for you. She'll make a fine companion for you to rule over Sabare with me."

Touched, Daiv placed his hand on Vaid's shoulder. "Thank you brother. He then paused before then continuing. "I want you to know before this duel begins that I love you, you will forever be a part of me and there is nearly nothing on this world that I would not do for you."

Placing his own hand on Daiv's opposing shoulder, Vaid then said "Thank you brother. And likewise."

The two then stood up proudly grabbing their weapons and placing on their armour and helmets.

"Now let's go kill this peace-loving weakling," Vaid growled.

Daiv fiercely smacked Vaid on the back and bellowed; "He is all but dead already."

The crowd that had amassed all cheered triumphantly as Daiv and Vaid readied themselves for the coming duel, roaring even louder when the two turned to face them lifting their weapons high in the air to acknowledge the cheers. They both wore terrific metal boots and gauntlets as well as metal plates on their shoulders, knees, and elbows. Besides the leather straps holding their armour in place, the animal fur around their waist covering their obnoxious areas, and their metal helmets, Daiv and Vaid wore nothing else; embracing the culture and warrior appearance they were fighting for, showing off their splendid defined muscles for all to see. Vaid had acquired another sword and so was armed with an axe and sword, to duel wield them over the fight whereas Daiv still brandished his signature twin bladed sword, the length of both its blades together being longer than most Elven spears.

As the break of dawn fully arrived and the morning sun now mostly lit up the sky, the gates to the chieftain's compound creaked opened once more and Turberus strode out into the dual arena. Wearing similar armour to his opponents and armed with a large kite shaped shield as well as his huge sword from the previous night, Turberus shouted from across the semi-circle;

"Are you two ready to die?"

"For our cause we would give our lives!" Vaid ferociously snapped back. "But today, fighting you for rule... Is not that day!"

"You are foolish to think you both have a chance against me!" Turberus rebutted.

"Quit stalling old man," Daiv chanted. "Close the gates behind you and let's do this!"

Turberus nodded and raised his shield baring hand. As he did the gates closed shut behind him and the three combatants all slowly began to pace towards one another, within the now completely confined dual arena. Vaid and Daiv started to spread out to occupy either flank of Turberus before then stopping as the chieftain himself stopped. About five metres away from one another, they all began fiercely facing down each other, starting attentively into each other's eyes.

There was a lull stillness in the air as the three indominable beings faced off against each other, beaming intently into each other's eyes and continually changing their stances for the most optimal way of attack or defence. The wind blew steadily through the arena, trailing some dust and loose soil picked up from the ground.

All of a sudden, the wind mystically picked up and a powerful gust blew dust right into Turberus. Flinching his eyes briefly from the irritation of the airborne soil, Turberus was then suddenly hit square in the face from Daiv's helmet which he had launched at him. So forceful was the impact that it reorientated Turberus's own helmet, impairing his vision as it had moved slightly over his eyes. Closely following the flung helmet, Vaid charged at Turberus, his axe and sword drawn by his side. As Vaid neared the Goliath chieftain, he quickly raised his weapons and smashed them down onto his target. But Turberus briefly saw this and raised his shield to counter just in time, yet the clash of weapons was so powerful that it was enough to knock Turberus to the ground. As soon as Vaid's axe and sword smashed into the shield, imbedding themselves into it, Vaid pulled them away and spun around to the side of Turberus, pulling his shield stuck on the two weapons with him. No sooner than doing this, Daiv immediately dropped from the sky slamming one blade of his twin bladed sword directly down into Turberus's now exposed prone body in a deadly downward motion. Turberus tried to shift his presence away from the incoming attack as well as remove his shield from Vaid's weapons but it was simply not possible to fully do and Daiv impaled his weapon through Turberus's metal boots as he landed, penetrating it through his foot and into the ground below, pinning the monstrous Goliath in place.

Turberus grunted out in pain and swung his huge sword at Daiv but Daiv positioned himself behind the other side of his twin blade that protruded high into the air, which deflected Turberus's strike. As soon as Turberus's attack rebounded off the firm implanted double bladed weapon, Vaid removed his axe from the shield and, with two hands, swung it from the ground upwards in a fleeting movement towards the chieftain's head. Vaid's axe struck Turberus's chin, whiplashing the chieftains head straight back and knocking his helmet flying into the gate behind him.

The crowd cheered tremendously and Vaid and Daiv grabbed their weapons, and stepped back from the prone chieftain, believing no one to be able to withstand a direct axe swing to the chin, not even Turberus. But to their dismay, but the crowds delight, Turberus rose up with a disgruntled, extremely angry look on his face; revealing the bloody axe shaped gouge and surrounding dent in his chin. Whipping blood onto his gauntlet and admiring it, Turberus then snorted; "Is that the best you can do?" Before then spitting out three teeth and charging head first into the two extremist leaders.

In shock but awe, Daiv and Vaid readied themselves to clash with their charging foe, brandishing their weapons behind them, ready to strike forwards with as much momentum as they could muster. They were about to swing their weapons at either side of Turberus when he was almost upon them, but just as he got within range, Daiv mysteriously, but as quick as a lightning bolt, shifted to one side, to his own surprise. But in doing so, Daiv had completely opened up Turberus's defenceless back to himself. The prestigious Samson spotted this and quickly slashed his weapon across the giant Goliaths back in a figure of 8 motion, severing all the leather straps holding Turberus's armour in place as well as gashing a deep grisly X shape into his back.

While Daiv did this however, Vaid had already swung his axe in one hand at Turberus, slamming it into his shield that Turberus had once again raised to defend himself with. Turberus, in the time between Daiv shifting behind him and striking him, used his other hand, which he was initially planning on striking Daiv with, to instead swing his oversized sword across his body to strike Vaid with. Realising this, Vaid just in time managed to raise his other hand armed with his sword to parry Turberus's strike away from him and into the ground. But Turberus skilfully and rapidly reversed his grip on his sword and, using the momentum from the parry, stabbed it straight back into Vaid again. Vaid thrust his sword down to lock hilts with Turberus and prevent his giant sword from impaling him. The two were then in a contest of strength, Turberus trying to stab his blade into Vaid's stomach and Vaid using his blade to prevent it. But alas, as strong as Vaid was among Goliaths, Turberus was stronger, and his blade slowly inched towards and then into Vaid's stomach. Before Turberus could get any deeper however, Daiv's strikes had made contact with his back and monstrous Goliath dropped his sword, recoiling upwards and backwords in pain. As his armour fell off him, Turberus spiralled in a painful, rage filled fury, slamming his shield into Daiv knocking the Samson flying backwards and punching his other arm into Vaid's wound with all his might, sending Vaid flying backwards as well and exploding blood out of his already serious wound.

As Daiv tumbled backwards, he blasted his weapon into the ground, gripping onto it to stop his flight back into the wall of stakes, creating an enormous dust cloud in his wake. Vaid however, reeling from the pain of his attacks sustained from Turberus, took no such action, and instead sored straight into the wooden spiked border of the arena. Plummeting back first into the stakes and being impaled by every stake he touched, Vaid smashed through spike after spike before eventually rolling to a stop. His back and sides were alike to that of a wooden spiked hedgehog. Daiv cried out in anguish for his brother-in-arms and sprinted towards him, leaping over Turberus, who himself knelt on the ground in agony. As Daiv landed from leaping over kneeling Goliath, he sliced his twin bladed sword across and behind him, cutting across the chieftains' cheeks and thrusting him to the ground in further suffering. Daiv reached for his brother, concerned as to the extent of his suffering, Vaid then steadily rose to his feet, yearning in pain. Blood tricked down slowly from all his wounds but he still showed no fear and was eager to continue the fight.

"Are you all right brother?" Daiv said in a concerned manner, attempting to help Vaid to his feet.

"Why? You aren't getting tried or too sore, are you?" Vaid coughed in as jokingly a manner as he could. Daiv smiled and handed Vaid his axe.

"Not at all brother, come, our journey together is almost complete!"

The two entered the duals arena once more and waved to the crowd, even throwing their helmets into them to show how stoic they were; revealing their red sweaty faces, and long braded breads and hair. Vaid stumbled over to his sword, used it to slice all the wooden stakes from his back and then launched it at Turberus shouting; "Give up yet oh great Chieftain of Sabare?" in a mocking manner.

Turberus raised his shield up once more to block the incoming projectile and then threw it to the ground, smashing the shield to splitters. Standing up gradually and raising his gauntlets up into a fighting stance, Turberus then exclaimed;

"Come at me you weak wounded puppy!"

Vaid then limped and charged towards Turberus, crying out in anger and Daiv followed suit. They both then leapt at the chieftain, swinging their weapons down onto him. Turberus however with his mighty metal gauntlets, grabbed both the swords blade and axe head mid-strike as they were thrusted towards him. He then squeezed them, partially crumpling them to bluntness. As Turberus did this, he jumped into the air, pulling Daiv and Vaid's weapons down with them along with them as they held on, while in the air, Turberus then and spear kneed both Daiv and Vaid in the sternums, dropping them both to the floor gasping for air. While convulsing on the floor, Turberus then brutally struck Daiv and Vaid both on the head with his gauntlets, his fists acting as hammers, until Daiv eventually dodged away and then pulled his brother to safety as well. The two then looked at each other, nodding and locking hands before letting go and launching themselves again at the formidable Goliath. The three then engaged in a devastating brawl, exchanging brutal strikes from all limbs they possibly could. The blows that landed were so powerful that they thundered across the whole surrounding arena. Fuelled by fury, anger, and desire, Daiv and Vaid eventually started to beat Turberus back, plunging powerful blows into him and slowly forcing him backwards into the sealed shut gates of his compound. So intense was their attack that their metal gauntlets, boots, knee, and elbow pads themselves began to crumble from their sheer usage on Turberus's body, legs, and head.

When his back was pressed against the gates and his body suffering tremendous damage, Turberus yelled out in maddening fury and grabbed both Daiv and Vaid up by the necks. He turned and faced the gates and slammed Daiv and Vaid continually into them. Eventually Vaid feel unconscious and went limp. Seeing this Daiv, prised himself away from Turberus's grasp, after throwing a distracting spike elbow into his bicep, and upon landing on the floor, kicked his metal boot into Turberus's inner thigh, spasming it outwards. Suddenly, with a new found strength mysteriously passing over and through him, reinvigorating him, Daiv then kicked Turberus's other leg, this time aiming for Turberus's knee which, in doing so, buckled his whole leg backwards and dropped the behemoth opponent to the ground. Vaid's listless body also then dropped by the gates. Daiv then hooked Turberus's head with his left gauntlet, then his right before then uppercutting him with his left again and then grabbing his head with his right hand, pulling it into a fatal strike from his right knee. Blood exploded from Turberus's face who then slumped to the ground. In sheer rage, Daiv picked up the huge Goliath and hurled him into the gates. As Turberus bashed into the gates and again fell to the ground he let out a whimper as all strength left him as he tried to get up. The beaten behemoth collapsed flat onto his bloody deformed face and broken body. Daiv then again approached Turberus and screamed in angst as he again picked up the huge Goliath and lifted his high above his head. Daiv then yelled again and threw Turberus directly down onto his knee causing a haunting cracking sound, like egg shells being crushed underfoot. Battered and bruised, Daiv then slowly limped over to his sword and then limped back to Turberus who was lying face up on the ground wheezing below the huge wooden gates, breathing heavily and spluttering blood. Daiv then stabbed the other still sharp blade of his weapon deeply into the wounded Goliaths stomach before pulling it out again. Delilah's soft voice then projected in his head saying;

"Back away my love,"

Daiv did so and then suddenly, somehow both the compounds enormous hefty gates collapsed down from their hinges and fell onto the limp bodies of Turberus and Vaid. The enormous weight of the log gates almost completely flattening them both into a disgusting bloody bony mush.

A wave of dust erupted from the gates as they smashed onto the ground. Nothing but silence followed as Daiv fell to his knees with his hands behind his head. The onlooking crowd started on in shock and wonder. Daiv's heavy panting grew louder and louder, eventually it turned into grunts, and then shouts, and then a roar of victory but also of pain and loss. Daiv rose to his feet, still staring at the place in which Vaid's dead body lay, and raised both his hands high above his head in a mighty, stoic, victorious stance. With blood dripping from all over Daiv's bruised and battered body, the crowd all erupted into a fierce uproar, welcoming their new chieftain. Daiv began to smile, a great feeling of accomplishment passed over him as the fact settled in that he had done it. He was now the chieftain of Sabare and he had done what his love Delilah had asked of him, his life was complete. He had finally achieved all he had been fighting for. He then heard Delilah's loving voice once more in his head;

"Well done my love. Truly you are the husband I dream off. Oh great, powerful, wonderous Chieftain of Sabare."

Chapter 10

Kyzus and the Dwarf Kings

Kyzus sat alone in his grandiose Roccano mountainside palace. He had just finished speaking with his daughter through the seeing stones they both held and was most intrigued at the useful information she had just told to him. The Dwarves were more stubborn than anticipated, their loyalty to their own kings and kingdoms safety stronger than their desires for riches and wealth. Yet this was seen as no problem to Kyzus. The wise ancient Half-elf knew exactly how to overcome this all be it small, but unexpected hurdle. If the Dwarves highest loyalty was to their kings and kingdoms, not to their wealth, then controlling the kings would in turn entail easy and total control over all Dwarves. Kyzus knew the Dwarf kings themselves desired nothing more than the riches and prosperity of their realms in as little hassle possible, so they only had to be reached to then be swayed. Mia-Myzus was right, the situation of both Dwarf kings being within Kossorlim discussing how to respond to the civil war presented a unique, convenient opportunity for Kyzus's plan and since Mia-Myzus had no chance of seizing it, Kyzus knew he had too.

    Kyzus grabbed two more seeing stones from the huge hall where they all resided and headed for Kossorlim; leaving orders for Barriel and Joell III to continue to rule in his absence. Kyzus dawned some long dark flowing robes and cast a spell over himself. Once done he quickly span around and, as he did this, teleported across Rodus and Nindir, arriving almost instantaneously just outside of Kossorlim's western gates. Kyzus smiled to himself, he had never travelled that far in a single teleport and he had done so with ease. The amount by which Kyzus had improved his magical ability was exponential, he was the only inhabitant in Terratopia that had discovered how to cast teleportation spells, as well as being the only one powerful enough to cast such spells upon himself to travel such vast distances.

Just outside of the grand sealed gates, before attempting to make contact with the Dwarves, Kyzus gowned his magical Awalatar guise once more. He approached the gates slowly and there he was halted and greeted by a band of Dwarf guards led by Korg, a familiar sight to Kyzus.

"Awalatar?" Korg questioned. "You have returned? Why?"

In the deep, yet frail old voice Kyzus put on, he replied; "There is a war on, your kind has been incredibly helpful to me previously. I wish to bestow upon your king's gifts to show my gratitude and to aid you all during these conflicted times."

Lowering their weapons, Korg and the Dwarf guards were enticed.

"What have you come to gift us old, yet wise and powerful man?" Korg asked.

Kyzus reached into his robes and in each hand pulled out a glowing seeing stone, their ever-changing rainbow hues intoxicating the gaze of the observing Dwarves.

"I understand both kings of the Dwarves, Kings Odin II, and Thor III, are currently here at the moment. Take me to them and I will gift these precious, magical crystals to your kingdoms," Kyzus demanded.

Korg was somewhat taken aback by Awalatar's knowledge of the kings' presence at the realm as it was a tightly kept secret, but he was too enthralled by the sight of the stones to let such thoughts distract him.

"Of course, Awalatar, follow me," Korg said, turning around towards the closed stone gates.

The orders were given and the monumental stone gates cracked open, allowing Korg to lead Awalatar inside. Such a trusted acquaintance was Kyzus as Awalatar to the Dwarves that he travelled alone with Korg. No Dwarven escort accompanied them both as they quickly turned off the wide grand straight road that spanned across Kossorlim and instead continually climbed a great many exquisite stone staircases that led to higher and higher levels of the enormous underground Dwarven realm. Huge, unspeakable amounts of the mountain peaks of Kossorlim had been carved out to form the upper levels of the Dwarves grandiose kingdom and Kyzus and Korg were to journey to the very tallest levels. The drop down into the forges and mines bellow was an unfathomable distance and it only grew larger the higher Kyzus and Korg travelled. The lower levels soom became impossible to see and only small flickering dots of orange from the monstrous great fires of the huge forges could be seen, as well as the glimmer of gold and sparkle of silver. As the pair climbed higher and higher, these dots and glimmers all shrank and eventually merged into a small orange dot in the depths of darkness.

The journey to the where the Dwarf kings resided took over a day of vertical travel through the subterranean kingdom and Kyzus and Korg rested for the night in one of the many Dwarven inns on their route. During the evening, Korg raised his earlier encounter with another one of the seeing stones; telling of the high Elf named Delilah who rode with the Wolfhound Rox's caravans and also with a mighty Samson and a couple of Goliaths. Kyzus, as Awalatar, explained that he had gifted many of his seeing stones to extremely powerful people that were his friends across all of Terratopia. Kyzus detailed how magically powerful the seeing stones were and of the abilities they gave to the ones who held them. Korg seemed fascinated, but skeptical of the incredible feats Awalatar claimed that the stones were capable of, and so Kyzus allowed to Korg to hold one of the stones to see for himself. Kyzus told Korg to imagine the very depths of the lowest levels of Kossorlim and that the stone would take his vision there when he touched it; and it did. As plain as day, Korg's vision, through his closed eyes, had instantly travelled down to the lowest level of Kossorlim that he knew of and he saw exactly what was going on there as if he was standing there himself at that moment. He saw the glistening shine of gold nuggets as they were poured into a giant fiery furnace which melted them down to become pure gold to then be moulded into whatever the Dwarven smiths desired. Korg saw the shine of emeralds, diamonds, rubies, and sapphires as they were all inspected by Dwarf jewellers through their monocles and tiny looking glasses. Every minute detail of every square inch of Korg's visions surroundings could be seen as clear as if he was himself there. His vision was also able to instantly move and travel wherever he desired and the clarity of detail always remained the same. Before long Korg eventually opened his eyes and took his hands off the stone. Speechless, he gazed at Awalatar in amazement and Kyzus nodded, understanding exactly what Korg had just experienced.

The next day the two finally arrived at the royal chamber halls of Thor III, within the very tallest heights of the middle peak of Kossorlim. Korg introduced Awalatar to the Dwarf kings who were curious to hear what this outsider had to say to them after Korg had held him in such high esteem. Just like before when entering Kossorlim, Kyzus presented the two mesmerising, magnificent and mysterious seeing stones and explained how they were his gifts to both the kings. Odin II and Thor III, similar to all Dwarves that had laid eyes on the stones, were captivated by their presence. Perfect rainbow glowing spheres of pure Magiccora, the rarest and most magical of material to be mined from the world. Kyzus allowed the kings to hold the stones and to try them out, similar to Korg the evening before. Both the Dwarf kings did so, being just as astounded by their ability as Korg was. Odin II was able to see his own kingdom of Dwaria and see his family with ease, despite it being on the other side of Terratopia. Thor III travelled his vision straight outside of Kossorlim and looked down upon its five snowy peaks as if he was an eagle flying high above them. Kyzus went onto explain how the stones were both linked as well and that if both kings were holding them, they could communicate with each other. The kings were more than sold and so graciously accepted and thanked Awalatar for his impressive gifts.

Kyzus then returned to Roccano, pleased with how things had gone. Upon his return into his palace however, Kyzus then grabbed his own master seeing stone from his robes sleeve. When holding it he activated another magical enchantment within it that all stones possessed. The two stones that now belonged to the Dwarf kings called to their very souls, beckoning the kings to hold them, a call that was irresistible not to follow. When both of the Dwarf kings held their stones, Kyzus unleashed one of the enchantments hidden deep within them. The magical spells inside the stones infused themselves into the Dwarves that held them and, as Kyzus was in complete control over these enchantments, Kyzus's will became dominate over the Dwarf kings own. Although stubborn and extremely strong willed, the Dwarf kings' souls soon bent to Kyzus's and his enchantment. His own magical power was too powerful for them to repel. With both the kings under his command, Kyzus detailed to them their role in his grand plan and gave them their instructions.

He ordered the Dwarf kings to rule their kingdoms in line with maximising their own prosperity at the devastating expense of both sides of the civil war. The kings were to aid both sides of the war equally, to supply them with deadly weapons and to minimise their wealth. The kings were to allow both sides to utilise all their Dwarven realms resources and access, but at an extremely costly price. The Dwarves where to milk both the Unionists and Liberalists dry, but to also supply them with everything they needed to ensure utter and total havoc and desolation.

The Dwarf kings would go on to do just as instructed by Kyzus and such was the nature of his enchantment over them, that no one ever knew of either king's true elegances. They had become puppets with unseen strings.

Kyzus also explained to the Dwarf kings that they could communicate with the leadership of the Unionists and Liberalists from their seeing stones, just as they could do with each other as the Unionist and Liberalist leadership possessed stones as well. The Dwarf kings were instructed to take full advantage of their close quick connections with both sides of the civil war, to coordinate and give both sides all the support needed to fuel them to fight each other to maximum devastation in as short of a time as possible. Finally, Kyzus also informed the kings of the Queen Delilah that was about to take over Sabare; he told how she was running an underworld crime empire that both of them should also support in any way they could, just like they were doing for both sides of the civil war, as well as utilise her own resources and access, as she too had her own seeing stone to communicate with. However, Kyzus also ordered that both kings keep any and all communications with Delilah and to her crime empire a secret.

Neither side of the civil war, nor any other peoples of Terratopia were to learn of her activities with the Dwarves.

* * *

In this time since the outbreak of civil war, Kyzus had himself been very busy as Lordbaron of Roccano. He had decreed and instructed to his kingdom that Roccano was against the civil war, his sons had clearly gone rough and so Roccano was to lend no help nor aid to either side. Although, he also vastly increases Roccano's military might to even further levels as well. Roccano's whole purpose was shifted into one that would resemble a war effort, yet no armies ever left for war. New, better, stronger defences where built. Even more powerful siege and war engines where engineered and constructed through the ingenuity of Men. Magic military academies spung up across the kingdom city where mostly Elves, but sometimes Men as well, learnt and practiced magical arts to extremely high levels under the teaching from Kyzus himself, though the power of these warrior mages paled pathetically in comparison to Kyzus's own power. Men now all trained to become fearsome knights their whole lives, as well as Elves. Additionally, the finest quality weapons and armour were forged within the kingdom by the greatest smiths from Dwaria that had been emigrated over to Roccano and now resided within the city. Roccano became host to the greatest standing army the world of Terra Tearia had ever seen so far. The kingdom hosted legions of knights of Men, clad in the finest amour and armed with the finest weapons in all of Terratopia, the likes of which were completely unique to Roccano. The kingdom boasted ranks of formidable Elven soldiers and mages, whom were among the most skilful warriors and powerful sorceress in all of Terratopia as well.

In addition to all this, Kyzus had also decreed the creation of new elite divisions within his Roccano army. These new warriors were selected from the mightiest Elven warriors, whom were also the most gifted and powerful mages. These Elves would be personally taught ruthlessly by Kyzus near enough every day for years to become even greater warriors and even more powerful sorcerers. They were to become his own personal guard and were known as the 'Paladins of Roccano'. The Paladins of Roccano gradually became the most formidable warriors in all of Terra Tearia, having the ability to defeat armies far greater in size then their own from any race, even of Samsons and Goliaths.

Barriel herself underwent the training to become a Paladin and rose to become the very best of them all. Because of this, by the time of the Liberalists invasion of Rodus, Barriel was given her own detachment of Paladins to command over and a given special assignment by Kyzus. The war was indeed having its desired consequences; breeding pain, treachery, and suffering all across Terratopia. But there were the beginnings of new developments happening that Kyzus had not foreseen and that the nature of which could potentially be detrimental to his plan.

The current situation across Terratopia was the perfect fertile landscape that Morur's Evil spirit needed for his soul to penetrate all beings that would welcome it. This was of course a good thing, for the short term, in Kyzus's eyes as it would empower the peoples of Terratopia to purse the very worse their state of nature had to offer, for all its horrors to be seen and experienced by all. But a consequence of Morur's increased Evil presence and power in Terratopia that Kyzus did not foresee, nor welcome was Morur's creation of warlocks and witches across the kingdoms of Terratopia. These Evil sorcerers served only Morur personally and created intolerable, gruesome, evil beasts thanks to Morur's teachings. These Evil magical practitioners and their creations of different Colossuses and Tyrants, neither loyal to the Unionists, the Liberalists or to Mia-Myzus's empire but instead devoted to Morur and pure Evil, were a problem. They had to potential to interfere and maybe even ruin Kyzus's grand plan if they grew powerful enough and their Evil concoctions grew large enough in number. It was these upsets to Kyzus's plan that were Barriel's and her detachment of Paladins special assignment. Barriel was tasked to hunt down and kill every Colossus, Tyrant, warlock, and witch throughout Terratopia. Which, over the course of the entire civil war, Barriel did; herself and her Paladins keeping any Evil magical partitioning well under control as well as the numbers of Colossuses and Tyrants throughout Terratopia to insignificant amounts, their impacts on the wider archipelago being insignificant as well.

Chapter 11

Kyzus and Mia-Myzus

A whole year had passed in the kingdom of Sabare since the revolution and the Samson Daiv was embracing his rule under the command of his wife Delilah. Sabare had changed much since its insurgency take over and Daiv being crowned the new chieftain. The warrior like culture of the kingdom had snowballed to even higher intensities as the ways of old were replaced with the new. Goliaths and Samsons now fully embraced the war effort that spread across the Terratopia. Clans and brotherhoods of terrifying warriors set themselves up and sold themselves off as elite mercenary armies to any kingdom that was highest bidder; every inhabitant within Sabare either went off to into Terratopia to join the war or they pledged themselves to Daiv's own personal army, which itself became the muscle of Delilah's crime empire. Life in Sabare became far more rough and unforgiving as well. A mentality of 'only the strongest shall survive' spread like wild fire across the minds of the kingdom's inhabitants. And it was Daiv who decreed this to be the case. The civilised ways of old were all but forgotten as the innate love of laughter and play within every Samson and Goliath was steered to a brutish love of warrior proses, combat, and war. Fighting was common place in the streets as well as the total disobedience of the old law. The new law of the land was that 'the strongest shall have the all that they could fight over and manage to keep'. All was 'fair' game. It was everything Daiv's inner extremism had envisioned. The weak within his kingdom were no more as they all either departed shamefully or were killed and the strong only grew stronger. The weak and lucky had gradually been weeded out. Daiv's duel with Turberus was so monumental, his abilities seemingly unnatural, that the kingdoms inhabitants held nothing but total respect and total fear for and of him; his authority and the following under his allegiance was absolute as he was clearly the strongest of them all, undeniably. None questioned it.

Mia-Myzus had executed her plan perfectly with Daiv, firstly with him as her puppet and secondly with him as her devoted husband. Sabare was indeed transformed into the capital of her crime empire and the whole of Terratopia knew it. Her empires reach was near limitless, its resources seemingly unending and its control outright tyrannical. Mia-Myzus's domination over the crime syndicates in Eastern and Central Terratopia, as well as over Thruck's trading authority and her partnership the Dwarves, all interconnected with Rox's caravans and backed up with the legendary might of a militarised Sabare made herself the most powerful Queen in all of Terratopia, a queen that ruled from the shadows, her existence being no more than a rumour to most. The vast majority of Terratopia was effectively at the command of her will and Mia-Myzus utilised this to the fullest extent.

Mia-Myzus made sure crime flourished across the lands, making Terratopia a truly miserable, helpless place for all that inhabited it, the ongoing civil war only added to the misery. Mia-Myzus, under her guise of Delilah also made her crime empires resources and supply available to the Unionists and Liberalists, as both sides inevitably turned to her underworld empire in an effort to one up each other. In just the span of one year, Mia-Myzus's own personal wealth had grown to an unfathomable level , there was literally nothing that she could not do with her truly insane amounts of wealth and control. This position, accompanied by the fact she was married to the husband of her dreams meant that soon Mia-Myzus truly felt she couldn't be happier, despite the unsustainable pain and suffering her happiness was built upon.

Due to the nature of the position Mia-Myzus had reached, the daughter of Kyzus Hobbes began to fundamentally change as a person. Her oaths to her father's plan began to slip to the back of her mind as she no longer felt she needed to fulfil them; she was already happier and more complete than she ever could imagine. Mia-Myzus, in her close relationship to Daiv, had also built up an incredibly strong bond to his kingdom and to the Goliath and Samson races. She grew even more enthralled with the new fanatic and radical culture they all adopted and began to buy into it, truly believing in it. Mia-Myzus began to maintain that not only should the strong survive but that ONLY the strongest should survive and that the very strongest should reap the rewards at the expense all others. Being the most powerful Queen in all of Terratopia, Mia-Myzus truly indulged this belief and her continual snowballing of power only solidified her new supremacist outlook on life and rule.

Mia-Myzus began to feel the strongest temptations of power. She desired more and more of it, the more she gained, the more it corrupted her. The daughter of Hobbes began to relish in the pain and suffering she caused to the wider peoples in Terratopia. She savoured it as it meant the more the peoples suffered, the more powerful she became, the more powerful she became, the more she desired nothing more than to escalate the anguish to grow her power further. This was only made worst by Daiv's radicalism mentality that she brought into. Those who suffered from her empire where the weak anyway, she was the strong. They 'deserved' to suffer and she 'deserved' to reap the rewards of it. She had worked hard to gain this power since she was six years old. It wasn't unfair. It was right. Mia-Myzus was truly starting to choose the path of Evil, her choices only encouraged by her husband who too enjoyed reaping the rewards of his loving wife's power. Morur's evil spirit was taking a hold of her soul and she continually chose to allow it, fully well knowing it was happening and welcoming its tight corrupting embrace.

During this time, Kyzus was sensing his daughters fall to Morur's ways and when it seemed that she truly would not rebuke her path of Evil, he attempted to intervein. He commanded to speak to her on her seeing stone but Mia-Myzus continually refused to acknowledge this, ignoring all attempts Kyzus made to talk to her. This however would not stop Kyzus who was determined to not only see his plan fulfilled for the benefit of all peoples for all time, but also to not allow his daughter to fully fall to Morur and choose a life of Evil, he loved his daughter and wanted her to stay by his side.

One fateful day, Mia-Myzus perched next to Daiv on his luxurious throne within Sabare. The lavish seat sat perfectly central on a raised platform at the very end of the chieftain's hall, the largest building inside the chieftain's compound. It was constructed out of fine polished bones and fur from previously hunted wild and monstrous predatory animals like bears and wolves. The tall wooden structure of the hall, with a base of stone that housed this throne was heavily guarded with Samson and Goliath guards that were positioned all around and inside it. It was right here that Kyzus made his appearance to his daughter.

It was around mid-day, just after the mid-day bells had sounded throughout the kingdom, that Kyzus teleported into the chieftain's hall. Appearing in a spiralling swish of mystical grey clouds right in the centre of the hall. Instantly the guards already in the hall charged menacingly at the mysterious intruder, but as the manifested being rose up and waved his hand non-saliently, the charging guards all magically flew backwards and smashed into the wooden walls behind them with such speed and force that they fell unconscious and splintered greatly the formidable timber.

After seeing this, Daiv and Mia-Myzus started at the dark grey robed hooded sorcerer that stood before them in concerned surprise. Kyzus then removed his large hood, revealing his face to the husband-and-wife rulers. Mia-Myzus instantly jumped to her feet in worry and annoyance.

"Father?" she exclaimed. "What are you doing here?"

Daiv looked at Mia-Myzus in surprise. "Father?" he questioned. "Delilah? This is your father?"

"What am I doing here?" Kyzus boomed in a mocking manner, his unique powerful echoing voices emanating throughout the hall. "You don't call and you don't respond to my summoning. How else am I meant to be able to speak to my daughter?"

"Maybe I don't want to speak to you father. Did you consider that?" Mia-Myzus shouted back.

"Come now daughter," Kyzus replied, his tone seemingly talking down to her as if she was only a small child. "You haven't forgotten your vows you took to me all those years ago, have you?"

Mia-Myzus snarled back at Kyzus, refusing to answer as

the eerie green mystical mist seeped from her upon the vows mentioning.

"What vows?" Daiv questioned. "What is happening? What is that?" Daiv shouted as he noticed the jade like fog clouding around his wife.

"Yes 'Delilah' what vows?" Kyzus boomed. "Have you not told your boyfriend why you are doing this?"

"What is this old man talking about Delilah?" Daiv demanded, angered by the intruder's audacity.

"My daughter is under oath to be under my command you brute. But she obviously hasn't told you that yet." Kyzus said in an insulting tone to Daiv before then looking at Mia-Myzus to speak; "Don't you forget your place daughter. Everything you are today and everything you have accomplished is thanks to me and don't you forget it!"

Mia-Myzus continued to stare intently at her father. Furious at every word that came out of his mouth.

"I laid this path you walk down daughter; I placed each and every stone slab you step upon, I built you up, I even taught you the correct way to walk it and I still continue to lay it out before you to this day!" Kyzus again then boomed.

Mia-Myzus's rage boiled inside of her, furious at her farther and despising how weak he made her feel.

Suddenly the doors to the large hall burst open and three Goliath guards rushed in.

"My chieftain!" one of them cried as all three of them hurtled towards the robed intruder that stood before the throne.

Kyzus continued to stare intently at Mia-Myzus and began to smile. As the Goliath guards neared him, Kyzus continued to stare at his daughter before then dodging out the way of all three of his attackers and their feeble attempts to strike him. Never breaking eye contact with Mia-Myzus for a moment and never dropping his smirk, Kyzus skilfully and easily avoided every attack thrown at him with speed and elegance before then magically gripping the three Goliaths. He raised them high up into the air and then violently crushed them with a magical compacting spell as he violently closed his fist. Daiv also rose to his feet at the sight of three of his kin being compressed into unrecognisable forms of their former selves and then further compacted into the size of small rocks; the haunting sounds of their bones crunching down under contorted metal armour a loathsome noise.

"Really daughter? These are the peoples you want to reside with?" Kyzus rumbled, again in a mocking manner as blood heavily began to drop from the disfigured balls of flesh and armour he held he in the air.

"ENOUGH!" Mia-Myzus roared leaping down from the thrones platform and smashing her presence right before her father, the sheer force of her magical leap cracking the stone beneath her and blowing Kyzus's robes wildly in a gale of wind. Although Kyzus himself stood firm and never so much as flinched. "I love them father. I love Daiv. I am happy here."

"Love?" Kyzus bellowed, laughing at the word. "No barbaric brute in this kingdom is worthy of the love or even to love no daughter of mine! But alas it is your life and I truly wish nothing more than for you to live it how you wish and to make yourself happy."

Mia-Myzus looked confusedly at her father, his semi-kind words not matching his stern tone or previous actions. As she stepped backwards however, Kyzus boomed his echoing voice one more;

"BUT! Happy as you may be here daughter, I will not lose you to Morur's Evil. You are making some very bad choices. VERY BAD CHOICES. No daughter of mine would ever choose Evil. I know that. I raised you better than that! Remember why you are doing what you are doing my dear. You have an oath to fulfil. An oath not for my own desires but for the benefits of all peoples for all time!"

The ferocity of Kyzus's proclamation shook Mia-Myzus to the ground and Daiv fell to his throne intimidated. Mia-Myzus slowly bowed her head in defeat, as the mist of her oath turned to fog and drowned her in it.

"What is it you have me do father?" Mia-Myzus mumbled, as she bowed to her knees.

"Excellent," Kyzus replied in a lower, more accepting but also ominous tone. "What you are doing here is perfect daughter, I am very proud of you. But do not lose yourself! You cannot! I will not have you fall to Evil and I will most certainly not have you betray my plan! Do not ever ignore me again!"

"Of course father," Mia-Myzus repented, again in a quiet, defeated tone.

"There is one more thing I need you to do as well daughter. The Kuk's Crime Clan has grown to an enormous size in the west. They all but control the underworld of Western Terratopia and have become a rival. A rival to your empire and a problem for my plan. See to it that this is no longer case." Kyzus said. His voice now being much calmer but still holding much authority.

With these as his parting words, Kyzus then lovingly placed his hand on his daughter head and stroked her cheek in a caring fatherly way. The powerful Half-elf then walked away, casting the teleportation spell over himself, and then spinning into nothingness, leaving only spiralling sparkling mist in his wake.

Chapter 12

The Journey Westward

Later that week Mia-Myzus along with Daiv travelled westward and sailed with some pirates from the Horn of Rodus with the Bane clan. The Bane clan were the latest brotherhood of Samsons and Goliaths from Sabare to hire themselves out for the war effort. They made for the city of Lendspen as the kingdom of Gweston had ordered their services, but they knew not for what end. Mia-Myzus and Daiv sailed with the Bane clan as they were seeking passage to Western Terratopia to seek out the Kuk's Crime Clan. There journey was long but uneventful. Both the Merpeople of Reeforiris and the Valkyries from the Sky Mountains of Terratopia were too preoccupied with the war effort to pay much, if any, attention to the small pirate fleet that sailed the long stretch of water from Rodus to Gweston.

Over this unnoteworthy journey however, Mia-Myzus's inner feelings turned to turmoil and rage. She was furious at her father. Furious that he had insulted her so much back in Sabare. Furious that he had insulted her husband as well. The most significant reason for her anger however was the fact she felt so embarrassed. So embarrassed, pathetic, and helpless. Mia-Myzus had always knew her father was powerful, but she had no idea to the true extent. Now that she had seen a glimpse of it, she was downright fearful of it. Fearful and filled with despair. Her father had not only been keeping much from all of his children, but increasing his own power significantly also. Kyzus's ability to teleport such incredible distances with seemingly little effort, as well as ability to dispel formidable Goliaths with the flick of his hands terrified Mia-Myzus, he was becoming all-powerful in her eyes. Mia-Myzus's rage and fear of Kyzus's actions soon also began to turn to jealously. Jealous of all the power he held over her. Jealous of the fact that not only did he control her, but that he could easily control her by force if he desired too. This turmoil building inside of Mia-Myzus caused her to plot. Mia-Myzus looked deep inside of herself, reflecting on her own position and power as well and how she could use it to get exactly what she wanted; to become the all-powerful Queen of her empire, answering to no one and having all she could ever desire. Having this, along with the eternal love of her husband would truly be all Mia-Myzus could ever want in her eyes, and so she schemed on how best to achieve it. She cared not for her farther nor his plan any longer.

Eventually however, the pirate's ships carrying their passengers of Goliaths and Samson arrived on the southern shores of the Gweston Bay. On their entry into the bay, they had all noticed a sea battle happening in the far horizon, just off the coast of Silvoud, it appeared to be several ships ladened with heavy cargo being bombarded from above by Valkyries. The pirates captain commented that this battle was more than likely the reason for their unusually peaceful journey, the wider surrounding kingdoms were too pre-occupied fighting each other to also try to fight piracy as well.

Mia-Myzus, Daiv, and the Bane clan all disembarked from the pirate's ships and made for the city of Lendspen that could be seen on top of the hill they all stood at the bottom of. The grand Elven city was a large grey stately looking gothic city that sat at the very end of the Lendspen Arm peninsula, atop of its high cliffs and overlooking the expansive sea Mia-Myzus's band had just sailed across. The Sky Mountains of Terratopia could also just be seen faintly in the distance, the huge floating islands hovering like sharp solid stationary clouds the size of mountains on the horizon.

By the end of the day, after many hours of hiking, the company of Samsons and Goliaths arrived at the gates of Lendspen. From there, they were all escourted through the grey, gothic style streets of the city to meet with the Elven lord of Gweston, Lord Gwasbeer. When arriving into Lord Gwasbeer's extravagant throne room, Mia-Myzus instantly recognised her brother Tyzus standing next to the Elf lord, them both dressed in fine tunics and wearing silky flowing capes. Quickly she hid behind Daiv and pulled him around to speak to him.

"I know that Half-elf next to Lord Gwasbeer," Mia-Myzus whispered.

"My my, is there anyone in this world you don't know Delilah," Daiv teased.

Mia-Myzus looked longingly at Daiv, lovingly assumed by his sarcasm but still trying to remain serious.

"I'm serious my love, this could be a problem, he's met me before in Embirith. He is Tyzus, the leader of the Liberalists and he thinks I'm married to some high Elf from Filnethias!" Mia-Myzus said, raising her voice slightly but still whispering.

"Well... are you?" Daiv replied.

"No, no! Of course not." Mia-Myzus laughed back.

"Then all's good, you have nothing to fear then, so what if this dude recognises you, you're my wife now and a Queen! Simple as that," Daiv lovingly explained.

"Yeah. Yeah, you're right! Sorry, I'm just overthinking and worrying a lot right now," Mia-Myzus explained.

"That's all right my love," Daiv replied. "I understand. But now don't you worry we'll be on our way to the Kuk's in no time."

Daiv and Mia-Myzus then turned around and faced Lord Gwasbeer and Tyzus who both in turn turned from their own conversation they were having among themselves to face the band of warrior Samsons and Goliaths.

"Welcome! Umm the Bane clan wasn't it?" Lord Gwasbeer said, gesturing his arms outwards. "We have a task we need you to fulfil."

"What is it how have us do?" the leader of the Bane clan replied.

"We need you to venture along with our masons to the Harpgar Mountains and protect them as they try to retrieve stone from there" Tyzus stepped forward and explained.

Daiv laughed. "You paid for the greatest warriors in all the land to babysit stone masons for you?"

"Oversimplification of things but yes," Tyzus replied in a serious tone.

"Can you not handle a few ruffians out in the wilderness? No wonder the Liberalists can't seem to take Cufle!" Daiv roared in laughter, a commonly known fact that had become an assuming joke to the inhabitants of Sabare.

Tyzus, unamused, sternly replied; "The problems you shall face on your 'babysitting' task will be far worse than what you can handle I promise you that, but I figured better someone else's men than my own."

This angered Daiv who, believing his people to be far superior to any Liberalist Elf, stormed right up to Tyzus towering over him, the Half-elf squared back, showing no intimidation, almost eager for a fight.

"Oh you don't want to do that my Samson friend," Tyzus confidently said in a cordial manner.

"Try me." Daiv snapped back, clutching his twin bladed sword.

Tyzus shrugged his shoulders, gripping tightly onto his own blade holstered by his side. Seeing the rising tensions, Mia-Myzus butted in-between them both quick shouting;

"Whoaw Whoaw Whoaw! This seems a bit unnecessary doesn't it?"

Daiv stepped back but Tyzus starred confusingly at the high Elf that had just butted in front of him.

"Do I know you? I swear I seen you before. I never forget a beautiful face." Tyzus said.

These flirtatious words annoyed Daiv who stepped back towards Tyzus again. Mia-Myzus outstretched her hand to stop Daiv and then turned to face Tyzus to speak.

"Yes, indeed you have. We met in Embirith before the war started."

Tyzus slapped his hands together, in excitement. "I knew I seen you from somewhere! Hang on wait a minute, weren't you married to some Unionist? What are you doing with these brutes?"

Daiv once again barged right up to Tyzus grunting "watch it Liberalist!" as Tyzus assumedly smirked back, squaring out his shoulders.

Mia-Myzus once again squeezed in-between them both in an attempt to keep matters civilised.

"Yes. Yes I was. But I couldn't stay married to some Unionist scum," Mia-Myzus then said.

Tyzus smiled approvingly before Mia-Myzus then continued;

"But this brute is my new husband and I really don't want to be responsible for the death of the great Tyzus, so please let us just get on our way."

"New husband?" Tyzus questioned, his expression sulking slightly. "And what makes you so sure I'd die? How about a duel for your hand oh beautiful Delilah, after all, I am the leader of the Liberalists and a son of Kyzus Hobbes. Surely me over some brute from the east" Tyzus then said with a smirk and a wink, outstretching his hand in a princely manner.

Daiv again barged up to Tyzus and rose his weapon above his head in anger. Tyzus quickly retracted his hand, threw his cape over Daiv's face, and then flipped away, drawing his own weapon as he elegantly landed and smiled at the development. But Mia-Myzus quickly stood in-between them both once again and shouted;

"As entertaining as that would be! We really must be going. Besides Tyzus. I actually love this so-called brute. So please, a Half-elf of your stature can surely respect that."

Tyzus lowered his blade, stood up fully and bowed his head at Mia-Myzus. "Of course my lady. May I wish you well on your travels. You know where to find me if you ever change your mind" he finished with a wink and he re-sheaved his blade.

As Tyzus finished speaking, Lord Gwasbeer spoke again, gesturing towards two Elven guards; "These two guards will show you to the masons and their wagons. Should you return with these wagons filled with stone you will be paid most generously? Now be gone!"

The leader of the Bane clan wasn't happy with this though. "No, you pay us now!" he shouted adamantly. Gwasbeer rolled his eyes and mumbled something under his breath no one could hear. He then ordered the guards to stop by the supply depot and gift the bane clan three barrels of ale as a down payment. The guards nodded and began to walk away with a now cheerful Bane clan all jeering to one another, which caused Gwasbeer to roll his eyes even more.

Mia-Myzus, Daiv and the Bane clan all then followed the Elf

guards out of the lofty palace with tall thin pointed towers that they were in into the streets of the grey gothic city once again. Not long after, the band, with their barrels of ale, arrived at the masons and their wagons. After fully learning of their task and of the details from the head stone mason, it was agreed by both parties that they would head for the Harpgar Mountains the next morning. The stone masons headed indoors to rest up for the night while the Bane clan and Daiv bust open their barrels of ale and got as drunk as they could.

During the night Mia-Myzus had other plans however. She travelled the dim dingy streets of Lendspen in an attempt to locate any Kuk's activities and sure enough she did. Wandering through the streets alone at night, Mia-Myzus soon attracted the attention of shady hooded figures that began to tail her. Mia-Myzus noticed this and led them into a dark, narrow alleyway between two tall stone houses. Once seemingly trapped by the hooded figures, Mia-Myzus lit blue flames in her hands that illuminated her smirking face and the alley around her. A voice then could be heard from behind the hooded figures that posed in front of Mia-Myzus.

"Back away!" the voice shouted. "I've met this witch before! Back away now!"

Mia-Myzus faintly recognised the voice and so leapt out of the alleyway, over the hooded figures and into the street. There in the street she saw another hooded figure, but this one had a slightly different silhouette as in place of his right hand was the distinct shape of a metal hook. The figure in the street lowered his hood revealing his face which was lit up by Mia-Myzus's magical blue flames in her palms. Mia-Myzus recognised the man's face instantly, it was the same man she had previously cut the hand off back in Embirith before she had ever travelled east.

"Very brave of you to come here alone miss," the man exclaimed. You're in Western Terratopia now! This is Kuk's territory."

"Oh I know" Mia-Myzus replied assuredly. "I'm here looking for you actually."

"Me?" the man said surprisingly as his fellow hooded men surrounded all around Mia-Myzus.

"Yeah. You see I'm looking for your bosses,"

"My bosses!" the man laughed out loud. "There is no chance they'd ever meet with the likes of you!" he exclaimed. "Unless of course you where their slave girl, which I can easily arrange for you."

"Don't you know who I am?" Mia-Myzus then shouted, bursting her blue flames to much larger intensities. "I am the Queen Dalilah of the Delilah Crime Empire. Your bosses should be honoured I seek their audience."

"I really don't care who you claim to be Elf. There is no chance they'd ever want to meet with the scum likes of you. Unless of course in chains and on your knees!" the man replied harshly.

Mia-Myzus sighed in annoyance. She then exploded her blue flames around her, knocking the surrounding hooded figures away and setting their cloaks and their faces alight. Mia-Myzus then instantly rushed towards the man with one hand and sliced his other hand clean off. The now handless man dropped to his knees in pain screaming.

"If that's going to be the case then please tell me where I may find them myself to pay them a visit."

The handless man looked up at Mia-Myzus and spat at her with all his hatred. Mia-Myzus rolled her eyes in disgust and drew her knife. The man only smiled, still refusing to talk so Mia-Myzus then promptly slit his throat and kicked his dead body away in annoyance and disgust as it fell onto her feet. She then walked over to one of the other hooded figures who was on the ground, clutching his burnt faces and rolling around to put his blazing cloak out. Mia-Myzus sliced the burning cloak off the man and then picked him up by the hair.

"Now please tell me where I can find you bosses. I'm really tired and really don't want to do this all night." Mia-Myzus said, her tone being totally unemotional and disingenuous.

"Our headquarters in is the ruined city of the Giants please, please let me go!" the man whimpered.

Mia-Myzus smiled and then dropped the man, proceeding to then wander back to the masons and her brethren that slept passed out on the wagons.

Chapter 13
Delilah and the Kuk's Crime Clan

Morning arrived the next day and so Mia-Myzus, Daiv, the Blane clan, and the stone masons all departed from Lendspen on their journey towards the Harpgar Mountains. During this journey, they all passed Jassett's partially constructed building site. The truly enormous structure had its monumental wooden skeleton completely erected but the laying of its stone body had barely been a quarter done. Elves and Men collectively scattered the construction site, covering all areas of the wooden frame with scaffolding and working tirelessly, placing huge formidable stones and slowly creating the soon to be impressive oversized fortress.

The Samsons and Goliaths starred in wonder and awe at the impressive building site whom were all amazed at the sheer magnitude of the military monument being created, despite it being but a shadow of its final form. Daiv was stupefied by the colossus fortress being built by the Liberalists, the vast size of the inner keep and towers put his own entire kingdom of Sabare walls to shame and he grew jealous. He underhandedly whispered to Mia-Myzus that he wished to transform Sabare's walls and defences into a behemoth structure, similar to Jassett but Mia-Myzus quickly rebuked this. She pointed out how long, arduous, and dangerous the construction of such a project would be, highlighting the substantial loss of life and suffering the building of Jassett had already caused the Liberalist's. Mia-Myzus then also proclaimed to Daiv how much of a waste Jassett was, belittling it to no more than an oversized, glorified castle in the heart of Liberalist territory filled with weak warriors. Mia-Myzus explained how Jassett served no purpose to the Liberalists other than a statement of might as it would never actually be attacked being so deep in Gweston. To Mia-Myzus, Jassett was more a project to fulfil the insecure, oversized egos of the Liberalist leadership. Daiv was amused tremendously from Mia-Myzus's analogy of Jassett and claimed that if it was true, then

Sabare required no such thing as its warriors were mighty, its defences at the forefront of its borders and its name a powerful enough statement in itself; its name resembling the capital of an underworld empire where only the strongest survived and the most powerful thrived.

It was during this time that Mia-Myzus explained to Daiv her new found knowledge regarding the whereabouts of the Kuk's Crime Clan bosses and they together plotted a way to visit them. Daiv wished for them to venture to the Giants Lands, along with the Blane clan, reasoning how pointless and insulting their task from Tyzus was anyway and so should just be abandoned. But Mia-Myzus disagreed, explaining how there was no need to venture with such a force. The Kuk's Crime Clan were indeed the most powerful underworld faction in Western Terratopia, but Mia-Myzus made clear that this was only down to a clear lack of any rivals or opposition to them, the Kuk's were not a mighty force to be reckoned with but rather a misfit gathering of the worst scum and villainy Terratopia had to offer and nothing more. Western Terratopia was only filled with lesser kingdoms of Men or Elves, there were no inherently mighty races since the extinction of the Giants besides the Dwarves or Great Owls but they resided only in their mountain homes. As a result the Kuk's strength was a glorified illusion due to the nature of the weak western kingdoms it infiltrated and inhabited. Mia-Myzus also reasoned that it would be useful for her and Daiv to see how the Blane clan handled the threats from the Harpgar Mountains, believing that they were likely hired due to troubles with the Great Owls that lived there. If the Bane clan were successful in their stone gathering task, then Mia-Myzus believed that perhaps the Great Owls weren't as fearful as a force as she had been led to believe from her early teachings under Kyzus and she wished to see if these stories were true or not.

Alas when the travelling company finally reached the Harpgar Mountains many days later, having crossed the miles and miles of flood plains within Gweston, they camped for the night on its foothills to prepare to start quarrying the next day. The curiosities posed by Mia-Myzus were soon answered no long after, although not to Daiv's likening. During twilight, Daiv and Mia-Myzus watched from afar as ginormous monstrous flying feathered beasts elegantly and silently descended from the clouds that covered the mountain peaks and completely obliterated the company of Goliaths, Samsons, and Lendspen's stone masons. The skirmish was a terrific horror scene to be witnessed by Daiv and Mia-Myzus from a distance; the bright fiery yellow and orange eyes of the Great Owls pierced through the evening dusk and their deadly beaks and talons were only illuminated by flickering torch light when it was too late for them to be avoided. In far too quickly of a time, not a single member of the masons or Bane clan survived, they all lay dead; scattered across the mountain foothills before the dark of night had even fully descended.

Mia-Myzus was slightly disheartened but mostly intrigued with the slaughter that had just transpired before her, the Great Owls had indeed lived up to their legend in her eyes. The infamous birds were perfectly beautiful, elegant, and silent but also truly deadly adversaries. Daiv was less enthusiastic about what he had just witnessed however. Watching his kin be killed so effortlessly wasn't pleasant and Daiv wished he had been able to help but he knew he never would have been able to do so. These feelings soon passed anyway as he came to reason that the Bane clan obviously weren't strong enough. They weren't worthy enough. They clearly weren't good enough as if they were truly strong, they would have survived. They were weak and Daiv was glad they were now gone.

After watching the Great Owls attack, Mia-Myzus and Daiv journeyed northward, travelling along the foothills of the Harpgar Mountains but making sure they never set foot into them. Mia-Myzus made sure of it as she had spotted several Griffins begin to slyly tail her and Daiv, likely making sure that they did not step foot into the Great Owls home. The couple eventually passed around the formidable mountains, squeezing between them and the woodland borders of the Silver Wood; from there it was a straight clear journey towards the Stepping Hills and the Giant Lands beyond them.

Several days later, after wandering through the empty landscape, still littered with old rusting weapons and fragile skeletal remains from the War for the sake of Thyzus, Mia-Myzus and Daiv arrived at the ruined City of Giants. They noted that for a land meant to be desolate and destroyed by a previous war, there was sure a lot of activity and this could not be more true than for the ruined, supposedly abandoned, former capital of the Giants. The two leaders of Sabare entered into the ginormous ruined city and wandered its busy but massively overly sized grim streets that dwarfed the size of the grand city avenues found in Embirith. The former city of Giants made Mia-Myzus and Daiv feel like mice due to its sheer size, despite it being in ruins. But the city was an awful sorry place to be however. The ground underfoot was all upturned and horrifically muddy. The humungous ruined buildings were haphazardly and partially repaired with timber, rope and, fabric creating much smaller shanty dwellings and slums within them. The occupants of the city were dingy, grubby, and squalid. Mia-Myzus was correct, this wretched headquarters of the Kuk's was a pitiful hub of an all manner of smugglers, gangsters, bounty hunters, scum, and villainy and it made Daiv sick with disgust.

"These people are the supposed to be a rival to your immaculate criminal empire? To my kingdom?" Daiv questioned with distaste.

"These people? No. No not at all. But what the Kuk's stand for is. These are a pathetic gathering of low lives not good enough to make it in my criminal empire. And so they ran from it. To here. The Kuk's is a refuge for the weak pretending to be strong," answered Mia-Myzus in assured distain.

"Ah I see," Daiv said with further disgust. "These are the weak that refuse to die off. Disgusting. But how does that make them rivals?"

"Because they stand against me. Against us. Against the strong. They flee, run, and hide in an attempt to survive because that's what the weak who survive do and because of that, the Kuk's will thrive. The weak will survive until they are stopped. The Kuk's also control the underworld in Western Terratopia and we cannot be having that! My empire should span the whole of this archipelago!" Mia-Myzus replied.

"Agreed, so it should my love. Only the strong should survive and the strongest should thrive." Daiv then said.

"There is yet one more thing the Kuk's undergo that needs to be stopped as well." Mia-Myzus then said. "The Kuk's are a feeble collection of Men, a collection of racist Men insecure about their standings in the world, after all their race is not immortal, mighty, wise, or inheritably strong like all others. They falsely lie to themselves and believe that they are the superior race in this world because they are the 'eighth born' and that all others are inferiors beneath them. Because of that they are ruthless slavers. They distain any race besides their own and enslave all they can, believing themselves to be above them." Mia-Myzus's words were filled with distain and loathing as she said them. "They are the weak and they know it. But through slavery, they act and believe themselves to be the strong. They must be stopped."

Mia-Myzus's words filled Daiv with rage, his disgust turning to repulsion at the hypocritic nature of the Kuk's Crime Clan that Delilah told him off. It was now that Daiv also saw how rife the ruined city really was with slaves. Elves were in rags and tied up with chains and claps. Dwarves were on their knees working without rest for their masters. Centaurs were limping with pain due to the wounds and scabs on their legs and bodies and collapsing in the mud with exhaustion. Pixies and Fairies buzzed around in tiny cages hung over balconies and in windows, their magical dust being harvested by Men for sale. Starving Gnomes worked tirelessly in the streets cooking foods but never being allow to eat anything they created. The slaves were all pale skeletons driven to exhaustion and starvation. Their bodies were covered in cuts and blisters, their hair was overgrown and muddy and their clothing was nothing more than cheap dirty rags. And all of them were ruthlessly reprimanded by their whip wielding masters.

It was also now that Mia-Myzus and Daiv realised the hostile following they had attracted since first entering the city, being a high Elf and Samson wandering freely without a master. They both continually kept a grasp of their weapons, being ever vigilant for a fight, but one never came. Soon however a representative for the Kuk's Crime Clan bosses approached them and offered to escort both Mia-Myzus and Daiv to them, which Mia-Myzus happily accepted, full well knowing the likely trap they were walking into. Daiv and Mia-Myzus were led into the truly huge ruined city hall, originally where the Giant kings would have resided.

Suddenly a rattling of heavy-duty chains could be heard as huge metal cages dropped onto them both as they entered through the enormous pillared doorway. Daiv quickly attempted to lift the cage off him but Mia-Myzus stopped him, projecting her voice into his head telling him to stop and to instead wait and see what would happen next. This proved to be a good move by Mia-Myzus as soon five monstrously fat Men waddled towards the two caged beings, scoffing blubberingly as they approached. The five Men all dressed in fine clothes and wore much jewellery. But their clothes were horribly stained and ill-fitting over their obese bodies and their jewellery was covered in grimy grease that seemed to seep from the corpulent sweaty skin. They were a ghastly blubbery mess, their site being more alike to five overly sized, overfed fed, fat slugs than to five Men and their laughs were just as slimy and distasteful as their appearance.

Mia-Myzus had never been so disgusted in all her life as she judgementally looked the Kuk's bosses up and down. A wave of anger passed over her and she couldn't believe she was sent by her father to deal with what she saw as such pathetic wastes of life. Mia-Myzus felt unbelievably disappointed that the infamous bosses of the Kuk's were nothing more than a drooling, flabby mess of slugs and so didn't even believe they deserved to be spoken too or offered a place in her empire.

As soon as the five Kuk's bosses had slithered up to Mia-Myzus's and Daiv's cages, Mia-Myzus shot out her magical prowess. The Queen of a criminal empire magically gripped onto the cages that trapped herself and her husband and tripped them onto the five fat Men before they could begin to wobble out the way. As the large heavy metal traps fell onto the bosses, they all squealed like pigs before then being crushed beneath them. But alas, the Kuk's leaders were so inflated, their bodies so blubbery, that their flab cushioned the cages that fell a top them. They all wailed in pain and attempted to slither away but their fat bodies were too enormously cumbersome to allow it. They were pinned down and slowly being squashed by the cages that Mia-Myzus continued to magically press down on. As the fat slugs and pigs squealed, wailed, and bawled, Mia-Myzus screamed at them to shut up and then for Daiv to kill them all to silence them when they did not. Which the great Samson did with much pleasure, stabbing his blade into them all one by one and then cleaning it clean of their thick greasy blood on their clothes.

Chapter 14

Mia-Myzus's Ultimate Betrayal

Another two years passed and still Mia-Myzus resided next to her husband within Sabare. She continued to rule over her crime empire, that now spanned from the edges of Western Terratopia to Eastern Terratopia. There were still many various different mafias and criminal syndicates across the archipelago, but they all answered to her. Any brigade of marauders, bandits, or ruffians out in the wilderness also answered to Mia-Myzus in some way. Any pirates out sailing the seas surrounding her empire answered to Mia-Myzus too. Her control was indefinite and absolute. Many welcomed her rule as it brought nothing but success and power to the underworld. Many distained her rule, with some hating that they still answered to a master other than themselves. But all feared her rule. Mia-Myzus as the infamous Queen Delilah had struck total terror into the hearts of all her subordinates and as a result, struck undying loyalty in them all as well. None dared to rise up and oppose her and none dared to betray or double cross her, those ignorant few who ever did where quickly and brutally delt with, making further disloyalty from anyone even more unlikely.

The consequences of Delilah's Crime Empire for the peoples of Terratopia that were not members of her operation was nothing short of ultimate and supreme suffering. Mia-Myzus's hand of the underworld penetrated into all levels of society in all kingdoms. The acts of corruption, cronyism, blackmail, fraud, theft, kidnaping, looting, pillaging, ransoms, torture, murder, and a great many other terrible criminal acts flourished without impediment across Terratopia. Even slavery continued, despite the full replenishment of the Kuk's leadership although now slavery was not a manner of Men enslaving believing themselves to be superior, but a manner of the strongest enslaving the weak.

Mia-Myzus's control over Thruck, the co-operation with the Dwarves and her relationship with Rox's caravans meant that she also practically had authority over nearly all trade within Terratopia. The black market exploded and became the default resource for the wider kingdoms that were gripped in civil war. Terratopia had been driven to a point where its kingdoms practically relied upon the formidable criminal empire to maintain some degree of order within the war-torn lands. Without it, Terratopia would undoubtably fall into chaos and the kingdoms leaders knew it, pleading ignorant to the empires true size, scope, and power. Through the people's greed and temptation to become strong and powerful, they had empowered Mia-Myzus's criminal underworld to what it was. Mia-Myzus had skilfully created her underworld to become the new standard of ordered society where the peoples now relied on it to survive. The cost of this survival and small degree of order it brung was the terrible and horrific exploitation and suffering throughout all of Terratopia.

To Mia-Myzus's eyes, this was perfect. She had truly become the most powerful and influential leader in all of Terratopia. This empire wide unchecked control accompanied along with her Samson husband whom she had grown completely intoxicated by, meant that Mia-Myzus truly felt happy and complete as an individual, she couldn't care the less about how she got there, what it had cost and what it was built upon. Yet this fact only filled her with dread as she knew this could not and would not last, despite the fact she wanted it too till her dying day. Mia-Myzus was still bound to fulfil her oaths to her father and to the completion of his plan. She knew that the empire she had built up was all a part of Kyzus's plan but she also knew that at some point it would be brought down to make way for his own untied society, free of war and suffering and filled with happiness and prosperity. But Mia-Myzus no longer wanted this, she no longer wanted her father to complete his plan and bring about his 'perfect society' under 'the Deity'. Her own version of society under her shadowy queens' rule was already perfect in her eyes. Mia-Myzus wanted what she had right now and for that not to change until her dying day. For her to remain the beautiful, all-powerful, indominable Queen and for her to reap the rewards of being in such a strong position with her loving husband for the rest of her time. But Mia-Myzus knew that this could not be and that Kyzus would never allow it.

Mia-Myzus's dread not only came from the fact that she knew her current life was doomed to end, but fearful and ashamed of the fact that she could not do anything about it. She was meant to be the strongest but yet her father could end it all at any moment, or so she believed. Even now her vast criminal empire could not penetrate into Roccano despite her now attempting to. Kyzus had completely shut off his kingdom from Terratopia, it was free of crime, war, and suffering. Kyzus himself was also simply too powerful for even Mia-Myzus to stand up to. His true control over Terratopia itself also was a mystery to her as well as to the true extent of his magical ability; although the glimpses Mia-Myzus had seen were enough to assure her that Kyzus's ultimate power was nothing short of God-like. Kyzus could teleport across Terratopia, he could dispatch of Goliath guards with ease, he could even somehow sense Mia-Myzus's own inner thoughts and turmoil. Furthermore, Mia-Myzus knew there was more to Kyzus's seeing stones than he already revealed to her, she could sense the vast amounts of powerful, unnatural magical enchantments within them and she knew Kyzus was in total control over all of the stones and all the spells within them. It was because of this that Mia-Myzus rarely if ever touched her stone, instead keeping it wrapped up and hidden away, despite it always subtlety called to her.

Mia-Myzus's worries about what she did know about her father paled in comparison to the fears of what she did not know. There were a great many seeing stones within the hall, she had first saw them in and she only knew of the location of four of them, or maybe six, guessing her brothers both had one and held them within their capitals as well. Who else had Kyzus given them too? Where else had he placed them? What actually were the other spells locked within them? And the civil war effort he had orchestrated, Mia-Myzus's brothers were mere puppets governing both sides of the war to Kyzus's own liking. The kingdoms of the Terratopia were mere pawns in Kyzus game. But when would the war end? Where else would it spread? What more would it cost everyone? And how would it ultimately somehow transition into a perfect united society? These unknown, scary questions rattled around Mia-Myzus's mind, but none bothered her more than the question of who or what exactly was 'the Deity' Kyzus spoke off? What was he creating?

These issues remained in Mia-Myzus's mind for a whole year long period, prolonging greatly how long time actually seemed to drag on. During this time, Mia-Myzus answered to her father's every requested and utilised her vast criminal empire to benefit both her brothers, who mostly fought each other around Carlin and Lemlee, but her distain and hatred towards Kyzus's control over her only grew ever more. But when the time came of Tyzus's invasion into Rodus and Mia-Myzus being ordered to send him a huge vast quantity of support from her empire as well as armies of Samson and Goliath mercenaries to Tyzus and Hyzus to utilise, her hatred finally snapped. Mia-Myzus could up hold her oaths to her father and his plan no longer.

Mia-Myzus was sitting casually in Daiv's throne with her seeing stone in her hand when she was given her instructs from Kyzus regarding aiding Tyzus's invasion of Rodus. After receiving Kyzus's instructions, Mia-Myzus felt her hatred towards her father snap. She agreed to Kyzus's orders apathetically but as soon as he terminated the connection to Mia-Myzus, she rose up from her lounging position on Daiv's throne and launched the seeing stone she held as far away from her as she could, letting out a terrifying, scathing scream of rage as she did. The seeing stone soared through the chieftain's hall and then passed through the wooden walls, continuing to hurtle to the very edge of the chieftain's compound. Daiv, who had saw the seeing stone fly through his halls wall and over his head and who had also heard his wife deathening scream, rushing into the hall to see if Mia-Myzus was all right. But as the Samson chieftain burst through the doors of his hall, he saw a truly alarming sight.

Mia-Myzus was magically levitating above his throne, her arms outstretched like a crucifix. A ghastly blue, purple and yellow fire swirled all around her like a thick cloud and it continued to grow larger as its flames were being produced from the outstretched palms of the terrifying T-shaped high Elf sorcerer. Mia-Myzus's body burned bright, emanating an orange hue and her eyes had exploded wide into burning blue fireballs. Her hair floated menacingly all around her head and transformed slowly into a rich jet-black colouration, becoming long wavy ebony vines attached to her scalp. All this time Mia-Myzus was letting out a painful, yet almighty screech at the top of her lungs with her mouth wide open and tongue sticking out. Daiv's throne beneath her rattled tremendously and loose paraphernalia around the hall started to levitate and swirl around the hall at an increasingly faster and faster pace.

Daiv stood in shock, admiration, and fear at the sight of his wife in such a powerful state. He called out;

"DELILAH! What has happened?"

Mia-Myzus replied in an unearthly deep beckoning voice;

"I forsake my vows to my father! I can take it no longer! I am the most powerful Queen in all of Terratopia's history and I will keep it that way! All will tremble and bow before me! All will suffer beneath my fist! None shall oppose me and my magical might! I am the Queen of all of Terratopia! Not of an underworld empire! I relinquish my oaths! I shall and will serve no one but myself and I will stop at nothing until I am the undisputed Queen over all of Terratopia!"

A thick bloom of black smoke erupted from Mia-Myzus as she said this in a deathening boom; the magical oath within her exploding in dismay and Daiv dropped to one knee and bowed his head. Nothing but pride passed over him and a sinister grin spanned across his face.

"Yes my love, oh most stupendous Queen Delilah of Terratopia!" Daiv boisterously shouted. "How can my kingdom and I be of service?"

Mia-Myzus dropped out the sky from her position, the fires surrounding her dispelling and the flying objects around the hall dropping to the floor loudly. The self-proclaimed Queen of Terratopia waltzed up to her menacing, smirking kneeling husband. She still gave off a potent orange hue from her body but somehow also glowed an eery blue silhouette as well. Blue fireballs still burned in her eye sockets but their intensity had faded much. Mia-Myzus placed her dedicate yet powerful hand under Daiv's chin and lifted him up gently till he stood fully up and towered above her. As Daiv starred down at Mia-Myzus, her blue fireball eyes slowly burned out and formed back to their normal appearance but then gradually and sinisterly they turned to a totally black and cold colouration, like windows into the Void. Then Mia-Myzus's irises slowly appeared back but in a fiery blue ball. Daiv had never seen such dire, daunting, yet dazzling eyes, Mia-Myzus's pupils and conjunctiva were a black and unforgiving void but her irises shone a bright, esoteric, beryl blue.

"You will and your kin help me take over this world," Mia-Myzus then said to Daiv and then she began to maniacally laugh in the most psychotic evil tone she had ever done and soon Daiv joined in with her, fully embracing the new truly Evil path they had both chose to run down.

* * *

Kyzus meanwhile, floating peacefully above the steps leading up to his palace, was hoovering in a meditative state with his legs crossed when suddenly he sensed a tremendous disturbance, and felt as if he had just been punched in the heart. The ancient Half-elf dropped clumsily and uncontrollably onto the steps beneath him and tumble down them. Kyzus knew exactly what had just happened. His worst fears had come true. His beloved daughter had been fully corrupted by her position and had given into Morur's spirit, fully accepting Morur's soul into her own. She had relinquished her vows to him.

Kyzus stopped his tumble down his grand palace steps and then proceeded to levitate up high into the sky. Kyzus rose higher and higher gaining faster acceleration the higher he went, so high that he acceded fully above the clouds and could no longer see the kingdom of Roccano beneath him. Once at this height, the great powerful Half-elf suddenly stopped and floated stationary and peacefully, listening to the sharp cool winds. Slowly a single tear developed in his right eye and then began to trickle down his face. As the tear dripped away from his cheek, Kyzus let out an awful desperate roar and shot an intense thunderous lightning bolt from his hands into the clouds below him. Tears then continually started to build up in Kyzus's eyes and then began to fall from them as well. The Half-elf of unmatched power, glory and wisdom felt tremendously lost and upset and began to uncontrollably cry for the first time since his wife Robin had died, feeling a similar way to then as well. In pain and grief Kyzus burst out a devastating howl and the tears he produced began to become so large and numerous that they formed a waterfall from his eyes. Kyzus then shot lighting once again at this waterfall of tears, disappearing it into rain.

Down below, in the city of Roccano, the inhabitants began to feel rain drip onto their heads before they then looked up to see that a sad grey gloomy storm had developed and was beginning to pour down on them. The storm was not violent, no lighting struck the kingdom and no deadly winds ravaged across the city streets. Instead, it was only rain, sad, heavy but gentle rain that fell straight downwards and never changed in intensity. The storm continued for many days, its thunder and lightning becoming a calm but brooding ambient noise for the kingdom's inhabitants and its rains cold but inconsequential.

Finally, one day the storm lamented, stopping as suddenly as it begun. It was on this day that Kyzus emerged in the kingdom once more and summoned Barriel and her Paladin's detachment to the Ruling Castle. Barriel and her Paladins made their way through the courtyard before suddenly being halted by Kyzus's foreboding command. They saw him up in the Regulatory Balcony, and noticed how hunched, saddened, and defeated he looked. None of them had ever seen Kyzus in such a state before and felt terribly uncomfortable at the sight.

"My truly loyal subjects. Over this war you have given me nothing but success and aided with my plans greatly. For that I am grateful." Kyzus said in a strong yet pessimistic manner. "Barriel, you have been like a daughter to me and risen to become as formidable as my own Mia-Myzus was before she left me. Your loyalty and devotion to my plan has been exceptional. You and your men have delt with the deadliest of sorcerers and monsters over the years and helped keep my plan on track."

Barriel and her Paladins looked at one another, slightly confused with Kyzus's kind words but sombre tone.

"BUT! I have been betrayed. I have been betrayed and it breaks my heart." Kyzus continued, in the same pessimistic but now also stern tone. "BUT AGAIN! More importantly this betrayal may stand in the way of my plan. I need you to solve this issue. Nothing must stand in the way of my plan! Nothing! NOTHING! And I can think of no better alternative to solve this betrayal, other than myself, than sending you."

Barriel and her Paladins again looked at one another restlessly. Only they knew of Kyzus's plan. He had shared it with them upon their creation into their special detachment. They were eager to help Kyzus, and even more eager to make the traitor pay. Whoever they would be.

"Of course, my Lordbaron!" Barriel replied. "Who is the one who's broken your heart so, betrayed you, and now stands in the way of your plan?"

Kyzus steadily looked up from his hunched position to make eye contact with the collection of fearsome Paladins beneath him; "The Crime Queen Delilah..."

Part III
The Deity

Chapter 1

The Plan Will Prevail

Kyzus, from the stone Regulatory Balcony he stood on high up from the ground, watched on as Barriel and her Paladins left the Ruling Castle's courtyard to leave on their journey to Sabare. Watching the last Paladin leave his sight was like watching the coffin close shut on his daughter. Kyzus truly did love his daughter with all his heart, especially since he had practically raised her alone since she was a small child. He had raised her, tutored her, and rigorously transformed her into the accomplished Half-elf she was today. Wise and cunning; strong and formidable; powerful and dominate. Mia-Myzus's intelligence, fighting skills, and magical prowess was second to none, believed Kyzus; he alone being the only one truly able to outmatch her. He was so proud, Mia-Myzus truly was all he could have ever dreamt of for a daughter. But. She had forsaken him.

Kyzus couldn't help but blame himself for putting Mia-Myzus in the position she was in and leading her down the path she was on. He believed now that he could have better prepared her to not be so tempted and corrupted by her position. He alone designed and orchestrated Mia-Myzus's actions to a large extent and trusted she was strong enough to rise above the role she played, for the benefit of his grand plan. But he was clearly wrong however. Kyzus had underestimated his daughters' independent desires as well as underestimated the powerful affects her role had on her, in addition to her unexpected, undying love for her extremist, radical, supremacist Samson love.

Still, Kyzus reasoned to himself, Mia-Myzus had chosen her path and as difficult as it was for Kyzus, he could not risk the delicate, intricate balance of his plan for the sake of attempting to save his daughter from herself. Like he had been justifying all this time, his grand plan was for the benefit of all peoples for all time, he could not risk all the sacrifice, pain and, suffering it had caused so far because of his love for his daughter. The united society under the Deity was just more important. Besides, Kyzus's own position and standing in Terratopia made him incredibly powerful and yet he had not let it corrupt himself, and he'd stayed true without needing told or have chances to redeem himself, which is far more than what could be said for his daughter. So, as much as it hurt him, Kyzus knew that Mia-Myzus was gone, but the Evil Queen Delilah in her place needed to be delt with.

Delilah's crime empire was incredibly powerful and could disrupt the whole war effort to have disastrous consequences for Kyzus and his plan if the empire shifted from its current status quote. A possibility that was all too real now that it wasn't under his control. Delilah's empire needed to be brought back under his leash and Kyzus could think of no one better to attempt this task than his trusted right hand Barriel and her detachment. Barriel and her Paladins had become so good at what they did; killing off any and all of the warlocks, witches, Colossus's, and Tyrants in Terratopia, that she had earned herself the nickname of 'Kyzus's Unchained Wolf' and her detachment of Paladins the 'Wolfpack'. Tittles given by the peoples of Terratopia upon hearing of their accomplishments over the years of the civil war. Yet, as formidable Barriel and her Paladins were, Delilah and her Sabare subornments would be unlike any other foe they had ever faced before, and, although Kyzus had faith in Barriel's ability, he had afterall trained her himself, he still worried about her chances of success. But in a way Kyzus needed Barriel to deal with Delilah; as although he continually said that nothing could stand in the way of his plan, he felt like could not face his daughter. Not after she had forsaken him and forsaken herself.

With these heavy thoughts plaguing his mind, Kyzus returned to his mountainside palace to delve into his study in an attempt to distract himself. Afterall, Tyzus's Liberalist invasion of Rodus was soon to commence and its success would be the make or break of Kyzus's plan, so he needed to be ready.

Luckily though, several weeks later, Tyzus and Hyzus's clash at Embirith had accomplished all Kyzus could have wanted and more. It was a near perfect result for what Kyzus desired and it brought him much peace of mind, his plan may well come to floriation and he may well save Terratopia from its state of nature afterall.

For Tyzus and Hyzus however, they did not quite share their father's peace of mind. What they had orchestrated, the massacre that they both had coordinated, troubled them greatly and weighed heavily on their souls. They both knew that together they had committed truly terrible acts and made apparent a side of their people that they never wanted to see, nor even truly believed to be there until now. Still, after their encouraging words from Kyzus and some time to let the intensities of emotions die down, as well as justify their actions to themselves; both Hyzus and Tyzus felt ready again to continue synthesising the civil war together.

Tyzus and his remaining Liberalist forces were re-embarking onto their invasion ships. Ships that were far far less in number and far far less filled with soldiers now. The coastline along Rodus where the mass of Liberalist ships had all originally landed was now a depressing sight. A considerable number of ships still remained deserted on the beaches, there former passengers never to return. Far more ships remained empty and on land than the sparsely occupied few that sailed back west. Likewise, for Hyzus, his standing garrison at Embirith had suffered devastating losses; the number of remaining high Men and Elves that left back for Rodus was disturbingly few also, and the formerly fresh new armies of Elves from Nindir and Nindar comprised of far fewer battle-weary Elves in numbers few and far between. But to the Twins of Hobbes, they would let such things no longer affected them as they knew they were truly the only ones with the will power and stomach to see Kyzus's plan through to its completion, second thoughts, regrets, and sympathy for what they had done were signs of weakness they now told themselves. Weakness that would not be brought into. For the sake of their people and to avenge their dead sister.

Chapter 2

The Unwanted Kindness of Fairies

News of the terrible events surrounding Rodus and Embirith spread across Terratopia like wildfire and by the end of the same morning Tyzus and Hyzus had called off the battle around Embirith, news of its devastation had reached the kingdom of Pixieland on Fairy Island. This innocent, quaint small island half a day's sail north of Port Thruck had been completely unaffected by the civil war so far. This was largely due to the fact that the Fairies and Pixies had separated themselves from the Terratopia Union and events within Terratopia at large since early on in the summer of the world. For countless ages their island remained mostly isolated from Terratopia, with its inhabitants only ever travelling into Terratopia for leisure and aid purposes. This was the case until the civil war broke out. Queen Eonway and her husband, Prince Varwin, the leaders of the Fairies and Pixies, decreed that no business into or out of Terratopia was allowed from their island and kingdom. They however, upon hearing the troubling news about the bloodbath that had occurred around Embirith could not bear to side-line themselves any longer. It was against their very nature, the Fairies particularly. They were a race of healing and of love and after hearing of the terrible suffering in and around Rodus and Embirith, the Fairies could bare to stay away no longer.

Eonway and Varwin put out word to their people that their island would now be entering the war effort. Not on either side as military partners but for both sides as relief allies. The Fairies and Pixies were to go the where their help was needed most; to provide aid, support, and relief to all those who were suffering. The Fairies and Pixies would give Magics and medicines to the sick and injured. Food and supplies to the weak and starving. And love and healing to the ones suffering and grieving.

And with this proclamation, plans where immediately put in place to send relief-aid teams of Fairies and Pixies to the worst affected areas of Terratopia. Cufle, Lemlee, Embirith, and settlements across Rodus were where the Fairies had identified they were needed most. A week later the first support teams had all arrived at their targets and were offering help to as many as they could. The smallness of their operations however was hardly enough to relieve the extremely horrific effects of the war and these small bands of Fairies and Pixies soon found themselves overwhelmed and drowning, but it did make the best of a terrible situation.

The upscaling of Fairy aid actively was welcomed by nearly all in Terratopia, but its appreciation was hardly universal. Tyzus and Hyzus especially were worried that the Fairies actions could be detrimental to their father's plan and were worried that they were taking away the truly desired negative impacts of the war. Furthermore, many within the Liberalists and Unionists leadership where disgruntled by the sudden help of Fairies. Those especially annoyed where the ones in military or leadership positions; in their view the Fairies were undermining everything they had been fighting towards, everything they had died for. Cufle for example had been under siege for years and was in a terrible state. It was filled with refugees from across Carlin, the city was in ruins and it barely ever had enough supplies to last. The Liberalists believed the city was close to a breaking point, finally all they had been striving for in the east could be over. But in the Liberalists eyes the Fairies had stopped this from happening by offering supplies and support to the people of the suffering besieged city. The same was also true for the Unionists in Lemlee. Fairy aid was mostly given to the Liberalist attackers as they suffered tremendously attempting to capture and hold onto the collection of woodland islands. The Unionist were furious that for all their defiance and countless attempts to defend the woodland kingdom of isles that had been under attack every day for years, the Fairies helped and supported the Liberalist attackers. The Unionist forgetting the fact the Fairies obviously did also help the Lemlee inhabitants, just not to the apparent same level.

These hostile feelings towards the Fairies for their aid was only felt by a small minority however as the vast majority of peoples; mothers, children, soldiers, and workers; all gratefully and gladly received the Fairies help. The fact there were however people not welcoming to the aid from Pixieland was predicted by Kyzus, it was a sign his plan was on the right track and he had also schemed just how to use hostilities towards the Fairies to make sure the war still had its desired effects.

Upon hearing of the news about the Fairies new relief-aid proclamation from Hyzus, Kyzus was surprised as he had expected the Fairies and Pixies would just stay out of the war completely, but he had suspected something like this might happen and had planned accordingly. Tyzus, whom was still sailing back to Western Terratopia at this time was contacted by Kyzus as he wanted to instruct both his twin sons how to best deal with the Fairies. Kyzus told how they'd be some who would distain the Fairies activities, and Kyzus ordered that Tyzus and Hyzus use this phenomenon. They were to be vocal supporters of its claims and to sway further distain towards the Fairies help and aid. Kyzus predicted that they'd never be able to wholly stop the Fairies in their aid missions because now that they were out, it be impossible to get them to go against their very nature of being. He also predicted that they'd never be able to fully turn everyone against the Fairies effort because after all they were providing valuable short-term help but Kyzus suspected that attitudes of a great many towards the Fairies aid could still definitely be turned hostile for both Unionists and Liberalists. This further fuelling division between them both and also anger towards the concept of help and aid. If Tyzus and Hyzus could succeed, the general attitudes of the people towards the Fairies activities of aid with the purpose of reliving suffering could be turned into attitudes of hatred towards help and the support of suffering. A devastating, toxic demeanour and notion for people to have and exactly the purpose the war was originally orchestrated for. To put on full show the very worst the state of nature had to offer, when in it, people could even lead themselves to believe that relief and aid was a terrible thing due to their selfishness, something it of course is the very opposite.

Chapter 3

A Tragic Misunderstanding

After just over a week since the Battle of Embirith, Tyzus and his Liberalist forces arrived back in Western Terratopia on their ships. But what they arrived back to was a shocking and wretched sight. The Liberalist fleet sailed through Gweston bay to find the kingdom of Suitear burning in the distance, Lendspen under ariel assault from an army Valkyrie's and Pegasus's and the great fortress of Jassett under siege by a combine force of Men and Elves from the Unionist kingdoms of Silvor and Silvoud. Tyzus was furious. How could Hyzus do something like that, ordering attacks on his Liberalist kingdoms knowing full well they had practically been emptied of military might for the invasion of Rodus and doing so without warning him. Tyzus was so flabbergasted with anger and confusion that he never called Hyzus from his seeing stone, he instead ordered his forces to land as soon as possible and relieve Jassett of its siege.

This was done as the armada of Liberalist ships beached themselves right on the southern shores of Gweston Bay and on the banks of the River Harpgar esotery. As the ships made land, they completely emptied themselves of the forces they carried and so Men and Elves from Arway, Suitear and Gweston charged straight for Jassett and for the Unionist forces that besieged it. As butchered as the combined Liberalist armies were from their events in Central Terratopia, they still matched the numbers of the smaller kingdoms of Silvor and Silvoud; and in addition, they were now battle-hardened veterans that had scorched Rodus and survived the bloodshed at Embirith. The Unionist forces never stood a chance; they had been besieging Jassett since they had first learnt of the Liberalist invasion of Rodus long ago and so were tired, exhausted, and halved in number at least. Jassett simply was too formidable of a fortress and too impenetrable of a construction, that it easily held the Unionists at bay, even with a sparse defensive force.

Almost as immediately as the Liberalist armies clashed with the backlines of the Unionists, the Unionist commanders ordered a full retreat and the Unionist Men and Elves fled back to the Silver Wood in a chaotic desperate spree. The Liberalists however, fuming with rage that the Unionist dared attack their proud fortress of Jassett and attack when barely anyone was around to prevent them, chased after them, trailing them across Gweston and into the Silver Wood and the southern burning borders of Suitear. Tyzus, who was still servery disgruntled at the Unionist actions did not try to stop his Liberalist forces, he instead gave them his blessing and ordered them to hunt down the Unionist scum that dared attack when no one was around. Tyzus demanded that the Unionists should pay for ruining the kingdom of Suitear and for burning its capital of Earwarth. He ordered this as Tyzus could see the huge towering tree that Earwarth was built up and around in flames in the far distance. A magnificent but disturbing sight. Tyzus also ordered that the Elves from Gweston not purse the fleeing Unionists but to instead follow him to Lendspen to fend off the Valkyrie's that were clearly pillaging the grand grey gothic city. In Tyzus's rage filled mind, these Unionist actions led him to believe that maybe his brother wasn't on the same page as him afterall, maybe Hyzus planned to betray him and their father and the plan. Tyzus reasoned to himself that this must have been Hyzus's ploy from the start; ordering his kingdoms to invade the emptied weakened Liberalist ones and occupy them so that he could win the war and take control of Terratopia for himself.

    A similar story however was happening in Central Terratopia but the opposite way around as Liberalist forces were the ones ransacking a Unionist kingdom. The Merpeople from the Great Eastern Bay, upon learning of the devastation around Embirith due to the two new Elven armies appearing from the north, pieced together that the forest kingdom of Nindar must have sent its entire army to Embirith; therefore, meaning it was practically defenceless. The Great Eastern Bay Merpeople then took it upon themselves to take advantage of the situation and pillage the coastline and the coastal towns on the woodland peninsula before any remaining Elven army got back. Which diligently happened with destructive and cataclysmic effectiveness. The unguarded woodland coastline was no match for the Merpeople assault, Merpeople that were veterans of war from their experiences in Carlin. Luckily for Nindar, the woodland realm had no rivers that drained into the Great Eastern Bay and so the Merpeoples incursion was largely only limited to the eastern coast.

The eastern coasts woodland of Nindar however was completely destroyed by the time the returning armies from Nindar and Nindir had caught word of the Merpeople offensive. And by the time the Unionist Elvish forces had made it to the coast, all the trees were burnt and toppled down, all its towns and villages were pillaged and any life that once resided there, whether Elf, animal, or Natures Shepperd, was all killed off. The slaughter of many Natures Sheppard's was particularly tragic to the Nindar Elves whose kingdom had built up a fine relationship with them and hosted possibly more in their kingdom than any other kingdom in Terratopia.

When Hyzus heard of the news of the Liberalist attacks on the coast of Nindar, he too was confused and angry, just like his brother and similarly factiously pieced together that this must have been some kind of ploy of betrayal to win the war. But instead of taking Tyzus's actions he instead attempted to contact his brother through the seeing stones to question as to why he ordered attacks on Nindar without first informing him. Tyzus answered Hyzus's call and before either of them could get the first word, they both yelled at each other for not warning them about their supposed 'planned attacks'. After this fierce exchange, they both were even more confused and so questioned what the other was talking about as they personally had in fact ordered no such attacks. Steadily the twins began to realise what had happened. Their kingdoms had taken it upon themselves to order and carry out the aforementioned attacks without any orders from their head leadership or even informing them of their planned attacks. The realisation shocked the twins as their following kingdoms had never done such things before and had always run everything by them as their leaders and had certainly never actively gone behind their leaders' backs. But nonetheless it had just happened and to quite tragic, terrible results.

Tyzus and Hyzus were disturbed. Their peoples were clearly changing to the very core. They now weren't fighting an organised war, their kingdoms were becoming war like, their people war like. Clearly not caring for the cost of life or destruction it caused, but instead caring for nothing else but victory at all cost; to take advantage of any situation they could and exploit it, without asking or clearing their actions via their allies and leaders. Doing all this with the sole goal of the destruction of their enemies and their homes. The Twins of Hobbes began to realise that their father was right, the state of nature was primitive and awful and it truly was changing the peoples of Terratopia, or rather the people were fully buying into it.

The comprehension of the fact that their fathers plan wasn't just some thought experiment or fun game that they were playing out but in fact a dangerous real concept that was having harrowing real world consequences began to dawn on Tyzus and Hyzus with even more weight. They began to question their fathers' methods. How could something so pure and good like his supposed united society come from something so ghastly and gruesome like pushing the peoples to 'change' for the worst? The twins still trusted in their father as they too were extremely wise from their studies in Aquata and they did see the logic in Kyzus's society under the Deity. But Kyzus's methods on how to get to that point were now beginning to trouble his twin sons and they began to truly question whether what they were doing was truly the right thing. Was all this really for the greater good? Could a greater good really be achieved from the current Evil that they were actively causing to occur? So much death. So much suffering. Actively causing people to become evil. Was it really the right thing to be doing?

Chapter 4

The Wolfpack

At about the time of the Fairies first beginning their relief aid to Terratopia, Tyzus arriving back to the war-torn shores of Gweston, and the returning Nindar Elves learning of the Merpeople attacks on their coast, Barriel and her Paladins were arriving on the shores of the Sabare Strait. The island kingdom of Sabare under the twin mountain peaks of Samson and Goliath, the sinister capital of the Delilah Crime Empire and home of the infamous treacherous Queen Delilah was within their sights. Hiding themselves from the surrounding world behind a series of sand banks, the 'Wolfpack' led by their 'Unchained Wolf' all plotted their next actions;

"How do you suppose we get over there?" asked one of the Paladins.

"It's way too heavily guarded to just waltz in, we hardly fit into this mindless rabble of criminals and brutes," pondered Barriel, trying to think of a solution.

"We could try to fit in," reasoned another Paladin; "Pretend us defectors or something, Queen Delilah will definitely want to see us then!"

A few other Paladins agreed with this concept, but Barriel did not. "I don't think we'd want to be attracting that attention and we especially don't want the crime queen to be expecting us," Barriel explained. "She is unlike any foe we have ever faced, and her private guard of Samsons and Goliaths also are unlike any foes we have ever faced as well. Our targets are no mindless goblins or trolls or some amateur witches, I think this task requires far more stealth, cunning, and wit. We want every advantage possible to us."

Barriel's detachment of Paladins all agreed with her, but then queried how to best do what she suggested. Soon though, after a little while of thinking, another Paladin proposed they simply cast invisibility enchantments over themselves and then simply wonder into the crime capital.

As simple as an idea it was, to Barriel it was perfect. They may be among the most powerful sorcerers in all of Terratopia, taught by Kyzus himself and capable of incredible feats like even teleporting across a room or building, but sometimes the simple most basic of spells are just exactly what is needed. And so that is exactly what the Wolfpack did. They cast invisibility enchantments over themselves and slyly hitched abroad some of the many loaded vessels sailing into the packed, busy Sabare harbour, filled with treasures, resources, cronies, and slaves of all kinds.

The harbour, much like the rest of the kingdom of Sabare was a chaotic mess. Rouse, bawls, and skirmishes happened along every boat, pier, street, and ally, within every shed, shack, and building. An all manner of beings from all races; Men, Elves, Merpeople, Valkyrie's, Dwarves, and even some Gnomes all ravaged, scavenged, and pillaged from one another. Food, Drink, loot, treasurer, weapons, slaves, pride, everything was being fought over by the kingdom's inhabitants. Whether as individuals or in groups or gangs. Some degree of order was kept in place by onlooking Samsons and Goliaths who were more than content with the fighting but still made sure that Daiv and Delilah's business continued to flow to some extent. Being the mightiest of all the inhabitants in the kingdom, the Samsons and Goliaths usually got whatever they wanted as well when bossing around other races. It also helped that they were respected and feared by Sabare's now rowdy populus and thus some degree of order was kept in the chaotic kingdom. As well as that, those that acted on behalf of Daiv or Delilah were not to be troubled, everyone in the scummy kingdom knew this, or face the crime queen's rath.

The Wolfpack all eventually gathered in a storage warehouse filled with barrels of cargo. They slew the few Men guards who guarded it before then locking themselves in to discuss what to do next;

"What a pitiful wretched place this is," scoffed a Paladin, rolling his eyes as the rest of the Wolfpack agreed.

"All too true," agreed Barriel; "In places like this we can really see the need for our Lordbaron's plan. It would bring such order and peace to this gratuitous community"

The Paladins again all collectively agreed before listening to their leader once more;

"Now, the Queen Delilah is somewhere in the chieftain's compound, most likely in the chieftain's hall, she will most definitely be heavily guarded by the most formidable Samsons and Goliaths as well as her puppet the Chieftain Daiv, again an extremely formidable adversary if even a fraction of his legendary duel with Turberus is true. We must be cautious; this is a delicate situation that could end in all our deaths. These are powerful savages we are dealing with here led by a cunning and formidable sorceress," Barriel explained.

"Nothing is too great of a task for the Wolfpack Barriel!" one of the Paladins asserted and the rest quietly cheered in agreement.

"That I agree with," Barriel chuckled; "but we still need to prove it! Now any suggestions about how we deal with Delilah?"

"I say we storm to compound!" proclaimed the same Paladin; "There are plenty of us! We quickly storm the compound with the sole aim of slaying Delilah and then we teleport our way out of the kingdom straight after. Forget the guards and Daiv, we only need to occupy them long enough to take out the witch. Without her this empire crumbles in on itself."

"A bold plan," Barriel pondered. "I absolutely believe we could storm the compound and deal with the guards long enough to find and engage with Delilah. But we must not under estimate her, she is more than capable of taking us all on and surviving long enough for her kingdom of scum and villainy to fly to her rescue."

"Why don't we teleport in during the dead of night," said another Paladin; "Minimise the guards and maximise the time it takes the kingdom to come to her aid."

"I like this idea," Barriel reasoned; "Some of us should teleport to the rooftops of the compound and attempt to locate Delilah, once we have done that, the rest of us could then teleport in to engage the guards on the walls, then those of us on the rooftops can drop down into the compound to engage the remaining guards and hopefully enough of us can also engage Delilah as well!"

"HEY, WHY IS THIS WAREHOUSE LOCKED?" boomed a loud foreboding voice from the other side of the warehouse doors.

The Wolfpack looked up from their discussion in horror as they saw several large broad silhouettes through the large stick and smeared glass windows of the warehouse doors. Almost immediately after that, the doors were smashed down and several Goliaths came rushing in behind with the splinters of the warehouse door. They instantly spotted the Wolfpack on the warehouse floor.

"RUN!" Barriel cried and her Wolfpack all scattered in all directions in a variety of ways. Some magically leapt into the rafters of the roof, some began to magically teleport themselves away, spiralling into a glittering grey cloud, and others followed Barriel as she blasted a hole into the back of the wooden warehouse with magical lightning and ran for it.

The Goliaths all chased after the intruders, splitting off to try and follow every single one of the Paladins. The Goliaths caused quite a commotion and many more nearby Goliaths and Samsons quickly joined the chase. "A handsome reward for anyone would can bring me any one of these intruders! DEAD OR ALIVE" a gravely voice called, clearly belonging to one of the Goliath captains.

The Paladins in the rafters all blasted holes in the warehouses roof to escape through it. The Paladins who teleported away could only teleport as far as the outside of the warehouse that was now swarming with the kingdom's bloodthirsty inhabitants and so only just narrowly manged to leap away to safety onto surrounding rooftops as well. Barriel and her group all sprinted through the narrow scrummy streets, splitting off into groups of no more than three. They leapt, dived, and dodged around all sorts of obstacles in the streets, quickly fending off any that attempted to stop them. The scattered Wolfpack all dispersed themselves across the kingdom, cruising through the streets and shanty towns and leaping across the rooftops and alleyways; all the while however being closely pursued by their Samson and Goliath adversaries.

Barriel and the two accompanying Paladins that fled with her had all managed to make their ways to the rickety rooftops of a shanty town within Sabare but they were still being pursued by Goliaths. Some of them had managed to make it onto surrounding rooftops as well. The might of the Goliaths was now becoming fully apparent to Barriel, and all the Paladins for that matter. As advanced and highly trained they were, for as fast, slick, and fit they were, even with all the magical assistance they possessed; the Samsons and especially Goliaths were matching them if not closing in on them, and without any assistance of supernatural magical leaps or short teleportation's, their supreme innate might and determination was more than enough. Even when the Wolfpack members managed to skilfully hide themselves whether through invisibility or teleporting into small hidden rooms, the filthy kingdom was so packed with shellfish scum that they were almost instantly spotted, found, or given away. They were trapped with nowhere to hide.

The chase went on for many hours after they were discovered and Barriel and her Paladins were beginning to fatigue greatly as they continually ran along the shack rooftops. Suddenly though, the most mighty Samson they had ever seen burst out from the roof directly in front of them just metres away. Barriel and the Paladins stopped immediately and guessed who stood before them was. It was Daiv. Panting with exhaustion the three mustered all the strength they could gather to teleport away as Daiv quickly advanced and reached to grab them. Barriel and one Paladin manged to spiral away to the neighbouring rooftop in a cloud of sparkling mist. But the last Paladin screamed out in pain as he had begun to twirl. A slick elegant Elven blade had been thrust through his foot and boot from the roof below him. The pinned Paladin stopped his spell and crouched down in pain to attempt to lift his foot off the blade that had skewed his foot in place. But all too soon, as Barriel and the other Paladin watched on in terror, Daiv approached and grabbed and pulled the immobilised Paladin up by the cape on his armour until he was lifted completely off the blade and dangling in the air. The Paladin reached for his own blade and sliced it across Daiv's stomach; but a single weak slice was easily shrugged off by the Samson and he grinned at the twinge he felt. The helpless Paladin stared in exhausted drained horror and he then slowly swung for another strike. But by that time another figure emerged from below the rooftop, armed with the slick, elegant Elven blade. Like a lightning strike she sliced the Paladins arm clear off, even through his spectacular armour, as he swung to strike Daiv.

Barriel screamed as the black-haired figure stared at her while she walked around the jarring daggling Paladin. Her piercing blue eyes surrounded by void blackness shot straight into Barriel's soul and the figure then smirked as she recognised who Barriel was. The figure slyly smirked as she faced towards Barriel with her back towards the powerless Paladin. Still with her sinister malevolent smile across her scarred face, the figure then stabbed her blade backwards into the side of the Paladin while she continued her staunch eye contact with Barriel. Barriel's terror turned to anger, there was only one person this evil figure could be she reasoned to herself. This must be Queen Delilah.

"You're going to regret that!" Barriel angrily shouted at Delilah.

"Oh, am I now?" Delilah manically chuckled. "I knew Kyzus would be taking some action against me, but this? Am I really only worth the effort of a few glorified Elf mages?" she sarcastically asked in a malevolent tone.

"Oh, you just wait!" Barriel snapped back. "You dare betray my Lordbaron and then have the audacity to kill one of my Wolfpack like that in front of me? ME? Kyzus's Unchained Wolf?"

"Unchained Wolf you say?" Delilah again manically chuckled, Daiv along with her. "Oh, I can't wait to find out the consequences of my actions," she again sarcastically added, talking in a similar tone to that of a parent taunting a child, using similarity sarcastic exaggerated hand gestures.

Barriel's anger was turning to fury at the queens' words and tone. By this time several other Paladins had also made their way to Barriel's side as well as the Goliath and Samson pursuers that now surrounded them as well.

"I'll tell you what," Delilah then said. "I'll throw your wolfpack a bone, why don't you and your friends pay me a visit in my hall in two days' time at the chiming of the midday bells? Would love to see what you have planned for me. In the meantime, why don't you enjoy your stay in my kingdom? Make the most of it my dear; ALL of Terratopia will be like this someday" Delilah's arms were outstretched and she spun around as she said this. "I'll leave you alone and so will my people" Delilah explained, in a coy nonserious manner; "well unless of course you get in their way or have something they want" she then jokingly added. "Only the strongest will survive in my kingdom, hope you make it."

"All right then," Barriel reluctantly agreed before then teleporting into the room directly below her and killing all the drunk Men within it that were enjoying the heated exchange above them. "I'll be right here!" Barriel then shouted aggressively out the window

Delilah pouted and nodded slightly in a semi-impressed, semi-sarcastic way. "Very well," she then replied happily before then looking towards the remaining Paladins on the rooftop; "Well?... Aren't you going to join her" she manically said before nodding at her Samsons and Goliaths to advance on them.

Immediately the Paladins all spun around and teleported into the building below them with Barriel.

Delilah and Daiv then turned and began walking back to their compound together.

"Lucky us my love! We got some fun friends to play with!" Delilah then laughed to Daiv as they walked away who too then also laughed in his deep roaring voice. The couples evil laughing being heard by the Wolfpack and unsettling them all to the bone.

Chapter 5

Barriel, Delilah and Mia-Myzus

Over the next two days, the remaining Paladins that had scattered themselves throughout Sabare in their escape from the warehouse all made their way back to Barriel and the rest of the Wolfpack. Although largely left alone by Delilah and her Samson and Goliath cronies as the crime queen issued no direct orders for the Wolfpack to be attacked, Barriel and her Paladins still continually found themselves getting into skirmishes with the local ravenous populous. There was after all no law in Sabare, just the order of that the only ones deserving of what they desire must be the strongest and fought for it.

Barriel and her Wolfpack recovered from their previous encounters as much as they could, but they constantly had to fight gangs of Men, Elves, Dwarves, Valkyrie's, and sometimes rouge Goliaths and Samsons for the time and space to recover. Altercations and brawls were constantly happening around the Wolfpacks building with the Sabare inhabitants all wanting a piece of the Wolfpack. Their exquisite gold, white, and silver weapons and armour became highly sought after and all wanted it either for themselves or to sell on for lofty fortunes.

These confrontations weren't without consequence either. As well as not allowing Barriel and her detachment time to fully rest and recover, they also cost the lives of three Paladins whom all fell to the scum and villainy of Sabare. One was swarmed by Dwarves with Gnomish potions; another was overrun and taken by determined Men and Elves and the last was brutally murdered by a group of Goliaths who desperately wanted his armour.

Finally, the day of their meeting with Queen Delilah eventually arrived and so the Wolfpack collectively made their way to the chieftain's compound. Although having less than ideal preparation to rest, recover, and plan, each member of the Wolfpack was feeling reinvigorated, determined, and ready for what lay ahead for them; they also had a rough plan. They would get Barriel and three more Paladins to duel and overrun Delilah; four Paladins to occupy Daiv to make sure he didn't intervene and aid his puppet master Delilah; and the remaining Paladins were to fend off the rest of Delilah's guards that she had brought for as long as they could. No matter how helplessly outnumbered they were.

Barriel's plan seemed desperate and she herself felt it. She really had no idea what she was leading her detachment into. She had no idea about her surroundings, no idea about how many foes she faced and she also didn't really have any idea about how truly formidable Delilah was. Barriel was nervous and tense. What's more was the fact that she really did not want to let Kyzus down. It was clear to Barriel, after having to attempt to survive in Sabare, just how needed Kyzus's united society was and so she really wanted to be successful in her task of dealing with Delilah's betrayal to him.

These thoughts plagued Barriel's mind her whole journey to the chieftain's compound in the centre of the kingdom. She led her Wolfpack as they travelled tightly together through the crime ridden, chaotic streets of Sabare. As the Wolfpack continued on their journey they were belittled, pestered, and assaulted from the crowds that swarmed all around them. The mass of riffraff never attempted to stop or impede the Wolfpack as they were eager to see Delilah kill them all, but they still hurled insults, rotten food, and rocks at them as they marched together.

Barriel and her Paladins all soon arrived at the huge gates of the chieftain's compound just as the mid-day bells began to ring. As the deathening chimes filled the kingdoms air, the enormous wooden gates that stood sealed shut before the Wolfpack began to creak open. Slowly vast numbers of armed and angry Samsons and Goliaths came into view that all crowded the courtyard of the compound in-between the gate and the hall. A Goliath then shouted down from the walls that Delilah was awaiting them in the hall. Barriel and her Paladins stood firm and tried not to show any of the fear that they were feeling, attempting instead to look as firm as possible.

Gradually the masses of Samson and Goliath warriors all began to part to form a clear passage to the halls grand, but decrepit doors. Seeing the clear intimidation tactics of the warrior guards Barriel instead decided to employ some of her own. She spiralled around and teleported right up to the doors in a puff of smoke, skipping the entire courtyard of merciless brutes. Barriel's Paladins then all followed suit, mimicking the actions of their leader exactly; these actions having the desired effect Barriel wished as the Samsons and Goliaths all stepped back in a gasp. Barriel then thrust open the halls doors which then collapsed under her forcefulness, as well as their own decay and disrepair.

Proudly Barriel and her Wolfpack waltzed into the hall to find Daiv sat confidently on his throne made of bones holding his infamous twin-bladed sword, he was surrounded entirely by formidable looking Samsons and Goliaths that lined the walls of the entire back half of the hall. Delilah was lounging comfortably on his right arm and shoulder. All of them were clearly armed and ready for a fight.

"Barriel!" Delilah confidently exclaimed as Barriel approached close enough. "Remember me dear friend? Thank you so much for my lift to Embirith all that time ago. I told you we'd see each other again!"

Barriel stopped suddenly in shock, recognising instantly who Queen Delilah really was, she was the high Elf from Filnethias she had journeyed to Embirith with all those years ago. "It's you?" she uttered sharply, the recognition sending chills down her spine.

"You look so surprised dear friend," Delilah teased. "Must be quite a shock wondering how I ever got here"

"How you got here makes no difference to me" Barriel snapped. "You have betrayed my Lordbaron Kyzus and I am here to rectify that."

"Betrayed Kyzus?" Delilah gasped. "I set myself free of Kyzus!" she then angrily shouted, stepping down off Daiv's person. "Kyzus and his stupid plan mean nothing to me. I betrayed nothing. I am now free of him! What he wants will take what I have away from me! I will never allow it to happen! Never! Delilah then screeched

Barriel silently stood, judging the clearly unhinged crime queen. "You and the way of life you have created shows exactly the need for Kyzus's plan and I will see to it that it is seen through to completion!"

Delilah giggled. "You think I did this? Dictated this way off life? My friend it's in our nature. The people themselves did this. They wanted this. They yearn and beg for it, they are pathetic. You all are like this. The only reason why I am Queen and they are not is because I am the only one enlightened enough to see it and powerful enough to rule over it!" Delilah again screeched as she exclaimed her last statement. She also lit up her hands into a burst of sharp blue flames as she did. "I believe Kyzus himself even calls it our state of nature" Delilah then said in a calmer tone "Why attempt to rise above it? We will only fall back into it again, so why not instead use it and rule over it instead of fight to overcome it!"

With the fiery sapphire glow of Delilah's fiery magic in her eyes, Barriel again stood silent and judged the queen before her. She began to struggle to believe that Kyzus would ever attempt to do business with her. "Whatever you say or believe," Barriel then said; "You have still betrayed Kyzus and he has sent me to deal with it."

"Oh yes" Delilah replied. "Kyzus's Unchained Wolf." She then mocked. "You don't want to do this though Barriel. You have to see that Kyzus is delusional and power hungry. Controlling us all. Controlling the war!"

Barriel stood confused, she had no idea Kyzus was controlling the war, she believed that Tyzus had forsaken him and that Hyzus was fighting for Kyzus's cause of uniting Terratopia together.

"Come now my friend," Delilah said. "You have no idea how much Kyzus is hiding from you. Hiding from us all! Forsake him Barriel, join me in my empire! I'm sure we could do great things and become great friends" she then said with an all-knowing smirk.

Barriel glared at Delilah and shot a magical bolt straight into her stomach sending the queen flying back into Daiv's lap. The surrounding Samsons and Goliaths all twitched and advanced on Barriel and the Wolfpack all readying themselves.

Delilah however laughed evilly as she got up from Daiv's lap, drawing her blade out and pointing it directly at Barriel as Barriel shouted out in anger;

"The beginnings of your empire killed my greatest friend! Killed Kyzus's daughter Mia-Myzus. She is dead because of the way of life your empire creates and trust me, if she was here right now with me you would be heading back to Kyzus already!" Barriel snarled.

Delilah malevolently laughed even more and even louder. "Oh Barriel" she exclaimed "You really have no idea." As Delilah said this, she then flashed her hand over her scared face and lifted her enchantment off herself, revealing her true identity to Barriel and the whole Wolfpack whom all gasped in shock, confusion, and horror.

"Traitor! How could you? Mia-Myzus you're alive? And you're the Crime Queen?" Barriel shouted in confused anger.

"That I most certainly am old friend!" Delilah replied. "But if only you could see Barriel! I am no traitor, I released myself from my fathers' bonds! I am free! I will grow my empire and my power to completely swallow Terratopia, destroy my father and rule over this whole land! We can do this together old friend! As sisters! We are together the strongest and the strongest deserve to reap the rewards of being so! My empire is a consequence of the true nature within all people, why not take advantage and live above them! Instead of fighting their nature in feeble attempts to be better than we already are! Join me Barriel! It's better this way"

After Delilah finished speaking, she offered out her hand, but Barriel continued to glare at her in refusal. Delilah retracted her hand in an offended manner and then spoke, her tone becoming more extreme with every word;

"A lion does not feel guilty for killing a gazelle. A bear feels no remorse when slaughtering a deer. You yourself experience no regret after squishing a fly. That means something Barriel! That really means something!"

Barriel again sharply glared at Delilah in a cold dead piecing look. She was confused and angry and she could not believe the words coming out of her old friend's mouth. She then pleaded;

"Please Mia-Myzus. Don't do this. Don't do this to yourself, to me or to your father and brothers! Come with me back to Roccano."

Delilah switched her expression and tone from her welcoming, desperate, and enticing one back to her unhinged stoic one. "I will never go back to Roccano or see my father again unless it is to defeat him! NEVER!" Delilah then switched again to her evil malevolent tone. "If you will not join me by my side Barriel my old friend, then I will destroy you and send you back to Kyzus in pieces!"

Barriel dropped her elegant white cape from her shoulders and drew her own formidable elegant blade. "You will try!" she proudly stated.

Delilah sinisterly grinned. Daiv boldly stood up from his throne grasping his large twin bladed sword. The surrounding Samsons and Goliaths all smiled eagerly, gripping their weapons, and shifting their weight from side to side in an agitated state. The Paladins, all clad in their magnificent gold and white plated armour, drew their own shining silver weapons and formed themselves into attack positions. The Wolfpack all looked at each other eagerly, ready to their upcoming battle. In their heads they all magically projected their plans of attack to each other to best agree on their soon to be ensuing moves for the coming battle.

Chapter 6

The Unchained Wolf and Queen of Crime

An eerie silence descended throughout the hall as the most indominable, stoic, formidable, and magical fighters in all of Terratopia stared each other down, impatiently eyeing each other up.

Delilah was first to break the silence. Yelling deathingly as she ignited her blade in a yellow and blue flame and charged straight for Barriel. Barriel then did the same, igniting a vibrant orange fire around her own sword and sprinting forward to meet Delilah. Daiv and his followers all then abruptly followed Delilah's lead, stampeding straight into the Wolfpack and then Paladins then all did the same back.

Just had they had originally planned, Barriel headed straight for Delilah with three Paladins charging up behind her. Four more Paladins all dashed straight for Daiv and the remaining Paladins split themselves into two groups. Some heading back towards the broken-down doors and attempting to use the entrance as a choke point to hold the courtyard of Samsons and Goliaths at bay, and the rest of the Paladins tried their best to tie up every other advisory in the hall for Barriel to have her best chance of taking Delilah down. The Samsons and Goliaths within the hall outnumbered the remaining Paladins three to one, but that did not stop any of these spectacular powerful Elves.

Delilah and Barriel roared at each other as they bolted towards one another with their flaming blades trailing besides them. They soon both leapt into the air and swung to strike each other, but as they did, Barriel quickly spun around and teleported to be just behind Delilah so that the queen was sandwiched between her and the three occupying Paladins. Delilah suspected this would happen however and was well prepared to turn herself around and deflect Barriel's strike with her blade, the yellow, blue, and orange flames clashing gloriously. As she did this, Delilah used her other hand to generate a huge explosion of blue fire which she slammed straight into the ground, just as the three Paladins were about to strike her, shooting them backwards and landing them flat on their backs far away.

As this happened, Daiv lifted his twin-bladed sword high about his head, so that either blade was sticking out directly horizontally to the side of his person, and he swung it down to smash into the four Paladins swords that they too had swung from above their heads. The six sword blades all locked as either side of Daiv's twin sword grinded against two great Paladin swords. The mighty Samson laughed out as his strength easily matched the highly trained Roccano Elves and he quickly overpowered them and swung his sword to the right in front of him, thrusting the four Paladins away. As he did this though, the Paladin on the most extreme left of Daiv managed to draw his dagger and stab it into Daiv's calf as he was thrust away.

Barriel and Delilah were furiously flourishing their blades around themselves and clashing, slicing, grinding, and stabbing them at each other at any given opportunity. Their blades were moving so fast that in-between their two extravagant, elegantly flowing bodies was an orange, yellow, and blue hue that ruptured sparks as the two formidable women elegantly danced around each other with deadly intent. Occasionally both of them manged to get an opening to unleash violent magical blasts at each other but they were always dodged away or blocked by a blade or magical counter and defensive spell. Delilah continually attempted to unleash her fierce blue fire at Barriel, who herself utilised lightning-fast golden bolts, magics taught to her by Kyzus. Together they were locked in their devastating duel, but it was clear that Barriel was fighting with all her might, attempting as hard as she could to only keep up with Delilah's insane prowess, who seemed more to be just testing her opponent. Luckily for Barriel though, her three accompanying Paladins soon came round and joined in with the fury, greatly turning the odds in the Unchained Wolfs favour.

Daiv's dagger wound had little effect to the hardy Samson whose race were already known for their insane durability in battle. From all sides; front, back, left, and right, Daiv fended off his four Paladin assailants. The speed at which he himself was able to move, as well as move his potent weapon was terrifying and any simultaneous strike from any of the four Paladins was nearly always blocked and returned. Even with their magical bolts and thrusts Daiv competently stood his ground and the few minor wounds he suffered were never enough to stop him in his fury, they in fact only seemed to add to it.

Delilah was in an extremely similar situation, fending off four advisories from all angles, though no spells or strikes ever landed on her. However, when she began to feel that she was becoming outmatched, Delilah attempted to truly unleash her magical prowess. She actively engaged and grinded her blade on Barriel's, and then another Paladins at the same time; Delilah then managed to direct the locked blades into the other two Paladins strikes through a combination of skill and pulling spells. With the might of Barriel and three other Paladins weapons grinding against her, the evil queen stood stubbornly behind her flaming blade. Her stance then gradually, however, began to physically slide backwards into the halls rear corner due to the combined strength of her advisories. Delilah made eye contact with the attackers and smiled; she then thrusted her own blade, and consequently, all the other locked blades into the air with one hand and then produced a ferocious, monumental, and continuous blue fire from her other which landed cleanly and fatally on the three Paladins and Barriel's chests, shooting them backwards in a wavey river of flame.

The four Paladins attacking Daiv meanwhile decided to switch up their strategy, vouching to start quick surgical teleportation strikes. A process of them all one by one teleporting away behind Daiv to an open spot, striking him and then teleporting a safe distance away again before then repeating. It was an extremely taxing affair as teleportation spells, especially in such quick succession where very draining; but for a while it worked and worked well. Daiv was suffering deep stab after stab, deadly slice after slice across his whole body from chest to feet, it began to drive him crazy with rage. Finally, after suffering one slice across his cheek from a Paladin, he spotted exactly where that Paladin teleported too and launched his huge twin bladed sword at him like a javelin. Quickly though the Paladin teleported to Daiv's back, narrowing missing the projectile sword and again stabbed his back. But, as the Paladin attempted to teleport away again, he was slightly to slow from being so exhausted and Daiv spung around, grabbed him by the neck and slammed him into the floor, cracking the stone below, doing this as Delilah unleashed her huge wave of fire in the back of the hall.

The whole hall seemed to stop slightly to either admire or check on their counterparts. Barriel and two Paladins stubbled up to face Delilah once more, their fantastic armour had saved their lives, though it was now severely dented inwards and blacken with scorch. Barriel's third Paladin counterpart did not get up, he had been crushed and burned by the might of Delilah's magic. The same went for the Paladin Daiv had slammed onto the floor. His body was completely broken, despite his armour's protection, such was the might of the chieftain in all his fury.

The battle then continued as Barriel let out a terrific scream and with both hands launched the biggest continuous magical bolt she had ever unleashed, its shining golden light slamming straight into Delilah. The infamous queen however manged to raise her blade into the frenzied bolt, protecting her but sending her soaring into the wall behind her, splintering the wood, such was the potency of Barriel's magic. She then returned with her own flaming spell but this was prevented from hitting Barriel by being dispelled from long bolts sent by both of Barriel's accompanying Paladins. The four advisories all then looked at each other panting heavily before then again unleashing monumental spells at each other. Delilah sent a huge tsunami of terrific blue fire towards Barriel and her two Paladins, and they countered this with an enormous combined bolt from the three of them that slammed straight into the fire stopping it in its track halfway between them all. Instead of give up though, the four powerful sorcerers kept up their spells, entering into a dangerous yet magnificent magical tug of war.

Daiv had re-engaged with the three remaining Paladins and very clearly had the upper hand now that their numbers were reduced and they were so exhausted from their teleportation antics. The Paladins still occasionally manged to hit Daiv with strikes either from their swords or daggers or magical bolts, but these again did nothing to the unstoppable, rage filled, formidable Samson. His movement and strikes had slowed as he too was beginning to tire and his substantial number of suffered wounds affect him, but Daiv was still as deadly a force as ever, especially to the exhausted Paladins who soon found themselves fighting for their survival and not to defeat Daiv like before. Eventually, Daiv, twirling his double-bladed sword around himself, managed to catch one of the Paladins with it and precisely lop his head clean off through the tiny gap in-between the grand armour and helmet of the Paladin. While the headless body collapsed to the floor, hitting it with a disturbing clinking sound, Daiv quickly dropped his weapon and grabbed both the Paladins by their helmets, crushing and compressing them so that the Paladins heads where painfully stuck inside them. They both screamed in pain as the once valiant golden and white helms that had protected them well now cut their heads and compressed their skulls. Daiv dropped them both to the ground as they squirmed in pain and attempted to pull their trapped heads from their helmets. Daiv then stood on both of their legs, pressing down on them hard, so that the wriggling Paladins were pinned in place, and then proceeded to strike down on both of them with his mighty fits. The grand golden and white armour cut and broke Daiv's fits significantly, but that made little difference to his hate fuelled agenda and one blow after another the Paladins armour and helmets caved in and the once lively, jerking, screaming body's suddenly fell completely motionless and silent, yet Daiv continually to pummel them.

 Barriel and her Paladins meanwhile were straining terribly to hold Delilah's magical fury at bay, slowly they found themselves being physically shifted backwards and their combined bolt was succumbing to Delilah's blue wave of flames. Eventually, despite Barriel and her Paladins giving it all their might, their magic power was overcome and they again found themselves on the receiving end of a devastating tsunami of fire, which hurtled them backwards across the vast hall and into the opposite wall of the hall, smashing into it, and then sliding to the floor like wet rags chucked at a screen.

Delilah laughed menacingly as Barriel slowly looked up dazed to see Daiv pummelling two Paladins to death on the floor. Her eyes began to shift in and out of focus but even then, Barriel could still make out that steadily, one by one, her exhausted Paladins from her infamous Wolfpack were becoming overran and killed brutally by the ruthless Samsons and Goliaths of Sabare. Although her Wolfpack had all fought valiantly and slaughter many Samsons and Goliaths that lay scattered around the hall, they were still hopelessly outnumbered and outmatched as the unending strength, fury, durability, and number of the Sabare warriors came into its own. Barriel looked for her accompanying Paladins that had been hit with Delilah's magic. One of them was very clearly dead, his motionless black charred body hard to witness. But the other Paladin was still alive and struggling to stand up. But as he got up to his knees, he was then brutally impaled from behind by a Samson, who had broken through the dwindling defence at the entrance way of the hall. A spear passed straight through his body and out the front of his armour before hitting the ground; leaving the now dead Paladin skewered in the air on his knees, blood trickling from his mouth.

Barriel screamed out in sorrow but her cry was cut short by being drenched by a waterfall of blue magical fire from Delilah, completely covering her whole body. Barriel lay face down on the burning stone floor, in too much pain, anger, and sorrow to even begin to fully comprehend her wounds. She knew that the battle was lost, but she decided that she couldn't let Kyzus down just yet, not while she still had breath in her. Somehow in a most unnatural movement she rose to her feet, spying Delilah and Daiv and they both menacingly walked towards her, but stopping in semi-shock semi-curiosity as Barriel rose up just in front of them.

In one fluent motion, with the speed of lightning, Barriel forcefully pinned Daiv in place with magic, stabbed her dagger into his chest and climbed upon it like a ladder rung while at the same time she threw and thrusted her blade into Delilah's hand.

The magical thrust had such force that it passed straight through Delilah's hand and lodged itself into the stone floor, pinning Delilah to the floor along with it. Barriel then leapt from Daiv's shoulder and chest from her dagger, spinning twice in the air, building up and even more unfathomable speed and momentum before than landing a clean blow with her closed fist on Delilah head, snapping it to the side and then flinging her through the air, only to then be halted and slammed into the ground like a rag doll by her own pinned hand. Barriel then collapsed onto the floor convulsing with exhaustion before then passing out.

Chapter 7

The Purge of Pixieland and Ransacking of Fairy Island

Barriel awoke again days later in a fatigued painful state. Her whole body still ached tremendously from her duel with Delilah and she was still exhausted. The more she came around however, the more pain she began to feel as the true extent of her wounds finally made it to her now conscious brain. Her whole body that wasn't covered by her armour, mainly her hands and face, were completely burned and singed from Delilah's fiery magics. Her face twitched with pain to even change expressions and it seemed to bleed slightly from areas and her hands were practically burnt and peeled back to the bone. Then Barriel felt that she couldn't move her arms at all, when she tried, she instantly felt tremendous pain in her forearms. She achingly opened her eyes wide and slowly moved her head to be able to see that her arms that were outstretch away from her. Horrified, Barriel realised that huge nails had been driven through her forearms and into a cruel wooden crucifix behind her. Barriel was freely dangling from her forearms and when she looked around more she recognised that she was crucified above Daiv's throne. Daiv was sitting in it beneath her and Delilah was standing and pacing in front of him screaming into a rainbow hued perfectly spherical crystal ball.

"Your feeble attempt to stop me has failed Kyzus!" shouted Delilah into her hand that grasped the stone. "Your supposed 'Unchained Wolf' now hangs like a scrawny pathetic lost puppy and her Wolfpack now all hang dead around the walls of my kingdom!"

These words upset Barriel terribly and her physical pain seemed to subside to a new grieving pain upon hearing the tragic news that her whole detachment was now dead and being displayed for the entire outside world of scum and villainy to see, likely being defiled with every passing minute. Barriel could not hear Kyzus's reply through the seeing stone but it clearly enraged the evil unhinged queen below her.

"ARRHHGGHH," Delilah screamed as she slammed the seeing stone into the stone floor. But the stone did not break or even scratch, the crystal ball instead perfectly embedded and lodged itself into the now cracked and broken stone floor beneath it, like a perfectly circular meteor in a snug crater

Delilah then swiftly turned and directly faced the fallen Paladin leader as she hung helplessly above her. Barriel however noticed something that brung a small smile to her face. She saw that the side of the face where she had struck Delilah with her final blow had partially crushed her left cheek bone and had closed and swelled up her left eye, perhaps permanently. This being said, Delilah's right eye still had a deathening piecing gaze, the hopeless blackness surrounded by sharp blueness that seemed to sit in an infinite dark void chilled Barriel to the bone.

"Why did you make me do this to you old friend?" Delilah pleaded in a surprisingly helpless tone.

Barriel refused to answer. She could not believe the crime queen that stood before her was her long thought dead best friend Mia-Myzus. Words failed to come to Barriel's mind.

Suddenly a spiralling mist of mystical sparking grey appeared around Barriel and her crucifix. Then Kyzus appeared suddenly in front of Barriel, himself hovering on a similarly twinkling grey cloud.

"Kyzus!" Delilah screamed with surprise and fury. "Finally, I am worthy of you to bless me with your presence!

Kyzus ignored this exclamation from Delilah however and instead magically levitated Barriel's crucifix from its fixed position above Daiv's throne and then teleported away with it back to Roccano.

***

Swirling back into the enormous entrance way landing in Kyzus's mountainside place Barriel tried to cry out in relief and regret.

"My Lordbaron," she muttered. "I am so sorry; I have failed you."

Kyzus shushed Barriel gently. Delicately placing her crude wooden cross laying down.

"What's done is done, you have nothing to be sorry for," Kyzus then said calmly as he then began to cast a warm comforting yellow magical dust over Barriel that emanated from his hands.

Barriel's pain seemed to instantly begin to subside and she felt warmth and comfort as if she was being hugged by all her loved ones.

Kyzus then proceeded to magically and gently pull the nails out of Barriel's forearms, freeing her from her crucified position. Then Kyzus levitated Barriel into the air and removed her hopelessly damaged, crumpled, and scorched heavy armour before then laying her down on a clean soft fabric stretcher.

Kyzus stood over Barriel and waved his hand across her laying body, producing a gentle white magical dust that settled all across Barriel; before then saying;

"Rest up now Barriel, you have done well."

Kyzus then produced a spell that peacefully sent Barriel into a deep sleep before the wise powerful Half-elf then cast more healing spells upon her and then levitated her stretcher from his palace to her home.

* * *

"NOOOO!" Delilah screamed as the ancient leader of Roccano teleported away with her prized prisoner.

Daiv stood up from his throne and fell backwards till his back hit the floor as he witnessed Kyzus's act. Speechless, the Samson looked towards his wife who had fell to her knees and started intently at the ground in front of her.

"What now?" Daiv asked in an annoyed manner.

"Assemble the army!" Delilah screeched. "The whole army! Every good for nothing Samson and Goliath in this stupid kingdom!"

"To do what?" Daiv asked

"To ransack somewhere! Anywhere! To scorch the earth of some lands and kill whomever we find in them!" Delilah again screamed in a psychotic manner.

"Yes, my love," Daiv quickly responded with a sinister grin on his face.

A few days later a vast army of Samson's and Goliath's had amassed themselves under Daiv's orders.

Sabare had practically been emptied of its natural inhabitants save for a few of Delilah and Daiv's most trusted guards to keep their compound safe from the mindless rabble of the rest of the wretched kingdom. A huge rag tag fleet of ships of varying different shapes and sizes had all assembled in Sabare's large harbour as well, these all belonging to pirate captains and pirate lords that happily rented their ships out to Delilah, as their feared empress with her sizable wealth.

Delilah and Daiv boarded their ships along with their vast terrifying army and headed for the nearest kingdom to them. The Fungi Forest. It was a monumental sight to see, all the pirate ships leaving Sabare's harbour packed full of barbarian like passengers all covered in war paint and filled with eager fury.

Soon the enormous army crossed the Sabare Strait and made land on the coast of the Fungi Forest. The peaceful Gnome inhabitants had no idea what was about to be unleashed on them though many Gnomes all stood frozen in fear upon seeing the huge force of angry Samsons and Goliaths amass on their shore. Delilah and Daiv disembarked first and wandered to the nearest giant mushroom they could see, completely ignoring all the small Gnomes that hurriedly jumped out their way in front of them. Upon reaching the foot of the enormous mushroom that towered above them, Delilah let out a huge relieving sigh before then unleashing a huge burst of blue fire from her palms directly into the mushrooms base, sending the entire thing up in flames, screaming psychotically as she did. Gnomes all around scattered and screamed in terror at the sight and the poor Gnome family inside the burning mushroom that was their home all desperately attempted to get out and roll away the fire that they had been set on. Daiv then rampaged through the scurrying Gnome crowds; kicking, flinging, grabbing, squishing, and slaughtering all the Gnomes he could mindlessly. The rest of the Samson and Goliath army then followed suit, disembarking from their ships and going on a rampage of destruction through the entire Fungi Forest kingdom. Destroying every giant mushroom there was and slaughtering every Gnome they could reach. It was too easy for them, but also somehow therapeutic to their savage, angry, war-like minds.

Days pasts and Delilah's rage and anger gradually began to subside the more she ravaged and burned. But it was replaced by a cynical evil enjoyment. Her screams turned to malevolent laughter as she too rampaged across the kingdom and brutally slaughtered every helpless terrified lost Gnome she could reach. After a few days the entire kingdom was destroyed. Completely raised to the ground and burning in flames. But Delilah, Daiv, and their army were having too much fun to stop now. They continued their destructive rampage day and night westwards along the coast, venturing into the most northern parts of Carlin and scorching it dry. Nothing was left alive. Even an occupying Liberalist battalion of Elves from Orthelian was completely wiped out, the quick battle being an enjoyable obstacle for the storming Sabare assault.

All too soon however, Delilah and Daiv's force had run out of land to ruin, they had reached the ends of Carlin and stood at the western most tip of a peninsula that made up the eastern coast and entrance to the Great Eastern Bay. Again though, Delilah and her army were having far too much fun, being too high of their sick enjoyment of destruction and genocide that they could not stop, especially as they could see the coast of Nindar in the distance. They were eager to continue their tempest killing spree into the woodland kingdom. So, as a result the pirate ships were boarded once more and made for the northern most tip of the woodland kingdom of Nindar.

However, Nindar's coast had already been completely ravaged by previous battles with the Great Eastern Bay Merpeople and so its limited destruction held little enjoyment of the berserk Sabare army, despite a quick and easily victorious battle against a small army of Unionist Elves sent to stop them. But again, standing on the coast, in the far distance they could see an island seemingly untouched by the war. A glimmering island that somehow gave off an innocent pink hue into the sky above it. Fairy Island.

Delilah and Daiv were both thinking the exact same thing and with such an intoxicating thought in their heads, there was no changing their minds or going back. The evil husband and wife ordered that they all sail for Fairy Island and completely wipe it and its inhabitants from the face of the world.

Which is exactly what happened. Exactly two weeks after Barriel had been recused by Kyzus and shortly after the same time that Tyzus and Hyzus realised their tragic misunderstanding between their sides of the war, Delilah and her formidable, unstoppable, and dreadful army landed on the shores of Pixieland on Fairy Island and what unfolded next was even worse than any of their previous raids on any land.

From the very east to the very west of the island, Delilah, Daiv and their followers tortured and slaughtered every Fairy and Pixie they could. Even managing to capture and easily kill the Fairy Queen Eonway and her husband Prince Varwin. The entire island was ruined and then burnt to the ground. By the end of Sabare's campaign and the genocidal enjoyment finally fizzling out, nothing was left alive on the island. No plant life, no wildlife and certainly no Fairy or Pixie life. Just a completely obliterated helpless former kingdom that sought to do good and bring healing and love. An innocent land that stood no chance against the evil berserk fury of Sabare's forces under Delilah's evil psychotic desires.

Satisfied, Delilah and Daiv ordered for the journey back home to Sabare, feeling no remorse or regret from their actions, and instead feeling the type of joy people felt after a relaxing holiday away from home.

Chapter 8

The Twins of Hobbes Deception

Hyzus and Tyzus, being cautious to avoid more huge battles like the one around Embirith and attempting to regain full control over the war again, had devised together that the war would move to smaller more local fronts. No longer where huge sieges and battles to take place that involved drastic forces from numerous allied kingdoms, instead kingdoms were ordered by the twins to separately attack and invade neighbouring ones.

This approach in many ways had the desired effects the Twins of Hobbes hoped for as nothing like the invasion of Rodus, the burning of Suitear or the pillaging of Nindar ever happened again and it brought the war right back under their control. They found their kingdoms were more than willing to engage in continuous, drawn-out smaller scale conflicts; largely due to the fact that they all wanted victory above all else and cared not for grand allied invasions to faraway lands but to instead attempt to crush nearby local kingdoms by any means.

Over the course of a year since Tyzus and Hyzus had realised continued to remain as devastating and horrific as before, probably even more so now that the war was far more wide spread. Carlin was still nearly fully occupied with Cufle still under its disastrous siege from neighbouring kingdoms of Orthelian and Lurtha. But the blockade around Lemlee was finally lifted and now the war around the isle's in-between Central and Western Terratopia took the form of brutal island hoping campaigns as Men from the Connecting Isles and Elves of Lemlee all attacked and defended every island they feasibly could, along with the help of their respected Merpeople allies of the Shore Mountains Atoll or Aquatatia. Large navel battles as well the raiding of supply ships and trade routes were also occurring in this war-torn area of Terratopia. The Great Eastern Bay now mostly gave up on their ventures in Carlin, instead they favoured attacks on Nindar after they had successful ruined its coastline before. Aquatatia was locked in conflict mostly with the nearby Shore Mountains Atoll kingdom as the other Merpeople kingdom of Reeforiris favoured attacking Filnethias and Rime as they were determined to take the grand cities after being defeated by them before at the previous invasion of Rodus. In Western Terratopia, the kingdom of Arway and Silvor had begun deadly incursions and invasions into each other's lands; pillaging farmlands, towns, and villages with continual but pointless success as both kingdoms were a part of the same large empty expanse of plains, only being separated geologically by the shallow Arway River. Within the Silver Wood, the two rival Elven kingdoms of Suitear and Silvoud were stuck in an awful stalemate along each other's borders with neither side now being able to break through into each other's woodland kingdoms, despite the terrifying costly battles fought. Gweston and Nindar were similarly largely left alone as the kingdoms were so deep inside either Liberalist or Unionist territory, but the draining, taxing effort of supporting the war effort made life miserable in these kingdoms as well. Further strain was continually added as both kingdoms continually received huge, uncountable amounts of refugees all the while their economy's crumbled in efforts to sustain the war effort for their allies.

As local as the war efforts now were, with kingdoms seemingly exclusively fighting one and other only, cross kingdom help was still apparent on both sides. Nindar and Gweston practically became the supply backbone of their alliances as they continually sent supplies and reinforcements to friendly kingdoms that needed them. These supplies having to take routes that were being fully exploited by the likes of the Dwarves, Thruckland, and the underworld which both sides of the civil war had come to fully rely upon. As well as this, kingdoms like Kondit Point, the Sky Mountains, and Aquatatia, all continually lent their support to their allies for the unique qualities they all had. Kondit Point and Aquatatia especially helped their allies in the Connecting Isles region as their naval forces were most helpful to the conflict there. The Valkyries from the Sky Mountains were obviously highly sought after as no other kingdom held the same ariel power that they did and so they became a valuable aid to all the Unionist kingdoms, and a highly sought-after target for the Liberalists.

The widespread costly war effort, along with the misery caused by the crime empire's indulged way of life, and the seemingly unbeatable power of the corrupt underworld truly had made Terratopia the worst place to inhabit in all of the world of Terra Tearia. Its peoples in all levels of society suffered tremendously. Even Hyzus and Tyzus suffered due to the conditions they had helped create, though they did not feel the same intensities of misery, suffering, and despair as a great many other inhabitants in the archipelago as they knew there was a supposed unseeable light at the end of the tunnel. Although, this being said, the state that Tyzus and Hyzus had created throughout the lands and witnessed all their people suffering in only made their questioning of Kyzus's methods towards his grand plan all the more certain. They began to doubt their father's wisdom, believing it to be completely flawed as for as good as an idea his united society was, they began to believe that the destruction and suffering his methods were causing were pointless and detrimental. Tyzus and Hyzus began to reason to themselves and each other that surely the united society Kyzus theorized could come about through more peaceful diplomatic means. After all, surely the peoples of Terratopia had suffered enough to see how bad their state of nature had become and how they had to rise above it and additionally, both Tyzus and Hyzus saw the greatness in his idea when Kyzus explained it to them, why couldn't the rest of the peoples of Terratopia if they too had it explained to them.

The Twins of Hobbes kept these thoughts to themselves and away from their father. But their certainty of that their father methods were wrong only grew in intensity as Kyzus continually pressed them to continue the war and maximise its destruction throughout the whole year. To Tyzus and Hyzus they knew of only a very select few in all of Terratopia that in fact lived comfortable lives. These people were Kyzus and the inhabitants of Roccano and perhaps the mysterious crime queen they had heard rumours about. Everyone else, including themselves seemed to be far far worst off because of Kyzus's plan, furthermore, Kyzus's methods had led to far worst things the twins had originally bargained for, like the horrific two-week long genocide from the Fungi Forest to Pixieland that had been caused by a terrifying unknown barbaric army from Sabare in the far east.

Terrible conspiratorial thoughts began to plague the twin brothers' minds; maybe their father had already created his perfect society in Roccano and deceived his sons to send the wider lands backwards in a great war to make his society all the more powerful, sustainable, and unstoppable, maybe their father had forsaken them, afterall he never allowed them back into Roccano and rarely saw them in person now. These ideas grew in the twins' minds. They both wanted to doubt them but their fathers' actions seemed to be confirming them with each passing month. It was because of these thoughts that Hyzus and Tyzus began to investigate all they could about their father without alerting him, including investigating their seeing stones gifted to them by him. When they discovered that there were more hidden, unnatural enchantments within them, Hyzus and Tyzus's minds ran wild out of control, they still could not bring themselves to fully believe that their father was somehow not who he said he was, but there was certainly more going on that he was not telling them and they certainly did not trust him, his word, or his methods any longer. Together the twins decided not to question Kyzus but to instead watch him and play along with his plan, if they, for whatever reason, believed their conspiracies where absolutely confirmed true, then they would forsake him and their oaths to him.

Hyzus and Tyzus knew extremely little about their seeing stones enchantments as well as the true powers of their father, so they together began to study to be able to fully hide their intentions and thoughts from him. Something they were quickly able to do from their own vast wisdom, magical power, and personal connections to Aquata's vast libraries.

Chapter 9

Treachery and Division

It had been a year since the genocide on Fairy Island and Delilah had been ruthlessly preparing herself and her kingdom under Daiv for an arrival from Kyzus. But the all-powerful Lordbaron of Roccano nor his fearsome army never showed. Because of this, Delilah grew restless, she was certain that Kyzus would confront her after she had so ruthlessly killed off his Wolfpack and belittled his right hand and gone on a rampage from Sabare to Pixieland. But it had been a year and Kyzus had not so much as attempted to contact Delilah through her seeing stone, let alone visit her filthy kingdom.

Daiv wondered why his beloved wife grew so agitated, to him, surely it was a good thing that her mysterious father didn't appear for any hostile altercation like the last time he did. But for Delilah, Kyzus's lack of effort to confront her and the lack of knowledge she had about him, his whereabouts, or his plans made her paranoid. She wanted to grow her empire and completely take over Terratopia; to become the 'undisputed' most powerful queen in all the land. But Delilah knew she could not do this with Kyzus around and especially with him wanting to execute an ulterior plan that was already in motion and would involve the crushing of her empire. Delilah needed Kyzus out of the picture and she knew she could only possibly be within a chance of doing this by confronting him on her own turf, similar to how she defeated Barriel and her Paladins before. Delilah knew that she could not possibly stand any chance against the supreme power of Kyzus any other way, and she definitely knew her kingdom, as mighty as it was, stood no chance of storming Roccano to confront Kyzus herself, she needed him to come to her, where she could best use her strengths and formidable forces.

Delilah reasoned that she had to find a way to provoke Kyzus somehow; to provoke him to face her and her kingdom on her own terms, then she could have a chance. And the infamous, cunning evil queen could think of only one way to do this, she would have to severely interfere with his plan that he cared so much about and spent his whole life making sure went off without a hitch. That way she could force his hand. But how to best do this? She pondered to herself. There was numerous ways Delilah knew she could impede Kyzus's plan as, for now, her criminal empire and its control was an integral part of it. But Delilah wondered to herself, how could she best do this without undermining her own position and power, afterall, she had grown so evil and power hungry in nature that she could not possibly bare to lose any of her gains for any reason. But then suddenly, it dawned on her, the perfect way to upset Kyzus's delicate war effort as well as strike a deadly blow deep into his soul. She would ravage Aquata, the ancient home of his mother Mia and a city that had so far been completely unaffected by the war.

And so, the sinister crime queen formulated her plan and discreetly put the word out. She ordered the assembly of every Merman and Mermaid she could muster as well as every Pirate vessel. Once gathered, Delilah dressed half of them in captured Unionist army clothes and armour and the other half in Liberalist army clothes and armour. Together this assembly were ordered and paid handsomely by Delilah to pillage, plunder, ravage, and ruin the great ancient capital of Aquatatia. Upon this being done, Delilah also ordered that messengers should immediately be sent to Jassett, Embirith, and Roccano bearing the 'devastating news' of the 'Unionist' or 'Liberalist' armies that had desolated Aquata'. This being the provoking strike that would surely bring Kyzus to Delilah's doorstep.

Upon receiving those exact orders from Delilah, the desolation of Aquata was set in motion as pirate fleets of ships sailed from Sabare to Aquata; some sailing northwards up and around Eastern and Central Terratopia, past Carlin, Nindar, and Thruckland, while others sailed southwards, down and past Orthelian, the Dividing Mountains, Rodus and then back up along Rodus's coast. And beneath these ships swam swarms of deviate Merpeople in their misleading armour hellbent on destroying the most grandiose Merpeople city.

And soon, as Delilah's ships arrived above Aquata, it happened. The pirate ships dropped all kinds of large, heavy, and destructive objectives from their ships which bombarded the untouched grand city below. Huge chucks of ruined buildings and towers sank with ferocious speed and smashed into the untouched wonderous buildings of Aquata. The pirates then continued this while also fending off attack from the Aquata defenders that had risen to safeguard their city. Delilah had coincidentally ordered her strike on Aquata at a perfect time as the entire kingdom was near empty of its main forces as they were off either helping their allies around Lemlee or battling Liberalist forces at Atoll City. It was when Aquata's garrison was largely at the surface and attempting to drive away the pirates that Delilah's own Merpeople force then attacked the city below the waves. They pillaged and plundered their way through the entire city in a destructive spree. Awe-inspiring ancient buildings, that had not already been ruined or toppled by the pirate's bombardment, were themselves toppled and ruined by the deviant Merpeople. The city of peaceful philosophers and thinkers was all but defenceless as their immaculate city was ravaged and ruined by Delilah's goons.

The infamous halls and libraries of texts that Thyzus, Kyzus, Lyzus, Tyzus and Hyzus had all studied in were luckily mostly saved however as even the deviate Merpeople on Delilah's pay roll and orders could not bring themselves to destroy such works of magnificence that all Merpeople respected and cherished. These stupendous building housed the most marvellous collections of knowledge and wisdom in all of Terra Tearia as well as history and legacy of Terratopia at large. No Merman or Mermaid, whether deviant, Unionist or Liberalist could ever bring themselves to purposefully damage or destroy this.

Despite this, the job Delilah had ordered was still done, Aquata was desolated and news of this very quickly reached both Tyzus and Hyzus, but Hyzus was first to learn and whom immediately in fury contacted his brother who pleaded his innocence and ignorance as he had ordered nor even knew of no such attack on Aquata. Both twins feared that a rogue Liberalist army had gone behind Tyzus's back once more and attacked Aquata. But this fear was dispelled when Tyzus too learnt of a now 'Unionist' attack on Aquata, not a 'Liberalist' one. Furious and confused he contacted Hyzus and the both of them raged at each other in confusion and anger as their beloved city of Aquata that held so much meaning to them both and their family had been ruined. Neither could wholly believe what the other was saying, instead starting to believe that their brother was instead lying to them and that it must be some kind of confusing new war tactic, signalling that they were no longer on the same side and that they were in actual fact now fighting a real war against one another. They now had completely lost trust in one another.

The raging twins where soon joined on their seeing stone connection by Kyzus however who explained to them both exactly what had actually happened, dispelling the accusations they were beginning to form about each other, but by no means repairing the broken lost trust. Kyzus explained to his sons that neither of their sides were to blame, as the events in Aquata were in actual fact a subversive, sinister, and cunning scheme of the crime empire. Kyzus also informed both Tyzus and Hyzus that he knew not for what end why the crime empire had committed such an unusual devastating act. After explaining this to his twins and calming them down, before then instructing them both to somehow use this event to further fuel the continued war effort, Kyzus ended his connection with Tyzus and Hyzus. But the twins stayed contacted.

"Are we really going to believe that brother?" Tyzus said angrily.

"Of course not!" Hyzus responded sharply. "I don't believe a word of it! How could Kyzus allow this to happen?" he then said in an extremely disgruntled, confused tone.

"I know! This is it. He has gone too far!" Tyzus then proclaimed.

"And..." Hyzus then said. "Even if it is true and he had no control over this, this still just shows our initial fears anyway! Kyzus's methods are clearly just too dangerous and unsustainable and unpredictable. What he has put in motion must be stopped! Its consequences are running out of control!"

"Agreed," Tyzus stated. "We must end this war. End this suffering and then crack down on this crime empire that has sprouted in the chaos we created."

"Yes brother!" Hyzus resounded. "Gather your Liberalist kingdom leaders and convince them to extend and offer of peace negotiations. I will make sure the Unionist accept."

"I don't see why my Liberalists should have to instigate the peace talks?" Tyzus questioned. "But still, I shall do that and we can finally end this war."

"Because your Liberalists where the instigators of this war?" Hyzus responded in a confused tone, seemingly genuinely believing what he said and that Tyzus was stupid to even question. "But yes. Together we can end this war and recombine the Terratopia union to expel this crime empire!"

"Whoa Whoa!" Tyzus responded. "You can't be serious brother? Why do you want to re-combine the Union? In saying that, we were not the instigators! Your Unionist were for not letting my kingdoms leave," he then said heatedly.

"Of course I'm serious!" Hyzus responded in an equally heated but also confused questioning manner. "We want to bring about peace and bring about a united society, just a different way to our delusional father, how else are we going to do that without re-igniting the Terratopia Union and then gradually bringing it closer and closer"

"But the union was failing brother!" Tyzus exclaimed. "It was failing and still is failing. We all need to take a big step back and then maybe try again later if ALL kingdoms want. BUT after we have rid the archipelago of the crime empire"

"The union was failing because of you Tyzus!" Hyzus shouted back. "Together WE can re-combine it. We were in total control of it with the Lord Delegate Petar, we tore it apart and we can make it work again! We need it if our kingdoms want to stand any chance of wiping out the organised empire!"

"I only used failings that were already apparent!" Tyzus retaliated. "The union was failing long before me and you know it, to quote our father, 'what we have created was inevitable anyway we just sped it up!' My kingdoms have been fighting a whole war and so many have died because they feel so strongly against it and they have a point! The Union needs to end. Our kingdoms need to flourish individually by themselves. They are all facing serious internal problems, we need to let them solve them first before we then maybe try again in the FAR future! And besides, we do not need a union to defeat crime together. My Liberalist movement are not in a union together, only allied towards a common goal they all want. No kingdom in Terratopia wants this crime empire, so we can all easily work together towards its downfall."

"The union was not failing! It just needed to right leadership, which we can bring brother! What has happened was maybe inevitable if nothing was done about it! Which we can now do and do properly!" Hyzus reasoned back. "And the crime empires grip is too vast Tyzus, its impeded too deep into all of our kingdom's governments and our own peoples all rely upon it. There's no way we can successfully bring the empire down without doing it together in an uncorrupted, untainted, re-combined union!" Hyzus boldly stated.

"Whatever reasons you give Hyzus and whatever you say to convince yourself, surely you can still see that my Liberalist kingdoms would never agree to re-join the union? Reversing everything that they have been fighting for. Suffering and DYING for. Furthermore, I would not re-join the union either! You are wrong brother! It needs to be disbanded! Terratopia's kingdoms need to go their independent separate ways!" Tyzus exclaimed.

"Why are you doing this brother?" Hyzus angrily questioned. "You sound just like a Liberalist! Come to your senses!"

These words brung fury to Tyzus's ears. "And you sound just like an ignorant Unionist!" he yelled back. "Why are YOU doing this? We both agree to forsake our father, our vows we took to him as children, because we want to end this war, but yet you still pursue actions that legitimately caused it in the first place?"

"Because it's the right thing to do!" Hyzus screamed. "In no way is working alone better than all working together and I will force us all to work together if I have too! Because like it or not we all need to work together brother!"

"Then force us I guess you will have to do then!" Tyzus retaliated. "I know you're wrong. Good luck trying to stop what the people want brother." Tyzus then said. "And good luck trying to do so with them now having my full support and leadership and me not informing you of all our actions!"

As soon as Tyzus said this he abruptly dropped his stone and ended his argument with Hyzus. Furious at his brother Hyzus then too dropped his stone. Both brothers then sat in their respected leadership seats and furiously thought the exact same things. "How could their twin be doing this? Why is he doing this? I am so certain I am right. And my people have been fighting this war for a reason. We can't just reverse what they have been fighting for? He must have been corrupted. He's fallen to the illogical ideals of his side's ideology. I shall continue this war! And see it through to its end. Then I can go about uniting Terratopia peacefully and not my father's way." As both the twins thought his last thought, a painful stabbing pain hit them both in the heart and an eerie green mist erupted from their hearts and surrounded them both. Both Tyzus and Hyzus knew exactly what had happened. It was now official, they had forsaken their magical vows, there was no going back now.

It was the dead of night as this happened, and as it did, Kyzus dropped to his knees in despair. A draining sorrowful feeling passed over him and he knew exactly why. Treachery had occurred. His sons had both deserted him. Madness and raged then came over Kyzus. This was all his fallen daughter's fault. She had ruined everything. And now Kyzus finally decided that it was time to make her pay. A burning orange fury passed over his eyes and Kyzus exploded out of his mountainside palace, powerfully thrusting open the enormous doors which produced a violent gust of wind that swept the whole of Roccano, wailing flags, banners, and curtains vigorously. Standing at the top of the mountainside steps in front of his palace overlooking his magnificent kingdom that was covered in darkness but lit splendidly by plentiful torch light, Kyzus then spiralled around quickly and vanished from view.

Chapter 10

The Lordbaron of Roccano

An ominous thunder storm was brewing over Sabare, its thick black and dark grey clouds blocking out the light of the moon and stars, making the disorderly kingdom almost completely pitch black, save for the odd fire and torch, but the noise of mindless ramble still polluted the night.

Daiv stood next to his throne made of bones while his wife Delilah sat on its comfortable furs hunched over with her head resting on her enclosed, interlocked fits, she was in deep thought and very nervous, she knew it was only a matter of time before Kyzus would make some kind of move.

Delilah suspected most that Kyzus would unleash Roccano's full might upon Sabare and personally lead it and so she had ordered all the Samsons and Goliaths to be on high alert and to guard and patrol the walls and streets of the whole kingdom, in case more Paladins teleported in at unusual places.

But, as the heavy rains of the storm began to fall down and the thunder became a deathening rumble overhead in the black night's sky, only being lit up by the instant strike of lighting, Kyzus arrived. But he arrived alone.

Kyzus had silently and slyly teleported before the entrance way into Sabare beneath the gatehouse. His dark grey flowing robes blended seamlessly into the darkness of night and so consequently was not spotted by anyone. Kyzus stood before the formidable closed metal portcullis of the gatehouse that imposingly stood in front of him but effortlessly, he waved his hands with two fingers on each hand pointing to either side of him in a calm gentle motion. As he did the stern metal bars of the portcullis twisted, contorted, and ripped apart before then pealing back and further ajar. The unnatural movement of the sturdy metal was not violent however and produced little sound, just a low uncomfortable squeaking and contorting metallic uhm. Kyzus then, with his long robes trailing behind him and hood over his face, calmly waltzed through the opening he had created, only to be greeted by three Samsons whom were directly guarding the entrance way before him and saw the whole thing. They boldly asked who Kyzus was while they approached the mysterious but old looking figure, whose stature was far smaller than their own. But Kyzus did not reply nor let the Samsons touch him. He instead raised his hands which in turn raised the Samsons up into the air by a magical grip on their necks and before they could make a sound Kyzus closed his open hands into fists with a tight grip, and in doing so, crushed the throats and necks of the three Samsons whom then all dropped dead to the floor. The only noise being the faint crunching of their necks and the squelching of their bodies falling into the wet mud. Kyzus then continued on his calm walk towards the chieftain's compound through the middle of the open and deserted soggy streets.

Kyzus on his composed walk towards the compound in the now torrential rain encountered many more Goliaths and Samsons often in isolated groups of no more than five, but no matter who he encountered or where he encountered them or how he encountered them, the result was always the same. Kyzus would barely bat an eye lid or break his slow smooth stride while also somehow dispatching mercilessly the most formidable warriors in all of Terratopia in a near instant. This was done through a number of means; whether through extremely powerful sever magics or clean, precise, lightning-fast strikes from his concealed blades. But no matter how Kyzus slayed the Samsons and Goliaths that stood in his way, he always did so silently and without delay. It was as if he was a grim reaper demi-god, slowly gliding through the streets and instantaneously killing all he touched, like an angel of death or ghost of oblivion. The ruin left in his wake was only briefly visible in the black of night through the flash of lighting. Dead motionless bodies littering the boggy streets, drenched in rain.

As Kyzus approached the imposing gates of the chieftain's compound, again completely unseen as the night was black and his appearance melded into the darkness perfectly, Delilah immediately sensed Kyzus's insane magical presence nearby and nervously rose to her feet rapidly.

"He's here" Delilah then murmured in an anxious manner as thunder seemingly applauded as if on que.

As she said this a series of loud individual thudding noises could just be made out from outside the hall over the sound of the rain thrashing down into the muddy ground. These thudding noises where the sounds of dead guards being dropped to the ground as Kyzus levitated himself up over the gates and put to death every guard he could see, in a similar fashion to how he dispatched the three Samsons at the front gate to the kingdom; lifting them high into the air, crushing their throats and dropping their corpses unceremoniously to the floor.

As the thudding ominous noises stopped, Daiv and Delilah readied themselves, gripping their sleeved undrawn weapons and bouncing nervously but in eager anticipation. A lull stillness filled the air as nothing but the serenity of the downpouring rain hitting the wooden roof of the hall could be heard.

But suddenly Kyzus flung open the recently repaired doors of the hall Delilah and Daiv stood at the end off, the force of his push producing a gust that rattled through the hall and past Delilah and Daiv. The flurry of wind violently blew past them and rattled their hair and clothes vigorously until the flurry dispersed away. But Delilah & Daiv's stoic stances remained the same, as if they were both solid stone statues. Lightning struck out and flashed up the night sky behind Kyzus in the doorway, producing a long daunting shadow that flickered across the whole hall, only stopping at Delilah's feet. Thunder once again rang vehemently as if to announce Kyzus's arrival.

Slowly Kyzus then approached his two adversaries, his footsteps on the cold stone floor echoing around the hall and the thunder and lightning in the background making his approach and appearance all the more perilous. In what seemed like an eternity later, Kyzus then stopped before Delilah and Daiv, standing collectedly behind his hood with his arms and hands hidden somewhere in his drenched grey robes. He then raised his head to look up at the evil queen and her brutish husband, his gaze just becoming visible to them, but his eyes and face showing no emotion.

"So, you have finally decided to come and finish off your dirty work your 'trusted' right hand could not," Delilah said in a strong malevolent tone.

In a small movement Kyzus, effectively gestured to Delilah's left eye that was now covered with a menacing black eye patch as her eye was completely sealed permanently shut and blinded, the patch also covered her crushed cheek bone.

"Barriel has done more than enough," Kyzus then boomed, his ethereal echoing voices surprising both Delilah and Daiv briefly as they had forgotten that was how Kyzus spoke.

"Then why dare show your face in my kingdom and my throne room." Delilah snapped back confidently.

"Because Queen Delilah..." Kyzus sneered; "You... and your operation... have... become... an... IMPEDIMENT!" he then growled before then suddenly leaping and spiralling up towards the empire's leaders, his two exquisite blades spinning around him in a silver propeller like blur. Kyzus was like a revolving twisting projectile and his actions were so sudden and fast that Delilah and Daiv barely had enough time to separate apart and avoid him, but the same could not be said for the sides of their hair which were cleanly sliced off and then floated down to the floor. Kyzus then collided and smashed through Daiv's throne which shattered into its separate bone pieces and threw up a cloud of dust.

Daiv and Delilah instantly drew their weapons and readied themselves for a duel, peering around to try and spot Kyzus in the spray. But behind the cloud of dust and falling rags of fur he could be seen nowhere. Suddenly though Delilah spotted him just in time as he shot down from the sky onto Daiv with both his blades drawn, pointing downwards like a spearhead.

"DAIV!" she screamed, which gave the mighty Samson enough warning to reflexively deflect Kyzus's attack away with his large twin-bladed sword. Kyzus elegantly landed in-between the husband and wife, rising both his blades up beside him to individually face both of the advisories that sandwiched him. Kyzus then slowly raised from his hunched landing position and raised his head up in a smirk, but he did not make eye contact with either Delilah or Daiv, he instead starred directly ahead of him across the empty hall and out the entrance way he had walked through. Delilah and Daiv yelled as they charged in to attack Kyzus in movements faster than the lighting strikes of the storm outside. But this was no problem for Kyzus who fended off the two facing sideways. He moved and deflected all their strikes with his own unnaturally faster speed. Nothing but the sound of rain, the swooshing of movement, and clinking of metal could be heard as Delilah and Daiv tried mercilessly to overwhelm Kyzus. But Kyzus stood firm, his robes waving around him elegantly like a sea of fine fabric as he danced a deadly dance with his advisories.

Soon though Kyzus manged to briefly thrust Delilah and Daiv backwards with his blades deflecting their simultaneous attacks, and in that brief moment of time, before their next strike, the powerful Half-elf wizard slammed his hands into the stone floor creating an almighty rippling wave that emanated through the air and stone flooring like an earthquake and pushed Delilah and Daiv violently back into the side walls of the hall. Kyzus then leapt into the centre of the hall, leaving behind the shattered stone slabs that once made up the platform around where the throne usually stood. Kyzus then removed his robes, dropping them to the floor revealing a fine tunic and other similarly exceptional fabric clothes beneath. Delilah and Daiv then approached him again through the rubble, shaking themselves off from their impacts into the walls.

The three fiercely starred at each other, exchanging no words. Kyzus's eyes burned orange and he grinned confidently as he glared at Delilah's menacing fiery piercing blue eye and scowling face. Delilah, followed by Daiv, again attempted to charge into Kyzus with their weapons drawn, but Kyzus instead of preparing to counter, quickly raised his hand so that his palm faced Delilah and then produced a potent thrust of an invisible magical force that slammed into Delilah and sent her flying back into Daiv, knocking them both to the ground. The speed of this magical strike was unlike Delilah had ever seen. The two had no time to gather their senses either as Kyzus vehemently followed up his thrust himself like a lightning bolt and speared himself into the laying couple. Delilah manged to stop Kyzus mid-flight just in front of her with her own magical burst of force, but Kyzus effortlessly passed around this and dropped to the floor continuing his attack again now sprinting faster than a cheetah, but by this time Daiv was now ready and he slammed his sword into the floor where Kyzus would have been if it was not for the Lordbaron's own supernatural speed who dodged away and stabbed straight for the mighty Samson. Delilah protected Daiv's exposed side with a rapid slice from her own blade, driving Kyzus's strike downwards towards the ground. But Kyzus was again unphased by this and used the momentum of this deflection to spin around and, like a windmill, he used his other outstretched arm, which held his other blade, to slice down on Delilah who herself just barely managed to move her body away. However, she could not move her hand away in time and so had the outside of her fingers were cut by Kyzus's slicing blade. Delilah yelped slightly and dropped her blade to the floor as the precise cleave from Kyzus cut painfully across the middle of her four figures holding her blade. Just as Kyzus was about to strike Delilah with his other blade, that Delilah had previously deflected away from Daiv but by now had windmilled around again to strike her, Delilah unleashed a potent burst of blue fire to defend herself. This was just what she needed as Kyzus then leapt up to avoid the fire and away from her. Even though Kyzus was so close to Delilah when she unleashed her spell, he was completely untouched and unharmed.

    With her hand now dripping with blood she picked up her blade again and Daiv pulled his from the stone floor he had slammed it in. Delilah using a small magical flame in one hand cauterised up her finger cuts and began to worry to herself. Throughout that whole series of events, Kyzus seemed to be serval steps ahead of them, everything she or Daiv did was avoided and used for another attack as if it was known and choreographed from the very beginning. The three advisories again found themselves in a face off, but this time it barely lasted any time at all. Kyzus dropped both his blades and produced a violent barrage of grey clouds from his hands. These deadly magical clouds hurtled towards

Delilah at a terrific pace and overpowered the small amount of fire she managed to produce in the time she had to react. Upon impacting Delilah, the grey clouds exploded into dazzling yellow lightning and smashed Delilah backwards, sending her soring into the wall behind her, crumbling the wooden wall with a big dent that she was now imbedded in. In this time, while Daiv was still briefly in shock at what happened, Kyzus slammed himself into the Samson with both his blades pointing forward. In a grey blur Kyzus had shot himself across the hall and impaled his blades all the way into Daiv, their tips coming out of his back dripping with blood. Daiv instantly twitched and flinched at this and directly starred down at Kyzus. Anger filled his body and he slammed his fist down to strike Kyzus, but again the Lordbaron's speed was unmatched and he threw himself backwards, pulling his blades with him, twisting them to gut out the thin wounds he had caused. Two slender, but opened, red slits then emerged from Daiv's stomach on either side of his monumental abs and blood began to seep and then pour from them at an alarming rate. Enraged, Daiv then charged towards Kyzus, who in turn smirked and directly met to engage with Daiv. Just as the two were about to meet blades however, Kyzus instantly teleported behind Daiv and stabbed one blade into his upper right trap before then deeply slicing all the way down his back and left leg with the other blade.

 Daiv fell forward to his hands and knees in pain and shock; feeling the imbedded blade still skewered into him and the deep continuous cut down his back and leg opening up fully and beginning to pour out more blood. Enraged further, Daiv screamed at the floor in front of him, ripped Kyzus's blade straight from his body, threw it away, and then swung his unique weapon behind him along the ground. Kyzus easily stepped out the way of this swing but it gave Daiv enough time to stand upright again and again Daiv swung his twin bladed sword down at Kyzus. But Kyzus gracefully and mysteriously shifted Daiv's sword strike to his side with his bare weaponless hand and sliced down with his other hand still holding a blade, chopping straight through the middle of Daiv's forearm. Then Kyzus, with his empty hand that had come up and around to face Daiv again, produced another violent tremendous grey cloud from his upside-down palm that blasted straight into Daiv's chest, hurtling him backwards in an explosion of sharp blinding lightning. This all being done in one beautiful and effortless fluent motion.

Such was the point-blank range that Daiv was stuck with by Kyzus's intense magic that the mighty Samson was sent straight through the hall's walls, smashing a hole right through them, and then landing some distance away in the sopping wet, deep mud of his compound. Delilah meanwhile had just come to her senses from being dazzled by Kyzus's magical strike. She was still lodged in the crumpled wooden wall high above the ground and had just seen the explosion that had sent Daiv soring out of the hall. Delilah screamed and launched herself from her position in the air, steaming straight towards Kyzus whose back was turned.

But Kyzus again gracefully moved and waved his whole body away from Delilah's missile-like strike. Delilah however, after landing controllably, continued her fury in a barrage of slashes, stabs, flourishes, and slices all aimed at Kyzus. But Kyzus nimbly, skilfully, and graciously evaded every strike from Delilah without having to utilise his blade for defence at all; his unnaturally swift body, head, and arm movement was more than enough. Delilah yet pressed on her attack. Fuelled by hatred, anger, and fear, her attacks grew faster and faster, and deadlier and deadlier, eventually even managing to press Kyzus onto his back foot and turn his confident smirk to a cold concentrated grimace. That soon changed however as when Delilah had dominated Kyzus into a corner and bended him backwards to evade being struck by her blade in a fatal blow across Kyzus's chest, Kyzus finally drew his remaining blade and locked it with Delilah's. The two deadly combatants grinded their superb refined blades against one another as they glared menacingly into each other souls. Delilah had a terrifying scowl on her face and was hell bent on slicing her blade into Kyzus, pressing down with all her might. But Kyzus, again with an unnatural amount of strength and power grinned and cackled as he rose back upright. Fear passed over Delilah's face as Kyzus then reached and grabbed Delilah's arm and somehow flung her to his side. The formidable Lordbaron of Roccano then with both hands produced more immense grey clouds from his hands aimed directly at Delilah on the ground. But the powerful queen dodged and leapt out the way but as soon as she landed elsewhere, she found that she had to jump out the way again as Kyzus had already shot his potent clouds spell towards her. Again, this happened. And again, and again. Delilah was becoming exhausted; she could not leap away any more; she began to slide and dodge out of the way of more of Kyzus's magical blasts but again found she had to suddenly continually move again and again. In a last-ditch attempt to evade Kyzus's magic and gain some much-needed space, Delilah leapt as hard and as high as she could to land as far away from Kyzus as she could. But as soon as she landed, she was struck terribly with a burst of clouds that had been sent towards her landing spot before she had even landed. A huge sparkling explosion of lightning occurred as Delilah was then flung out the entrance way of the hall like a ragdoll.

Chapter 11

The Plan Must Prevail

Delilah landed face first into the muddy ground of the chieftain's compound because of her blow from Kyzus and then continued to slide and tumble along the slippery slimy ground until she hit the solid log compounds walls that stopped her suddenly. She sat up exhausted, covered in mud, and her whole body was mercilessly bruised. Delilah was now becoming drenched in rain, but she welcoming it as the chilled waterfall of water cooler her off and rinsed the mud off her body. In the distance she could see Kyzus smoothly emerge from the entrance way of the hall and stride straight towards Daiv. The Samson had gradually managed to harrowingly crawl to his weapon and rise to his knees by now. He was mortally wounded but still had fight within him. Covered in rain, mud, and a lot of blood Daiv grunted and raised himself up to meet Kyzus. But by now Kyzus was eager to end this fight as soon as possible and went on the offensive mercilessly. Kyzus had retrieved his other blade that Daiv had previously thrown away and was more than ready to finish off the great Samson chieftain once and for all. Daiv desperately swung at all angels at Kyzus, but the all-powerful ancient Half-elf brushed all the incoming strikes off and always returned with a deadly stab or slice of his own, each afflict weakening Daiv further and further. All too soon Daiv was suddenly brought to his knees as Kyzus spung around him and sliced the back of them. Delirious, close to death, and defeated Daiv noticed Kyzus boldly stand before him and grab his head.

Daiv accepted that he was beaten. It had finally happened. But he did not feel despair nor jealously and instead smiled. With blood beginning to emanate from his mouth, Daiv managed to splutter some words at his great advisory;

"Only the strongest deserve to survive," he chocked as he also lowered his head in sorrowful defeat awaiting his demise, before Kyzus then sighed and sarcastically replied rolling his eyes;

"Sure."

Kyzus then rapidly sliced numerous deep fatal slashes across Daiv's whole body from head to knee. The swift slicing sounds were unsettling to hear and haunted Delilah as she finally rose up out her exhausted dazed state against the compounds wall. For a moment nothing happened and even the rain seemed to stop. But then blood began to seep out from Daiv's whole body, covering him in red, but still, he did not die. Daiv had truly shown how durable and formidable the Samson race could be. Despite the fact that he could no longer see, Daiv sensed Kyzus's disturbed reaction and mild annoyance. The impressive Samson laughed out in a thunderous applause that even drowned out the thunder storm around him before Kyzus then impaled both his blades into Daiv's open mouth and then sliced then apart in a brutally gory scene; finally ending the monumental, colossal, legendary, mighty warrior and chieftain that now lay in a puddle of mud, blood, and gore.

Delilah screamed out in grief at the sight and cried out in heartbreak and anger as Daiv's body splatted into the muddy ground. Kyzus then graciously began to walk back into the hall out the rain. Delilah sprinted towards her husband's body to grieve over him but as she got close to him and saw the true extent of his brutal wounds, the most insane feelings of hated and anger she had ever felt past over her. Fuelled by her new found heartbreak and despair, Delilah desired only one thing now, absolute revenge on Kyzus. He had taken away the thing she had truly loved the most in her world, even more than her position of power as crime queen. Fierce blue and yellow fire explode all around Delilah's body and then continued to emanate directly from her, like a thick inferno layer of armour. Delilah could not find her blade as Kyzus had knocked it from her with his lighting explosion but that did not matter, the infamous crime queen levitated her beloved husbands twin-bladed sword towards her, snapped it in half to form two great large swords and then hovered towards the great hall to face down Kyzus, leaving a trail of dried burnt-out mud in her wake.

Delilah entered the hall in a berserk fiery frenzy, the wooden building all gradually began to burn all around her. The fire was only kept from burning out of control by the thunderstorms torrential rain outside. Kyzus turned to face Delilah and smiled in a pleasant surprise. Kyzus then formed a magical grey cloud beneath him and rose up to meet her on it. The two most powerful sorcerers in all of Terratopia, and perhaps that Terra Tearia had ever seen faced off against one another once again.

"You. Took. Everything. From. Me!" Delilah menacingly growled angrily, pausing after every word, and breathing heavily in fury.

"You have brought all this on yourself you evil low life! Besides isn't this the kind of life you strive for? The strongest reap rewards and all that. You hypocrite. You make me ashamed!" Kyzus then replied before then harnessing stupendous lighting strikes from the storm above him directly into his hands. Kyzus's eyes seemed to turn a bright flickering electric golden yellow, and the magical grey clouds beneath him turned into actual thunder clouds that emanated lighting. A truly legendary sight

"You have but one chance!" he then beckoned, his voices frightening to the bone and announced so epically that half the surrounding kingdom could hear; "Serve me or face my ultimate vengeance!"

Delilah screeched psychotically and unleashed a hail fire of blue flaming waves towards Kyzus from Daiv's swords. Kyzus thusly lifted his own blades into an X shape in front of him and produced lighting all around them. The exquisite blades covered in crackling yellow lightning absorbed all the magical blue fire shot into them with ease and then Kyzus swiftly returned, blasting a cascade of terrific lightning bolts back towards Delilah that were so unbelievably powerful that they over-came her own X shaped defence of fire covered swords and smashed into her. Delilah dropped backwards from the sky and slammed into the floor. Her magical fire flickered around her, but as she stood up and roared with anger, it burst right back into all its glory.

Kyzus too lowered himself to the ground to face Delilah and he too was swarmed all around by layers of magical prowess.

Grey clouds of varying shades, from light, misty, and transparent to dark, foggy, and foreboding, surrounded around Kyzus with lightning periodically flashing out from all them. Kyzus approached Delilah slowly. Once again, the two engaged themselves in a furious duel of blades and magic, but Delilah immediately found herself on the back foot fighting for her survival as Kyzus was not playing around any more. Dual wielding Daiv's swords around herself saved Delilah for a small while as she was able to match Kyzus's own armaments, but the Lordbaron of Roccano that had lived since the Summer of the world and done barely anything else but study and practice ancient magics and combat his whole life was simply far too superior for Delilah to ever hope to beat. One by one Delilah found her swords disarmed and swung away by Kyzus's insane skill and before she could get a chance to desperately unleash her signature blue fire with all her fury in a last-ditch attempt to fight on, she was magically frozen in place by Kyzus, his power being simply too vast and strong for even herself to attempt to overcome.

With one hand Kyzus held Delilah in place and with another he placed his blade on Delilah's throat. Delilah's hatred and anger quickly turned to fear and despair. She truly was beaten and was completely outmatch, she knew that she could never hope to defeat Kyzus, his true prowess had now been shown to her and it truly was all-powerful, she had lost.

"Please!" she cried. "Please have mercy on me! Spare me!" she then squirmed. Kyzus only snarled silently in return.

"Please father! It's me. Your daughter, Mia-Myzus! Have mercy on me please!" Mia-Myzus then genuinely cried out in despair and horror as the realisation that her own father may well actually kill her because of who she had become.

Kyzus's expression briefly turned to fragility before he then forced it back to sternness; but that did not stop a tear coming to his eye. Kyzus truly faced the biggest challenge he had yet to face. Was he really going to kill his daughter whom he still loved with all his heart? Whether she was an evil crime queen named Delilah or not, she was still defeated and now begging for mercy. Kyzus pondered to himself while he also strained to keep Mia-

Myzus in place and keep a stern look on his face; No. No, he decided. He could not risk his grand plan that would benefit all people for all time for the sake of maybe saving his daughter, one person. Afterall, as he had been continually telling his sons, they and himself were the only ones with the power, strength of will, and stomach strong enough to do what needed to be done. To see his plan through to the end. And they had to always make the right call no matter how difficult the decision may be. His daughter had forsaken him and had caused his sons to betray him also. She had to be delt with.

"You are not Mia-Myzus. No daughter of mine would ever fall so low into treachery and despair," Kyzus then boomed and he pressed his blade slightly harder into Mia-Myzus's neck. "No daughter of mine would betray me and seek for my own downfall. No daughter of mine would allow herself to be so corrupted and choose to become so evil. AND! No daughter of mine would beg for mercy like a lost child after doing all that!" Kyzus's blade pushed even harder into Mia-Myzus's skin, it was on the brink breaking it.

Mia-Myzus managed to flinch at the pain and again pleaded; "It is me father! I am sorry! Please spare me!"

"You are not Mia-Myzus." Kyzus harshly replied. "You are not worthy of the Hobbes family name. And you are not worthy to share the name of my mother!" Kyzus then boomed loudly again, even more sternly. "You, 'Queen Delilah', are of no relation to me!"

Anger passed over Mia-Myzus once more as the sight of her father renouncing her made her furious. "Well just kill me then!" she then screamed as blue fire returned to her eye.

"Oh, I will not kill you" Kyzus then said. "My plan is still yet to be complete and you still need to serve your purpose. Delilah! And you will do so now that you know your place!" he then stoically finished.

Delilah bowed her head in total defeat and remained motionless, even as Kyzus released his magical bond from her. Kyzus then produced his master seeing stone and from it unleashed a horrifically powerful and unnatural spell that shot straight into Delilah whom absorbed it all willingly.

Once the spectacular sight was over, Delilah fell to all fours before then raising up tall in a plain and tame manner. She then faced Kyzus;

"I am at yours to command my master, Lordbaron Kyzus Hobbes" she then said in a monotone voice.

Chapter 12
A Stalemate That Only a God Could Break

The war waged on across Terratopia for another year, being just as brutal, destructive, and unsufferable as it always was, except now the stalemates between kingdoms that had spanned the entire war effort were beginning to shift. Tyzus, more enthusiastic than ever to actually win and end the war, and to no longer prolong it, led his Liberalists to significant victories all across the archipelago. Without Unionist support and prior knowledge to Liberalist attacks, the grand city of Cufle finally fell to its siege. The last bastion of the Unionist in the East had finally fallen to its Liberalist besiegers and it was a crippling blow to Hyzus. In addition to this, Tyzus had swung the war over the Connecting Isle's region also. This was due to Aquatatia's forces, which had been of great value to the Unionist, now all permanently guarded their capital city at all times to make sure that it could never be ransacked again. This fact along with Tyzus combining the might's of his Liberalist kingdoms in that region meant that Lemlee soon found itself in a very desperate position once more. The men of the Connecting Isles, with the assistance of the Merpeople of the Shore Mountains Atoll and from Kondit Point's still impressive navy once again continually assaulted the woodland islands of Lemlee, completely isolating them from the Unionist with an even more impenetrable blockade and even managed to re-capture many of the smaller outer woodland islands.

The war wasn't all Liberalist victories however, Hyzus had managed to shift the war effort in Western Terratopia dramatically in his favour, despite the region being a Liberalist strong point. Hyzus managed to break the stalemate between the two Elvish kingdoms in the Silver Wood and had pushed his forces to ravage the majority of Suitear once more. The Liberalist city of Earwarth still stood but besides that, the majority of the Silver Wood was now under his Unionist control. A consequence of Hyzus's actions was that now he had cut Western Terratopia in half, isolating Gweston, the Liberalist's capital region, and effectively bringing the war right onto Tyzus's doorstep as Lendspen and Jassett where now permanently under serious threat. Tyzus had attempted to relieve his capital region by ordering armies from Arway to either attack Silvoud from behind or venture over the Harpgar Mountains to aid Gweston's own forces. But alas, neither plan seemed to work. Although Arway had mostly captured most of Silvor, they could not break through into the Silver Wood or capture the capital city of Thozon; a situation all too similar to what had occurred in the east with the successful invasion of Carlin but unsuccessful capture of Cufle for a great many years. Likewise, Arway's armies that attempted to cross over the Harpgar Mountains were all prevented by the Great Owls that again refused any war effort to enter into their mountainous realm. The Sky Mountains Valkyries now constantly raided Lendspen unexpectedly as well now, ravaging several districts of the grandiose gothic city. The high capitals of Men and Elves, Rime and Filnethias, had now completely repelled the Merpeople of Reeforiris as well. Reeforiris's forces were now far too few in number to stage any more assaults, there armies were all but wiped out by the formidable defence of Rodus's two grandest cities.

The criminal underworld and neutral kingdoms continued to fuel the war effort but now it seemed that they both seemed to favour Hyzus and his Unionists. The Dwarves refused to communicate with Tyzus and his Liberalist, seriously hampering his efforts to win the war and Thruckland too seemingly turned a cold shoulder to Tyzus, not allowing his Liberalists to utilise any of Thruckland's trading lanes, ships or, merchantry access.

And so once again by the end of the passing year, the civil war across Terratopia found itself in a stalemate. The Liberalists held all Eastern Terratopia but could not cross through or over the Dividing Mountains into Central Terratopia and they were also nearly completed isolated from the remaining Liberalist kingdoms as Kossorlim had completely sealed its gates. Central Terratopia remained completely in Unionist hands and the Liberalist had no way to disrupt that, but the Unionist also had no way nor any forces to venture out of Central Terratopia. The Connecting Isles were now all but ruled by the Liberalist's as well with Wefalime's fall inevitable in the coming months. The seas across and around Terratopia were all but Liberalist as well with only some Unionist bastions remaining that were not likely to fall at all. Western Terratopia was split into two with neither side being able to successfully or fully break the other. The war had simply gone on for too many years and caused too much damage, destruction, and death to kingdoms that neither side had the capability to be victorious over the other. They had both ground themselves into submission but still neither side would dare yield. Some Unionist and Liberalist leaders were beginning to request that Tyzus and Hyzus open up peace talks to end the war but by now both brothers were far too stubborn and bitter towards their twin that they would never agree or allow peace talks to commence. To Tyzus and Hyzus they were now fighting for something they whole heartedly believed in and would not give up until they were either killed or victorious.

It was at this point that Kyzus demanded his twin sons to talk to him, which eventually they both did. The three all agreed to meet in the secret cavern in the Thruckland range they had all historically met in previously before the war was first declared. One by one the three relatives arrived in the cold untouched cavern. Hyzus, then Kyzus, then Tyzus. They all refused to exchange words with each other and consequently created a cold, thick, and tense torturous atmosphere. Eventually however Kyzus spoke, his voices echoing commandingly throughout the cave;

"You have both forsaken me my children. You have let me down. I am going to give you one chance to come back to me and fulfil your vows."

Tyzus and Hyzus looked at each other angrily before Hyzus then spoke.

"We have forsaken you father because you have lost your way. Look at what you yourself have caused in the pursuit of your thought experiment. You have turned Terratopia into a wrenched and evil place. You have transformed the people into evil shadows of themselves and we could stand it no longer!"

"And you allowed us to suffer along with them! And you allowed Aquata to be ruined! How could you allow that to happen father! You to allow your own children, your only two descendants left! Allow them to suffer! And allow the sacred city of your mother, a city that holds great meaning to us all, all the Hobbes family, to be attacked and ruined!" Tyzus then angrily added.

Kyzus stared blankly at his two sons. He could see that similar to his daughter, he had pushed them both too hard and underestimated the toll their positions would have on them. But he would not show this dismay to them.

"I allowed it for the greater good my sons! You know that! And I thought you two of all people would be able to cope with that! I have been through too much to allow my archipelago, a land filled with kingdoms and peoples whom I cherish dearly to also experience anything like I had continually throughout all time. To lose my father, mother, wife, and daughter, to allow entire races to be driven to extinction! I could stop all that with my plan! I could bring Terratopia back to its summer heights of happiness and prosperity! I could do all that and you both were doing an amazing job of helping me!" Kyzus proclaimed before then continuing, "There is still time my sons! Please I beg. Join back with me, help me produce my united society under the Deity, for the benefit of all peoples! I beg of you my sons, I don't want to lose you as well," Kyzus said, lowering his head in sadness.

"Father," Hyzus then said, "can you not see that what you have caused has put the people of Terratopia through more suffering than what you have endured?"

Kyzus's eyes darted at Hyzus in fury. "How dare, you son! You have no idea what I have endured," he said sharply before then continuing, "And so what? Like I have been telling you both all this time, all this suffering was inevitable. This state of nature I have push you both to show, its worst side, was within all peoples! Like it or not! I didn't cause this. The people could have stopped at any time. They could have deposed their leaders and rebelled and stopped fighting. But they never did. They never will. Without my Deity, the peoples are not better than this and never will be!

Not that now Morur's Evil is apparent in the world. If we didn't create this together, I assure you plenty of others would have! And would have continually for centuries, millennia, and ages to come! We all need a society where we are all united together under the Deity and live under its strict laws that benefit us all, with harsh consequences if not obeyed. In the end it would do nothing but benefit us all and thrust us ever forward and never backward! We would overcome this horrific state of bickering, distrust, war, and death! We need that! We as a people need to be kept in check so we can pursue the prosperity we all also desire because if we are not, the people will continue to blindly fall into the primitive state of nature within us all."

"Even if you are right, father," Tyzus butted it. "Even if you cold heartedly believe that we as a peoples need this society you speak of in order the best live our lives, even if that was true, there are surely better methods to go about bringing it to life! That is what we forsook our oaths to you over. Not your grand final plan, but your methods. You have caused so much death, torture, and suffering that we could not take it any more! It's too much! There is too much destruction! There must be a peaceful way to bring about your society and so that is what we are pursuing!"

Kyzus laughed. "HA! If that is true, why do you both continue to fight one another then? And besides, not everyone has been brought up in the wisdom of us three. We see the logic in my plan but the vast majority of other peoples would not, they would never trust it as they have no trust, their state of nature is shellfish above all else. No matter what we do they will always find a way to go against it. They will find perceived short comings, justify them to themselves and then fight against them. They will see the freedoms they lose and feel they were better off before, despite this not being the case. Just as what happened before with the Terratopia Union. The only way we can bring about my society is if all the people actively want it and sign up for it! If they do that, they will see the laws as their own, if not then they will call them unjust and it would all come crashing down. The only way the people will want it, is when their state of nature could not be more worst as they'll want to not only be lifted out of it and lifted above it, but for it also to never be reachable ever again! This is exactly what my society promises, it would be unsatiable if not. In order to flip people to an extreme that is the very best for them, we must push them to the extreme that is the very worst for them!" Kyzus finished his speech by lowering his arms back down and facing his twins' sons, his tone was desperate, not like previous occasions of when he had been explaining his grand plan. Now Kyzus was trying in vain to get his children to agree with him and continue along their paths with him.

Hyzus and Tyzus shook their heads. "You are wrong, Father," Hyzus said disappointingly before then Tyzus also agreed. Kyzus hunched over and sighed deeply into his hands in defeat. He could not believe what was happening, his own sons were now totally against him. Tears began to come to his eyes and he once more raised up to face his sons.

"Please I beg my sons, I can't lose you both as well, please come back to me" Kyzus said in a sombre fragile tone.

"I am sorry, Father," Tyzus said, "but we can't, you've lost your way and we are now going to go about things our own way, a way we 'know' to be right. You will be proud of us in the future, I am sure."

As Tyzus said this, he then slowly walked past Kyzus and placed his hand lovingly on his shoulder before then continuing out of the cave. Kyzus then looked at Hyzus who too also shook his head and tried to avoid eye contact. Hyzus then also walked past Kyzus placing his hand softly on his father.

"I too am sorry father; I only hope you'll be proud of us both when either of us wins this war," Hyzus said softly before then continuing past Kyzus and out of the cavern.

All by his lonesome in the dark cold cave tears slowly trickled from Kyzus's eyes.

"I already am proud of you both" he mumbled softly to himself in a loving tone before he then teleported back to his mountainside palace.

Over many days Kyzus gradually recomposed himself. He was totally devastated that both his sons truly had forsaken him and his plan, but as was the same case with his daughter, Kyzus would not allow this stand in his way. His sons had chosen their path and they must now be delt with as they were no longer a controllable part of the plan.

Kyzus knew that his grand plan was nearing completion, the war was truly at a terrific stalemate and both sides were now at their worst, the state of nature had reached its evil peak and it was clear the people were ready for peace by any means. It was the perfect opportunity to complete his plan. But now, without the help or endorsement of his two sons, Kyzus would again have to adapt his plan accordingly. And so Kyzus plotted. The infamous Lordbaron secluded himself in his study and adapted his plan to now bring about his society without his sons help. After a few days he had done this, his grand plan was simply too inevitable at this point that even his sons' betrayal could not stop it, only alter its methods. Kyzus, now with his clear fully redevised plan reached for his master seeing stone and held onto it.

"Delilah," he called, "I am a mission for you..."

Chapter 13

The End of the War

Another two weeks had passed since Kyzus and his twin sons meeting and, in that time, much in Terratopia had changed; the war was finally coming to an end. The Liberalists were beginning to crumble to the Unionists, thanks in no small part to the entire Delilah Crime Empire undertaking new actions that were somehow exactly what the Unionists needed for victory. This was of course all of Kyzus's doing. The Lordbaron had cunningly ordered Sabare to commit to a huge invasion campaign across all of Eastern Terratopia as well as ordering the Dwarves of Kossorlim to join in. Kyzus had also ordered that all pirates and Merpeople in the service of the crime empire to ravage the Connecting Isles region. The effects of this on the Liberalists were devastating; their control in the east collapsed and fell into total chaos and the blockade around Lemlee was destroyed as all Liberalist forces were pushed back to their homelands. It was in this chaos that Hyzus seized the seemingly perfect opportunity that was presented before him. All Unionist forces within Central Terratopia where drained either through Thruckland or Kossorlim and they pushed deep into Liberalist territory, easily capturing and holding everything their armies seized upon. The forces of the crime empire had done their part, they had not the strength to souly take over the areas they were ordered to invade, but they certainly had the ability to plunge the Liberalists into total disarray and weaken them to be easily crushed by the advancing Unionists armies.

In just two weeks, the civil war of Terratopia had swung so dramatically that no one, not even Hyzus could quite fully believe it. Eastern Terratopia was now completely in Unionist hands and under their control, a complete role reversal. And Liberalist forces in the Connecting Isles were all but wiped out, save for Xephex who now found itself under siege. Liberalist Merpeople forces had all abandoned their efforts and retreated back to their home kingdoms where they remained and what was left of Kondit Point's grand navy now resided entirely hidden within Kondit Bay. To all the peoples of Terratopia it was clear, the war was finally ending. Most didn't even care who's side they were on or had fought for; whether they were the 'winners' or 'losers', the peoples of Terratopia were just glad that an end was in sight, a small degree of optimism and relief was in the air of the archipelago.

This was not the case for all however, most particularly Tyzus. At this desperate time for the Liberalists, Tyzus had gathered all the remaining Liberalist leaders that had not been trapped, captured or killed to Jassett where he decreed that an emergency council needed to be held to re-evaluate the war effort and to desperately try to find a way to fight on. The gathered leaders in Tyzus's council however largely had different ideas; most simply wanted to surrender and end the war with Hyzus, they saw no hope for victory and were by now fed up with the war. They also believed that maybe if they did surrender now, then maybe the leaders' kingdoms may not be forced to re-join the union once more. Tyzus vehemently rebuked this however, demanding continually that the Liberalists should continue to fight on. They afterall still controlled most of the seas and most of Western Terratopia, they were not totally defeated just yet. Tyzus adamantly believed that the Liberalist could easily stave off any Unionist invasion into their western lands and perhaps maybe now they could overrun Silvor and Silvoud with the Unionist being so pre-occupied trying to control the rest of Terratopia.

This council raged on for nearly two days with Tyzus garnering some support to continue the war under his plan but not enough to fully lead and commit the remaining Liberalist Alliance to his cause.

As the combined leaders of the Liberalists all raged and argued with each other in their Jassett stronghold, Delilah had skilfully and successful infiltrated the great fortress remaining completely undetected and soon she found herself outside the imposing doors to the chamber where Tyzus and his subordinates were. Delilah could hear them all arguing and bickering neither of the two opposing views ever listening to what the other had to say, instead themselves just attempting to rant over the other louder than they could retaliate back.

It was during this childish bickering that Delilah burst through the chamber doors and silenced the arguing Liberalist leaders whom all turned and starred in unison at the mysterious cloaked figure that had interrupted them.

Delilah, with her black cloak surrounded all around her, completely concealing her figure and instead making her look like a black cone with a head, stared intently and silently at the stunned Liberalist leaders, her fiery blue eye piercing to behold. The shocked Liberalist leaders all began to tilt their heads in confused curiosity, they had never seen such a mysterious figure before. A bold face scarred from cheek to hairline, black eerily waving hair, a black concealing cloak, and a black eye patch covering her left eye and cheek. A most mysterious figure indeed, so perplexing and cryptic that some leaders even considered her to be some sort of unknown spirit, especially since her hair seemed to blow mystically without wind and her one eye burned as bright as a small blue star. Tyzus then spoke to break the silence;

"And who might you be?"

But Delilah did not answer, instead she slowly began to walk into the chamber and approach the Liberalist leaders that all stood together before her, roughly in the centre of the grand expansive room. As the mysterious figure came closer, Tyzus again spoke, this time in a more commanding tone;

"Can we help you? Who are you?

But again, Delilah remained silent and continued her slow approach to the leaders. As she got closer, her cloak began to open up at the front more and more and her formidable slender physic began to become more apparent. The Liberalist leaders all began to become slightly nervous and agitated, some even backed away slightly. Tyzus held his ground however and stood forward stoically;

"As leader of the Liberalist Alliance, I demand you tell me who you are before you dare take another step!" Tyzus proclaimed.

Delilah took notice of this announcement and stopped immediately. She also stood up stoically and starred right back at Tyzus, she then undid her cloak and let it drop to the floor revealing her full self but also revealing her elegant blade strapped to her side. Delilah waved her hair and placed one hand on her blades hilt and her other on her hip.

"I thought you never forgot a beautiful face?" Delilah then said bluntly before then smirking afterwards.

Tyzus's eyes widened as he instantly recognised her voice and gradually began to recognise the female high-Elf before him.

"Delilah?" he exclaimed in a calm but surprised manner. "Oh, what's happened to you?" he then asked eyeing her up and down. "You've changed your hair I see... and your looks," Tyzus then added as he inspected Delilah even closer and then gradually began to walk up to her. "Love what you've done with your eye, the blue and black is dazzling." As Tyzus got within arm's reach of Delilah whom was smiling friendly back at him, he spoke again; "Where's your brutish husband? You finally decided to come live in my own extravagant city?" Tyzus asked while gesturing his arms out wide and spinning around to show off the whole chamber.

Delilah's smile however instantly disappeared and turned to an unemotional scowl.

"My perfect husband is dead," she then snapped, surprising Tyzus greatly with her tone's ferocity. "Your father Kyzus killed him" she then coldly added.

Tyzus turned and faced Delilah again and tried to seem as understanding as possible;

"I am so sorry to hear that, truly. I have fore-shook any connection I have with my father. His actions have nothing to do with me nor mine with him, I in fact wish to put an end to Kyzus's actions" Tyzus said calmly, then extending his hand out to Delilah; "Would you care to join me and help me put an end to him?"

Delilah smiled and placed her hand in Tyzus's open grasp, but she still held one hand firmly on her holstered blade. But then, in an instant, a malevolent look passed over Delilah's face and her eye burst into a rich blue flame.

"NEVER!" Delilah then screeched as she then drew her blade and attempted to slice it across Tyzus's body. Tyzus however, himself being an extremely powerful and accomplished Half-elf and descendant of Kyzus managed to just back out the way of Delilah's strike, her blade only just scuffing his thick fine tunic before then hitting the ground and creating a pool of sparks in an awful clanging sound. Tyzus then quickly leapt up and far away from Delilah to the other side of the chamber and drew his own blade with a look of shock on his face.

Delilah raised her blade up in a composed manner and then grunted as she lit a blue flame in her other hand. The other Liberalist leaders were by now all panicking tremendously at the sight and were backing hastily away from the powerful high Elf witch. The two Elf lords of Gweston and Suitear drew their own blades, the two leaders of Men from Arway and Kondit Point drew their swords and the two Merpeople kings had hoped back to their watery tanks where they usually sat for the council, reaching for their own tridents before then hopping back out.

There Delilah stood in the centre of the chamber facing off against two Men, two Elves and two Merman whom all had their weapons pointed right at her and, additionally, behind all them, Tyzus stood confidently with his own blade drawn by his side. With a smile Delilah then flicked her wrist and in an instant all the doors to the chamber slammed tight shut and a mysterious magical barrier appeared in front of them as well. These magical actions made the Liberalist leaders shake a little in fear and they all shuffled even further back from Delilah.

"Bold of you to lock yourself in this chamber with all of us" Tyzus then chuckled in a confident manner as he was not afraid.

"You think I'm locked in here with you?" Delilah then smugly laughed before she then unleashed a terrific blue flame through the Liberalist leaders and towards Tyzus. The leaders all clumsily managed to leap to the side out of the way but Tyzus, frozen in shock and fear at the violent magic heading towards him, was hit square in the chest and flung into the back of the chamber, slamming into an extravagant stone carved wall which crumbled beyond repair upon his impact.

In the chaos Delilah then began to calmly approach the congregated Liberalist leaders. As they all came to their senses and saw Tyzus motionless body at the back of the large room, Delilah swung across her blade and sliced the Merman king of Reeforiris clean in half, his large fish tail and Elf-like body becoming completely separating in a bloody and watery mess. The sight horrified the remaining Liberalist leaders whom all immediately lost all confidence and bravery they had and they all ran to the nearest door they could find. Like a pack of petrified dispersing prey, the Liberalist leaders separately ran in all directions to find a way out the lavish oval shaped chamber they were trapped in, of course though, there was no way out. Gradually and calmly, Delilah pursued after her mortified prey who all desperately tried to break through the magical barriers Delilah had erected or smash through the walls off the room. Slowly however, one by one the Liberalist leaders were all slain, their terrified last ditch attempts to escape or fed off Delilah's quick blows all in hopeless vain as they were no match for her.

Tyzus meanwhile was slowly coming too and opening his eyes to the massacre that was occurring in his chamber before him. Also terrified, Tyzus instead did not try to escape but rose up and tried to brush off the flickering flames on his lightly burning tunic that had singed his chest. Just as Delilah slit the Duke of Kondit Point's throat, the last remaining Liberalist leader, and dropped him dead, she locked eyes with Tyzus and smiled once more.

"How could you do this!" Tyzus cried out. "Look what you have done! I was the only thing standing in the way of my father and his brutal unhinged methods. Now look!"

Delilah maintained her smile as she waltzed up towards Tyzus. "I know you were Tyzus, that is why you must go. But let me also tell you, if not even I could stand up to and defeat Kyzus, you by yourself had no chance."

Anger passed over Tyzus; "what makes you think you have more of a chance than me?" he grunted at Delilah as he flourished his weapon around himself

"Because I am the most powerful and formidable witch

and combatant in all of Terratopia!" Delilah exclaimed back without hesitation.

Tyzus smirked at the confidence of Delilah; "Oh you have no idea! If my sister Mia-Myzus was here you would not be saying such things! And if her and I were together, Kyzus himself would stand no chance!" he proclaimed boldly back.

Tyzus's words shook Delilah and she stubbled back slightly as if tripping over something she had no idea was there. Her blue flaming eye flickered and she herself felt a relapse of lost memories she never realised she had had or had completely forgotten about. This anomaly quickly passed however and everything she was feeling in an instant vanished and was replaced with her evil ferocity of being the crime queen in Kyzus's service. Her eye burst into blue fire once more.

"But your sister is dead!" Delilah snapped back sharply. "I know this because I killed her! She was weak and obedient to Kyzus. Just like you were! And you too will die just like her!"

These disturbing revelations pressed down on Tyzus like he was being squished by a giant and all fight and determination left him. Tyzus sank to his knees in defeat. True despair passed over him. It was over. His Liberalist movement was dead, his leaders' dead, his kingdoms dead, his vision dead, and now he found himself also at deaths door. At the hands of the one who murdered his beloved sister. Tyzus knew he could not stand up to this mysterious High Elf sorcerer Delilah if she truly had been the one to kill his sister and she had obviously been sent by Kyzus to kill him for betraying him. Feelings of great sadness and defeat flooded Tyzus's head and he looked up to Delilah whom by now was standing over him with her blade pointing down on him.

It was at this moment that Kyzus teleported into the chamber in a puff of grey sparkling smoke. Tyzus tilted his head and looked over to see his father and even more sadness passed over him.

"Come to see your own son's execution," Tyzus whimpered in defeat. "I was right to betray you."

Tyzus's harsh words pierced Kyzus's soul and made him feel a sharp tightness in his heart.

"Not at all my son," Kyzus said as softly as he could. "Like

I said before, I can't bear to lose either of my sons as well so I am here to offer you one last chance to re-join me. I can still make you a part of my plan and we can live together happily in a prosperous Terratopia. Please. Come back to me my son." Tears were again beginning to pool in Kyzus's eyes and now they were also appearing in Tyzus's eyes.

"Will the suffering you've put Terratopia's people through end right now if I say yes? And will you kill this witch that killed my dear sister?" Tyzus sombrely asked.

Kyzus's heart sank and he tore his gaze away from Tyzus.

"Soon my son, their suffering will end soon, I promise you that. My plan is not yet complete, but it is so close. And I really don't think you want me to kill this witch..." The infamous Lordbaron then said.

Tyzus's expression turned to sternness and his heart also sank at Kyzus's words.

"Just kill me then" Tyzus said in defeat, looking directly into Delilah's blade that hovered just a few inches from his face. "I would rather die and be with my sister than be with you and prolong the evil suffering you have created," Tyzus then spat.

Kyzus turned away with a heavy heart and also sighed in defeat and in grief. The ancient all-powerful Half-elf then began to spin around and then teleported to his palace home in Roccano.

"Oh, my son, if only you knew," Kyzus then mumbled to himself before he then started to weep heavily.

Meanwhile as Kyzus teleported away, Delilah mercilessly thrusted her blade into Tyzus's face, skewering his head and killing him instantly. The last remaining Liberalist leader was dead.

Chapter 14

Aftermath

News of the Liberalist leaders' mysterious deaths within Jassett's own walls spread like wildfire and surprised all within Terratopia greatly, including Hyzus, whom was particularly saddened to learn that his brother had been killed and there was nothing he could have done about it to save him. Hyzus may have disagreed with his brother Tyzus and been enraged by his decision to continue to wage war against him, but he still loved him dearly and never wanted him to die, he himself certainly never would have sought Tyzus's death and was certain Tyzus had the same attitude towards him. But alas Hyzus knew that he could not dwell on such matters, there was now a huge power vacuum in Terratopia and he knew he had to fill it properly in order to bring lasting, uniting peace to Terratopia once again.

Shortly after the terrible news of what had happened in Jassett, every remaining Liberalist kingdom all unconditionally surrendered to Hyzus and his Unionists. With their unconditional surrender, Hyzus decreed that every kingdom in Terratopia once again re-join the Terratopia Union in the name of friendship so that they could all start to rebuild and recover from their costly devastating war. The former Liberalist kingdoms still largely did not want to be a part of the Terratopia Union but they knew they had no choice but to follow Hyzus's decree. Something Hyzus did not foresee however was how hostile the already Unionist kingdoms would be to the re-joining kingdoms. Hyzus's dream of all the kingdoms within Terratopia coming together once more to rebuild and join together was on a thin knives' edge. So, as a result of this, Hyzus demanded all the former Liberalist kingdoms new leaders and all the Unionist leaders to all meet in the Lord Delegates Chamber in Embirith once more for Hyzus to give his first post war address to everyone.

Begrudgingly, every kingdom agreed to this, either because of the fear they felt from the unbeatable might of Hyzus's forces or because they simply had no will left to argue otherwise, the war had simply just drained everyone. And so, at exactly one month after Tyzus's death, Hyzus stood up in front of a cramped, packed, and still divided Lord Delegates Chamber. Hyzus reprised his role as the Prime Lord Delegate and opened his arms out wide, gesturing for silence and attention which he again got as everyone was too depleted to do otherwise.

"My friends... And I mean that, we are all friends here in this chamber. We have had a costly and devastating disagreement that I am sure we all wish didn't happen, but alas it did..."

The chamber roared up into outrage as Hyzus finished his sentence as the Unionist all shouted and pointed figures at the former Liberalist representatives across the other side of the chamber, blaming them for the war and its costs. This being something the Liberalists angrily rebutted and of course blamed the Unionist's instead for. Hyzus fell silent and let the frenzy go on for some time before he then rose up again and shot a small bolt of magical lightning into the air to grab everyone's attention.

"Have none of you people learned ANYTHING!" he furiously shouted. "A clearly divided chamber like this, arguing and contradicting mindlessly what the other side says without merit or reason is exactly how our costly war started! It cannot stand! Now, all of you grow up! Act like the leaders of kingdoms you truly are!" As Hyzus shouted his words he clearly looked at and gestured towards all the members in the huge chamber building, not just the Liberalist's but his own Unionist was well.

"Now I will not stand nor allow this once great archipelago to destroy itself again and again because its leaders all act like little primitive children; constantly bickering, needlessly blaming one another, and refusing to work together. Instead dividing themselves, picking sides, and refusing to acknowledge the other sides merit or stance. It is what caused our terrible war and it is what will continually hold us back until we overcome it!" Hyzus again continued to shout to the whole filled chamber that seemingly seemed to calm down and listen to his frank blunt words.

"This union has survived since long before I was born and

that is because it is the right thing for us all! It is not a power grab for certain kingdoms. It is not something meant to benefit someone more than another. It is not a tool of power for any one or kingdom. It is not something that takes anything away from our own local kingdoms. It is not something that holds back or restricts anyone either! It is instead a system of us all to come together in the name of friendship to best find ways for us all to work together to benefit each other and not just ourselves!" As Hyzus said these powerful statements he continually banged his fists onto the table before him and became more and more emotional as he truly whole hearted believed in everything he was saying.

"Our beautiful union can work and I will do everything in my power to make it work! Just like my founding grandfather and then father before me. I will work within the union until my dying day in whatever position you all want me in! I will give this union my whole support and I expect you all to do so as well! Again, not for your own individual benefit but for the benefit of us all and because it is the right thing to do! It may be more difficult but that is just the point! There will never not be a time when working together is worse than working apart, alone, and separately!" Hyzus's emotional state and the wisdom of his words began to garner much support across the chamber from all peoples whom all began to nod and sometimes cheer in agreement.

"We together have the power to enact incredible change and incredible feats! We are the archipelago of Terratopia! We once were the greatest land in all the world of Terra Tearia and though we may have swerved from that path there is no reason why we cannot build back onto it together! Every land is not perfect and every land makes mistakes, but the best ones are the ones where they learn from their past, not hold it against one another, and never allow themselves to repeat it again! I believe we can all do this together! If I am capable of it then so are all of you! I know we are all capable of it. We just need to come together and get over ourselves. You all need to trust one another again and work together for selfless reasons! Not shellfish ones!"

By now Hyzus's speech had completely flipped the

atmosphere of the Lord Delegates Chamber. All members had begun to congregate together to face Hyzus, no longer dividing themselves with Liberalists opposing Hyzus and Unionists behind him. Everyone was cheering in agreement side by side and some began chatting 'long live the union!' 'Long live friendship!' Long live Terratopia!'

The sight before him brung a tear to Hyzus's eye and he then continued, "My friends! Together we can re-build our kingdoms, we can share resources, we can help one another, we can rebuild all that was broken, we can make amends, we can do all that and if we do, we will all be better because of it! And make no mistake my friends, we need to! We must restore ourselves because due to our civil war, we together created a new enemy that now only we together can defeat. The Delilah Crime Empire!"

As Hyzus said this, the chamber erupted in belittlement and boos to the criminal underworld and so Hyzus then continued;

"We created it as a consequence of our terrible actions and we have come to rely upon it. But make no mistake, the criminal underworld and the crime empire it has created has no place in Terratopia and we must and will put an end to it! We must dispel it from our city streets, we must dispel it from our rural lands and we must dispel its corruption within our kingdom's politics!"

The chamber again erupted in agreement and Hyzus fell back onto his seat in satisfaction and disbelief. The noisy ramble of the chamber all coming together was drowned out as Hyzus collapsed into his hands. He had done it, he believed. He had brought Terratopia back together again in one fell swoop. Hyzus couldn't help but smile to himself and despite feeling slightly hollow cause his father, nor sister, nor dear twin brother was here to see him and what he had just accomplished, Hyzus still felt great achievement and for the first time in years, peace of mind.

Kyzus meanwhile was also within the Lord Delegates Chamber as all this was happening, he had cast a similar identity hiding enchantment over himself like what Mia-Myzus had done previously years before and was mingling within the cramped crowds of the chamber building. He blended in seamlessly although he still made every effort not to draw attention to himself by trying to stay within the background of the rowdy grand parliament building and crowd within it.

After watching Hyzus's speech play out, Kyzus couldn't help but feel proud of his last remaining descendant. To Kyzus's eyes, although his son's theory was fundamentally flawed as Kyzus knew that the people of Terratopia could not be better than they already were any more, his son was still very wise, very morally bond to what he saw as right and clearly had a skilful hand for politics. But this pride for his son soon diminished and was replaced with sadness and pity, Kyzus felt so ashamed that his last son had also betrayed him and betrayed him for the goal he was currently pursuing of reuniting the Terratopia Union once more. Kyzus knew for certain in his mind that it would never work, not in the current climate of the world and what's more, Kyzus grew greatly saddened that he was now going to have to be the one to tear down what Hyzus was attempting to re-create for his own superior plan. But alas, as Kyzus had continually justified to himself, his plan must go on and come before all else; especially now as it had cost him nearly everything and cost Terratopia at large so much suffering, there was no turning back. But even then, it was not like Kyzus could turn back, his plan was in motion and had been for years, there was nothing he could do to stop it or alter it. Either he had to make it succeed or watch as life in Terratopia would remain in its state of nature forever, and everything up until this point had been in pointless vain. Life that was primitive, cruel, unfair, nasty, brutish, and short would continue.

The rambunctious, loud-mouthed crowd, invigorated by Hyzus's powerful speech had by now spilled out of the immaculate chamber building and spread across the whole parliament complex. New enthusiasm for the Terratopia Union spread like an infectious disease and poured out into the wider city of Embirith. Change was clearly in the air and thanks to Hyzus, it was being grasped favourably with both hands by everyone, at least for now. Chats of 'long live the Terratopia Union!' extended throughout the whole marvellous city as for the first time in a long time The peoples of Terratopia, races of all kind, joined together in friendliness and partied happily throughout the day and long into the night. The land was at peace and hope on the horizon.

Over this time Kyzus easily slipped away and back to Roccano where he called to address the whole kingdom. Terratopia at large was changing, it was time Roccano started changing its position in Terratopia also...

Chapter 15

Terratopia in Misery

Seven years pasted after Hyzus's grand speech and the Terratopia Union fully re-uniting itself, but unfortunately for Hyzus and the peoples of Terratopia, not much changed. The once prosperous, immaculate, beautiful lands remained desolate, ruined, and void of all former exorbitance. Spoiled fertile grasslands refused to grow back and remained churned up boggy messes. Burned and dilapidated forests did not replenish themselves, instead they remained dead, baron, and charred. Ruined settlements, villages, towns, cities, even kingdom capitals remained in their decayed botched state. Even the rivers, bays and seas that flowed in and all around the archipelago seemed to remain in their cold, dark, murky bloodstained state.

The Delilah's Crime Empire continued to run rampant out of control and there was seemingly nothing Hyzus alone could do about it. The criminal underworld was profusely embedded too deep into every kingdom's society and into the union itself that it was impossible to get rid of. Rife and corruption flowed through the union and simply never allowed any meaningful actions with any goal of change to be taken by anyone. All the while the empire only stepped up its activity and power. Entire kingdoms seemed to owe their leadership to the crime empire and powerful leaders all found themselves in the ruthless pockets of Delilah.

The main problem for Hyzus, or anyone wishing to end the crime empire, was that a lot of Terratopia's inhabitants were perfectly fine with the criminal underworld controlling presence and in fact wished it to remain, though they would never outwardly show it. This was not the vast majority of peoples however, just the controlling sway of those in ruling authority and positions of power, those that were actually able to enact change. It was these dominate influential people that prevented Hyzus, or anyone really, taking down the sinister crime empire and its vast underworld. They themselves weren't suffering, nor were the ones they cared about or were truly loyal too, in fact they were all benefiting tremendously and would lose out considerably or be forced from their positions of comfort and power if Delilah's Crime Empire of corruption, rife, and cronyism was to end, so there was no chance they would ever allow such a possibility to even occur, no matter what anyone did to change it. The Delilah crime empire would always find ways to remain.

Things only seemed to fall apart more and more for Hyzus as well. All across Terratopia, the initial optimism for a brighter future faded and turned into despair and anger as everyone's life didn't seem to improve. The changes that were promised never came to fruition. People once again turned violently on one another; riots and civil unrest broke out across Terratopia's various kingdoms almost weekly and many more brought into Delilah's crime empire, seeing it as the only thing that could bring their individual lives back into their own control. Terratopia's peoples largely became even more selfish and its kingdoms even more selfish. Everyone began looking out only for themselves or for their own once again to an even more extreme degree. Cities and kingdoms turned to exploiting each other as much as they feasibly could to benefit only themselves, not considering the long-term consequences of their actions in the slightest. What made matters worse was the fact that all of Terratopia had become so militarized because of the war and that when the war was suddenly over; armies, weapons, and resources weren't turned over to start rebuilding Terratopia, instead they were scrambled chaotically for entirely selfish reasons to intimidate and enforce power. This only making Terratopia's state even worse. For everyone, even Hyzus, hope for a better bright tomorrow faded, this was clearly just the way things were now. The way things had to be and the way they always would be. Kyzus was right Hyzus began to concede to himself.

In a way, all of Kyzus's children got exactly what they wished for and fought for, just not in the way they would have intended. And in ways none of them would have been happy or satisfied with. In fact they would more than likely be sickened with them as Terratopia was nothing at all what they had envisioned or wanted.

For Hyzus, all of Terratopia was once again reunited in a union, although not for the reasons he wished for; the union survived as it could be used as a tool for kingdoms and individuals to get exactly what they wanted by easier exploitation or blackmail of others, the exact opposite of what Hyzus desired. For Tyzus, if he was still alive, all the kingdoms in Terratopia were indeed taking back total control of their kingdoms and focusing more on themselves, prioritising what was happening within their own borders, though again, not for the reasons, or in the ways he envisioned, as they did this with the intent to be the best and to hold power over other kingdoms, not to be friendly or allied with them. And the power kingdoms held onto wasn't used for good and betterment. It was used for powers own sake. For rulers to fuel their greedy or dominating desires. And for Mia-Myzus, if she was aware of the empire she was running as Delilah, she had mostly successfully captured all of Terratopia and thrust it into her empire, just as she wished. She had pushed all within Terratopia to buy into her philosophy of that only the strongest should survive and in fact reap the rewards of their position. Although once again, Mia-Myzus would not be satisfied as her entire empire and her actions were still entirely under the control of Kyzus and what's more, Terratopia's people largely weren't buying into her barbaric philosophy to fully and completely reap the rewards of being the strongest like she always intended. Instead, they were doing so to merely survive and get by comfortably, something Mia-Myzus would have despised and considered weak and undeserving.

Of course, Terratopia's state of misery was entirely down to Kyzus's plan and his influences. Kyzus had full control over Delilah, her crime empire, the Dwarven Kingdoms, Thruckland, and had also grown his significance in the shadows of many other kingdoms as well by having loyal or brainwashed subordinates in key positions throughout Terratopia's kingdoms with their own seeing stones. Kyzus's actions and plan was simple enough; using Terratopia's current state of nature, he facilitated and gave its kingdoms the tools their peoples needed to stay in or worsen their conditions, to buy into the state of nature and not rise above it, which of course the vast, controlling majority did.

Kyzus knew that his plan would collapse if Hyzus got his way and Terratopia's inhabitants chose to bind together, trust one another, and work together selflessly, but alas they never did and Kyzus knew for certain that Terratopia's peoples never would. The people by themselves just simply could not be better than their state of nature, despite also wanting to rise above it. They needed to be put in check by one they all trusted. Kyzus knew that ultimately Terratopia's people couldn't be better than their own selfish desires and distrusting nature, despite their stronger desire for peace. And they themselves continually proved him right. And so, Kyzus's plan would continue till its completion so that he could finally lift Terratopia up out of its primitive state of nature.

Over this seven-year period of misery and disarray, Kyzus as Lordbaron, for the first time in years, began to gradually open up Roccano once more to the wider world once more and he re-entered his kingdom into the Terratopia Union. In doing so, Kyzus cunningly exposed the entire union and archipelago at large to the near heavenly wonders of his rule and the haven of a kingdom he ruled over. Roccano indeed was entirely untouched by the war and the criminal underworld and had seemed to have grown in prosperity in its isolation under Kyzus's sole direction and rule. With Roccano gradually opening back up to Terratopia, Kyzus ordered that his kingdom aid and help the struggling surrounding lands, and within the union his kingdom rose to become the spearhead for change and prosperity, overtaking even Hyzus's own efforts as the concept's apparent figurehead. Of course, Kyzus deliberately and expertly made sure his kingdoms actions were ultimately useless or frivolous, changing nothing that really mattered in Terratopia. Importantly instead, his kingdoms actions gave the positive illusion of help and change and Kyzus made sure that these actions reflected positively on him personally as well.

Steadily, Kyzus rose in prominence once more, rekindling a spark of hope in Terratopia peoples and in-turn raised himself to a near mythical status due to his apparent benevolence and the sheer marvellous wonder of his kingdom. This storied, allegorical status seeped and spread to his kingdom and its peoples. Roccano citizens became visionary saints to the wider Terratopia populous and Roccano's mages, soldiers, knights, and paladins grew into guardian crusaders of prosperity, unity, and tranquillity. Roccano's image became that of a symbolic emblem of what Terratopia should be. And Kyzus, as Roccano's legendary Lordbaron became this exemplary concepts' figurehead.

As opinion seemed to turn to Kyzus in admiration, attitude towards Hyzus gradually began to fall, then collapse. He began to be seen as completely incompetent and his ideals, philosophies, and leadership as inept and inadequate. His ways were seen as clearly not being good enough to defeat the Delilah Crime Empire and to rebuild and restore Terratopia to glory.

Over this time, with all these wider factors, elements, and components beginning to add together and boil over, the climate of Terratopia was once again beginning to spoil into one of war like frenzy. And so, in seeing this and desperately wanting to avoid it, Hyzus called for an emergency meeting in an extremely public event to urgently attempt to simmer down the toxic, obnoxious rising climate. This event was due to take place on a large makeshift stage, built right in the centre of Embirith on the outskirts of the Terratopia Union Parliament complex, and it was to be done like this with the aim of making Hyzus's meeting seem like it was of the upmost importance and for everyone to be involved in. Not just the relatively few leaders in the Terratopia Union, but Terratopia's wider populous as well. The event gave the impression of being Hyzus's last desperate plea to Terratopia's peoples, it was not just another political council summoning for members of the union parliament.

The advice and reasoning for all of Hyzus's actions however, although somewhat of his own thought, was largely down to Kyzus himself who, through his connections, influenced the whole event into being. And Kyzus, of course, had his own big plans and agenda for Hyzus's upcoming event that he was more than ready to act upon.

Chapter 16

A Leader Emerges

Soon the day of Hyzus's grand emergency meeting came. Embirith was packed and filled to bursting, the city streets were bustling with inhabitants and races from all across the archipelago, resembling what Embirith used to be like in the cities far earlier days. There was a small degree of hope and optimism in the air as vast hordes of people had all converged on the grand city and swarmed to attend Hyzus's call. Flags and banners for all kingdoms and for all races were strung all across Embirith's large streets, avenues, and impressive buildings, and even friendly marches and gatherings began to take place with no hostilities or violent uprisings springing up anywhere. The noisy yet positive atmosphere gave Hyzus hope that maybe he could turn Terratopia's troubles around, especially now that his father's kingdom seemed to have loosely joined his cause, though Kyzus himself had yet to reach out and contact Hyzus personally.

This was until that very morning. While Hyzus was in his private residence within the parliament residences complex, Kyzus teleported into the small hallway Hyzus was practicing his introductory words to the gathering in. Shocked, Hyzus stumbled backwards.

"Kyzus? Father!" he exclaimed. "What are you doing here?"

Kyzus spoke as softly and unconfrontational as he could.

"I have come to offer you one final chance my son. My plan is near its final completion. There is still yet time however, I beg of you, please renounce your ways and come back to me. You're all I got left."

Hyzus expression had turned from pleasant surprise to sadness and disappointment.

"You still want to stick with your 'grand' plan, despite all the pain, suffering, and misery it has caused? If it wasn't for the things you set in motion, I would be already leading Terratopia to a better brighter future!"

Kyzus sigh. "You have to know that's not true though son," he then said in a deflated manner.

But Hyzus did not listen or consider his father's words, he was too disappointed in him for continually sticking to his own plan and not working with his own son instead. Hyzus's pride was also beginning to cloud his own judgement.

"Look at what I alone have done!" Hyzus exclaimed; "I won the war! I have reunited the union! And look! Out there an all manner of peoples and beings have come together to try to work together again."

Kyzus once again sighed. "It really not what you think it is son please trust me." Kyzus then asked.

"Trust you! After all you have put me through, after all you have put everyone through!" Hyzus then retaliated back, his voice raised and tone shifting to anger.

Kyzus let his head fall and he turned around to face away from Hyzus. "If that is how you really feel and you really won't re-join me" Kyzus paused, his tone one of disappointment; "then I bid you farewell my son." Then as Kyzus said this he gently teleported away leaving Hyzus once again all alone in his small lonesome hallway.

All of a sudden Hyzus could hear voices approaching from outside, it was time.

In a grand precession, Hyzus and other notable representatives of the Terratopia Union that were closely aligned with him all made their way to the grand stage that had been built in Embirith's city centre. They arrived to pleasant cheers and applause and were personally greeted by many leaders from all of kingdoms and races. Finally, Hyzus arrived on the large, expertly crafted wooden stage and overlooked the crowd before him. The sight was truly monumental to behold and made Hyzus extremely proud to witness. As far as his eye could see, inhabitants from all across Terratopia, from all kingdoms, from all races, from all levels of society, had all banded and grouped together to hear what Hyzus had to say and to hopefully work together again. Everyone from grand high kings to rugged peasants, from lords and union members to farmers, miners, and merchants. Everyone all stood together and prepared to listen to Hyzus. There clearly was yet still some good and unity left in the world Hyzus thought to himself.

But, just as Hyzus raised his hands and prepared his voice to speak, an enormous ferocious blue fireball exploded in the centre of the stage, rupturing, and shattering the wooden structure and sending its deadly broken pieces flying in all directions. Hyzus was sent flying into the panicking and dispersing crowd and landed harshly onto some fleeing Dwarves. With his bare back burnt terribly from the explosion that had just happen right behind him, Hyzus still rose up as quick as he could to survey what was happening and what he saw broke his heart. All around Embirith's centre, an army of large formidable menacing Samson's and Goliaths encircled the fleeing crowds and forced them all together like trapped insignificant creatures in a cage. And right where the huge explosion had occurred, the infamous mysterious Queen Delilah stood on the remains of the annihilated stage with a powerful blue fire emanating from her hands and then surrounding all around herself.

Without hesitation Hyzus shot himself straight at Delilah, darting towards her despite his injured state and despite the fact that he had no weapon as he did not bring his blade, believing he wouldn't need it for such a peaceful event. Hyzus screamed in anger and ferocity and shot a small magical bolt from his hand. This of course was easily deflected by Delilah insane power, like a parent swooping aside a small child's feeble tantrum outburst. All too soon, Hyzus was within arm's reach of Delilah. The sinister sorceress smirked and, in a move, as quick as lightning grabbed onto Hyzus's head, spun him around in the air and then slammed him into the charred, fractured remains of the stage that were formerly blasted into the ground from Delilah's explosion. In an instant Hyzus was incapacitated. He was swatted onto a bed of razor sharp fractured wooden stake like shards and pinned in place, his death now all but sealed.

The crowds all gasped and screamed at the sight, cowering together and as far away from Delilah and her warriors as they could, crushing each other together mercilessly in the process.

The small degree of hope and optimism that was apparent leading up to the event was completely destroyed and instead filled with total and complete panic. Not even Terratopia's leaders were safe from Delilah's empires wrath and the empires power was enough to even completely take over an event such as this one.

Delilah watched on over the fearful crowds and laughed maniacally, terminating her fierce fiery enchantment around herself, and placing her hands on her hips confidently. But all of a sudden, a small bright burning yellow star seemed to fall from the sky and shoot straight onto Delilah's head, slamming her into the ground as if she had been struck by a meteor. And also, in that moment, just above where every Samson and Goliath stood, a magnificent Paladin, clad in shinning white and golden armour that seemed to gleam brighter than the sun, with an elegant flowing pure white cape attached to it, teleported down onto the all Samson's and Goliath's shoulders in a spiralling puff of white glimmering mist. Before any of Delilah's minions could even register what was happening, they were all impaled with sharp slick blades and had their throats cut with stainless exquisite knives. One by one as all the once terrifying Samson's and Goliath's fell dead onto the floor, Kyzus himself emerge from the dust around Delilah's body, showing himself to be that burning bright star that had slammed into her.

The crowds of people all stood up in shock and awe at the sight. Silence loomed over Embirith as everyone tried to process and register what had happened. Before long though, the whole city erupted into gleeful cheers and applause.

"The evil queen is dead!" they cried. "The witch is dead! The empire is dead! Kyzus is our saviour!"

Kyzus smiled and raised his arms to acknowledge the boisterous crowds and then shot playful and celebratory magics from his hands to please them, which his colourful spells certainly did. Embirith's city centre began to resemble that of a playful and joyful festival despite everything that had just occurred in it. The Paladins were all thanked graciously and soon also joined in with the celebrations of the crowd, only adding to the new found joy within Terratopia's peoples.

Hyzus, still clinging onto life, not able to fully die just yet, could not see, but could hear everything going on and guessed accurately exactly all that had happened. It was all a setup, everything. His meeting, Delilah's disruption, and her own death at the 'rescuing' hands of Kyzus. Hyzus could not believe it, his own father had used him.

"Father!" Hyzus barely managed to splutter out, his cry being completely drowned out by the crowd but still being heard by Kyzus. As Kyzus learned over his son, Hyzus could see the saddened look on his face and he again just managed to blurt out a sentence;

"How could you father! Your own son!"

Kyzus sighed painfully, not in disappointment but in shame and disgrace at himself. In a self-loathing tone Kyzus muttered;

"You left me no choice my dear son. I am so sorry."

Tears began to trickle from Kyzus's eyes and then from Hyzus's as well, as he saw and recognised the true distress Kyzus was in.

"For the greater good right?" Hyzus crackled in as understanding of a tone as he could and then trying to hold a smile for as long as he could before he then began to painfully cough up blood.

Kyzus smiled in affection and placed one hand gently behind his son's head. "For the greater good" Kyzus then repeated and nodded sombrely. "You can rest now son, the plan is all but complete, you, your brother and your sister all did me proud."

Hyzus again tried to smile and felt a warm feeling pass over him. In the background Hyzus could just make out the crowd's chats. Their cheers had gradually changed from 'Kyzus is our saviour' to 'Kyzus is our leader! Kyzus is our protector!' Hyzus's thoughts all clicked together in his mind, his father was right and had executed his plan flawlessly, its true magnificence being now fully apparent to him. The people now wanted his total rule.

"It's complete then," Hyzus whispered as his body grew weak.

Kyzus nodded "I promise you my son, I will bring Terratopia to its former Summer-like glory, the people are now ready. It is all thanks to you and your siblings," he then said calmly. "Now go. Be with them."

Hyzus smiled and closed his eyes, steadily his breathing got lighter and lighter and all too soon, he took and expelled his very last breath.

Kyzus, still holding his last descendants' body, leant over and kissed Hyzus on the forehead before gently laying him down. The swarms of people all calmed down and nodded their heads in respect as they all saw Kyzus holding his last, now dead heir. Silence loomed over Embirith once more as the whole of Terratopia seemed to watch Kyzus and waited for his next move.

Collectively Kyzus rose to his feet and then levitated himself up into the air. Once high enough for all to see, Kyzus spoke, projecting his impressive magical rich voices all across the city;

"People of Terratopia! You know who I am and you know my past! Our once mighty, magical, and magnificent land has not been the same since summer turned to autumn. It changed us all and put us through an awful lot. It has cost me more than I can ever imagine or ever get back. As I'm sure it did for you all too. In this time wars have been fought, races driven to extinction, great noble leaders slain, kingdoms ruined, our lands desolated, and above all else, good people have all suffered or died. It is not the end however! I stand before you now as a citizen of Terratopia like all of you, a citizen sick of what has become of my beloved land which I love so much and once knew to be the most grand land in all the world! I also stand before with a plan. A plan to unite together. A way to restore ourselves to former glory! A way to reach our former prosperity, our former splendour, and our former happiness!"

The crowds all smiled and gleamed faces of hope

"You call me your saviour, you call me your leader, you call me your protector. And you are right. I am those things! I am those things because I will do whatever it takes to save the lands which I love, to look after the peoples in which I hold dear, to rescue and restore our lost ways and protect us all from falling away again! I will do whatever it takes and as you can see, I am capable of such things as well! In my kingdom of Roccano, it is as if autumn never happened! And with your blessing my people I can and will extend that to be the case across all of Terratopia!"

An eruption of cheers broke out and thunderous applause empowered the noise even further. Steadily, one by one all the leaders of Terratopia's kingdoms that had all gathered to Embirith approached Kyzus.

"If you can lift us from this misery, restore us to glory and protect us from such harm ever occurring again... then I pledge myself and my kingdom to you Kyzus. My ruler." The high king of Filnethias, Glorthelian said, placing his blade into the ground kneeing before Kyzus.

"And I too," the high king of Rime then said, following suit.

"And I," another leader said.

And again, and again, one by one every ruling king, queen, lord, duke, baron, and magistrate of every kingdom across Terratopia pledged themselves to Kyzus and kneed before him.

"I can lift us all out of this state of despair we have found ourselves in and I will protect you all! To prove it I shall wipe every last remaining remnant of Delilah's crime empire from the map and never allow them to return!" Kyzus boomed to the leaders beneath him and to the crowds all around him.

Suddenly, as if ordered to, though they were not, the entire crowd in unison knelt down to Kyzus and exclaimed;

"Long live Kyzus Hobbes! Our ruler and protector!"

Kyzus welcomed this and raised his arms out wide to acknowledge the crowd's proclamations. Kyzus couldn't help but smile giddily at the sight and what was happening to him. He had done it. He had finally done it. His plan was completed. Everything he had thought over and worked on since Robin had died. Though it had cost him everything, Kyzus knew that now he could finally achieve his dream and restore Terratopia to a time like that of when his father Thyzus ruled. He now had the power and ability to fix it.

Chapter 17

The Deity

And so, the Delilah's crime empire crumbled without their infamous queen. It stood no chance and was crushed by the efforts of Roccano under the leadership of Kyzus and the actions of Barriel, who herself had grown into a legend due to her heroic duel with Delilah. With all the military might of Roccano piled behind Barriel, the empire collapsed with ease. One after another, every kingdom was liberated from the empire's clutches and the clutches of any other form of organised crime remanets. To maintain this freedom from the crime empire, a battalion of Roccano soldiers and knights, Elven mages, and Paladins remained in each kingdom. These battalions also led the initial rebuilding, recovery, and reformation of the kingdoms they resided in. The result of this was that the battalions from Roccano were hosted with much enthusiasm by the kingdoms they stayed in as they were seen saviours and as extensions of Kyzus's good will, rising their kingdom out of its misery, kickstarting its recovery, and implementing real, actual, and notable change that the people felt immediate benefit from.

 Finally, when the very last of the crime empire was destroyed by Barriel and new Wolfpack detachment within the Ruined City of Giants, Kyzus was voted in and crowned the 'Supreme Protectorate of Terratopia' and it's one true 'Sovereign Overlord'. With this new elected power over the peoples of Terratopia, Kyzus immediately moved to untie all of Terratopia kingdoms into one united society, with Roccano as its capital and Kyzus as its head. Which Terratopia's peoples all wished for and agreed to, even the kingdoms that had formerly departed or isolated themselves from such arrangements in the past like the Dwarves or Centaurs. And with that, Kyzus's grand plan was finally completed. He had united all of Terratopia into one collective society under one ruler. And with this, Kyzus immediately set about implementing his new rule and the laws of his united society.

Kyzus knew he had come into rule for two reasons. The main one being that he would protect Terratopia from its inherit state of nature, prevent it from arising again, and not allow the people to fall back into it again. To do this, as Kyzus previously continually reasoned, the people needed rules and a ruler to keep them all in check, but unlike before throughout history, Kyzus's rule would be total and absolute, it needed to be. But it was also welcomed and trusted.

The people needed rule with laws to rise above their inherit primitive state of nature but they also continually needed to obey the rule of law that had been put in place without question and follow it through, which throughout Terratopia's history, they rarely did. Instead, because of the people not directly obeying the rules that they put in place and questioning them and trying to circumvent them, the state of nature remained, just in a different form, a form of complaining, disobeying, avoiding, evading, denouncing, and backtracking any rule and all its laws they did not like or trust. This was because rule was never perfect and never suited everyone's own individual desires exactly, as it never could, but nonetheless it still left perfect opportunity for the people to be influenced and swayed to come together and demand new rule again and again, no matter if what they believed or fought for was true or not, or beneficial or not. And no matter whether the rule was good for them or not. This was why Terratopia's rulers and its unions where always historically deposed, overthrown, fell apart, or otherwise failed, because the state of nature remained, just in a different face. Rulers, governments or unions inevitably never lived up to the people's desires, and so were gotten rid of, with them never being given a chance by the people anyway.

Kyzus proclaimed that without total and absolute rule, the people had the power to dispose of any ruler they did not even mildly like which in a state of nature would always be the case as the people couldn't trust one another, let alone the ones in power over them, even if they had empowered them there in the first place. All it took was one inevitable setback or some mild discontent and the snowball of deposition would already be rolling downhill. The people collectively could not be trusted with this power and so needed to give it up and be ruled over totally and absolutely. Further to that, the rule needed to keep them all in check, away from their most primitive desires. Kyzus told all this to Terratopia's peoples and further proclaimed that: 'Protection requires obedience and thusly total protection required absolute obedience.' To protect the people from their own, inherit shortcomings due to their state of nature, they needed to give their submission and obedience to rule. Total protection from themselves thusly required total submission and obedience to their ruler; so long as the ruler delivered on their purpose and really did protect society and the people from themselves. And so thusly Kyzus's rule was total and absolute. It requiring total and absolute obedience from Terratopia's people and because they had all experienced the true horrors and consequences of the state of nature Kyzus spoke off, they all resoundingly agreed and brought into Kyzus's theory, voluntarily giving him the total and absolute power, he needed to rule to protect them.

Terratopia's people were further content with this situation because Kyzus's total and absolute rule didn't extend to all aspects of life. All aspects of his united society and his rule also couldn't also be abused, corrupted, and contorted to suit himself or anyone else. This was because the laws of Kyzus's absolute rule only extended out to cover protection of Terratopia and prevent its people from falling into the state of nature. Just as Kyzus had first reasoned years earlier to his children in his study within his mountainside palace, Terratopia's people only had to give up some small freedoms, these freedoms being the ones that played into the state of nature and allowed it to flourish. But besides these relatively few freedoms that were given up equally by all people totally obeying Kyzus's laws, Terratopia's peoples were completely free to do whatever else they liked, to live their lives however they liked. And they now could do so comfortably, in peace, and in good faith as they all trusted on another again. They did this and could do this because it was impossible to not trust each other as such monumental selfish distrust only came about within the state of nature but under Kyzus's rule, with everyone following his laws absolutely without question, it would be impossible for this to be the case. Distrust was mitigated. It was made irrelevant.

To aid Kyzus enforce his rule and to best watch over his united society of Terratopia, Kyzus placed one seeing stone in every kingdom all across Terratopia and a 'Grand Paladin' to keep and watch over it. These Grand Paladins were commanded to be seen, and indeed they were seen, as literal extensions of Kyzus himself and so were treated as though they were him by Terratopia's peoples. It was these Grand Paladins who communicated and informed Kyzus of their kingdoms business on a local level and then enforced Kyzus's rule locally in these kingdoms as well. Kyzus additionally utilised advisors from all across Terratopia, as well as his Grand Paladins, to best create and retract his laws for ruling Terratopia as he knew that, for all his ages, wisdom, and experience, he could never know everything and he certainly could never know everything about every race from every kingdom across the whole archipelago and what was best for each of these kingdoms and their inhabitants. But despite the people advising and helping him, Kyzus was the Supreme Protectorate, ultimately, he alone was the law, it was ultimately only his final words and actions that required total and absolute obedience.

To enforce Kyzus's laws and to seek out and punish harshly those that disobeyed Kyzus's absolute rule and caused civil unrest was the job of his Paladins of Roccano; of which there were a plentiful amount as their numbers had been built up continually throughout Roccano's history since they were first created. All the Paladins were personally selected and trained by Kyzus himself as well, lending to their own impressive ability and the respect and submission the people of Terratopia held towards them.

The other reason Kyzus knew he had been empowered to supreme rule was because, not only could he protect Terratopia from falling back into its state of nature and the misery it entailed, but that he could also lift Terratopia to greater and greater prosperity once more, to the heights of Summer-like levels in the days of old and days of his father Thyzus. Kyzus distinguished his rule to meet this end, however, as it was not totally absolute. This change in rule was because that due to the already total obedience he had from his rule of law set as the Supreme Protectorate to lift the people above their state of nature, Terratopia and its people were back to what they were like in the Summer of the world and so did not require absolute rule to reach prosperity again, as they never did before. They themselves would achieve summer prosperity again naturally, as they would want to strive for in. Furthermore, they would in fact not allow or stand for total rule in this area anyway as then they would be giving up far too many freedoms and it would break the perfect society Kyzus had created.

Terratopia's peoples had inherit desire for peace and an inherit desire for continual prosperity and greatness. Kyzus knew this. Now that the people's desires for peace was being accomplished by them electing him as the Supreme Protectorate to power, and his rule mitigating the inherit state of nature, thusly giving them peace, the people themselves would strive for prosperity naturally now and so they did not need absolute and total rule for this. Kyzus did however, as the one Sovereign Overlord of Terratopia attempt to replicate the lands to be exactly what they were like in the summer of the world when Thyzus ruled. Leaders and advisors from all across Terratopia's kingdoms gathered once again in the very first parliament building of the first Terratopia Union within Roccano and all together worked with Kyzus as the Sovereign Overlord to bring Terratopia further and further together, to reach greater and greater harmony, and higher and higher prosperity. Just as was done in Terratopia's earliest history in the first Terratopia Union under Thyzus's leadership.

With all this, Kyzus's true plan and philosophical brilliance could be seen. Kyzus ruled over Terratopia as its Supreme Protectorate and its Sovereign Overlord, two separate roles with two very different rules of law, with very different purposes.

As Terratopia's Supreme Protectorate, Kyzus's rule was total and absolute, his laws required total obedience. The result of this was that Terratopia as a whole was lifted to what it was like in the Summer of the world, before Morur's Evil made apparent to all the inherit state of nature within all people, and before Morur empowered them all to chaos, selfishness, and ruin. The people of Terratopia totally obeyed Kyzus, and eventually nearly all did so completely willingly, not because they felt had to, even though they of course did. The people's willingness to give absolute submission to the Supreme Protectorate's rule was because living under his absolute rule gave them peace, peace to pursue anything they desired without fear of the state of nature hindering or preventing them and without distrust dictating their views and actions. And because of this, it allowed them to reach heights they never could of before. Kyzus's rule became seen as the very pinacol of what Terratopia should be and so his actions became to be literally seen as Terratopia's peoples own; afterall it was them who collectively propelled him to his position of power anyway. Enforcement of Kyzus's rule was done with strict laws and harsh consequences when they weren't totally obeyed. This enforcement was advocated and carried out by his forces of many Paladins. Because they were all trained by Kyzus himself, they were incredibly skilled and prestigious and held total respect from Terratopia's peoples but also struck total fear into those who disobeyed or caused unrest. For Kyzus to best fulfil and serve his role as the Supreme Protectorate of all of Terratopia he was advised by representatives from all peoples from across all kingdoms and he utilised his many seeing stones, possessed by his Grand Paladins, in all kingdoms, to best know exactly what was going on within them and to best enforce his rule locally in them. But again, as Kyzus's Grand Paladins rule was seen as a literal extension of Kyzus's own rule, and Kyzus's own rule seen as literally the peoples own; his actions the peoples desired actions, and himself being all that Terratopia should be; Kyzus's Grand Paladins also held the same total obedience as him from Terratopia's peoples. Kyzus had successfully created and implemented the perfect and sustainable cycle of rule. Kyzus's total laws were continually kept up to date to best serve all of Terratopia and its people's due to close communication and work with his Grand Paladins and Kingdoms Advisors, which the people happily obeyed as the laws were seen as their own laws that they themselves had collectively put in place.

Kyzus as the Sovereign Overlord of Terratopia didn't demand or require total obedience however as because of his rule as the Supreme Protectorate, Terratopia had risen and restored itself to what it was like in the Summer of the world and so thusly could be ruled like it was back then, not requiring total, absolute rule. And Kyzus made sure to make such a thing happen as he thoroughly believed that the ways in which his father had set up and ruled Terratopia, through the very first Terratopia Union in the summer of the world, truly was the best way to do so. All the individual leaders of Terratopia's kingdoms were free to rule their realms however they wished, so long as it was within Kyzus's Supreme Protectorate laws and they still answered to him as their Sovereign Overlord. However, unlike his laws and decrees as the Supreme Protectorate, Terratopia's leaders and peoples could question or even disobey Kyzus's Sovereign Overlord laws and decrees if they wished and could do so without harsh consequence. They could disagree with them without penalty and without fear of punishment, after all they weren't selfish leaders any more and so likely must have good reason to disobey. A solution always being worked out peacefully and diplomatically for the benefit of all. And just like in Terratopia's days of old, the Terratopia Union of kingdoms sprung up again, its capital being Roccano, and Kyzus as its head. And once, again just like in Terratopia's days of old, the kingdoms all united together and empowered themselves to prosperity once more. The unions collective efforts under the guise and advise of Kyzus's vast wisdom and experience made insane progress towards greatness and far larger continual progress than what ever could have been made otherwise.

 Days passed under Kyzus's rule, days turned to weeks, weeks to months, months to years, and years to decades, and centuries and still Kyzus remained comfortably in his position of power. Terratopia's peoples never opposed or disobeyed him for they knew and felt that life under his rule was a far cry better than what life without his rule in Terratopia was like or would ever be like. But even as Terratopia's peoples came and went and inhabitants who had never experienced the misery of Terratopia when it's state of nature was at its worst came into their own; they still did not oppose or resist Kyzus's rule. It was just the way life was and life was as close to perfect as it came. The people had near total freedom, this freedom being in a setting of peace that was impossible to break and the lands in which they lived were prosperous and great. Even when Kyzus and his advisors made mistakes, it was never seen as his fault directly and it never led to resistance, retaliation to his rule, and calls for him to be disposed. It was instead seen as inevitable. Terratopia's peoples were much calmer and wiser now, they were more patient and as a result they all more clearly saw that they were all, even Kyzus and his advisors, imperfect beings, making imperfect decisions, living in an imperfect word, with imperfect opinions and desires, no matter how pure they believed themselves or others to be. The people had grown to be far more forgiving and understanding. Each mistake made was not seen as a fault by Kyzus but an inevitable fault by all and a valuable lesson to now be learnt from and to rise above. Also, with only Kyzus's himself being the law, any mistakes he made he could then easily backtrack on and fix. Able to do so without criticism and his actions being portrayed against him as incompetence. In fact, backtracking was seen as the opposite, it was a clear sign that Kyzus had made a mistake and listened to his people to recognise this and rectified it. As time passed however, less and less mistakes were made as everyone, including Kyzus, strove to do better and to not instead use any mistakes against one another.

 Kyzus himself and his rule seamlessly fitted into the two different roles it filled, as the Supreme Protectorate and also the Sovereign Overlord, so much so that even Kyzus's own identity and the persona the people saw in him split into the two roles as well. As the Sovereign Overlord of Terratopia, Kyzus remained Kyzus Hobbes; the grand, immaculate, and wise son of Thyzus Hobbes, the former impressive ruler of Roccano and the enlightened, selfless, and powerful ruler that empowers Terratopia to greater and greater prosperity. But as Terratopia's Supreme Protectorate Kyzus very identity turned into 'The Deity'; the mysterious all-powerful sorcerer that saved Terratopia from its troubles and misery. The absolute yet benevolent ruler, elected by the people, that restored and continually maintains Terratopia's very nature high above and away from the clutches of Morur and his evil ways; the unfair, selfish, cruel, nasty brutish, and short lives in the state of nature evil thrived off.

As the centuries turned to millenniums and millenniums to ages, there were times when Kyzus wished that he had managed to accomplish his plan with his children by his side as he wished for nothing more than for them to be with him and aid him rule over Terratopia. In fact, Kyzus had originally planned for his three children to be the Sovereign Overlords of Terratopia and himself to be The Deity and nothing more. But alas that was not the case and it never would be. There may have been ways for Kyzus to save his children from swaying from their oaths to him and in hindsight, through his own wisdom, Kyzus could think of many. But at the time Kyzus knew he did not have the benefit of hindsight and at the time he still made the right decision because after all, he still managed to bring about the united society under the Deity just as he had envisioned and it was all he imagined it to be. If Kyzus had risked that, if he had risked the unity and prosperity of all of Terratopia's peoples for all time for the sake of just three people, three people that had actively chosen not to be a part of it and had chosen instead to hinder it, even when given warnings and chances not too and even when knowing it was for the better, to Kyzus, that logically and morally made no sense. Furthermore, although Kyzus missed his children, he still basked in the joy and happiness of knowing that he had succeeded in his plan and his plans succession meant the ultimate happiness and prosperity of all. Kyzus may have lost everything dear to him, but through his efforts he also felt completeness, he felt as though his life was fulfilled and it would remain so as long as he maintained what he was doing, No one would ever loose what he had. No one would ever suffer as so many had done before.

Throughout the ages, Terratopia's splendour fully replenished itself to what it was like during the heights of its summer. All kingdoms that were destroyed, ravaged, and ruined rebuilt themselves to marvellous glory. Dead, burned, and decayed forests and lands regrew themselves into areas of beautiful stunning grandeur. Bright, powerful, radiant flowers sprung up and grew magnificently upon former battlefields and former sights of suffering and death. All urban areas from villages to capital cities, no matter how ravaged and wrecked by previous events, exploded in marvel and wonder. Grand, glorious, gargantuan architecture sprawled the land. Soon Terratopia, its kingdoms, its lands, its nature, its cities, looked as if nothing wrought had ever come across them since their first creation. Even the Giant's Lands were reinhabited by all races and Fairy Island was rebuilt, regrew, and repopulated with the few remaining Fairies and Pixies that had survived. And, even though Terra Tearia was in its autumn, Terratopia's land and nature still grew in magnificence. Although it would never be as warm, bright, lush, and green as it was before during its summer, Terratopia now irradiated a different kind of beauty, one of striking bright vibrant colour and wonder. Terratopia's glory spread throughout all of Terra Tearia; it became a land of legend; a land where everyone worked together in perfect harmony; a land where there was no war, battles, fighting, or bickering; a land of complete unity and happiness; a land of prosperity unheard of; a land of unparallel natural beauty with lush bright landscapes, vibrant colourful forests, and rich blue rivers, seas and sky; a land home to all races and an all manner of creatures birds, and beasts, a land where all this was possible under the mysterious yet somehow benevolent rule of the Deity. Terratopia was once again the grandest, most marvellous, most magnificent, most magical, and impressive land in all the world of Terra Tearia.

Even as Terra Tearia's Autumn turned to Winter, and brought with it new strengths of evil and new challenges for all the world to face and often suffer from, still Terratopia remained strong, its lands rich, plentiful, and prosperous, its people united, happy, and strong.

And so, ages continued to pass and Kyzus's rule remained, himself becoming an incredibly ancient being, perhaps one of, if not the, oldest being in all the world. Kyzus had indeed created the perfect cycle of rule for his people in Terratopia and it would always last and be sustained until either his rule and laws became worse than the state of nature, something he would never allow or ever be allowed due to the amount of Kingdom Advisors he had; or he no longer held the power to enforce his laws and protect his people from the state of nature.

A situation which would never occur until during the dawn of the apocalypse, Vangrol Abril, when his long-lost brother Lyzus returned and the great beast Tarragon emerged and laid waste to all of Terratopia...

War of Terratopia Timeline

Summer of World begins.
Thyzus awakens near Mount Roccano.
- 100-years pass

Roccano is founded.
Thyzus befriends Aquatatia Merpeople and Magistrate Solomon I.
- 100-years pass

Thyzus studies in Aquata, meets and marries Mia, and devises Terratopia Union idea with her.
Terratopia Union idea is proposed to the kingdoms of Terratopia.
- 2-years pass

Terratopia Union is created and set up with Thyzus as its Prime Lord Delegate.
Mia falls pregnant with Kyzus.
- 3-years pass

Centaur kingdoms leave the union.
- 2-years pass

Fairies and Pixies kingdom leave the union.
- 100-years pass

Mia falls pregnant with Lyzus.
- Multiple Ages of Summer pass (tens of thousands of years)

Terratopia Union prospers.
Hobbes children grow, study, explore, venture around, and work within Terratopia Union.
Lyzus creates the Merpeople kingdom Alliance.
Kyzus becomes the new Prime Lord Delegate.
Lyzus meets the Cherub and Gnarth and leaves with them to create the Baubles of Terra Tearia.
Lyzus leaves for Valhalla to become a Bauble Guardian.
- Entirety of Summer passes over many more Ages

Terratopia Union continues to prosper.
- The Autumn of World begins

Chaos and panic sweeps across Terratopia.

Chroniclers explain the chaotic situation on Mount Roccano's slopes.
- 4-years pass

Chaos continues to sweep Terratopia.
Giants formulate their rebellion plan.
The Autumn crisis meeting is organised by Kyzus.
- 6-months pass

Thyzus and Mia are visited by a Grim Reaper.
Roccano, Filnethias, Aquata, and Rime build up small armies.
- 6-months pass

The Giants' rebellion begins.
Thyzus is killed.
- 3-days pass

Mia is killed.
The Giants flee back to their kingdom.
Kyzus awakes and locks himself in his palace, giving Premier Joell command.
- 3-days pass

Kyzus meets the Wraith sent to him.
Kyzus invites Robin into his home.
- 40-years pass

The War for the sake of Thyzus rages on, and the Giants are pinned into their kingdom.
The city of Embirith is constructed.
Kyzus and Robin begin their courtship.
Hyzus and Tyzus are born.
- 4-years pass

Mia-Myzus is born.
- 6-years pass

Kyzus and his family venture out of his palace.
- 1-year passes

Kyzus marries Robin.
Kyzus resumes command of Roccano.
A peace treaty signing is agreed with the Giants.
- 1-week passes

The Giants betray peace treaty negotiations.
Robin is killed.

Kyzus begins his journey back to Roccano with his children.
- 2-weeks pass

Kyzus and his children arrive in Lemlee.
The Giants are driven to extinction.
- 1-week passes

Kyzus and his children arrive in Melian with the Valkyries.
Kyzus begins formulating his grand plan.
- 1-year passes

Kyzus finishes working on first part of his plan.
Hyzus, Tyzus, and Mia-Myzus all take their oaths of Kyzus.
Tyzus and Hyzus are sent to Aquata.
Mia-Myzus and Kyzus travel back to Roccano.
The Terratopia Union begins operation again.
- 100-years pass

The twins finish their studies at Aquata.
Mia-Myzus continues her ruthless tutoring under Kyzus.
The Terratopia Union ticks along smoothly with some discontent.
- 20-years pass

Mia-Myzus discovers Sabare and falls in love with the kingdom and its people.
The twins explore Terratopia and live within various kingdoms.
- 30-years pass

Kyzus summons his children and details to them his grand plan.
The Terratopia Union continues but to limited progress.
- 1-year passes

Kyzus and his children learn, formulate, and finalise out Kyzus's grand plan.
- 50-years pass

Mia-Myzus rules over Roccano.
The Twins advance their political careers within the Terratopia union.
Kyzus explores and learns new powerful magics.
Kyzus creates the seeing stones with Kossorlim Dwarves.
- 1-year passes

Tyzus becomes the Terratopia Union parliament Speaker.
Hyzus becomes the Terratopia Union parliament Prime Lord Delegate.

Mia-Myzus learns of her next role within Kyzus's plan and leaves for Sabare.
- 1-day passes

Mia-Myzus meets Barriel on the road and arrives in Embirith.
The twins meet Mia-Myzus and learn of Kyzus's summoning.
- 1-day passes

Mia-Myzus meets Rox and secures passage to Sabare.
The twins continue travel to Kyzus.
- 1-day passes

The twins learn of their sister's death.
Mia-Myzus departs from Kossorlim.
- 3-days pass

The twins learn of their next role within Kyzus's plan.
Mia-Myzus meets with Daiv and Vaid.
- 1-day passes

The twins arrive in Embirith.
Mia-Myzus takes over Sons of the East crime syndicate.
- 3-weeks pass

The twins sow division within the Terratopia Union.
Mia-Myzus fully takes hold of all crime in Eastern Terratopia.
Mia-Myzus develops affectionate feelings for Daiv.
Mia-Myzus travels and arrives in Embirith to meet Rox.
Kyzus begins to build up Roccano's military in secret.
- 1-day passes

Mia-Myzus assassinates Lord Delegate Petar.
- 1-day passes

Civil war is declared by Hyzus and Tyzus.
Embirith falls into riots.
Mia-Myzus travels to the Thruckland range.
- 3-days pass

Embirith riots begin to subside.
Kyzus meets with his children within their secret Thruckland Range cave.
- 3-days pass

Mia-Myzus arrives in Thruck and locates Viceroy Charles VIII.
Tyzus arrives in Xephex.

Hyzus begins co-ordinated defensive preparations for Carlin and Lemlee.
- 3-days pass

Mia-Myzus arrives back in Embirith and begins expanding her crime empire.
Tyzus arrives in Lendspen and decrees his first war orders to the Liberalist leaders.
Kyzus begins to create his Paladins of Roccano forces.
- 1-weeks pass

Attacks around Lemlee begin.
Carlin is invaded and Cufle falls under siege.
Mia-Myzus seals her crime empires control in Central Terratopia.
- 1-week passes

The Sabare revolution takes place.
Kyzus gains control over Dwarf Kings.
Turberus and Vaid are killed.
- 1-year passes

Lemlee is isolated and attacked ruthlessly.
Carlin is fully conquered and only Cufle remains.
Jassett's wooden construction stage is finished.
Mia-Myzus begins slipping into evil ways and is confronted by Kyzus.
Mia-Myzus and Daiv arrive in Gweston.
- 1-week passes

Mia-Myzus takes over the Kuk's Crime Clan.
- 2-years pass

Jassett is completed.
The Invasion of Rodus is decided upon and planned out by the twins and Kyzus.
- 2-weeks pass

Rodus invasion preparations continue.
Mia-Myzus renounces her oath and betrays Kyzus.
- 4-days pass

Barriel is sent to stop Mia-Myzus.
The Invasion of Rodus begins.
- 2-weeks pass

Suitear, Gweston, Jassett and Lendspen are attacked by the

Unionist kingdoms Silvor and Silvoud.
The Invasion of Rodus and Battle for Embirith conclude.
The twins question Kyzus's plan.
Barriel arrives in Sabare.
- 3-days pass

Mia-Myzus and Barriel duel.
Tyzus departs Central Terratopia aboard invasion ships.
The Fairies and Pixies issue their aid proclamation.
The Merpeople of the Great Eastern Bay attack Nindar's coast.
- 1-week passes

Fairy aid begins.
Tyzus arrives back in eastern Terratopia.
Kyzus rescues Barriel.
Mia-Myzus orders the assembly of a pirate fleet and her army.
- 1-day passes

The twins realise their misunderstanding and further question Kyzus's plan.
Mia-Myzus departs for the Fungi Forest kingdom.
- 2-weeks pass

The civil war splinters into wider reaching but small-scale fronts.
Fairy Island and Pixieland is totally destroyed by Mia-Myzus and her army.
- 1-year passes

The twins truly question Kyzus's methods and decide to deceive him to investigate what they can.
- 2-weeks pass

Aquatatia is ravaged by Mia-Myzus's deviant forces.
The twins totally renounce their oaths to Kyzus but fall out and go their separate ways to continue and win the civil war on their own terms.
- 1-day passes

Kyzus confronts Mia-Myzus.
Daiv is killed.
The Delilah crime empire is brought under Kyzus's control.
- 1-year passes

Cufle falls to the Liberalists.
Lemlee is pushed to surrender.

Gweston becomes isolated.
The crime empire stops deals and communication with Liberalists.
Kyzus meets his twins in the secret Thruckland Range cave, and the twins refuse to rejoin Kyzus.
- 2-weeks pass

Sabare attacks Eastern Terratopia.
Pirate fleets ravage the Connecting Isles region.
The Unionists retake control across nearly all Terratopia.
Mia-Myzus assassinates the remaining Liberalist leadership and kills Tyzus.
- 1-month passes

Hyzus reformulates the Terratopia Union.
- 7-years pass

The crime empire continues and escalates in power.
Roccano opens up its borders and sores in power and political standing.
The emergency meeting is organised in Embirith city centre.
- 1-month passes

Mia-Myzus disrupts Hyzus's meeting and kills Hyzus.
Kyzus and his forces 'save' Terratopia's people from feared destruction and Kyzus is elevated to supreme leadership by the people.
- 6-weeks pass

The crime empire is totally crushed by Barriel.
Roccano's forces begin rebuilding kingdoms.
Kyzus is made the Supreme Protectorate of Terratopia and finally completes his plan by setting up the united society under the Deity through his forces and Grand Paladins.
Kyzus is made Sovereign Overlord of Terratopia and re-creates the first Terratopia Union.
- Ages of Autumn pass

Terratopia prospers beyond measure under the Deity and Kyzus.

About the Author

This is his second book. He is very excited to have another out there. This book takes place within the fantastical world of Terra Tearia, the fantasy world he created in his first book, and is one of the first stories he wrote within this world over his spare time at university. He is a huge lover of philosophy, the thoughts, and questions it can provoke. He hopes by the end of this book, it provokes some thoughts within you too. But don't worry, it is far more exciting than a boring philosophy essay.